EVERYBODY'S
ALL-AMERICAN

D0958311

EVERYBODY'S
ALL-AMERICAN

FRANK DEFORD

DA CAPO PRESS
A Member of the Perseus Books Group

Designed by Brent Wilcox
Set in 11.5 point Dante MT by the Perseus Books Group

Library of Congress Cataloging-in-Publication Data
Deford, Frank.
    Everybody's all-American / Frank Deford.—1st Da Capo Press ed.
        p.   cm.
    ISBN 0-306-81375-0 (pbk. : alk. paper)
        1. Loss (Psychology)—Fiction.   2. Football players—Fiction.
3. North Carolina—Fiction.   4. Married people—Fiction.   I. Title.

PS3554.E37E93   2004
813'.54—dc22

                                                                    2004011657

First Da Capo Press edition 2004
First published in 1981 by The Viking Press
Reprinted by arrangement with the author

Published by Da Capo Press
A Member of the Perseus Books Group
www.dacapopress.com

Da Capo Press books are available at special discounts for bulk purchases in the
U.S. by corporations, institutions, and other organizations. For more
information, please contact the Special Markets Department at the Perseus
Books Group, 11 Cambridge Center, Cambridge, MA 02142, or call (800) 255-
1514 or (617) 252-5298, or e-mail special.markets@perseusbooks.com.

1 2 3 4 5 6 7 8 9—08 07 06 05 04

For Alex, for her memory
For Christian, for his future

PREFACE

Invariably, the first thing anybody asks me about *Everybody's All-American* is who is it *really* about? I don't know why people so naturally assume that any work of fiction must be based on some real person, but it appears to be a normal curiosity. I guess it makes a reader somehow feel in the know if one thinks he or she is really getting the veiled truth about some celebrity.

People are, in fact, terribly disappointed (if not disbelieving) when I tell them, sorry, Gavin Grey isn't anybody in particular. He's just Gavin Grey, a composite of so many great athletes I have known. Ironically, in fact, because I covered basketball more than any other sport in the years before I wrote *Everybody's All-American,* more of what I had learned about athletes adjusting to their new lives came from my knowledge of basketball players. Once I began to form the idea of the book, however, I planned it as a football story because indisputably football is the heroic American college game (and was even more so in the 1950s).

Those people who are absolutely sure I'm fibbing and that Gavin is really based on the late Choo-Choo Justice, the great University of North Carolina running back, should know of the odd coincidences that led to my choice of North Carolina as the site. First, just as I thought my hero should best be a football player, so too did I think I should locate the story in the South, inasmuch as that is the area of the country where the college game has been most popular. Besides, although I was raised in Baltimore, my family has Southern antecedents.

I was particularly familiar with North Carolina because I had used it as my model state for a nonfiction book I had done on the Miss America Pageant, because I had written often about the Carolina basketball team, and because I had a couple of good friends who had played football for the Tarheels. Basically, I chose Chapel Hill and Carolina because it made my research job easier. I really didn't know jack about Choo-Choo. Still don't.

But conspiracy theory is always more fun, and when the first plans for a movie developed, the University turned the producers down because they *knew* for sure that I had been writing about Choo-Choo Justice. (Nearby Duke was happy to serve as the location, by the way. Kevin Costner had agreed to star as Gavin Grey, with Michael Apted directing. But various Hollywood-type conflicts arose, and the film was junked at that time.)

When the movie plans were revived, with Dennis Quaid as Gavin, under the direction of Taylor Hackford, the story was shifted to Louisiana simply because the shooting schedule would last well into the winter, and North Carolina wasn't warm enough. Immediately, then, all the insiders who weren't familiar with the novel decided that the movie must be about Billy Cannon, the old LSU star. Sorry. Don't know Billy Cannon any more than I knew Choo-Choo Justice.

The second question I'm asked is whether I liked the movie version. Well, frankly, I don't think authors who sell their works to Hollywood have any kick coming if Hollywood rearranges the story. If you want to protect your precious literature, then be like

J. D. Salinger and don't take the movie money. But, in fact, I thought that Hackford and Tom Rickman, the screenwriter, did a terrific job. If I had to quibble, I would say that the latter part of the film becomes more of a domestic drama, where I think my book continued to concentrate on the conflicts of being a hero—but that's small potatoes.

I've been pleased, too, that both the novel and the film seem to have grown in appreciation with time. We like formula sports stories—different as they may be in tone, there's really no plot difference between *Rocky*, *Hoosiers*, and *The Bad News Bears*—and so the travails of Gavin and Babs may seem jarring. But I think the story, although set in a time past, is just as applicable to any modern period. Athletes get so much adulation early on and must adjust when the spotlight dims. So *Everybody's All-American* is not a tale crimped by time. It seems to travel well through the years, and I hope you enjoy it now as much as the first readers did a quarter of a century ago.

Frank Deford
February 2004

PART ONE
THE GREY GHOST

1

The dawn of May 8, 1864, brought a heavy fog, but it lifted soon enough, and it was almost a summer heat that bore down on the civilians of the county as they made their way to church. Several of them saw Stuart near Todd's Tavern, riding toward Spotsylvania, with Garnett and Lomax, Hulliben and Venable. All of their uniforms were splattered with spring mud, had been torn and patched and torn again, and while Stuart was no cleaner than the others, he still carried himself with the style and élan of the cavalier. Certainly, he affected no concern over the Yankees, who, in far superior numbers, now pushed hard on Richmond.

Up a hill leading to the Church of the Redeemer, the local Episcopal parish, he and his men overtook a group of women walking to the morning services. Garnett and Lomax, in the lead, slowed and saluted the ladies, but Stuart immediately reined in his huge chestnut, Skylark, and called for the others to do likewise. There was no time to linger, either. They were already lagging behind schedule for meeting with Bragg, and Venable started to remind the general of their tardiness.

Stuart must have sensed what was on his mind, however, for even as he dismounted, he turned to Venable. "Major," he said, "we owe these ladies an apology. All that they have heard of us—and now, what must they think of Jeb Stuart's cavalry, not to hold a dance on a Saturday night, nor to join them in Scripture on Sunday? What's the sense of fighting battles if there's no time for music or prayer? Isn't that what we fight for?" He took off his plumed hat and shook his head. "Ladies, you have General Stuart's personal regrets, but we have been troubled by a host of tiresome military details."

He asked them, then, if they would like the use of the horses to ride the rest of the way up the hill, but the women all declined, for in their long, full skirts there was no acceptable way for ladies to have sat the cavalry saddles. But Stuart would not be satisfied with that. There was one child in the group, and he impulsively reached down and gathered her up, and together they climbed onto Skylark, where he held her in his lap. The child's name was Madeline McAdams, and she had just turned five earlier that spring of '64, but she never forgot those moments for the almost full century more that she lived.

Whatever materials would strike her as she grew older—talking pictures, television, an airplane ride, a chance encounter in Atlanta with Margaret Mitchell—Miss McAdams would only shake her head, smile, and say, "But of course, I saw General Jeb Stuart ride with his cavalry one fine spring day in '64." For nothing could ever match that vision: Always, Stuart was the largest in her life. Always, too, she spoke of him as a great, tall man, and surely he must have loomed as that to a child. Besides, even if he did stand short of six feet, he had a long trunk and short limbs, and so he appeared all the taller in the saddle of the huge beasts he always sought out to ride.

And, indeed, he was transformed there upon their backs. Even as a young boy, he was known for his courage and horsemanship alike, and though he passed an indifferent tenure at West Point, his greatness had been recognized almost immediately upon his commission to the cavalry. For Jeb Stuart could do this one thing well: Just getting astride a horse, he was another man; going to battle on one, he was an exceptional man. He was a colonel of the Confederacy at twenty-eight, a brigadier before he was thirty, and a full legend by the time Madeline McAdams found herself swept up into his kind, dusty arms. Stuart was extraordinary at this single thing in life, and it was his good fortune that it was a romantic thing and that history gave him a chance to exploit it when he was hardly past being a boy.

So the general bade the others to escort the ladies up the hill on foot, and with one arm holding the child firm at the waist, he snapped at the reins and cantered off toward the spire. When his men reached the church several minutes later, they found Stuart sitting in the shade of the graveyard, back up against a tombstone, with little Madeline facing him, resting against his knees. She would reach out and touch his thick, cinnamon beard, mesmerized by his soft blue-gray eyes and by the sweet Virginia voice that was telling her of the great balls and cotillions he had graced, of the belles in their beautiful gowns, and of the dancing till dawn. There was no talk of the fighting, nor either of his own little Flora, who would be just this child's age had she not died the mean winter before last, when the general was with his horse troops in the Shenandoah.

His aides and the ladies approached only so close. If Stuart realized they were there, he showed no awareness, only concentrating more devotion onto the little girl. At last Hulliben nudged Venable, and the major took a tentative step forward. They had to meet Bragg. But just then Stuart finished recounting a story, rose, held Madeline by one hand, and began to sing to her. He sang his favorite, "The Girl I Left Behind Me." No one moved a muscle. Some old men and some women and children were already settled in their pews, but they came out and stared, to see General J. E. B. Stuart himself singing full voice to a child in the May morning. The song lifted out over the tall trees, past dogwoods, where the fresh petals lay on the ground, and then down over the fields that were bare from no men or mules to handle the spring planting.

Lieutenant Hulliben simply thought, "If the Yankees could only see this."

When the general finished the song, he kissed the little girl, ripped a shiny button from his coat, and gave it to her. "I'm sorry we couldn't dance last night," he said. "When this war is done, Madeline, will you save a dance for an old man?" She smiled at the ancient fellow of age thirty-one. Then Stuart moved to the chestnut, a glorious golden in the sun. The others waited impatiently for him to climb upon the horse, but he gently admonished them to walk their mounts until they were a polite distance away from the church. "I'm sorry, sir," Venable said, "but we really better mount, for there may even be Yankee patrols back up in here."

"Major," Stuart replied evenly, walking Skylark, "I appreciate your concern, but you must know by now that there are two things I'm not the least bit frightened of. One is Yankees, the battle. The other is what the Yankees can give me: death. I have faced them both enough to grow very familiar with what both have to offer. I feel content to give the Blues back whatever they risk with my encounter, and I feel just as peaceful a resignation if I must go at God's bidding to join my darling little Flora."

"I know well enough you're not scared, sir," Venable hurried to say.

"Oh," Stuart replied, "I have my fears, Major. Only, most men fear the battles; I fear what lies after them. The music can't ever again be so sweet for us, can it?" And then abruptly he sprang into the saddle, snapped up the reins, clucked to the chestnut, wheeled to the left away from the road, and started to cut across field, going full gallop, as the crow flies, toward the Chickahominy.

—DONALD MCCLURE,
The Life and Death of the Knight of the Golden Spur

EVEN NOW, LOOKING BACK, THERE HAS NEVER been anything so exciting in my life as the weekend when I was wide-eyed and fourteen and visited Gavin Grey at Chapel Hill. I still measure all my other memories by it.

In that autumn, when he was twenty-one and in his senior year at the University of North Carolina, it stayed Indian summer right up through the Duke game; Gavin Grey was famous, handsome and heroic, and in no ways a man or a real person. He stood six foot even and weighed one hundred and eighty-five pounds, a body perfectly proportioned, and as agile as it was classically formed. He played right halfback and was the fastest man on the Tarheel team, number twenty-five. We always said, "Gavin Grey, number twenty-five in your program, number one in our hearts." The two previous years he had been chosen an All-American, but now it was something else again, now he was known as *everybody's* All-American; when anyone referred to him, they always said, "Gavin Grey, everybody's All-American," as if the apposition was part of his name. But then, the feats he performed between the sideline stripes were incredible, and the whole world (as opposed to merely the sports world) knew of him, because he was on the covers of *Time* and *Life* and on *The Ed Sullivan Show*.

The latter especially certified him. Even years later, when people would meet Gavin, they would not mention how they saw him play Virginia or Wake Forest or whatever; instead, they would say, "I saw you when you were on *Ed Sullivan*." They said that as if that appearance was what had made him famous. "And all I done was stand up and wave," Gavin used to protest.

He was known far and wide as "The Grey Ghost," which immediately conjured up images, not only of his elusive ball-carrying abilities, but of the transcendent glories of the Old South as well. In those days—the 1950s—it was still permissible to celebrate the Confederacy. All the teams that played football—each one's marching band played "Dixie" to specifically salute their team. It was everybody's song, and went on all during every game, first one side

playing "Dixie" and everybody jumping up and waving Confederate flags, and then the other side doing the exact same thing.

There was a very old lady from Virginia, a Mrs. Madeline
Stringfellow, who lived in Chapel Hill. She was well into her
nineties, because this was 1954, and the point of bringing her up
here is that when she was a little girl she had seen General J. E. B.
Stuart ride off, full steam, going after Sheridan near Spotsylvania.
Stuart was the last cavalier: Into battle he wore white buckskin
gauntlets, a silk saber sash, gold spurs, and a cloak lined with scarlet. Flowers were woven into his horse's mane, and two buglers
rode with him as heralds. Mrs. Stringfellow met General Stuart
when she was on her way to church with her mother in the spring
of '64. The general was to be mortally wounded within the week
and laid in the ground at the age of thirty-one. Perhaps this made
the memory all the more vivid for the child. She never forgot that
handsome face and the gallant figure, majestic in the saddle, who
turned and tipped his hat to her as he rode off to meet the Yankees
one more time. Lord, but she even recalled the black ostrich plume
he always wore in his hat, standing out against the clear blue
Southern sky.

The local newspaper went to interview Mrs. Stringfellow on
the occasion of her ninety-fifth birthday, and as she had done for
years, she recounted this dear old recollection. It was a litany with
the old lady by now. But then, this time she suddenly added, "All
my born days, I never thought these old eyes of mine would see
such a sight as General Stuart riding to Spotsylvania, and they
didn't, either, till two weeks ago when I saw The Grey Ghost in the
second half against State." She had been there, with a corsage,
when he had torn up North Carolina State single-handedly. Gavin
was immediately rushed in to pose for an Associated Press

wirephoto, with Mrs. Stringfellow kissing him on the cheek and presenting him with an ostrich feather that someone had hurriedly turned up—with assurances that General Stuart had worn it into the fray at South Mountain. Soon, wherever Gavin appeared, everybody waved ostrich feathers (or reasonable facsimiles), and they planned to paint one on his baby-blue Carolina helmet until he vetoed that as ostentatious.

GAVIN WORE A crew cut, flattop style. He had bright blue eyes, a clean face, a dazzling smile . . . but on the field, when he had the black grease painted under his eyes (to cut reflection), he magically took on the bold, menacing countenance of a warrior. I could imagine him with Jeb Stuart, riding a great steed to battle, wearing his football uniform, number twenty-five, shoulder pads and all, with the black under his eyes. I could just imagine the damn Yankees seeing that coming at them alongside Stuart. (The Yankees, I knew well enough, were not a very bright bunch and could be easily rattled.)

Generally speaking, at that time Gavin Grey was faultless. The fame and attention of one whole state and much of a nation did not appear to have gone to his head. It was often written in the Carolina papers that he still wore the same helmet size as he had when he had first appeared on campus (in fact, it was written in those exact same words every time). Gavin was conscientious about his appointments, he made passable grades, dressed neatly, did not smoke, and owned to an occasional 3.2 beer only so long as it did not conflict with his training regimen. He identified himself as a Christian, and, during an interview before the midterm elections that fall, he came out solidly for democracy in general and, specifically, for the value of every single vote. In the off-season, he addressed youth groups. In the spring, he ran the one-hundred-yard dash for the university track team. This was still a time when, apparently, white people could run as fast as black people in the United States. It was the last of the good old days, although we did not know that at the time.

Beneath the fairest breasts in North Carolina there beat not a heart that did not beat—yea, flutter—for The Grey Ghost. But, as you might expect by now, there was only one girl for him. Babs. Barbara Jane Rogers, from High Point. Her father was prominent in furniture. She went to the Women's College at Greensboro, about an hour away from Chapel Hill. This was an ideal arrangement, notably from Gavin's point of view. He could see Babs all weekends and special times, but he could also sneak off with some of the other players and enjoy what they called "poontang." For this purpose there were a number of agreeable local backwoods girls and one immoral Yankee with huge tits from Wilmington, Delaware, over at the Duke Nursing School. On special occasions, after a great deal of the 3.2 beer, there was also a colored whore-house in Raleigh. Of all the things Gavin counseled me in, I think what left me with the most wonder was when he said, "Donnie, you just haven't lived until you've split black oak."

But perhaps you will not be harsh on Gavin and will forgive him these wild-oats-sowing hijinks if you understand that Babs was a virgin. Of course. This was common knowledge. This was known. She would not put out, even for The Grey Ghost himself, until they were officially married the next June. Because she is a girl, I can describe Babs better than Gavin. First of all, she was five foot seven, one hundred and twenty-three pounds, and measured thirty-eight/twenty-three/thirty-six. I know this precisely because this information was all revealed when Babs became Queen of the

Blueberry Festival at White Lake. On account of this singular honor, she had to take her sophomore year off and travel all over the country—"from Maine to Mexico"—extolling the virtue of Carolina blueberries. This was why she and Gavin were no longer in the same class and why she never graduated from the W.C., which is what we called the Women's College (and without ever knowing that more sophisticated travelers would think it was a double entendre). Babs had another year to go in school and was planning to shoot for Miss North Carolina when Gavin finished at Chapel Hill, but she left and went with him into the pros instead.

Babs had black hair, a peaches-and-cream complexion, and a way about her. I guess I have never stopped fantasizing about her. Close my eyes now, I can visualize her perfected the way I saw her that last football weekend, lying on her bed, still, eyes closed, there in the white sheet Gavin had wrapped round her. In the South, when I was growing up, we fell back on the word "creature" as the ultimate compliment. I cannot improve upon that, although if you have not heard the word employed in quite that way, I may not be able to fully convey its meaning. But everybody used to say, "Babs Rogers must be the most beautiful *creature* that God ever put upon the face of this earth."

The day Babs posed with Gavin for the *Life* cover at the Old Well, the campus landmark, a crowd of a thousand or more assembled to watch, and when Babs idly allowed at one point that she was just a teensy-weensy bit thirsty, several boys ran off to get her a soda pop, and there was a really considerable commotion when they all came back, trying to break through the crowd to hand her their drink. She accepted the first half dozen that came, sipping in turn from each—a Nehi, an RC cola, a Pepsi, and so on—rather like a president signing a bill with a score of fountain pens. For his part, Gavin spent most of the in-between time auto-graphing items and kissing the ostrich feathers that were pressed upon him. He and Babs loved every minute of it, and the Tarheels were undefeated on the year.

I CAME OVER to Chapel Hill to visit Gavin for the Clemson week-end from Wilson, where I lived, in the eastern part of the state. Gavin was my uncle, my mother's younger brother, and my going to see him, to be with him at the height of his glory, was the first unordi-nary thing (never mind outstanding) that had ever happened to me. At that time I was a freshman at Fike High, but "small for my age," which was fourteen. I was skinny, my voice had not changed, and—unlike, say, Gavin—I did not have the head for a crew cut, which I had to wear nonetheless because everyone did, and my mother made me. As a consequence, my life went in cycles: The more distant from my last haircut, the longer the scrubby brown shoots on my pinhead, the happier I was. I carefully planned my visit to Chapel Hill so that my coiffure would be at its most extreme length.

While many people claimed that I was the first genuine celebrity-type person to come out of Wilson since 1946, when Trudy Riley went on from being Miss Wilson to become Miss North Carolina, the fuss made over me was not all flattering. Much of the high-school elite chortled at the silly ironies of Mother Na-ture, that she could possibly fashion a Gavin Grey and a Donnie McClure out of the same family clay. More than ever I felt short-changed, and in my despair too often became what was known in my family as "cross."

"Don't be cross with your mother," my father said.

"But she—"

"Don't call your mother 'she.'"

"Yes, sir."

"I'm tired of you being cross."

When Mother then began to suggest that I would need an early haircut in advance of my trip, I gave up the ghost and began looking for an excuse to get out of the visit. I might have found one, too, but for our next-door neighbor, Judge Frank R. Pace, Jr., who called for me to come over one day when I returned home from school.

Judge Pace was the first grown-up ever to accept me as a person, and not just as the son of Edna and Kinloch McClure. I don't suppose he was yet fifty years old then, but so evenly did he treat me that it seemed to me that he must be a venerable as he was sage. He exhibited an omniscience that struck many of his contemporaries as overbearing, but it didn't bother me a bit because I didn't have the nerve to dispute any adult under any circumstance. He was "the judge" manifest. Had he in fact not been a judge, had he just been a tobacco warehouseman hanging around the Moose Lodge or kicking tires down at the Betholine-Sinclair filling station, I'm sure he would have still been known as "Judge" to his cronies.

He was a widower, and he lived alone, except for the maid, Clarissa, who looked after the judge and called me "Cake," to my constant mortification. She was a dear old black lady, nearly illiterate, who had been in the Pace family all her life. The judge had suggested that she go take care of his niece, Dolly, over in Rocky Mount, who was having a baby and couldn't take care of herself (which is why she was having a baby) but Clarissa had finally grown tired of being shuffled about the Pace family, and had vowed to stay with the judge. Clarissa's funeral insurance had just been paid up, so she could exert herself. And anyway, she adored the judge.

When I approached his porch, where he was sitting on the top step, I saw that he was carving up a jack-o'-lantern for Halloween, which was a few days off. "I admire jagged, uneven teeth," he said, notching out a mean incisor. He carved nimbly with a kitchen knife, and from the motion, I glanced down at his wrists, which were uncommonly powerful for a man so lean. Judge Pace was supposed to have been a great baseball prospect in his time— and even more of a musician. He was a piano player and a crooner, the only person from Lenoir County ever to have won on *Ted Mack's Original Amateur Hour,* but he had given up "show business" for marriage and night law school, and I never even once heard him play the piano that sat so prominently in his living room.

"Let's give him a scar thisaway on his cheek," Judge Pace said, with great enthusiasm for the task. I only nodded grave assent. As I said, and particularly early on in conversations, before I got my feet wet, I was reluctant to actually speak, because I was embarrassed about my soprano voice.

But I felt comfortable with the judge. Merely by including me in this little pumpkin enterprise, he had given me the distinct feeling that I was an intimate. What was different about the judge from all other people I knew was (as I figured out much later) that he arrived at various and sundry conclusions via thinking. It was an extraordinary break for me that I had encountered such an individual, for very few children ever meet anyone who actually thinks. Thus, for most children, thinking is as foreign a venture as making an H-bomb or attending a network TV show in person; some people do these things, but not you. Of course, in the adult circles around me in Wilson there were always *views.* Then too, teachers delivered set ultimatums, and no one, certainly, was lacking for opinions—which were always identified by the holder as "considered" opinions. But only the judge *thought* as such.

With the knife, now, he etched a fine line that just broke the pumpkin skin, and then he drew back, like an artist from his easel, to inspect this scar. "Just about right, wouldn't you say, Donnie-Me-Boy?" The one thing I disliked about the judge was that he called me that. Understand: Amidst his thoughts, he thought a lot of weird things.

"Looks okay to me, sir."

He dug in then, to complete the job. "You know, of course, that you're becoming quite famous," he said.

I blushed. "Shoot."

"No indeed. I hear all ovah how you're goin' to visit the intrepid Mistuh Gavin Grey himself this weekend. Here, steady this punkin for me."

I grabbed the pumpkin firmly in both hands and said, "Now I ain't real sure about goin' atall."

"It isn't easy to make scars on punkins, you know," the judge said. "Too thin, you can't make them out at any distance. Too wide, they appear to be some kind of Band-Aid, which is completely out of character for a jack-o'-lantern."

"Yes, sir."

"Y'all don't sound very enthusiastic about your trip to Chapel Hill, Donnie-Me-Boy."

"Well, I jes don' know, Judge."

"Don't know what-all?"

"Well, it was my mama set this up with Gavin, and I ain't real sure he wants me."

The judge looked up from his scar work and peered down at me over his glasses, which he wore on the tip of his long nose. He said, "Go."

"Sir?"

"Go to Chapel Hill. Gavin Grey is fast becoming a phenome-non, and to have the opportunity to study a phenomenon from up close, from the inside, so to speak—that's a rare privilege." I nod-ded, if not altogether confidently, for I was not quite sure what a phenomenon was. I thought they were, basically, comets, or the swallows coming back to Capistrano. "His implications are large," the judge went on, "and I envy you this opportunity."

"Yes, sir."

He put down his knife in mid-scar and pulled out his pipe and monkeyed with it. I was fourteen then, am nearing forty now, and do not to this day possess a fair notion as to what it is exactly that pipe smokers do with their pipes. Whatever, Judge Pace did it often, and usually as a prologue to some profundity. "Understand what Gavin Grey is to us," he said. "He is Alexander, Robin Hood, General Washington; he is our old lady's friend, Jeb Stuart. He is Sergeant York; or even, if you prefer art to life, Gary Cooper. Same difference. Our young Mistuh Grey is the modern equivalent of that crowd."

"You mean . . . like a legend?" I had seen it written regularly and heard it often enough on radio and TV that The Grey Ghost was "a legend in his own time."

"No, no, no, Donnie-Me-Boy. That is precisely what he is not. In another time, any other time, he might have been a legend, but now we're too literal to produce legends. Do you know what that means?"

"No, sir, I don't b'lieve I do altogether."

"It means that we are not very imaginative any longer, and leg-ends are, by definition, the product of imagination. Legends must be distant to survive. Even Jeb Stuart, saber and gold spurs and all, would have been done in by television long before the Yankees could have put him away."

I nodded: encouragement more than understanding.

"You see, we *see* entirely too much nowadays, Donnie-Me-Boy. We used to buy what we could afford and live with our dreams, but now we buy our dream items on credit and thus are confined by all our purchases. We will soon enough no longer accept anything unless we can actually witness it. Well, you cannot televise character and principle any more than you can televise bravery on some distant battlefield. And always before, that was the stuff of legend.

"So you see, Gavin Grey has the opportunity to be accepted as a hero—he better than some general, better than some statesman. It makes us all very frivolous, perhaps, that our civilization is reduced to worshiping athletes and entertainers . . . but then again, maybe that is the first sign of an advanced culture. Perhaps if we stop drawin' our heroes from wars, we will no longah see a need to fight wars. Now, I'd call that progress, wouldn't you, Donnie-Me-Boy?"

"Yes, sir, I 'spect so," I said with great thought.

He fooled with his pipe again. "So go to Chapel Hill," he told me. "It's your chance to be with a bona fide hero, and for those of us who could only read of those gentlemen in Plutarch or could only stand on a street corner to catch a glimpse of General of the Army Douglas MacArthur goin' by in his limousine, you will be far ahead of us." Then, straightaway, he went back to carving the pumpkin and inquired if I had a girl friend yet.

2

ONLY BECAUSE MY FATHER, WHO SELDOM INVOLVED himself in such child-rearing minutiae, stepped in on my side, did my mother relent and permit me to put off my haircut until after my return from Chapel Hill. And even then, she was a bad sport about it. "I declare," she said, "my own child goin' off to Chapel Hill lookin' like a wild hoo-rah's nest." It was her favorite expression to identify any aspect of my appearance, although I never knew what a wild hoo-rah's nest was (nor how to spell it, either).

Mother was Gavin's sister. She was Edna Grey, the oldest of her family, closely followed by two other children; Gavin had materialized many years later, a flat-out mistake. It seems that he had been conceived on a vacation trip to the Blue Ridge Mountains of Virginia. Really, I always thought of him more as a cousin than as an uncle. And besides, until about this time we had had little connection with one another. Not only was Gavin several years older than I, but Mother's family all lived at the other end of the state from Wilson—in Charlotte. Mother had come from Charlotte, but then she had married a tobacco man and left the Piedmont.

Mostly, Gavin and I saw each other only at family functions, when I knew he was assigned to "look after Donnie." I hated those trips we took to Charlotte, to my grandparents' dark old house on Tryon Street. Invariably, we were there either because of sickness or death or, worse, upon the occasion of some national (and school) holiday, when I least wanted to be removed from my friends and fun in Wilson. Even now, I think of Charlotte as a gloomy, depressing place; I can still smell the distinct stale odors that that dusky house on Tryon Street held. I have always believed that our senses are most vivid in childhood, and that what characterizes great artists is merely that these people can remain as alert when grown-ups as they were as children.

In that way, I expect I can more accurately tell you what Gavin was like as a teenager than how he had been in recent times. Most people recall him from that time on *The Ed Sullivan Show;* I remember him from Charlotte. I was in awe of him for being older—simply that—and a high-school star, but I remember him best for being so especially kind to me. Gavin always treated people decently, as equals; he was not afraid to be considerate. He was really a shy kid, already baffled by the attention being paid him. He showed me dirty funny books (Archie Andrews, Jughead, Betty and Veronica doing all manner of things salacious to one another), took me to a record store, and once, when I was nine, he even encouraged me to come along with him and his steady girl to the Friday-night picture show. She wore his high-school ring on a chain around her neck and snuggled up close to him as soon as we settled into our sticky theater seats. I was mortified. It is impossible to feel any more unwanted than when accompanying a teenage couple to a movie theater. It was then, anyway. Gavin appreciated my position right away. "Straighten up now, *Lou*-ise," he snapped at her. "There's the three of us chickens." He never put his arm around her during the entire performance, and afterward, he took her directly home—which burned her up—and then drove me back to the house on Tryon Street.

We nodded to our parents and went upstairs to watch TV. The Friday-night fights were on from the Saint Nicholas Arena in New

York City. I assured Gavin that I hadn't meant to be any trouble, I didn't want him to take Louise home on account of me. I felt unbearably guilty. Gavin replied, "To be truthful, Donnie, I'm dang glad y'all are here, because I wanted to see this boxing bout a whole lot more than I wanted to be with old Lou-ise."

"Why?" I asked incredulously, on reflex. Even to see TV—and they had a nice set—even for that, to pass up the company of a girl, a girl with breasts, a girl with breasts who liked you, a girl with breasts who liked you and therefore might even let you touch same . . . well, that was beyond my comprehension.

"Let's wait till after this round," Gavin said, and, keeping to that, he started up talking promptly as the round ended, answering my question as if I had just that moment asked it. We talked on that way, too, for the rest of the fight, conversing in one-minute segments between the rounds while a parrot sold razor blades. The fight went the distance—ten rounds—Chuck Davey winning a clear decision.

After the first round, Gavin said, "Lou-ise is gettin' too bossy, Donnie. She's an old Baptist girl, and she and that daddy o' hers are tryin' to get me to go ovuh to Wake. Sometimes, it dang seems that she'd do 'bout anything I wanted if I'd go to Wake."

I looked at him, shocked, unbelieving, able only to ask with my eyes: Anything? Really? *Anything*? "Yeah, I 'spect 'bout anything at all," he answered my eyes (I have great eyes). "I'm just now findin' out what-all girls are a-liable to do if you're a football player."

Eyes: Really and truly?

"You oughtta be one, Donnie. Bein' a football player for a boy is every bit as good as havin' big tits for a girl. And that's a nat'ral fact."

"I didn't know that," I declared.

"Oh, yeah," Gavin went on. At that time, of course, he appeared as sage to me as he was certified heroic. Now, looking back, I can see, of course, that he was not all that bright. Oh, he was clever enough. Gavin seemed to sense, most of the time, what was going on around him. He had his wits about him sufficient even in teenage passion to realize that Lou-ise what's-her-name was not above using her wiles to help steer him to Wake Forest. But here's the point: Even full in this knowledge, I guarantee you, Gavin still would have taken the carnal path to Wake Forest if somebody else hadn't come along with inducements that could direct him to Chapel Hill or State or Duke or wherever. Athletes develop so young that their decisions are made for them. They react, they respond. Blow the whistle, fire the gun, scream "Play ball," and they proceed upon the field to do their stuff. But they lose, it seems, the need to initiate thought. In time, they don't even bother coming up with considered opinions. Gavin always needed a coach to tell him the plays. Sometimes the coach was in fact a coach; sometimes the coach was a wife; sometimes it was a "business partner"; sometimes it was even me. But whoever: Somewhere, sometime early on, what is known as native intelligence was shadowed by what is known as natural ability, and only the one was allowed to blossom.

"But as much as I'd like to get into old Lou-ise's drawers, I ain't gonna go to Wake to do it," he went on. "That's the last place I want to go on the face o' the earth, old Wake."

"The last place on the face o' the earth?"

"Well, leastwise the last place in Carolina," Gavin said, qualifying the answer a bit. But then, except possibly for parts of Virginia—which was out of the question here, since there weren't any good football schools in Virginia—and most of South Carolina, North Carolina was the face of our earth. This place was known as

Carolina (it most particularly did not include South Carolina, any more than that Carolina included North Carolina), and as best I can spell it phonetically, it was pronounced Kowlinah.

You must remember that this was just at the beginnings of television, and my place, this Kowlinah, still felt different from all other places. It was before everybody all spoke like the six o'clock news and lived in ranch-style houses and ate at the salad bar. There was still a sense of being, a sense of Carolina.

"Well, if you don't want to go to Wake, where do you wanna go?" I asked, and while I knew I was being indecently curious, even then I understood that Gavin didn't mind talking about such deep private matters with me. There was a great gap of age and experience, but, however remote, I was family: thus, the ideal confidant. And: Blood is thicker than water. Gavin liked me well enough, too, and he even came to depend upon my counsel as I grew older and accumulated the mantle of wisdom that advanced degrees conferred upon me in his mind. But basically, to him, I was just a safe outlet, a place where he could try out his thoughts, sure that they would rest with kin in trust. I never told any of this until now.

The bell signaled the start of the second round, postponing his reply for the moment. This was still only Gavin's junior year in high school, but already he was a local celebrity: all-Mecklenberg County, all-Carolina. Already he was gaining some recognition of how his peculiar abilities related him to the world at large. Athletes in this country—good athletes—really don't make anything of the fact until they are advised that they should. That is because it comes so effortlessly to them that they think it is natural. That is the natural part of being a natural athlete: *not* that you are capable of performing naturally, but that you are natural in accepting the fact. There are natural actors, natural moneymakers, natural

singers—natural everything, I suppose. Hell, there is natural child-
birth. And, of course, it is extremely painful. Only natural athletes
simply proceed. That gift is displayed at the earliest age; it is just always there, a part of things. Natural athletes really have no con-
ception of how they can use this ability. Ultimately, they are pow-
erless before it.

Already, Gavin struggled with how unnatural athletes assessed
what he had. When the bell rang after another round, he said: "I'll
tell you something, Donnie, something about the old gridiron.
Grown-ups treat me like I was the grown-up and they was the boy.
It's upside down. And then folks come to say, Ain't he one wonderful boy 'cause he ain't changed none? Well, I ain't changed. I
just take aholt of the old pigskin and run with it. It's just what I
can do."

I nodded. The bell rang and he stopped. When the round
ended, he started up again. "What-all can you do, Donnie?"

"Me? Oh, I can't do nothin' good."

"Aw, shoot. I reckon ever'body can do somethin' real good. You
just don't know what-all it is. Most things don't have an all-this-and-
that like they have an all-Carolina in football. You don't know Mr.
Edward Turnbull, do you?"

The bell rang as I shook my head. When the round ended,
Chuck Davey sniping at the midsection, Gavin said, "Well, there really ain't any reason for you to know Mr. Edward Turnbull, since
you don't live here in Charlotte."

"No."

"Well, listen up. My daddy bought a DeSoto from Mr. Edward
Turnbull. You know that green DeSoto V–8 my daddy drives, the
one out yonder in the driveway?"

"Sure." That was easy.

"Well, my daddy says he didn't have no mind getting a DeSoto, not after driving Fords and Mercs all these years. But he met Mr. Edward Turnbull at the KI-wanis one day, and Mr. Turnbull come down on Daddy like a duck on a june bug about test-driving his DeSotos. Daddy said he wasn't goin' to buy a DeSoto any which way, but he would come and look if Mr. Turnbull wanted to waste his own good time." The bell rang.

When the round ended two minutes later, Gavin went right on. "So my daddy went to see Mr. Turnbull, and in fifteen minutes he had gone and bought hisself a DeSoto—financing arranged and all—because, as he tells me, Mr. Edward Turnbull had got to be— *got* to be, Donnie—the finest automobile salesman in Mecklenberg County, if not the whole Tarheel State."

"See? Ever'body knows I can play football real good, but there's a lot of things people can't do till they're growed up more." He shook his head.

"You're lucky you can do somethin' so glamorous," I said. "That's the different part." The bell rang.

At the end of the round, Gavin said: "No, it ain't different. I don't feel no different because I ain't doin' nothin' 'specially different. The thing of it is, all the other people is treating you so different, you figure, well, you sure must be. It's all gonna go straight to my head."

"Shoot no, Gavin," I said. I was mad he could say a blasphemous thing like that. "Ever'body says that even though you're the best gridiron prospect in the Tarheel State your hat size hasn't changed one little bit. That was written right out in the Raleigh *News and Observer.*"

"Yeah, and what-all do they know?" he asked inscrutably. I didn't know what to reply. Never in all my born days had I heard anyone dismiss the Raleigh *News and Observer* so absolutely. Even Judge Pace gave it some passing credit. The bell rang.

After the round, Gavin said: "You see, it ain't so much how you appear, Donnie. If you was brought up right, not common or tacky—shoot, the actin' is easy. Actin' real humble is easy as pie. It ain't no less nat'ral than runnin' with the ball. It's the people start actin' different 'round you. They're the ones that change. You don't. Already, like I say, they treat me like I was the grown-up. See, you don't have to change. It's all done for you. That's very hard for people like the Raleigh *News and Observer* to see."

FOR THE CLEMSON game, I sat with Babs and fantasized that those few strangers in Chapel Hill (the ones just in from the moon) who did not know whose girl she truly was thought she was my date. My God, but she was beautiful. She was made for this. Oh sure, of course I believe in women's rights; I sign the ERA petitions whenever the college kids bring one around; I believe that women are just as smart as you and me and less likely to initiate nuclear holocaust. Just the same, to be perfectly honest with you, ideally, the best of all worlds, women should all be dolled up and sent to watch football games with color in their cheeks.

I read once that we fight wars because the women are watching, and, after all, football is a little war. It always seemed to me that warming up before the game, when players bang their helmets and their shoulder pads against one another, they are like great bull moose rattling their antlers in mating season. As a skinny kid, I was limited to sports like golf and tennis, basketball and baseball, and it always upset me that girls never swooned over us the way they did over football players. I didn't mean me personally, of course; but, Lord, those basketball pros: tall, lithe, lean, powerful men, nearly nude, their bodies glistening, and so close to the fans you could almost touch them. I would think women would prefer them, but perhaps basketball players are too close, too real. The football players are distant, masked, anonymous forms—and they have stylized, classical masculine bodies: V-shaped, great-shouldered, powerful-legged. If Walt Disney had drawn people instead of animals, I'm sure all the men would have looked like football players. No wonder the women love them so.

And for the player, football must be even more satisfying than battle is for the soldier. So what that women watch wars: Men and women alike are watching football, and while any man can be conscripted for the battlefield, only the very special qualify for the gridiron. It always seemed to me, in fact, that Gavin's prime delight came from pleasing other men, in being supreme among his fellows. Oh, sure, he liked the fuss the girls made, but it did not affect him in the same proud way. To star athletes, women are merely booty, something else they come to expect naturally. Very few of them like women, enjoy their company. Women intrude upon athletes. Teams are company. Teams are comfort. Of course, athletes do like to screw women, and they do that left and right, but that is something else again.

Athletes and pretty girls probably share too much, so that it would be hard for them to contribute anything but sex to one another. They both possess this rare physical bounty that society prizes, but they have done nothing to earn it, and don't even know that it will fade away as magically as it came. Being beautiful or being a natural athlete is, past a point, only a matter of trying to stay one. Those of us who are neither can go about the simple business of living in a much freer way. We don't have to agonize about losing our magic—just our youth.

Oh, but you should have seen Babs and Gavin together—they were so ideal: not only looking the part but speaking it too. I remember that especially. I think that came with the franchise. Damn, we have seen so many love scenes in so many movies that none of us is any longer capable of original expressions of love. Babs and Gavin—and you and me—could be so innovative at times in uttering thoughts of hate or joy or anger or exasperation. But never in what they said of love. They both spoke only in the finest Hollywood clichés, as if it was their understanding that nothing else was permitted. They were the best two at being In Love I ever saw. She always called him "Precious," and there was a regular large amount of vowing about forevers.

I remember one time, several years later, when my mother dragged me to church one Sunday when I came home from Vanderbilt, where I was taking my master's in the Civil War, and the subject of the sermon was something like Can You Find Love? Can We Touch Love?—some damn fool title like that. And the minister, a Rev. Eugene Willoughby, was carrying on (I'm just hitting the intellectual highlights here): "We know love is there because we've all felt it in so many ways—as a child or as a parent, as a man or as a woman. There are so many different kinds of love. But yes, we know it's there, all around us. But we can't see it, can we? We can see nature, we can see money, we can see the great works of man, but love is like the wind. We cannot see it, but we can see its effect upon this world."

And sitting there, in my one suit, half asleep from a normal late Saturday night's revels, I thought to myself: Look, I don't care whether love passes by disguised as a whiff of aftershave lotion or as a Trailways bus, but don't tell me I haven't seen love, you dumb Reverend Sonuvabitch, because I saw Gavin Grey and

Babs Rogers walking across the campus at Chapel Hill hand in hand, during the football season, the year he was everybody's All-American.

SITTING WITH BABS at the Clemson game, I sensed early on that she, of all people in the stands, could least afford to concentrate upon watching Gavin. Too many people were watching her as well. And so Babs looked on regally, with a sort of disciplined devotion, the same way she kept from being laid. She exuded rather than cheered. She did not have to advertise her allegiance; she wore no special Grey Ghost pin, nor waved any ostrich feather. Whenever Gavin made an outstanding run or scored a touchdown, the people in the section turned instinctively to look at her, and she took to nodding back, accepting his acclaim by proxy. After awhile, I got the strange feeling that Babs was somehow in charge. We had been studying Roman history at that time at Fike High, and it seemed to me that at any moment the referees might look up to Babs for a thumb signal to advise them what exactly they were to do with the Clemson Tigers.

We were located in the right place for that sort of gesture, too: almost dead on the fifty-yard line on the south side, in the section reserved for officials, for the chancellor and the university president, the governor when he came, and so on. (The fat cats, the ones who donated to the athletic program, were seated directly across the way.) Only where we sat, in all the stadium, was there cover: Tarheel blue-and-white bunting stretched above us, like the canopy the king of England always had when he attended jousts and archery contests in medieval movies.

But never mind the protection, what a glorious day it was: late in October, not a cloud in the sky. I had been schooled in exactly where Chapel Hill was located: the Southern part of Heaven. I had heard that truth all my life. I knew we were the most favored of people: If God isn't a Tarheel, then why is the sky Carolina blue? I believed these things in my heart even as I chuckled at them in my sophistication. But today—my God, Gavin Grey rampant upon the gridiron, a stadium full of Tarheels, the heavens unmarred. Was there anywhere else in the world this joyous day?

Kenan Stadium sits in a natural valley, hidden away from mankind. If you were a stranger, you would not even know that a stadium was there until you came through the woods all around, through the gates, and looked down upon the bowl. There are pines all about it, and some sycamores, poplars, and cedars, as well, and today, just this week, the first color was coming to the sycamores, so there was a crown of fire running around the top of the stadium.

First with Choo-Choo Justice, who had been a Tarheel All-American a few years previous, and then again with Gavin, there had been demands to double-deck the stadium, to add another ten or fifteen thousand additional seats, but this could not be accomplished because it was in Mr. Kenan's deed that his stadium could never rise above the treetops. A lot of important fans fretted about this and searched for loopholes in the deed, and Judge Pace assured me that the tobacco companies would spring for the cost of a top deck in a July minute as soon as this nagging little legal obstacle could be brushed aside, but no one ever did find a way around the late Mr. Kenan's best intentions. It is a good thing, too, because as long as a stadium has trees above it, it is easier to keep the feats below in perspective. Lord only knows how much more we would have lionized The Grey Ghost if there were not God's own trees rising in such bright autumn glory.

Gavin was never better this day. He ran the opening kickoff back ninety-eight yards for his first touchdown, and he poured it on the poor Clemson Tigers from there at scrimmage. The stadium was beside itself, cathartic. At the half-time it was 27–0, Carolina, and a number of people began to come to Babs for autographs. Some actually bowed, a few of the younger ladies curtsied, and most called her, deferentially, "Miss Babs." She reveled in this, although I did not completely appreciate why until much later. You see, the worst part of being a star's girl is that you and the star are constantly in competition for the attentions of the same men. This was all the more apparent when Gavin got to the pros. Babs and the other players' wives never seemed particularly upset by all the pointy-breasted blondes who buzzed about their husbands. What bothered the wives was that whenever other *men* were around, they would ignore them, beautiful women, and congregate only about the husbands. Now that just wasn't fair. Even then, at Chapel Hill, before they were married, it was evident that Gavin was as much a threat to Babs as he was her passport.

She could radiate more when he was required down on the field, when they had to be separated. "Isn't this a glorious afternoon, Donnie?" she asked me near the end of the game. The remark came apropos of nothing. Gavin and the first string had been taken out, and the action at the moment was even quite desultory. So more people were looking toward Babs. She touched at her hair. Where it curled up in a bounce, she just touched at it, in a way that only very pretty girls know how to do. "I do hope I look all right, Donnie," she said. "It just wouldn't *do* for Gavin Grey's girl not to look attractive."

"You look . . . fine," I said. I started to say "beautiful," but backed off to "fine" lest I sound too forward. No matter. She wasn't listening anyhow. Pretty girls never listen to the answer when they inquire how they look. They already know. And besides . . . !

"Hush, Donnie," Babs whispered as soon as she heard it.

It had just begun across the way, as the clock ticked down the final seconds: "Ghost . . . Ghost," the crowd was chanting. Merely the one word, over and over, with each tick of the clock. This special form of adoration had never been employed before. It had started with some students way up high in Section Eleven, near the end zone, and had swept down from there, engulfing the whole stadium, section by section: "Ghost . . . Ghost . . . Ghost," growing from a distant mumble to a rumble to a more distinct chant and now into some kind of universal murmur. "Ghost . . . Ghost . . . Ghost . . ." The words drifted away, over the treetops, past the Bell Tower, which chimed the alma mater in victory, above the campus, on to Bynum and Cary, to Raleigh and Durham, all over Kowlinah, all over the world—words that need not be carried by the wind, but moved quite by themselves, as if they were another of nature's acts, like sunshine or rain.

The tingles went up and down my spine. Babs let a slight smile of benediction cross her ruby-red lips. She did not join in, nor did I. It would have been inappropriate for family to participate in such a hymn of praise.

On the bench, Gavin did not move except to drop his head, properly humble at the gesture; as you know, he did not come from a common or tacky family. The lowering autumn sun came just over the trees, bounced onto his crew cut, and made it seem that God was beginning to wrap a halo around his head, starting with just the one side first. "Ghost . . . Ghost . . . Ghost . . ." I put my head down with my tears, shamed to death that Babs might see Gavin's male cousin, a teenager, crying. And then there was a great burst as the game ended, a raucous roar supplanting the rolling chorale, and I could look up. The Carolina team started to run off to the locker room, but Gavin himself could not get far before various of the Clemson players—the opponents—came out of their way to stop him and clasp his hand. And then the children, who had crashed down onto the field, swarmed upon him, reaching out just to touch, calling to him, repeating his name. All around me people pressed upon Babs, and, to themselves, spoke about witnessing a legend in their own time.

MANY YEARS LATER, far from that day and from Gavin and Babs, I saw it all again. It came to me in this way. It was Christmas Eve, 1968. In the weeks just preceding, Karen and I had moved into our first house ever, in Charlottesville, and had (at last) our first child. It was a boy, too, robust and as handsome as we could expect, genetics being what they are. We put up a little tree and decorated it, drinking too much in the process, and then, on a rug in front of a roaring fire, we made love for the first time in our house, the first time since the baby, the first time in weeks.

Afterward, Karen went and got the baby and nursed him before the TV. Borman, Lovell, and Anders had gone to the moon and disappeared around the far side. "They'll be all right," Karen said, blithely blessing them with our own joy. The baby was done with his meal, but she held him still, my son and heir, gurgling over her shoulder. With her other side, she snuggled up against me. It is difficult to believe that Norman Rockwell, at the height of his powers, could have reproduced a more adorable scene. There was even a puppy dog at our feet. I forgot the puppy dog.

Nearly beside himself, even as Karen and I, Walter Cronkite tensed at a sudden cracking, and then listened to Borman's metallic voice, bringing us a report of their safety and a call for peace on earth. Baby. Wife. Love. Fire. Puppy dog. Christmas tree. Walter Cronkite. Astronauts. Peace. Happiness. First house. Karen leaned over and kissed me, and we both cried with joy. "My God," she sobbed, "what a glorious, happy day. Darling, in all my life, I've never had a time like this."

I do not know what possessed me. All I know is that before I realized it I had opened my mouth, and this is what I said, verbatim: "Well, yeah, but of course you weren't there the day Gavin Grey played Clemson."

For the balance of a somewhat foreshortened evening I tried to explain how probable it was that you really had to have been there to have understood that.

3

"WHAT DO YOU WANT TO DO, DONNIE?" BABS asked me early that evening, after the Clemson game.

"Well, I just don't want to get in y'all's way."

"You get out of here, Donnie McClure," Gavin said. "You're with us."

"What picture show's in town?" Babs asked.

"Shoot, picture show," Gavin said. "Donnie can see a picture show any old time in Wilson. If he's come to college, then let's do something real collegiate."

I nodded enthusiastically to that. We were at Babs's aunt's house. Her uncle was an associate professor of sociology. Babs came from a very learned family—relative to Gavin and me. The Greys and the McClures were mostly commercial people. But all of us were good Southern people, what was simply called "nice." Babs had not only come out in Greensboro—introduced to society with the cream of Carolina girlhood—but she had also made a debut in South Carolina too, at the St. Cecilia's in Columbia, where her mother came from. The McClures and the Greys were the same sort of families as Babs's: better off in social standing than in wealth. At the time, in the South, except for the white trash, who were common, pretty near everybody stood higher socially than they did economically.

The change in the South, the signal change that was coming, was hardly just a matter of improved racial attitudes. It had just as much to do with Southerners beginning to carry on like Yankees, emphasizing money at the expense of breeding. Imagine that! And air conditioning. It's easy to be more compassionate and compatible when you're not so damned hot all the time. I don't believe we ever would have fought the Civil War if we had had air conditioning then; cooler heads would have prevailed. My wife, who never lived in the South until it was the New South, gets very angry every time I say air conditioning was more important than Martin Luther King. But you couldn't put air conditioning on the six o'clock news.

Of course, Gavin and Babs were not just Southern. Above all, they were generic characters: the great American athlete and the great American pretty girl. And not tacky either. They were much more than what Joe DiMaggio and Marilyn Monroe ever could have symbolized—him being Eye-talian, her a service-station calendar bimbo. Besides, at that time, good pretty girls and nice athletic boys meant more to the South, for the same reasons that social status also counted more there. If there is any difference now, it is that the great athletes tend to be black and the pretty girls all let themselves get laid at an early age, so nobody takes either quick moves or beautiful faces quite as seriously as they used to.

In any event, Gavin decided that the collegiate thing to do was to take me to a fraternity party, and so he began checking around on the phone. Naturally, he didn't belong to any fraternity himself. The athletes seldom did, for they would be welcomed most anywhere without having to be inconvenienced by paying dues. As a rule, the worst people for spoiling athletes are women, fraternity brothers, and clergymen.

Gavin called Lawrence and Finegan. Just like you and me, they had first names, but except perhaps in the football roster, they were never utilized. Certainly, I never heard anybody actually speak their first names. Lawrence and Finegan were linemen on the team, old friends and classmates of Gavin. He adored them, as they worshiped him; they had blocked for him all these years, sacrificing themselves for his glory. I always think of football linemen as being palms, stretched out on the ground, cushioning Jesus' triumphal procession into Jerusalem.

Ostensibly, in the game program, both Lawrence and Finegan were seniors, but in point of fact they were no more than in the suburbs of their sophomore year. There was something known as "quality points" that you had to obtain a parcel of if you wished to stay athletically eligible, and somehow, through summer school and friendly professors (who were in the debt of coaches), Lawrence and Finegan and the other lummoxes who blocked for The Grey Ghost cadged enough of these to remain Tarheels.

They obtained no education and scratched out no future—neither was good enough to even dream of making the pros—but belonging to the football team prolonged their adolescence for four years, and so they were satisfied enough with that reward. Finegan, the right tackle—the right palm, if you will—had somehow been recruited to North Carolina from Rockaway, in Queens, and he returned to New York shortly after the Sugar Bowl and took up bartending, *around.* (He did show a certain native intelligence some years later by opening up a gay bar before that was easily tolerated . . . and making a killing by being in the vanguard.) Lawrence, who came (or "hailed," as he always had it) from way out in the western tip of Carolina, left the university at the same time as Finegan, but thereafter he would frequently reappear, if in no known capacity, until he became partner and manager of the Grey Ghost Inn, Gavin's steak house, which they opened five years later with his bonus money from the National Football League. Gavin and

Lawrence really loved each other as brothers, in ways I never could fathom. I think you had to play on a team together.

Lawrence was always celebrated at Chapel Hill, though—not only for being the right guard, but for being a prominent part of the local folklore. When Lawrence was a sophomore, a teammate, St. George Randolph, got married. Football can be, after all, something of a democratic experience, and Lawrence was invited to be in the wedding party, to be a principal in the social event of the year in Winston-Salem. The bride was tobacco. Lawrence was decked out in a rented tuxedo for the first time in his life (he refused to acknowledge it as anything but a "monkey suit"), and domiciled at an estate belonging to the great-aunt of the bride. Three of the groomsmen were put up there, each in his own private room. It was a huge place. The hostess was an aristocratic old maid who lived alone with a retinue of servants and her pet chihuahua, whose name was General Beauregard.

Lawrence had never in his life been intimidated by anything as he was by his fancy room, by the whole house, and by all the lovely people. Even though a whole pride of his teammates was on hand, and even though everybody in the wedding party went out of their way to make him feel at home, Lawrence felt impossibly uncomfortable. He weighed two hundred and fifty-eight pounds, and for the first time in his life he felt fat. And he just plain knew for a fact that he was common. If you were common in the South at that time, you were well aware of it—every bit as much as Gavin and I knew that our family was not common. You knew these things. Lawrence, who was renowned the state over for his ability to consume inhuman amounts of liquor, was in his cups before the champagne toasts were done. Gavin had never even seen him tipsy before, but now Lawrence knocked over a glass table; spoke incoherently, even when propositioning the bride's fifteen-year-old cousin (he couldn't enunciate "finger fuck"); and goosed the one bridesmaid who was extremely pregnant. Following that last unto-ward episode, the other players were able to subdue Lawrence, more or less, and get him to his bed at the great-aunt's house.

In the middle of the night Lawrence woke up and, feeling sick, reached for the light on the bedside table. Instead, he knocked over a glass of water, and then, staggering into the bathroom in the pitch dark, he threw up over much of the plumbing. But at least he felt somewhat better, and, feeling a bit guilty as well, he took a towel back to the bedroom, got down on his knees by the bed and made at least a cursory effort to mop up the water he had spilled all over the rug.

The next morning, when Lawrence awoke with the first light, his head splitting, he looked down and discovered that he had not knocked over a glass of water; he had knocked over a fancy old inkwell, and then he had mopped the ink all over the fuzzy white rug. That is, a white rug formerly-wise. And vomit was splattered over the bathroom walls. Lawrence paused before this scene only long enough to throw some water on his face, then he dressed and departed, hastening back to the friendly confines of Shelby, Encee. He did not even wait around to attend the wedding.

That was in June. In August, at preseason practice, St. George Randolph assured Lawrence that everyone back in Winston under-stood about the ink and the spit-up. It was accepted as an uninten-tional mistake; everybody is allowed at least one drunk. The pregnant lady he goosed had enjoyed an uneventful delivery, notwithstanding. The little cousin didn't mind at all being propositioned by a Tarheel. And so on. St. George got Gavin himself to offer additional assur-ances, and they all finally convinced Lawrence that he must apolo-gize to the great-aunt, clear his name as a Kowlinah Christian gentleman. So, at Christmas vacation, on his way back to Shelby from Chapel Hill, Lawrence detoured to Winston-Salem and, gritting his teeth, drove up to the great-aunt's estate. He got out of his old car, straightened his tie, and strode to the door.

The butler recognized Lawrence at once and gasped in fright. He would not let him in, only crack the door. By now, Lawrence was up to almost two hundred and eighty, and with his crew cut almost sliced down to his skull was an even more terrible creature than before. "Sir, I just want to apologize to Miss Susan, sir," he mumbled. The butler told him to wait there and closed the door on him. When the butler returned, he told him that the old lady would see him; she would come downstairs and meet him in the sitting room. Then the butler let Lawrence in, giving him a wide berth, and waved him in the direction of the parlor. The room was crowded with fragile bric-à-brac, and Lawrence, terrified that he might knock something else down, crossed to the largest chair as gingerly as his bulk would permit. The chair, ample in size, loaded with a number of furry pillows, could obviously safely contain even the full Lawrence. Relieved, he sank into it, *kerplop*.

Right away he knew something was amiss. He reached down in the vicinity of one of his huge thighs, and there, in the environs, he felt something warm and foreign. Also limp. It was General Beauregard, Miss Susan's chihuahua, whose custom it was to nap in this chair. Lawrence had sat on General Beauregard and broken his little neck. General Beauregard had gone quickly; he was graveyard dead.

Under these swiftly changing circumstances, Lawrence felt that an apology about the inkwell might not be accepted in the spirit in which it was intended. Therefore, and without further ado, Lawrence picked up the late General Beauregard by the scruff of his neck and dropped him in the umbrella stand in the hall by the front door as he departed.

The great-aunt was just beginning to negotiate her way to the stairs as Lawrence peeled out of her driveway, Shelby-bound. General Beauregard was located somewhat later by a sharp-nosed retainer.

THE CHIHUAHUA STORY soon became a part of the oral history of the state. Gavin never tired of the telling, just as he could listen for hours to Finegan—in his Noo Yawk accent, all the r's in the middle missing—relating quaint tales of the big city, of gang wars and subways, homos, foreigners, Mafiosi, bookies, and other alien people and features. Plus Finegan knew the sexual secrets of every celebrity in the world—these gleaned from those indisputable authorities who patronized the saloons of Rockaway, Queens. And what Gavin loved was that all this inside information was certified correct. Guaranteed as sure as Hadacol.

In their spare time, Finegan and Lawrence did not go to class. Instead, they broke up fraternities (or sororities, as the case may be), crashed parties, totaled cars, got in on all the available gang bangs, harassed colored people, and ate prodigious amounts of everything. Finegan could eat even more than Lawrence. He had slightly outbound teeth, and Lawrence maintained he could "gnaw the bottom out of a fryin' pan." Lawrence, on his behalf, was undisputed champion of chug-a-lugging and passing wind. Whatever, Gavin laughed uncontrollably at all their antics, and rather came to view them as modern Renaissance men: that they could carry on so spectacularly and still be good Tarheel football players as well! So:

"Ugh," said Babs, when Gavin informed her that we were going to a party with Lawrence and Finegan. "They're vulgar. They'll give Donnie a *totally* wrong impression of *our* Chapel Hill."

"Ah, don't be hoity-toity," Gavin said.

Whereupon, Babs threw her arms about me, saying, "Well then, y'all can be with them, and Donnie'll be my beau tonight."

"Hey, Donnie," Gavin hooted, "I hope you can get more off'n her than me."

I didn't know how to react to that. Babs herself backed away and glared at Gavin. "Gavin Grey, that is the commonest piece of tacky thing I have ever heard in my life," she said. "Sometimes you talk like a Yankee."

He just smiled. In fact, of course, he knew that Babs was delighted, for whereas she surely was a nice girl, as advertised, some sort of testimony to that effect was required periodically. Likewise, it was his obligation to test her chastity, under game conditions, each time they were along. Otherwise: Does a tree falling in the forest make a sound if no one is around to hear?

We drove down Columbia Street, turned onto Fraternity Court, and met Lawrence and Finegan outside Sigma Nu. It was a red-brick building—like so many of the fraternities, in the style of a gracious old plantation, or reminiscent of the gorgeous old town houses in Wilson that lined Nash Street. I suspect, at least until that time, that the fraternity houses in the South were the architectural sons of Dixie's men. You could not always marry your ideal, and it was chancier still that you would sire a classic Southern child (a Gavin Grey, say, or a Babs Rogers). Indeed, few enough could buy a dream house, there being only so many, even in tobacco towns. But at least for a few of the *formative* years, every southern man could belong to a fraternity, reside in a house built to look like the antebellum plantation dream he had been raised on. Maybe that was why at that time in the South, throughout a man's life, whatever his accomplishments, he was liable to be identified first by his college fraternity affiliation: "This is Mr. Jones, a Phi Delt from State." Or: "I'm sure y'all will like Benjie Smith. He was a St. A at the University." No more was necessary to say.

Gavin had selected the Sigma Nu house because of the band that was playing there. Sigma Nu and Sigma Chi were the most influential jock fraternities, but this Saturday night Sigma Nu had the Hot Nuts, a black band that was very risqué and demanded top dollar. They would sing such choruses as, "See that man, dressed in tan / He won't do it, but his sister can." I mean, that was vintage Hot Nuts. That drove us crazy. Then the refrain: "Hot nuts, hot nuts, get 'em from the peanut man." And we would cheer our fool heads off some more. You've got to remember that fun required more of an imagination in those purer, halcyon days. Once it became all right for the good girls to screw (and often as not, just for fun) nobody had to work as hard at anything anymore. Diligence went all to hell. It was right after that that the college board scores started to go down, for example.

To Babs's additional disgust, Lawrence and Finegan were not only parked out front, consuming beer upon beer, but they were accompanied in this and other joint endeavors by a dumpy little high-school girl known only as "Turtle." Her reputation as a county punchboard preceded her, and Lawrence was quick to advise me that she was "jailbait," but while I expressed my gratitude for this intelligence, I was also altogether unaware of what it meant. I remember Turtle so especially vividly only because, in all my life, she was the first girl I ever heard say anything stronger than "damn" (and few enough even said that). I don't know who was more mortified, me or Babs, when Turtle first lashed out at Finegan for his spilling a bit of beer on her dress. "You common fucking Yankee cocksucker," is how Turtle began her tirade, sending

Gavin and Lawrence and Finegan into spasms of giggles and snorts and encouraging Turtle to unleash more obscenities.

Babs, genuinely disquieted at this display, but also putting on some for show, turned heel toward the haven of Sigma Nu, and we all hastened after her. Certainly, from the monstrous forms of Lawrence and Finegan to the dwarflike Turtle and skinny little me, we formed a bizarre phalanx as we entered the building. We could hear the music downstairs. Here, in the common room, couples relaxed away from the crush of the dance floor; a few necked innocently. But all stopped whatever it was they were doing as soon as Gavin walked through the door. By reflex, it seemed, some of the boys appeared to touch their hands to their hearts as he passed, as they would salute Old Glory. All fell silent.

Downstairs, the dance floor was dark, and so few could immediately comprehend that a deity was in their midst. Lawrence remedied this by heading directly to the stage, appropriating the microphone, and pointing out Gavin to the head Hot Nut. Instantly, he stopped the music. "The Grey Ghost: number twenty-five in your program, number one in your heart," Lawrence screamed.

In the ensuing tumult, Gavin dropped his head and said, "Shoot, Lawrence." He loved it. The girls and boys alike smiled at his becoming modesty and commented on the unchanging size of his helmet.

The Hot Nuts sang, "See that man, name of Grey / Everybody loves him in the U.S. of A." The place exploded again, and the change of "Ghost . . . Ghost . . . Ghost . . ." obliged Gavin to stop merely holding his head humbly and to be convoyed to the microphone by Finegan. There, he spoke one word: "Kowlinah." He may have had more in mind, but that was all he said for the moment before the room tore apart. The Hot Nuts broke into fight songs, Tarheel songs, and one ponytailed girl, a cheerleader, jumped up and did a split in her pleated skirt. Lawrence took the microphone back and, pointing to Babs, still down on the floor, stuck there with Turtle and me, hollered, "And how 'bout a cheer for the loveliest lady in all the Tarheel State?"

And they exploded for Babs.

"Thank you, Sigma Nu, God bless you," she cried out, waving to the crowd. It was good and proper that Lawrence had not forgotten her.

The Hot Nuts sang, "See our Babs, dressed in green / Prettiest girl you've ever seen." Gavin came down from the stage and wrapped one arm around her, then clapped the other about my shoulder. He left Turtle there for Lawrence and Finegan, and began to steer Babs and me back upstairs.

"I gotta pee," he whispered to me. "You gotta pee, Donnie?" I nodded in the affirmative even though the thought had not recently crossed my mind. But what the hell, you can always take a pee, especially when everybody's All-American invites you along. So we left Babs there in the common room, and she stood off by herself. There were many boys about, but they dared not approach her. She smiled. They looked away. Her whole life, her every instinct, her upbringing, even, was that men, in such circumstances, would come to her, be solicitous at least, fuss over her. But now she was Gavin Grey's girl, and they would not mess with an institution. I saw a little grimness set upon her face, and for nothing to do, she went to the ladies' room.

In the men's room, there were three urinals. The one on the right was taken. I chose the one on the left, and Gavin moved to the center. The young fellow on the right glanced over idly at us newcomers. Then he looked again, his head sort of swiveling, as in a cartoon. Next, he merely uttered Gavin's name, and, in his excitement, exercised bad aim. Out of politeness and good raising, Gavin stared ahead and called no attention to this benign miscue. But the boy would not quit. "Gavin Grey," he sighed. "Wait'll I tell folks back home I took a piss with The Grey Ghost hisself."

"Ah, come on," Gavin said.

"People pissing all ovuh Chapel Hill, and me, I get to take a leak with Gavin Grey." He shook his head, awed at the odds and at Gavin alike. Then he kind of backed out of the bathroom, neglecting to zip up his fly all the way.

"Ain't that the shits?" Gavin asked. "Ain't it?" I nodded. "Carryin' on like that ovuh me takin' a pee."

"Well now, it wasn't just you takin' a pee, Gavin. It was you and him takin' a pee *togethuh*. The two of you."

"What's all that?" Gavin replied, zipping up. "There's nobody on God's green earth I care to take a pee with. No reflection on you, of course, Donnie. I wouldn't care who-all it is, peeing. Man or woman."

"It's just that you're a HE-ro, Gavin."

"HE-ro! You think people got all excited when they got a chance to take a leak with Robert E. Lee? With George Washington? Nobody ever said, 'George Washington peed here,' did they? Did they, Donnie?"

"Not that I ever heard."

"You see. There's just so much of this 'everybody's All-American' shit I can't understand."

We returned to the common room. It was an ornate place, high-ceilinged, with sweeping draperies and heavily upholstered chairs. Babs was waiting near the door to the ladies' room, standing alone, lost and somewhat indignant. As soon as she saw us emerge from the men's room, she came toward us. There were a lot of people scattered around, and they hushed again to stare reverently at Gavin and Babs together. In the corners, some were kissing and holding hands; otherwise, they sipped beer and smoked. In North Carolina, in those days before anybody knew there was a fellow known as the Surgeon General, pretty near everybody smoked all the time. Considering the disrepute come to singing "Dixie" and smoking cigarettes, it's amazing that we Southern folk have ended up at all stable.

Gavin took Babs's hand. "Come on, y'all," he said. "Let's go get some beers from Lawrence." She nodded and reached for my hand too, and it was in that very instant, as Babs's hand touched mine, that the awful flash came from across the way. I saw the flames exactly as they burst. I was looking, by chance, right at them, because I was too shy to look at Babs when she actually touched me. It was right by a large sofa, where a girl named Caroline Cross was sitting, next to her date, who was a Beta. (He was identified that way in all the press accounts.) The sofa ended right where some rich, pleated, shiny curtains fell, and somewhat in front of them there was a standing ashtray. Somebody had put some gum or candy wrappers in it, and without looking, Caroline Cross's date, the Beta, had leaned over and laid a lighted match in the ashtray. Seconds later the papers burst into flame, and Caroline, startled, jumped back in her seat.

Her legs knocked the ashtray over onto her, the fiery paper tumbling out and spilling down her dress. It was of a soft material, with two or three crinolines underneath, and they caught fire as if made of kindling. In another instant, the flames leapt above her head, and she screamed in such a way that Babs squeezed my hand in terror.

The people around Caroline Cross turned to look at her, and they froze at the sight. As though reflexively, then, she jumped up, and somehow she stumbled and fell back against the curtains, which went up like a torch, the flames climbing up toward the ceiling.

I cannot tell you how long this all took. Certainly, it takes much longer to recount than the events themselves lasted. Ten seconds, maybe? Five? Who knows? I only know we all stood transfixed, all but one of us in that room—and there must have been ten or fifteen people there. I was so shocked that I did not even comprehend at first that it was Gavin who jumped by me, almost knocking Babs aside. He dashed to an alcove and from the wall grabbed one of those little red fire extinguishers. I had never seen it—who had?—and how Gavin knew it was there, I will never understand. In three more steps he was upon Caroline Cross. She had fallen to the floor and was writhing there, a pyre, it seemed. But till now the flames had only consumed her dress and crinolines; it would be another instant before they would be burning her body.

In that last moment, Gavin ripped open the extinguisher tab and fired a long burst of foam upon her, killing the fire dead. Then, that accomplished, he turned from her and reached right up and grabbed the curtain, thrusting his hand into the very heart of the flames, I thought. It looked like that; it was that close. Whatever, he found enough material intact to take hold and give it a mighty yank. It was like Samson pulling at the temple pillars in the Bible picture books. The burning curtain ripped away, saving the flames from reaching the draperies that ran across the top. Had they gotten there—and they were just below—there would have been no stopping them short of fire engines coming and much of the building going, for sure, and maybe many of the people crowded downstairs, too.

The curtain fell, still blazing. Gavin fired the rest of the extinguisher upon it, holding the trigger until it was spent. Then he hurled the gadget aside and, in one more motion, pulled off his own sports jacket. With it, he fell upon Caroline Cross, who lay on the floor, sobbing, her skirts smoldering. He pressed the jacket around her, smothering her charred clothes. And then, at last, he sighed and rested there, limp, upon her.

It was only then, after all of that, that any of the rest of us reacted. It was all over and done with before we even moved. Two Sigma Nus stamped out the last cinders from the curtain. Caroline Cross sobbed louder, but she was not hurt. Then she opened her eyes and recognized who lay on her. "Ghost," she cried in a startled whisper. And once more: "Ghost."

Immediately, Gavin rose up from her. "Excuse me, ma'am" is what he said, as if he had taken liberties. Carefully, he pulled his jacket down, so that it shielded the lower part of her body, where her clothes had burned away.

He got to his feet. A few people had come up the steps from the dance floor. They had heard the screams and crowded at the top of the stairs: "What's going on?" "Who is it?" "Lemme see, y'all." But the rest of us, those in the room who had witnessed it all, said not a word. Gavin looked around at us, and then down to Caroline and the curtains, at what he had done. His eyes were full of wonder, although possibly fear, too. He seemed as startled as the rest of us.

At last, unsure, even tentative, he raised his right hand, beckoning toward Babs. She nodded and, picking her way through the others, who stood stock-still, moved to his side and took his hand. He looked back over at me, and when he realized that I would not move without a personal invitation either, he pointed at me and then jerked his thumb. I obeyed immediately. I walked to the door with them, although, out of deference, a half step or so behind.

Still, there was not a sound. Even Caroline Cross, lying on the floor, covered by The Grey Ghost's own jacket, kept her peace till Gavin was gone.

In the car, I got into the backseat. Gavin started the engine up right away, without a word, but he only drove it around the corner, onto Columbia, out of sight of the fraternity. He cut the engine there and flicked off the lights, and then he looked toward Babs and fell into her arms. He cried for some time. "My God, what I did" was what he said at last.

She held him and soothed him for a long time more, until at last he raised up and began to pull himself together. "You know, Babsie," he said, "I'm scared to death of fire." For emphasis, he turned around to me. Maybe it was the first time he remembered that I was there. "I am, Donnie, I'm scared to death of fire. Isn't that funny?" Then he fell back down into her arms and cried even more, but laughing a little nervously, too.

She patted him on the back once and simply said, "Gavin Grey, you can just do no wrong."

He nodded, too, in response, as if very much that he was up to these days was out of his hands. "I s'pose so," he said.

THE NEXT DAY, when I was alone with Babs, she said, "Now Donnie, don't y'all ever tell anybody about Gavin in the car last night."

"No ma'am," I said, and I shook my head vigorously. And I have kept that promise all along, until now.

4

A S THE TALE OF THAT NIGHT AT SIGMA NU SPREAD, the legend of Gavin Grey grew all the more. A ballad was written and records actually pressed. Caroline Cross's dress—what remained of it after the fire and after those present sliced off souvenir patches—was hung up by the cash register in the Goody Shop, the most popular hamburger emporium in Chapel Hill, and people came to marvel at the stark evidence of the tale, which grew in heroism with each repetition.

Gavin could no longer move about freely. Grown people came from all over the state, on expedition, merely in hopes of catching a fleeting glimpse of The Ghost strolling the campus in his cardigan letter sweater, his khakis, and his white bucks. The first casualty of fame is modesty; the second, privacy; and so he appeared in public only for obligatory classes—moving swiftly, from a different direction each day, and in the hulking escort of Lawrence and Finegan. By now, they had given up all pretense of scholarship, and had taken to convoying Gavin full time. Much to Babs's dismay, he had even moved into their off-campus apartment with them.

Moreover, he compounded his avatar complex by playing a game against Wake Forest the likes of which could not have been dreamt up, much less put in the Sunday paper. It was on national television, too. Gavin scored four touchdowns in the first half and appeared to add a fifth when he made a diving catch in the corner of the end zone. The official nearest threw his hands up: TD! The stadium exploded. The band broke into "Dixie." Gavin walked over, handed the referee the ball, and informed him that the pass was incomplete: He had not caught it fairly but had trapped it on a short bounce off the ground. This action won over every moralist and mother not already in his camp, and he likewise charmed the win-at-any-cost skeptics by allowing to the press afterward, "Well, it ain't real hard to tell the truth when you're ahead twenty-eight to zero."

Next, the Tarheels and The Ghost left South Carolina in ruins and then utterly annihilated Virginia. I was blessed to see that game in person, too, because even though my parents had little interest in football and were suspicious of Chapel Hill as a Communist outpost, even they longed to see The Grey Ghost play one last time at Carolina, for Carolina. We went to a party afterward at Babs's uncle's house. It was only family, on both sides, with just a few ringers. Gavin suffered this as long as he could, as relatives and putative relatives squeezed him like a supermarket fruit, and then, to my delight, he snuck over to me, took me by the arm, and spirited me up a back stairs to a room with a television set, where we sat and watched the June Taylor Dancers do terpsichorean formations (like flower buds opening) on *The Jackie Gleason Show*. "And awaaay we go," Gavin cried.

We perused the dancers and the opening monologue. At the commercial, Gavin said, "I get so tired of family and all, don't you, Donnie?" I nodded agreeably. "And Babs is down there like a pig in shit. Family!"

"Hey, I'm family too," I reminded him. Listen, I didn't want Gavin Grey's company under any false pretenses.

"Naww, you're good people, Donnie. You're one of the few people around 'sides Lawrence and Finegan who don't get all over me."

I nodded enthusiastically. Obviously, it was part of my enduring charm for The Grey Ghost that I was almost pathologically reticent with him, and so I did my best to institutionalize this attribute.

"You know what it is," Gavin went on, when Jackie Gleason retired for a singer—a "guest vocalist" in TV parlance. "It ain't just the people all around me, and making a fuss and all. Hell, that's even nice sometimes. But it's that they're always talkin' 'bout me. So I gotta talk 'bout me, too. That's the hardest part of being everybody's All-American. That's why I like sneakin' up here with you, 'cause I know you and me can just sit here and watch old Jackie Gleason. You know what I mean?"

I said I did.

"See if everybody's interested in you, well, after a while, you get that way, too. It's not that I think I'm special, it's just that folks won't let *me* get away from *me*. Now, I've already started wonderin' myself how I'm gonna do 'gainst Duke, 'cause that's all anybody lets me think about. And the trouble is, I can see that I get like in a groove. Already, I'm *expecting* people to ask me about it."

The thought stirred him into action. All of a sudden, Gavin reared up and said, "Let's just get our little red asses outta here."

"You mean leave?"

"Yeah. I'm just plain tired of bein' The Grey Ghost." And he told me to go downstairs and call up Lawrence and Finegan and get them to come over and pick us up. The roof of the front porch came right up under the window of the room we were in, and Gavin looked out and figured he could jump off it to a tree there, and climb down the rest of the way.

I called Lawrence straightaway, ducking Babs on the way to the phone. Finegan was out with what was described to me as "motor-sickle snatch" (I believe that meant a tough lady in a leather jacket), but Lawrence was only too delighted to rescue his pal. In fact, when I explained the situation about the roof and so forth, the first thing he said was that he thought he knew where he could steal a fire truck—steal a fire truck!—so he could hoist a ladder up for The Ghost. Thinking on my own initiative for a change, I volunteered that I really didn't believe that was necessary; just get the car and bring it around.

The getaway worked to a T. Everybody's All-American climbed out onto the roof, stuck a leg out to the tree, got a toehold, then pushed himself out, bridging there for just a moment until his body firmly committed itself to the direction of the tree. He grabbed hold then, and clambered down with no damage to his person, and no witnesses either. Gavin wanted me to follow in his footsteps, but since, in the first place, nobody cared whether or not I stayed at the party, and, in the second, I was reasonably scared of high places that swayed, I went downstairs the orthodox way, told my parents I was going out with Gavin ("and tell Babs if she asks," I added over my shoulder as I ducked out the house), and dashed out to the waiting car, the famous Plymouth which had once spirited a crazed chihuahua murderer away from the scene of the crime.

"You ever been to Coloredtown, Donnie?" Gavin asked leaning forward with the seat so I could climb into the back.

I sure hadn't.

"Maybe we'll get us some black oak for Donnie to split," Lawrence said.

"Naw we ain't," Gavin declared, at once relieving me and disappointing me. "We're just gonna go see that colored boy."

"Oh," I said. Now I was just plain scared to death. To go to such a place at any time was unwise; any night, foolish; but to be so dangerous as to go on a Saturday night: Why, of all the hundreds of Rastus jokes I had ever heard, most involved some reference to Saturday night. But, not to betray my manhood, I kept my fears to myself and trusted that however casually Lawrence might view my life (not to mention his own), he would surely do nothing to jeopardize the health of The Grey Ghost.

"We're goin' to a place called the Three Corners," Lawrence told me. "There's a boy from back near my home in Rutherford County who kinda runs it. I sees him ever' now and again."

"You know him too, Gavin?" I asked.

"I ain't never met him, but Lawrence been tellin' me 'bout him all these years," he said. They were riding up front together, and I was in the back of the old Plymouth. It was an off-maroon, I would say, with a large pair of fuzzy dice hanging down from the rearview mirror and a necker's nob on the steering wheel. Once it had even had a foxtail trolling from the aerial, but that had been removed as passé. However tacky Lawrence might have been, he could not have been accused of being unfashionably so. He was one of these people (there's a great many of them, really) who was always tacky *au courant*.

The Plymouth negotiated back roads out of Chapel Hill toward Durham. The two of them were drinking beer out of bottles, and I just hung on, getting really scared when I could tell we had gotten into a black neighborhood. The roads were bad, that was how you could tell right away. If it were poor-white, the houses might be just as ramshackle, but the roads would be better, and almost certainly paved. The Plymouth jostled over the ruts and holes, skidding in the dirt around corners. "Slow down," Gavin cautioned Lawrence. "You sure don't want to hit any nigger on a Saturday night."

I had expected, I suppose, a regular sort of establishment, with a neon sign and the other accoutrements of normal white commerce, but the Three Corners was barely more than a clapboard house, with no sign I ever saw indicating that it was a place of business. The location was not ideal either. It was at the end of a cul-de-sac, though two footpaths led away from it through the surrounding fields, the one going to a black elementary school, the other to some kind of small plant where the neighborhood black men could find some work whenever the worse jobs opened up. Somehow this configuration had led to the name of the Three Corners.

But there surely was a lot of activity: a bunch of cars out front and a number of black folks milling about them. Music was blaring from the place—rhythm and blues, or what had been called "race records" to right up about this time, when the whites started to appropriate it. "Earth Angel," by the Penguins, was playing as we drove up, then "My Babe," by Little Walter, and "Pledging My Love," by Johnny Ace, who did himself in playing Russian roulette. Presley was still a couple years away. I heard Ray Charles for the first time that night at the Three Corners. Scared as I was, I was more tingling with wonder, even as some of the young men came up to the Plymouth. One tall fellow spoke to us, menacing and polite at one and the same time, which was about the only way a black could deal firmly with trespassing whites back then. "This ain't no place for college boys," he said, leaning down toward Lawrence.

"Hey, y'all, I just wanna see Blue. He's a friend of mine," Lawrence said, bringing with it a strange ripple of cynical recognition from the crowd. I didn't know it then, of course, but at that time Blue was what passed for what we later called a "black militant"; hence the snickers—that any fool white man would claim to be his friend.

"That *po*-lice, Junie?" a voice farther in the back inquired.

"Cain't be," Junie replied. "There be a little boy in the backseat." Junie was looking directly at me now, his dark eyes trying to sort me out. And funny, now that I could see him one-to-one and deal with him that way, I wasn't frightened at all. I remember my thoughts turned to his pink and black outfit, and it filled up my mind that that was positively the commonest apparel I had ever seen in all my life.

"I just wanna see Blue," Lawrence told him. "We both come from down yonder in Rutherford County."

A young woman heard that and came up to Junie. "Blue do come from there," she advised him.

"Well, I'll set some store in that, then," Junie said. "I'll tell you what, gentlemens: Let me take the little white boy in after Blue."

Gavin and Lawrence turned around to me, expecting me to cringe at the proposition, but I signaled that it was perfectly agreeable for me to play the hostage. As I got out, earning my stripes, Lawrence told me, "Donnie, you just tell him it's Lawrence here to see him."

Junie ushered me into the Three Corners, past people who stared at me with a passive kind of curiosity. For my part, I tried to act as if I did this sort of thing all the time, imagining myself rather like the adventurous boy in *Treasure Island,* cast amidst friendly buccaneers. In my self-consciousness, I barely noticed the surroundings, except that they were dark, and it was crowded and noisy, and redolent of greasy food. Blue, in fact, was occupied in the back, in what was the kitchen, and when I first saw him he was just coming out, wiping his hands on an apron. "He come with two college boys lookin' for you," Junie said to him.

"Lawrence," I said. I got it out in a hurry, a password.

"Oh, big ole Lawrence from Shelby?" Blue asked. "Shit, come on." And he took off the apron and cut back through the crowd to get outside. He was exceptionally dark, not spared of the thick Negroid facial features we thought so ugly, but he was a lean young man, thin-wasted, wide in the shoulders, perhaps six feet, no more, and he walked—rolled—with a pronounced pigeon-toes gait. I followed close behind him.

He spied Lawrence, still sitting in the car. Lawrence waved to Blue and called his name; without any such corresponding regard, Blue merely beckoned for him to get out and come over. Lawrence did, bounding, jiggling happily, his great mass now revealed, rather astounding the crowd still gathered about; he tended to settle into a car seat. "Lawrence, my man, you got a nerve bringin' this boy with you, huntin' for colored girls," Blue said, and I could tell that he was not pleased. I had never seen a black man talk to a white in such a way. It was not the anger (and that faded soon enough), but the tone, which was so maddeningly confident and natural. It was odd: Blue then spoke with every bit as much inflection as any young black man in Carolina, but his manner, just that, made him sound so altogether different to me.

"I didn't come for no girls, Blue."

"You ain't never come here for *my* company afore."

"No, I brung you somethin'."

"Is that a natural fact? You brung me somethin'? I know you sure didn't bring me no white girl." And Blue laughed some at that, baring a mouth chock-full of holes, with tarnished and twisted teeth. It was shocking, because every other part of him was so sound and beautiful. Lawrence laughed with him, and took him over to the car, and told him to look inside. Blue peered down for just an instant, and then he roared again. "Lord, you done brung me De Ghost," and he stuck out his hand, and Gavin took it through the window and pumped it, laughing back. "De Ghost hisself."

Blue opened the door for him, and Gavin stood up, and for an instant they just hung there, looking one another in the eye.

"I done watched you, Ghost, and you is some player."

"I heard tell the same 'bout you." And curiously, to me, for I still didn't know who Blue was, they shook hands again.

Lawrence came over. "We brung our own beer," he said.

"You mean, you're a-fixin' to stay?"

"There ain't no place we can go without everybody makin' such a fuss over The Ghost. So we thought maybe we could come out here, and just sit in the corner and listen to some R&B."

Blue thought for a moment, and then he nodded a qualified assent. "You're welcome, but you keep in mind that there ain't no police comin' out to Coloredtown of a Saturday night, and if one of these young gentlemens gets a little whiskeyed up, he might get hisself disagreeable to a white man. It ain't likely, but—" He shrugged. "We ain't never had a white man in the Three Corners."

"Can I get some dinner?" Gavin asked, purposely not even bothering to acknowledge the dire warning.

"We ain't got nothin' but colored food."

"No mind. An old colored lady brought me up, and I ate it all, pigs' feet, chitlins. You got any kale, Blue? I'd like some colored food again."

"Is that so? Is that a nat'ral fact?" Blue said, and he looked at Gavin in an even different way, as if they were friends or kin, or could understand one another. I was never scared at all the rest of the time at the Three Corners.

Blue took us inside and found us a table back in the corner. He introduced us to the people in the vicinity (just casually), and then he went away, but came back in a minute with a Nehi orange for me, which he said was on the house.

"Who *is* he?" I whispered to Lawrence as soon as he walked away.

"You never heard of Narvel Blue?" He was incredulous.

"Never, and that's the God's truth."

"Narvel Blue come from down in Rutherford County, outside of Shelby, and he was the best football player ever to come out of the Tarheel State."

"The best?" I gasped, incredulous at this blasphemy.

"The best *at the time,* right after the war," Lawrence said, amending his remarks. "I'll tell you what, though, he was better than ole Choo-Choo. No question 'bout that. He was three years ahead of me, and I seen him play three seasons for the colored school. It got so, so many white folks was comin' out to see Narvel Blue play, that they had to switch the colored games less'n there wouldn't be nobody at the white games."

"Is that a fact?" Gavin said.

"They took the colored games from Saturdays to Fridays his last two years. I seen Blue score eight touchdowns in one game, and he didn't hardly play the last quarter."

"But he wasn't better'n . . . Gavin," I said, frightened of the answer.

"I was sure I wouldn't never see no man play football better than Narvel Blue, but now, like I done told Gavin a lot of times, I'd hate someone to put a pistol to my head, 'cause I don't know at all what I'd say."

"Did he ever play after high school?" I asked.

"There was talk that some Yankee schools was lookin' at him, but he done real poorly in school, and then he knocked up his girl friend and got hisself married while he was still in school. A & T wanted him, I believe, but there was no way he could support a wife and baby in college. No, I don't believe Blue done ever played so much as a lick since high school."

"Ain't that a shame," Gavin said.

Suddenly, there was an old black lady standing there next to Gavin. She was so ancient she seemed almost tinted gray, and her hair was falling out, so that what was left was done up in those hedgerows—though with more skin between than rows of hair. But she moved pretty good, and her eyes were bright and gay, and she was having a whale of a good time. What she wanted was Gavin's autograph, and as soon as she spoke to him, he jumped right up out of his chair. He called her ma'am, and he treated her exactly like she was a white lady, and it so shamed Lawrence and me that we found ourselves rising to our feet, too.

Gavin said he wouldn't give her his autograph unless she gave him a taste of her snuff. She was chewing a little snuff with her glass of beer. It didn't have any foam left; she'd probably nursed it all night, just sitting there, watching the dancing and listening to the gossip and the rhythm and blues.

"You want snuff, Ghost?" she asked, cackling. "Young folks don't take snuff no more. Leastwise no colored."

"There was an old colored lady brought me up down yonder in Charlotte," Gavin said. "A Mrs. Belle Hargrove, from Chester, South Carolina. She used to take snuff too, and she'd give me a little now and again."

The old lady giggled—snickered like a schoolgirl—when he took that tin of snuff from her, and put some in his mouth, like it was all he ever did in his life. In all the time he was everybody's All-American, I never saw him more relaxed and natural, and it didn't seem like there was a person in the place who didn't look on him with favor.

The old lady looked him over, chewing, and finally she just upped and said, "Mister Ghost, I do declare, would you mind if an old colored lady kissed you." Why, she was downright coy by now; she was carrying on with him.

And, for his part, Gavin said, "I never said no to any good-lookin' woman ever wanted to kiss me." And if that didn't do it: The people nearby who could hear him hooted and hollered, and out of the corner of my eye I saw Blue come out of the kitchen and stand there and watch in some wonder as the old lady reached up and kissed Gavin on the cheek. The musical selection at that time was "Close Your Eyes," by the Five Keys. By now, we were all laughing, and there wasn't a soul on the dance floor who didn't stop to look over. Gavin reach down, picked up his beer off the table, and poured some into her glass, leering a little as he did it, as fine as I ever saw him play any part.

The old lady reeled back, pretending to swoon—she played her part pretty good, too—and said, "Lord 'a mercy, now The Ghost gonna get me drunk as a monkey!" And Gavin raised a toast to her with his beer.

Blue came over and wrapped an arm around the old lady. In an odd way he was kind of annoyed at Gavin for daring to take center stage, yet he was all the more pleased and proud of him that he had fit in so comfortably. "I thought I tolds you white gentlemens that y'all could visit if you didn't go about mo-lestin' the young girls. Right, Miss Edna?"

She looked up to him. "There's more devilment in Mister Ghost than there is even in you, Blue. He is one mischievous boy."

"I 'preciate your comin' by, Miss Edna," Gavin said, and he sat back down. Lawrence and I followed his lead, and Blue kissed the old lady himself, and she went back to her table, clutching the autograph.

"Y'all want somethin' to eat now?" Blue asked.

"I was hopin' you'd sit with us awhile and talk," Gavin said. "Come on, Blue, have a beer"—and he took a bottle out of the six-pack.

So Blue nodded, pulled up a chair, turned it around, and sat down backwards, arms across the top of the back. "That was right kind of you with old Miss Edna. You spend any time with colored folks?"

"I said out yonder, there was the old lady raised me from the day I was born. And then I played with colored boys when I was growin' up. But you know."

"You ain't never played no football 'gainst them?"

"Never so much as a one," Gavin replied.

"Did you ever play after high school?" I asked.

"The last time I played was in Rutherford County, the fall of 'forty-seven. I married then. I got me two calls from up north, Illinois and some other college university, but I wasn't studyin' nothin' 'bout no Illinois. I was just a dumb nigger never been much past Rutherford County. Three years later, after me and my wife broke up, I tried Canada. I had me a good car, that Dodge I got set out yonder, and a white man I knew from Greensboro told me 'bout Canada, so I rode up there, and I went to three teams, and not a one of 'em would so much as let me on the field. I said, Let me just run in my stockin' feet. But they wouldn't tolerate even that. They only allows so many Americans, and they had alls they wanted. And they said, Where'd you play, boy? And when I said Rutherford County, North Carolina, they 'bout laughed at me, so after the third team, I jus' climbed back in the car and drove clear through to Carolina. And to tell you the truth, I never give it another thought, football."

He paused for a second and sucked on his beer. "Well, I be dead honest with you. I started let it cross my mind this fall, when I seen you play."

"You came out to see me play?"

"I had to see for myself 'zackly how good you is."

I started to ask the question myself, but Gavin anticipated me, and laid his hand on my wrist to silence me. "How good am I?" he asked directly—the only time I ever heard him ask such a question, the only time I ever even heard him encourage someone to talk about his prowess.

"You was ever' bit as good as Lawrence says you is. I 'spect you's jus' 'bout as good as me."

"What I say?" cried Lawrence. "Ain't but a cunt hair could separate you two."

"I come back and seen you play Wake, too, and I seen you on TV. I watched you, and there's some things you do better'n me."

"Like what?" Gavin said, much too anxiously.

"Pick a hole better. I could see that. Follow your blockers. I was always gettin' out ahead of 'em."

"Gavin can catch a pass better'n you, too, Blue," Lawrence said.

"That's true, and you might be a little bit stronger at breakin' tackles. I was more liable to try and fake my way round about a man."

"Jitterbug," Lawrence said.

"But you's not as good in the open field as me. If there's one or two men to beat, I didn't never get caught. Never's I can remember. I seen you fail at that once." Gavin nodded, acknowledging the criticism as fair. "And quick as you is, you ain't no ways up to what I could do off'n the ball. Why, Lawrence, if it was you playin' in front o' me, I'd run right up your ass."

This frame of reference did not bother Lawrence at all. On the contrary: "Ain't no one in the world could come off that mark like Blue. The ball snap, and zip, he was at the line."

"When we had a new official refereein' our games," Blue said, "the ole coach, Mr. Meriwether, he had to take them gentlemens aside afore the game and have us run off a play or two on the side-lines so they could see I wasn't goin' in motion, beatin' the snap."

"And neither one of you never fumble," Lawrence said.

"Who's the faster?" I asked.

"I be a bit faster," Blue said.

"Naw, I don't reckon so," Lawrence said. "I never in my life thought I'd see anybody faster on the gridiron than you, Blue, but I played with The Ghost four years now, and I come to think he'd catch you in the secondary. Not to the line, but with the longer strides: in the secondary."

By now, Gavin was just sitting and listening, interested in a dispassionate sort of way, as if it weren't him they were talking about. But Blue was not so unmoved—especially now that he and Lawrence had come to their first dispute. "You might set store by that judgment, Lawrence, but you ain't ever gonna get me to think thataway."

"It wouldn't be by much now," Lawrence said, trying to placate our host somewhat, "but I do believe The Ghost would whip you over any distance of ground."

"A football field?" asked Blue. "A hundred yards?"

"Yeah, he'd beat you a step or two."

"You bet on that judgment, Lawrence?"

"Sure I would."

"How much?"

Lawrence ruminated for a few seconds, but then he replied firmly: "Fifty dollars. I got fifty dollars says The Ghost can beat your black ass at a hundred yards." Gavin giggled. I gasped: fifty dollars!

"Shit, any fifty dollars," Blue said.

"That's all I got."

"You got that car, you got that Plymouth out yonder, and that must be worth three-four hundred."

"What'd you got to drive, Blue?"

"I got a 'forty-nine Dodge with sixty-some thousand on it."

"That's an honest readin'?"

"Honest as the day is long. Alls it needs is points."

"My Plymouth has fifty-eight and change."

Gavin clapped his hands. "Sounds fair to me," he said. "Fair bet."

That sort of reminded Blue that Gavin was the other principal, and right there on the premises, too. "Whatdya think, Ghost?"

"I don't know, Blue. You seen me run. I ain't never seen you."

"I mean, will you run me, sure 'nuff?"

Gavin looked him square ahead, and what he said quite astonished me. He said, "I'd rather race the one and only Narvel Blue than I would play Duke." And he reached out his hand and shook that black man's. "So let's go."

My heart was fluttering to such an extent that I felt I must be bouncing up and down off my seat. But Lawrence had a second thought. "Now wait just a cotton-pickin' minute," he said. "The Ghost been drinkin' beer all night. You ain't had but the one." Blue sighed. Without a word, he chug-a-lugged the half or so left in his bottle, and then, one by one, he reached out and took what was left of Gavin's and Lawrence's, and, for good measure, washed them down with the half of a Nehi orange I had left.

Gavin laughed and declared, "Ain't no more argument here at the table, Lawrence."

5

THE ROAD TO THE THREE CORNERS, THE ROAD we had driven down, the road where the two of them would race, was relatively flat, with a slight incline going away from the restaurant. "You want to run uphill or down?" Blue asked Gavin.

"No matter, really."

"Got to be one way or the other."

"Uphill, then. Make it a little bit harder on us."

"Then we'll start over yonder," Blue said, and he drew a line in the dirt with his foot, and ordered two or three people to move their cars from where they appeared to be in the path. The area was already jammed with people; word of the race had completely emptied the Three Corners.

"Let's get 'em to turn on their lights for us," Gavin suggested, and Blue promptly ordered it: "It's only gonna be a few minutes, y'all. Ain't gonna hurt no batteries."

With the road lighted now, we could see it clearly, and the four of us walked the race route. There was one bad hole, about forty yards out, but it was to the side of the road, and they could skirt it easily by starting a little to the left. It wasn't till near the end of the course that the road started to bear up, but it was hardly more than a drift; perhaps the race finished three or four yards higher than it started, no more.

We traced our way back to the starting point. "What y'all gonna run in?" I asked. Gavin had on white bucks and Blue some kind of fancy wing tips. This hadn't occurred to anyone until now, and so they sort of examined each other's shoes until they decided that the disadvantages were even on either side. Then Blue ordered a bystander to go inside and find some string to raise across the finish line, he asked Lawrence to walk off a hundred paces, and he hollered to Junie to get a pistol to fire at the start of the race. One materialized quickly enough, and then Blue called Miss Edna over, and put his arm round her.

"You gonna be the startin' judge, Miss Edna."

"What's I do?"

"You stand right 'bout here," he said, stationing her about ten yards in front of the starting line, "and you keep your eyes on me and The Grey Ghost. And when you hear Junie fire that pistol, you holler if either him or me goes off too soon. Your eyes good enough for that?"

"I know they is to see the white boy," she chuckled, "and I 'spect they is, even to spot a nigger as dark as you is, Blue." Blue and Gavin roared in tandem at that, and Gavin allowed that he would gladly accept her as the official arbiter of the start.

"From all I hear tell, you gonna beat me off the blocks anyhow," he said.

A pretty young woman returned with some string, taken off a package of meat, and Blue called two fellows over and ordered them to set up the finish line. Lawrence stopped his striding at precisely this moment, dug a heel in and turned back, calling: "Here it is. A hundred paces."

"Pull out that string there," Blue shouted, and several of the younger people in the crowd dashed off in that direction then, so they could be close to the finish. Many others by now had clambered onto their cars, or stood between them, so that almost the whole route was lined with spectators, and the place reeked with a kind of sudden drama I had never sensed before in any sort of official arena, where tickets had to be printed in advance.

"All right, Ghost?" Blue asked. It was time.

"Well, all 'cept first I got to take me a leak."

"Good idea," said Blue, and he hollered for everybody to wait a minute, and then the two of them walked behind the starting line, back in the dark, where one of the paths led to the school.

I hung back, but in a few seconds Gavin called to me, and I ran up, and he started emptying his pockets of change and keys and other junk, and handed it all to me with his coat. Blue was in his shirt-sleeves, but he took all the stuff he had out of his pockets, and gave me that and his big watch. "You think The Ghost can beat me, too?" he said.

"I reckon so."

"You gonna bet me, too?"

"I only got eight dollars."

"You be on for eight, then," Blue said, and that transacted, he unzipped his fly and stood next to Gavin.

That's all Gavin was doing, too—just standing. "Damn," he said. "I ain't never in my life been pee shy before."

"You ought to be nervous, white boy," Blue said.

"No, I ain't nervous one bit. I'd be nervous if I was scared of losing to you. And I ain't scared. I'm just very curious, Blue. I'm excited, is what I am."

"You gots nothing to gain and everything to lose," Blue said. "If I beats you, the word's gonna get out that The Grey Ghost done got whupped by a nigger. But if you wins, ain't nobody gonna care,

'cause they just gonna say, well, The Ghost beat some nigger, too."
He paused and finished his business. "It was Lawrence put you up
to this. You can still get out. You wanna call it off?"

"No, soon's I pee," Gavin said, and, in fact, he finally started at
that moment. There was no more conversation till he finished and
zipped up. "Blue, I want to find out." And he clapped Blue on the
shoulder, and for just an instant they looked into one another's
eyes, but there was nothing I could see that passed, because whatever it was, you had to be one of them to understand.

They were nearly back to the starting line when Blue said: "You
know, I plumb forgot to get somebody to call the finish. I got Miss
Edna at the start, but I didn't get no one for the finish."

"Don't make no difference," Gavin said. "You and me gonna
know."

"Yeah, but let's get somebody anyhow," Blue said, and he called
over to an older fellow, of a distinguished stripe. "Mr. Tisdale, you
go up at the finish, and you call the winner. As close as it be, you
call a winner."

The man agreed and ambled off, dedicated to the task. Then
Blue spotted me there. "You go with him. You call it 'longside Mr.
Tisdale."

"Donnie don't have to go," Gavin said. "I trust your man."

"Be more comfortable this way," Blue said, so Gavin nodded to
me, and I ran off and took my post opposite Mr. Tisdale at the finish line. Behind me, Lawrence and a large crowd of others clus-
tered about, angling for the best view.

The two of them set up at the start like halfbacks, side by side,
Gavin nearest to me, Blue just over from him. The place was absolutely still, hushed, with the car lights illuminating the path they
had to run. Miss Edna had taken her place on the other side, af-

fecting, it seemed to me, the posture of a traffic cop, which she was surely more familiar with than a starting judge; I don't imagine she had ever been to the Penn Relays. And then on my side, at the start, I could see Junie raise the Saturday-night special, and both men hunched down in their places and tensed a little more, and listened to Junie call out, "Take your marks . . . get set . . ." and another beat and the gun exploded.

There was nothing I ever saw like it. Gavin Grey was renowned for being the halfback fastest off the ball in all the country. When he ran track, he had the same kind of reputation with the gun. But as fast as he came up now, Blue was already in stride before Gavin started to put a leg down. The black man had come away clean, too, and Miss Edna was right to stand clear and let them fly. She was stationed about ten yards out, and when Blue passed her he was already one more step ahead of Gavin, probably a full two strides in front.

And then, at that instant, Gavin went down. He was down so fast there was no time for any of us to react. He hit a patch of loose dirt, and his white bucks came out from under him, and he kind of skidded to a heap. Whether Blue sensed the accident from the crowd's reaction or saw Gavin go down out of the corner of his eye, I don't know, but he looked back in the next instant, and as soon as he did, he eased himself to a halt and went back to him. Lawrence ran all the way back from the finish line, and they helped Gavin to his feet.

"I'm sorry," he said to Lawrence. "That cost you the Plymouth."

"A man got to run the race to win," Blue said. "We be goin' back to start again."

"That's not fair to you," Gavin protested. "You were ahead."

"We run it out," Blue said, and he went back directly to his starting place.

Gavin had tiny little cuts on the heels of his hands, where he had tried to cushion his fall, but otherwise he was fine, and he pawed over the loose place in the road where he had gone down, smoothing it out, and then he went back to take his place next to Blue. He shook his head at the black man. "Lawrence was dead right, Narvel Blue. No man ever come off a mark like you."

Blue just smiled back, Gavin got down, Mr. Tisdale and I and Miss Edna froze in our positions in the tableau, the full silence fell again, and Junie raised the little pistol and called them to their marks once more.

Bang! And this time, if it were possible, Blue reached out to an even greater early lead. It was as if Gavin was so intimidated by what he knew was coming that he let himself be shamed all the more. By the time he reached his full stride, out about where he had fallen the time before, Blue was full heels ahead and pouring it on. The noise changed from a roar for the race to a cheer for their man, and by the time Blue went by the hole—which I had estimated was about forty yards out—he was yet another step in front, a good three yards or so on top, I would say.

In the flat stretch that remained before the closing incline, though, Gavin began to make up some ground. It was barely what you could see, but he had cut the lead enough for himself to realize that he was back in the race, so long as they did not run out of territory first. They both ran very much the same, so perfectly balanced in a headlong way, each with a remarkably calm, fixed expression. The only difference was down with the legs, where Gavin, with his long strides, seemed to slide over the ground, while Blue, with his pigeon toes, looked like he was gobbling up distance, the feet like a mouth chewing wide open.

The road bent up that little bit the last thirty or forty yards. I knew I was supposed to fix my eyes upon the finish, but I couldn't take them from the two runners, especially since I could tell by now, the closer they came, that Gavin had cut into the margin even more. And . . . now there wasn't any space between them: They were in the stretch and Gavin had reached Blue's flank.

It was only in the last strides that I turned away from them to look straight down the string. From the corner of my eye, though, I could see them bearing down on me as one. Gavin had caught him. My God, he had caught up. His neck veins were ridges, and his legs were reaching out more each step, like lungs gasping for air, eyes searching in the dark. I've never again seen legs operating on a man quite like that.

In all the tumult around me, I heard only one distinctive cry, Lawrence shouting, "Ghost got him!" And then, in another instant, they both flashed in front of me. But there was no doubt. It was Gavin's breast that crested the meat string. He was two feet ahead of Blue, and I was made all the more certain because Blue threw himself at the line in desperation, and a step or two past the finish he had to pay for this, losing his balance and stumbling head-on, crashing toward the ground.

Only, Gavin caught him before he fell. He reached out with his left arm, and let Blue grab ahold of it and find a mooring. I heard the first thing Blue said, then, when he was safe on his feet. It was "Lord Jesus, how did a body catch me?"

By now, many people who had been watching along the course were running up to the finish, and since almost all of them had been at positions where Blue was clearly ahead, they ran in antici-pation of hearing of his victory. All of a sudden I realized that everybody was looking at me and Mr. Tisdale. He was senior, so they called to him for the verdict first.

But Mr. Tisdale wanted no part of this, that was for sure. I stared across the finish line at him, and he was trying to look away. Finally, he did raise up his head, but he shook it, too. "That was too close for these old eyes," he said.

So then everybody turned to me. Blue and Gavin were still catching their breath and tending to one another, and I don't believe they heard what Mr. Tisdale had said. But I spoke up as firmly and authoritatively as I could: "I saw Gavin Grey win," and when I did a lot of people hooted at me and others grumbled, but it was only for a few moments, because then Blue held up his hands and said: "Hey, the little white boy be right. Let's have a hand for The Grey Ghost." And he started the applause himself, so the other people began to join in, perhaps only politely at first, but more and more in genuine admiration for the battle, keeping it up until, one by one, the headlights went out and the place turned back to darkness.

We walked back to the Three Corners then—Blue and Gavin side by side, sweating; Lawrence and me, and Mr. Tisdale, he who had taken to holding his hands yea far apart, as if he had caught a big one, to confidently indicate the margin of victory. He had seen exactly what I had. It was by almost a clean yard that Gavin Grey beat Narvel Blue.

IT WAS PAST midnight when we left the Three Corners. Blue would not let us depart without feeding us, while someone fetched the title to his Dodge from where he lived. Lawrence protested that there wasn't any rush, but Blue would have it no other way, and made him take the keys on the spot. Gavin drove this car, the Dodge, when we finally left, and I accompanied him. He was going to take me back to the motel, to my parents, but the apartment was on the way, so he swung by there first to see if Finegan was back. He wanted to tell Finegan about the race; even in the car with me, he spoke almost compulsively on the subject. It was so unlike him. He was thrilled with himself, and almost common.

Only Babs was at the apartment. She had been there, she said, going on two hours, sitting on the couch, watching the TV flicker. But it did not matter how angry she was, or even how worried, for Gavin was so excited, so anxious to tell her all about his adventure, that he paid her attitude no mind; soon, in frustration, Babs had to turn her ire upon me. "You ought to be ashamed of yourself, Donnie McClure, takin' off with Gavin like that, disappearin' off the face of the earth!"

"Hey, he didn't do nothin'," Gavin protested.

"Well, sometimes I think Donnie has more sense than you, Gavin Grey."

"I'm only fourteen years old," I said.

"Your uncle's a child too. Sneakin' out a window, climbin' down off a roof. How old is that?" Gavin just smiled at me. "I'm sure Lawrence was a big part of this."

Boy, was Gavin glad she brought that up! "Hey, Lawrence won hisself a new car—a 'fifty Dodge, A-1 shape."

Babs wasn't listening anymore. "Precious, sometimes I think you love Lawrence more than you do me." The reason I knew she wasn't listening is that even then I had learned that whenever a pretty woman says you love someone or something more, she does not believe herself for a moment, and is certainly not going to stop and listen to you discourse on a premise that was patently foolish to start with. (On the contrary, what a woman really wonders is how, if you love her at all, you could possibly love anything else.

How could Gavin possibly want to spend a few hours with Lawrence this evening?)

Anyway, she stomped away, turning her back, staring off in the distance, even though a wall, unfortunately, got in front of the distance, four feet away. This was the climax to her scene, and Gavin was supposed to be driven to abject apology or (just as good) to throwing up his hands in exasperation and arguing the point with her. Instead, though, he came over to her very calmly and laid both his hands on her back—just set them there, up by the shoulder blades, and kept them that way while he talked softly. "Babs, let me tell you somethin' first off: You got no business sayin' that to me and embarrassin' Donnie."

"I'll leave," I said.

"No, Donnie, I'd just as soon you listen to this too. Babsie, I love you more than anything in the world. I sure never loved a *girl* like I do you." I could see her soften and squirm a little, sorry it had come to this, because she wasn't really mad anymore now that he was back and it was obvious no other woman had been involved. "You gotta understand that it ain't just that Lawrence is the best friend I ever had. It's the whole thing of him, of y'all. 'Bout the best thing I do with Lawrence is go out runnin' 'round, laughin', drinkin' beer. Now suppose one day he upped and told me, Ghost, we can spend a who' lot of time together doin' this and that, so forth and so on, but we can't do no runnin' 'round, laughin' and drinkin' beer. Do you understand what I'm sayin', darlin'?"

"I understand you just want me to be a bad girl."

"Yeah, I do," Gavin said, absolutely sotto voce. And he took his hands off her.

"Ohh," she whined. This one time, Gavin had turned Babs every which his way. Now he didn't say another word, so she had to start coming back, and she began by kind of peeking around to see what he was up to. He just smiled ever so nicely at her.

"Babs, I know you ain't gonna understand what I say. Maybe Donnie will, because he's the smart one. There's two things I could never know for sure. One was what it would like makin' love to you. The other was nigras—"

"Making love to nigras?" she screeched, holding her head in her hands.

"No, no, no. Playin *ball* 'gainst nigras. People say, Well, you and Miss Babs sure is America's sweethearts, the perfect couple. And people say, Gavin, you are the finest player of them all. But in my heart I couldn't never believe either. You understand?"

"I think I do."

"You Donnie? I makin' any sense?"

I thought I understood the football part, so I nodded my head to it all.

"I know how you feel, Babs. I was so scared out there tonight. You didn't know it, Donnie, did you?" I shook my head vigorously this time; I sure hadn't. "I wasn't myself, Babsie. All my life I hear about Narvel Blue, how good he is, how fast he is. 'Spose he whipped me five yards tonight? 'Spose he beat me an inch? I'm 'sposed to be the best there is, everybody's All-American, but I never could come to believe it. People say, Gavin, how you gonna do against Maryland, how you gonna do against Duke, and I say, well, such and such, gonna try and win, and all the time I knew egg-*zactly* how I was gonna do. Oh, I don't know the score or how many yards 'zactly, but I knew just about. But I didn't know out there tonight, and there was a part of me, a big ole chunk, sayin', You get outta here, Gavin Grey, you pass it up, you just go on bein' everybody's All-American and don't you fret about it. I couldn't pee aforehand.

"And you seen it, Donnie. Tell her. That nigger come out o' there on top. I mean he was out there, Babs, he was way out yonder, and my heart was down to my knees. And I beat him still. I beat that nigger clean, didn't I, Donnie? I beat him. And he run like a deer, Blue did. He like to run a hole in the wind. I never run so fast in all my life. I showed myself all I ever needed to know.

"Babsie." He pointed at her, and his tone changed. "I love, you, but I ain't gonna make you say no to me again till we're married. I don't gotta. I beat Narvel Blue tonight, and you ain't never gonna know what that was like till you sleep with me. And you can wait all you want, sweetheart, because I got mine."

And he jerked his head toward me, turned, started to take a step, and crumpled to the ground. He went down like he was shot. He grabbed his thigh there, and Babs ran to him and threw herself down next to him. "I fear I strained a little muscle running against Blue," he said.

"Oh, Precious," she said.

6

B Y TUESDAY, THREE DAYS LATER, GAVIN HAD RESTED
his leg, taken some heat treatments, and appeared whole
again. My own stature, locally, was increasing with each game The
Grey Ghost played, and it reached a veritable crescendo after I was
interviewed for an article in the school paper, wherein it was revealed that I had been present, in person, that famous night at
Sigma Nu:

"Not many Fikians would call themselves lucky ducks for being
at a fire, but this does not include Don McClure, ninth grade.
Don's uncle is none other than Gavin Grey, who, as everybody
knows is the Grey Ghost for the Tarheels, and Don was visiting in
Chapel Hill for the Clemson Tigers game when the horrible accident in the frat house we have all heard about by now took place at
Sigma Nu.

"'My uncle and me had just come out of the lavatory [I was
horribly misquoted; I never said "lavatory" in all my life; my
mother thought it was a tacky word, and so I'm sure I said "boys'
room"],' Don told this reporter, 'and we saw the flames just plain
leap up. . . .'" And so on.

It was in this spirit of my growing recognition that I was sought
out by Bolling Kiely as I came out of school that Tuesday. Apparently, someone had instructed him in my appearance, because he in-
spected me carefully before venturing to say my name. I recognized

his face, but could not recollect from where, and so I responded by tilting my head, rather as any pet animal will do when it is called near dinner time. Then he thrust out his hand: "Bolling Kiely, Donnie. Of Kiely Chevvalay"—that was the only way I ever heard the car's name pronounced in my native precincts. And quickly then: "I seen your momma and daddy up at the club."

"Yes, sir!" Why, it was Bolling Kiely himself. Everybody in town recognized him, because he always had his face in the Kiely Chevrolet advertisements in the Wilson *Daily Times:* The Tarheel Deal!

"I was just a-drivin' by Fike here, Donnie, and I suddenly had an idear that involves you, and I'd like to explain it to y'all if I can. I'll buy you a Co-Cola." I was leery, but curious more, and before I even knew it, Mr. Kiely had steered me safely away from my friends, Edgar Sampson and Jack Sydnor, as sure as if I had been a customer being guided from a stick-shift Chevy with no accessories over to the fluid-drive Pontiac area of the showroom.

In the car, as he drove, he kept up a constant chatter about his products, for the new 1955 models had just now come in, and he described them to me in all their finned glory. In fact, much of this was wasted on me, for I was that odd child of the South who had no interest whatsoever in matters automotive. Cars to me were never more than mobile containers, only vehicles that spirited you from one location to another, all the while entertaining you with songs over the radio. (If only it was made federal law to prohibit radios, tape decks, and other entertainment centers from cars, automotive gasoline consumption in the United States would drop by a third.) I knew nothing of engines and little more of brands; cars to me only came in colors: That was a big green car and that a small blue one.

But car fanciers assume everyone else is equally entrenched in the subject, and I found it easy to pass as another authority by always keeping to myself, except when it came to slamming doors and kicking tires. Bolling Kiely never solicited a word from me, babbling on himself about the wonders of the '55s and how he would help me get a deal on such a beauty two years hence when I was eligible to drive. And he showed me how all the dashboard gadgets worked, till suddenly, to my surprise, I found myself at his showroom: The Tarheel Deal!

There he ushered me through the showroom with the twisted shiny silver streamers that looked like they were turning all the time, and sat me down with a Co-Cola in his paneled private office. The room was filled with only two types of artifacts: those pertaining to the sale of GM cars and trucks, and those relating to football at Chapel Hill. Plaques upon plaques—this many pickups sold, this many used cars turned over, this much in gross sales—with Carolina gridiron photographs betwixt and between, every one of them of a Tarheel player or coach standing with Kiely, every one of them inscribed to "My good friend, Bolling Kiely" (although occasionally with the *i* and *e* transposed) or to the more formal "Mr. Tarheel Football."

By now, Bolling Kiely was sucking on a Nehi grape and smoking a Camel, which, at this time, was always celebrated as the best-selling cigarette in the country, although you never saw anybody smoking it, and certainly you never saw anybody *nice* smoking it.

But then, as you might have gathered by now, Bolling Kiely was not nice. That was his problem. He was common. That was why, as I soon learned, he couldn't get into the Carolina Country Club. Indeed, he had seen my parents there, but only on those occasions when he had been a guest of his friend the widowed Mrs. S. E. Flowers III. He certainly couldn't be a member. He came from no family whatsoever, and he was a divorced individual who put his picture in the paper. He had been nothing but a mechanic late in the Depression when he took over County Motors and then single-handedly built it into Kiely Chevrolet, The Tarheel Deal!—the largest dealership in eastern Carolina—and he would forever remain a mechanic.

But luckily for Bolling Kiely, S. E. Flowers III had, some months before, been mortally wounded in an unfortunate hunting accident by his friend and neighbor Taylor Moncrief. S. E. Flowers III was the scion of the oldest and finest family in all of Wilson County, and he only made two mistakes in his life, the second being the dalliance with Mrs. Taylor Moncrief. The first was the former Darlene Merrihew, a frowzy beautician from Columbus, Georgia, whom S. E. had knocked up and married when he was a kid away from home, drafted to fight World War II. Oh, the wages of sin, the perils of democracy!

There was another child hastily conceived upon S. E.'s return from overseas, and so when he returned to Wilson in '46, he had a whole family in tow. Darlene hung on, but thereafter she lived a tenuous existence, content to remain only as the titular Mrs. Flowers while her husband carried on publicly with everyone loose, immoral, and Episcopalian in eastern Carolina. His demise did not either bring Darlene the family fortune—it was passed on to the children—but it did leave her the great house and the interest on the children's trust and a great deal of time on her be-ringed hands.

So, in many ways (whether or not you were being snotty when you said it), the Widow Flowers and Bolling Kiely were truly made for one another. And anyone would have thought she would have married him just for the support and consolation: Oh Lord, but she could be treated shabbily at the country club! The best that she ever received was condescension. Whenever anyone stopped

long enough to acknowledge her—to avoid her would be tacky—
and inquire into the health of her offspring, they were usually referred to as "the Flowers children," as if she had not been involved
in the enterprise.

You would have thought, under the circumstances, that Darlene would have been anxious to accept Bolling's loving attentions,
but she had enjoyed a comfortable tenure above the salt and was
reluctant to marry beneath her new self. And this is where I came
into the picture.

"I was just a-thinkin'," Mr. Kiely said to me, standing behind his
desk, hitching up his pants in a circular way, as if he were searching for
a groove in his waist. "I'm gonna be in Chapel Hill this Sad'dee for the
Maryland Terrapin game, and it could be beneficial for your cousin
and me to have dinner together afterwards at the Carolina Inn."

"Who, sir?"

"Your cousin, *The Ghost*," he said impatiently, as if I didn't even
know the man.

"Oh, he's not my cousin. He's my uncle."

"Well, pretty near same difference, son," he said, and he dipped
into his pocket, extracted a wad of bills and peeled off a twenty.
"Now, this is for you, Donnie, if you can arrange this all."

A twenty-dollar bill! "Shoot, Mr. Kiely, I sure don't know anything about this."

He packed another Camel tight, rapping it against the face of
his watch. "There'd be the use of a new 1955 Impala Chevvalay
convertible in this for your cousin."

"Just for comin' to dinner after the Terrapin game?" I was so excited I skipped right over the continuing confusion as to my exact
relationship with Gavin, while, in the heat of the moment, reaching out and taking the bill. "A new Chevvalay?"

"The *use* of a new 1955 Impala Chevvalay for one year, twelve months," Mr. Kiely replied in firm clarification. But softer now: "But, boy, that don't mean there won't be the use of a 1956 this time next year, and a 'fifty-seven the year after, and so forth and so on. Maybe me and The Ghost can go into business together."

This was way over my head to start with, and the dirty word "business" advised me anew to be wary. While I didn't know the first thing about commerce, I surely did know that college athletes could not go around accepting cars willy-nilly. Then they wouldn't be certified amateurs. In college athletics, the only thing you can legally accept in payment for your services is an education—indicating that it is not considered worth much. Certainly not so much as a shiny new car. Any college athlete accepting that would become a shameful, grubby professional, and, when caught, all the games he played in would be forever forfeited, his college and state discredited. To the best of my ability I politely tried to school Bolling Kiely in these truths.

He was disappointed in me. "Boy, you don't think those niggers who play for those Yankee schools—who can't nearly read nor write—you don't think they're not gettin' money and cars and white girls and I don't know what-all? And them R. C. Eye-talians and Polacks who play for Notre Dame? So what's wrong with a good, white Methodist Carolina boy gettin' to *drive around* in a car?" I shrugged in confusion at this persuasive rebuttal and sipped some more from my pop bottle. "Remember now, I ain't givin' him no car. I'm givin' him the *use* of a car."

"Yessir."

"You see, you're a bright young man, Donnie. How old are you?"

"Fourteen."

"Fo'teen! I cain't believe it. You're much smarter than any fo'-teen." I knew by now to be wary of such a drift. If an adult told you you were big for your age, he wanted you to carry something heavy for him; smart for your age, he expected you to prove it by agreeing with him. I braced. Mr. Kiely did not disappoint me. "I want you to tell your cousin that I'd like to give him the use of a new 1955 Impala Chevvalay convertible. It'll be a weddin' present for him and Miss Babs.

"But they ain't bein' married till June."

"An early weddin' present. Not even the SU-preme Court can tell a body when you can give a weddin' present to a friend, can they?"

"Nosir!" I fairly chanted. After the school-integration decision of a few months earlier, anyone in Carolina who invoked the Court in any sort of negative manner was guaranteed agreement.

"You bet. Donnie, you just tell your cousin that I'll have the use of the 'fifty-five Impala convertible all set for him and Miss Babs if they'll just meet me for dinner at the Carolina Inn after the Terrapin game Sad'dee."

I DIDN'T DARE call Gavin. I palmed the twenty and took it to the five-and-ten-cent store to get it broken up into a lot of silver, so I could call Babs from a pay phone. The man in the store asked me why I didn't go across the street and get the bill changed at the bank, which certainly was a more sensible idea, I agreed, only I had never been to a bank before, and so going there to transact business had not immediately occurred to me.

Then I called Babs at the W. C. from a pay phone that night. She was intrigued and aghast with much I had to say, but she certainly did like the idea of the '55 Impala convertible; the use of the

convertible, I explained. Still, the Carolina Inn was about the fanci-
est and most visible restaurant in Chapel Hill, and the last place
Gavin would want to appear the night after a game. Babs mulled it
all over, and narrowed it down to the nub. "Donnie," she said, "tell
me one thing."

I had to put in another thirty-five cents. "Yes ma'am?"

"Is this Mr. Kiely a gentleman?" That was a hard question, and I
paused to ponder it. Babs did not care for the delay. "Well, is he,
Donnie? You're either a gentleman or you're not."

"Well, yes and no, Babs. I mean I got to tell you, that he is divorced." I could hear Babs sigh into the receiver. "But he sees my
momma and daddy up at the Carolina Country Club, and the club
sure wouldn't take no common people, would they?"

"Well, I certainly don't believe so," Babs said, and, thereby satisfied with Mr. Kiely's cultural credentials, she advised me to inform
him that they would join him for dinner that night. But I, as the
contact man, must come along too. This left me with horrible
mixed emotions. On the one hand, I was thrilled at the opportunity
to see The Grey Ghost play another game, but on the other, and
notwithstanding the Supreme Court, the idea of coming along
with Bolling Kiely left me feeling a bit soiled.

The money especially worried me. While I felt that the *use* of a
car was something of a cloudy ideological issue, the sort of sticky
business that nagged at King David and people like that in the Bible
(without ever doing them in), money could be traced. So I took the
sixteen dollars and change that was left after I called Babs and
placed it in my secretmost nook, there with a rubber, my color
photographs of actual naked women, and the picture books Gavin
had bequeathed me of Archie and his friends perpetrating imaginative acts of sodomy, and I never touched so much as a penny of

that money until months later, when Gavin was officially ensconced on the pros. Then, with another ten dollars I had picked
up from relatives and godparents on my birthday, I took out a
money order and sent away for the Charles Atlas Dynamic Tension
muscle-building course. Somehow, I convinced myself that the
physical improvement of the temple that housed my soul, that
spending for this noble purpose cleansed whatever taint the money
might have possessed. It was sort of a moral job of laundering.

A MECHANIC NAMED Barney drove the '55 Impala convertible
down to Chapel Hill Saturday morning. He was accompanied by a
fellow with a camera. The Impala was two shades of green, em-
bossed in chrome. Darlene Flowers and I rode with Bolling in his
best demonstrator. We followed the gift car, all the way listening to
Mr. Kiely discoursing about cars and football players—interchange-
ably, it seemed to me after a while. Soon, the cars took on very personal characteristics, while the players began to come off as assem-
bly-line models, and little else. There were even times when Mr.
Kiely could not help himself: Gavin was, for example, described as
having a great deal of horsepower and "gridiron roadability."

Mr. Kiely winked at me whenever he mentioned Gavin, because, as he had privately informed me before our convoy departed
Wilson, the Widow Flowers did not know whom she was going to
dine with this evening. It was not easy for him to manage a wink to
me, though, as I was in the backseat, while Darlene snuggled up
close to him, like a teenager. She would even light his Camels, take
the first drag, and pass them on to him. I had never before seen a
grown-up lady ride this way; she was right on top of him, a veritable copilot, the proximity emphasized all the more by her two
huge breasts, which spilled over onto Mr. Kiely.

It was this outstanding aspect of Darlene which, I understood, had first attracted the young and discerning S. E. Flowers III to her. She mentioned her late husband occasionally as we drove along. She was, for instance, so especially pleased to be taking this trip to Chapel Hill, inasmuch as Mr. Flowers had never taken her any-where, except for the one trip to Myrtle Beach, South Carolina. So many memories were invoked of that visit that I gathered it was the high-water mark of the marriage.

Darlene liked the game better than Mr. Kiely and I did, because she enjoyed the spectacle more than the football, and the game was, sadly, the only real lackluster effort Gavin put forth all year. His longest run was a measly twenty-three yards, and he even fumbled once. I wondered: Had beating Narvel Blue sapped his interest in the game? Did his secret leg injury really bother him? It must have, I decided, and I longed to tell Bolling Kiely, tell the world, that they were not seeing a 100 percent Ghost. But nonetheless, the Tarheels won 21–10, and sustained their number-one ranking. "I liked when the Merlin band played the medley," Darlene said after-ward, and soon enough the slovenly game details were forgotten, and by the time the three of us arrived at the Carolina Inn, the con-test had been raised to its lowest common denominator: another victory, like all the others.

When Babs and Gavin entered the dining room a few minutes later, the whole place shot to its feet, alumni shouting, "Ghost! Ghost!" and, "I'm a Tarheel born and a Tarheel bred and when I die I'll be a Tarheel dead, so rah-rah Kow'linah, 'lina, rah-rah Kow'linah, 'lina, rah-rah, Kow'linah, rah-rah-rah." Notwithstand-ing the pandemonium, Bolling Kiely was almost immediately at Gavin's side, placing his hand around his shoulder, while urging me to explain who the hell he was. Gavin smiled the best he could, and from nowhere, the fellow with the flash camera who had ridden down on the '55 Impala convertible with Barney appeared and snapped the picture that was, by Tuesday, featured in all the Kiely Chevrolet newspaper advertisements: "Two Big Winners! The Grey Ghost of Chapel Hill and Bolling Kiely of Kiely Chevrolet— A Real Tarheel Deal on all new '55s (and the few remaining '54s still in stock)!!"

Mr. Kiely steered Gavin over to a seat between Darlene and himself and provided introductions. "I'm so thrilled—The Grey Ghost hisself," she said.

"How you?" Gavin said, more or less addressing her bosom, re-membering to lift his eyes only when the flashbulbs started up again.

"Well, you sure showed them Po-lacks, all the *skis*, how to play football," Kiely said, pouring himself a bourbon from his brown bag. While Maryland was indeed south of the Mason-Dixon Line, it had shown its true colors by not seceding a century previous, and, worse, its roster was speckled with ethnic coal-miner types from the backwaters of anthracite Pennsylvania. Playing Maryland was not at all like playing Duke or State at all; I don't believe that the Maryland band even played "Dixie"—certainly not as a matter of course. Mr. Kiely reached over Gavin and poured Darlene a drink, too. "Hardly got any real Americans on that Terrapin team," he said. "Dirty-lookin' boys."

I saw Gavin wince just a little. It was not that he was above prej-udice; the saints in heaven would have been inculcated with a cer-tain amount of prejudice had they resided in Dixie then. But like any competitor, Gavin possessed a certain respect for the opposi-tion that transcended any residual bias he might have picked up in the outside world. Athletes are not any better than you or me, that's for sure. Neither are soldiers or cops or cowboys and Indians. But athletes learn to respect rivals for virtues they would admire in themselves—courage, sacrifice, rising to the occasion. As a rule, the farther one is from the action, the more he personalizes the contest—and as often as not with regard to race, color, and creed. But to someone like Gavin, smack in the action, action was about all there was to it.

But even when Gavin did not go along with Mr. Kiely's sentiments, the Chevrolet man did not understand, and he pressed on with the subject. "I 'spect you gonna even have to play jigaboos in the pros next year," he said, screwing up his face to show his disgust.

"Reckon so."

"You never did play no niggers before, did you?"

"Well, I never played on the gridiron against any, but I run a footrace once against Narvel Blue, who was 'bout the best football player ever to come out of the Tarheel State."

Bolling Kiely snorted and guffawed at that, and tried to explain to Darlene what a preposterous thing The Ghost had just said: a nigger the best football player ever in Carolina. And he guffawed again. Only when he got ahold of himself did Kiely ask Gavin how he fared against Narvel Blue.

"We raced twice," Gavin replied, without any real expression. "He beat me the first time, I beat him the second."

My mouth flew upon in protest. Gavin Grey didn't get beat! He slipped and fell! Wasn't his fault! I started to correct him, but he looked at me from across the table, and I understood that I was to stay silent. Gavin turned his face away from me, and I think he was planning to speak to Darlene's cleavage again, but suddenly, two little boys had materialized at his elbow, standing between him and the lady.

There were almost no children in the room. These two had on little blue blazers, each with the seal of a private school from Winston-Salem on the breast pocket. They were regimental ties and gray flannel pants, and their hair was brushed. They were scared to death. The bigger one, who was possibly eleven, shoved the smaller one, who was eight or nine, in a little closer and prodded him. "Mr. Grey, sir, can I have your autograph, please?" he asked.

But then, from behind Gavin, Mr. Kiely's beefy left hand shot out and planted itself on the younger boy's neck. "Hey, boy," he snapped brusquely, "The Ghost is havin' dinner with his friends. No time to bother him for autographs now."

The older boy backed off in fear, mumbling apologies. The little one's eyes clouded up with tears. Without a word, Gavin reached back, and took Bolling Kiely's hand off the boy. He took that hand away from the kid and let it drop—just let go of it, as if it were an unattached object that would crash to the floor. Then he stared the man dead in the face. "Don't you tell me who my friends are," he said. "These boys are my friends."

Gavin snapped it off so quickly and without raising his voice that I don't even believe Darlene took it in. Mr. Kiely put a sickly grin on his face, but Gavin had turned his back on him by now and was asking the boys their names and where they lived and what they thought of the Tarheels and did they play football and what position and would they come to Chapel Hill when they got old enough for college and several more things. And then he signed personal autographs and shook their hands and wished them well.

"There you got two well-behaved boys," Bolling Kiely said.

Gavin still didn't look over at him. He rose, and to the whole table in general, he said: "'Scuse me. I gotta see a man about a horse." But he ended up looking at me, and he nodded his head in the direction of the men's room, and so I excused myself and headed after him. Gavin walked right past the men's room door and led me outside. "I didn't have to pee," he said, and he headed across the driveway, out of the lights. "I'm sorry, Donnie, I just don't like that man. Who is he, anyway?"

"That's Bolling Kiely of Kiely Chevvalay in Wilson."

"Oh yeah. I knew I seen him, kissing the coaches' asses before. What's he mean to Sister and your daddy?"

"He don't mean nothin'. They just see him up at the club."

"They ain't big asshole buddies with him?"

"No."

"Well, what the fuck is Babs doin' to me?" he cried suddenly, banging his right fist into his left palm. "The last goddamn place on the face of the earth I wanna be on a football weekend is eatin' dinner at the Carolina Inn with a bunch of alumni all liquored up comin' round makin' a mess over me. The only reason I done this was because Babs said I owed it to Sister and your daddy to go out with their good friends from Wilson, and now—"

"Is that all Babs told you?"

He turned on me. "What else is there?"

"She didn't tell you about the Chevvalay?"

"What Chevvalay?"

"The 'fifty-five Impala Chevvalay convertible Mr. Kiely was going to give you?"

"What *are* you talkin' about, Donnie?"

"Well, he said he'd give you the use of a convertible for a year if you'd come have dinner with him and Mrs. Flowers."

"Who's Mrs. Flowers, the one in there with the big tits?"

"Yeah, she's a widow lady."

"And he's gonna give me a Chevvalay?"

"The use of a Chevvalay. He brung it down here. It's down here in Chapel Hill right now. It's an early wedding present."

"Does Babs know all this, Donnie?"

"I called her up and told her."

"Well goddamnit, why didn't you call me?" I tried to explain, but I couldn't talk. I couldn't say anything. He pounded his hand into his palm again and rocked back and forth. "You think I'm just a dumb jockstrap who couldn't know how to handle this. That's what-all you think."

"No, no, Gavin." And I could feel myself starting to cry, and I thought, Please, don't cry. But of course I did, and it was horrible. "I'm sorry," I said, and by then I was sorry mostly about crying in front of him.

"It's all right, Donnie."

"I just didn't think you should be bothered before a game. I thought I could—"

He wrapped an arm around me. "It's okay, Donnie. You're good people."

"I let you down, didn't I?" I asked.

"A little bit," Gavin said, very truthful. "I thought you knew better about treatin' me like everybody's All-American. But don't fret, Donnie. Let's go back and talk to that Mr. Kiely 'bout the Chevvalay."

"You can't take it, can you, Gavin?"

"Well, it ain't likely anybody would find out about it," he said. "But you could never be sure."

"But it'd be dumb to take it, wouldn't it?"

"No, not dumb. But what it would be, would be common. See, if I got caught, wouldn't nothin' happen to me. They can't say, you can't play pro-fessional football because you already are pro-fessional. They couldn't punish me no way. But they could take the whole season away from the team, from Lawrence and Finegan and the coaches and the Tarheels. And that would be common as cat shit."

"Sure would that," I said.

"But I tell you what-all, Donnie. I don't suppose there's no harm in me takin' the use of that Chevvalay if I'm not the one doin' the using."

SOON ENOUGH, BACK at the table, Bolling Kiely brought up all the business about the car. He said that all Gavin had to do to get it, legally and formally, was to sing a one-dollar lease for the year, and Gavin pointed out that he didn't want to sign anything, lest nitpickers get the wrong idea and incriminate the entire Tarheel team. "I'm gonna get me a friend to do the signing and the driving," Gavin said, tucking the lease in his pocket.

"Why, you got a heart as good as your legs, Ghost," Mr. Kiely said, and so we all piled into the demonstrator and the convertible and drove off toward where Gavin directed us. I assumed we were going to meet Lawrence or Finegan at the apartment.

"Where we goin', anyhow?" Mr. Kiely asked after a while.

"Coloredtown," Gavin said.

"Now, why we goin' to Coloredtown?"

"Because we're givin' the car to a colored boy," Gavin said.

Mr. Kiely laughed at that because it was such a good joke. He was still chuckling a little bit when we pulled up at the Three Corners and Blue walked out.

"That's the boy who gets the car," Gavin said.

"You ain't givin' my new 'fifty-five Impala to that nigger?"

"I'm givin' him the *use* of the 'fifty-five Impala."

"Well now, wait a JU-ly minute, Gavin. Nobody said anything about smokes."

"Right, nobody said nothin'," Gavin said, and he climbed out of the car and went over to where Blue was standing.

"Well, Ghost, come back to race again?" Blue said.

"No. Just sign this," Gavin said, whipping out the lease.

Blue shook his head. "I ain't signin' fuck-all."

"Sign it, or I'll whip you upside the head, sure as I can beat your ass," Gavin replied, and he turned me around like I was a dummy and laid the paper across my back. Blue signed it right there where Gavin pointed. Then Gavin grabbed the paper back, took a dollar bill from his pocket and thrust it at Bolling Kiely, as he strode past him to the Impala. There, Gavin reached in over Barney, pulled the keys out of the ignition switch, stood back a step, and tossed them high in the air over to where Blue still stood.

"Blue," Gavin said, "just you make sure you get this Impala back to Mr. Bolling Kiely in Wilson next November 12."

7

IT CANNOT BE IMAGINED, THE EXTENT OF THE
depression which inflicted the state, when, twelve days later, on
Thanksgiving, in the last game of the regular season, against Duke
over at Durham, Gavin was hurt. He took a pitchout around right
end and was brought down by two Duke tacklers—one high, one
low—just as he made the corner. The ground was soft from a rain
that had fallen much of Wednesday, and his cleats caught for an instant. He did something to his left knee, the one he was turning on.
He went down in a heap and had to be helped from the field, hop-
ping on his good leg.

There was a hush upon the stadium so pronounced that suddenly the radio announcer began speaking in whispers, as if he
were covering a state funeral or a golf green. The Tarheels still
went on to win rather handily, remaining number one in the nation, but I forget the details because as soon as Gavin went down
I lost interest in the game. I heard it all, but I was only waiting for
what is known as a "report on his condition," how he is. To the
best of my recollection, that was the last time in my life that I
ever genuinely listened to anything on the radio. Oh sure, I push
radio buttons in cars, and I hear traffic helicopters and Accu-
weather summaries when the clock radio fires in the morning,
but I have never listened to a radio for a sustained period since
that Thanksgiving afternoon. This is to the good, I guess. It

makes those events more substantial, as if they were coming from another era.

In the days after Thanksgiving, all that concerned us was whether or not The Grey Ghost would be ready for the Sugar Bowl on New Year's Day. The careful consensus was that his chances were fifty-fifty, and each day in the newspapers, doctors, trainers, coaches, and Gavin himself advanced fifty-fifty opinions.

Only one man in all the state of North Carolina knew all along that Gavin would play in the Sugar Bowl. I became the second person privy to this dope a few days before Christmas. Judge Pace was outside doing yard work this Saturday morning. It was still an uncommonly mild autumn, for I remember that neither of us wore winter coats, just sweaters. He beckoned to me, and when I came over, he exchanged his rake for a pipe and welcomed me inside for some coffee. I drank coffee with the judge before I did with anyone else; at this time, under similar circumstances, all other grown-ups would still proffer hot chocolate—which is one reason why I never got the chance to like it.

I had two cups with the judge this day. Over the first, we discussed the sad state of affairs in Washington, D.C. There was not a mention of football, of The Grey Ghost. With the judge, of course, the state of affairs in Washington, D.C., was invariably sad (at best), mixed with the hopeless and abysmal, and inasmuch as I would volunteer nothing on the subject, we both enjoyed these conversational critiques. In eastern Carolina at this time, political commentary was pretty much restricted to nigger-this and nigger-that, and so topics of any other sort—no matter what—could not fail but sound downright Promethean. I always appeared so intelligently agog at all the judge said that, two years before, he had invited me to go with him to Raleigh to hear Adlai Stevenson deliver a campaign address.

My father was flabbergasted at the invitation. The judge's wife had been dead many years, he was never seen in the company of women, and there is just no telling what considered opinions were held in the community about this side of him. (As it was, the judge just did things quietly in his own time. Several years later, when I was away at college, he married Jennifer, the new librarian in town, a winsome, long-legged divorcée many years his junior.) Anyway, Dad finally agreed to let me go with Judge Pace to hear "the governor," and I had a marvelous time. Stevenson spoke outdoors, downtown, from a low platform into a bad microphone, and I heard little of what he said. Neither, I'm sure, did the judge, but he was somehow able to extrapolate much from the speech, sufficient to deliver his version of the remarks on our drive back to Wilson.

The judge endorsed virtually everything he had heard Stevenson say, and so I ventured to ask him why exactly he planned to vote for him instead of Eisenhower. The judge sucked on his pipe that he had placed in his lips as we left our parking space (he was the most precise driver I have ever met; he never took either hand off the wheel, he drove exactly six miles over the speed limit, and he never had the foggiest idea where he was going). "I didn't say I was going to vote for the governor," he replied. "I didn't say that, did I, Donnie-Me-Boy?"

This put me aback. "I thought you were for the governor . . . sir."

"Favor him, yes. His policies. But I think I'll vote for the general."

Dare I ask? I paused. At last: "Why, sir?"

"That's a good question, Donnie-Me-Boy. A very good question. The governor is no doubt a more capable man than the general— wiser—but this is not necessarily a time for wisdom in Washington, D.C. Periodically, it seems, we need a HE-ro at the tiller. I don't mean just us Americans. It appears to be a human condition. There are times when we look ahead with our leaders. Mr. Franklin D. Roosevelt was such a chief executive. Times, I'm afraid, when we look back—or away, in any event—when we ask not to be troubled: You have your Mr. Harding here, your Mr. Coolidge. And then, at last, there are times when we do not look ahead or away, but when we peer straight up. And this, it seems to me, is just such a time. Would you like a bite to eat?"

"Yes, sir."

The judge pulled in ahead at a roadhouse, where (I learned somewhat later) he slept regularly and discreetly with the proprietress, a devout Roman Catholic lady named O'Reilly, who had been married once to a no-good good-time Charlie who had long since been thrown off the premises, but who remained her Church's husband in perpetuity. Nor surprisingly, then, the lady, who had been expecting us, greeted us in a most friendly fashion and gave us a choice table. The judge had brought with him a bottle of J. W. Dant bourbon, which remained encased in a brown bag, as required by state law, one sustained by the joint efforts of Baptists and bootleggers. (There was a certain parallel between how Baptists viewed liquor and the Pope disenfranchised wives.) The judge asked for a highball glass with branch water, administered it with the "Doctor Dant," as he called it, and ordered me an RC. Following another bourbon, and after no discussion with a waiter that I recall, full plates of fried chicken, mashed potatoes, and peas magically appeared. The judge mixed his peas all up in his mashed potatoes, and then drowned the consolidated mess in gravy.

"Why is it that right now we look up, for the general?" I asked, after we had had a few good mouthfuls.

"That's a good question, Donnie-Me-Boy." I nodded. "So, you want to know what I think on that subject?"

"Yes, sir."

"Well, the newspapers and the historians will give you a lot of who-shot-John, all based on the premise that we create HE-roes because we need them. I don't buy that, Donnie-Me-Boy. Never did, not for a minute. It is my experience that you can't sit around and wish up a HE-ro any more than you can conjure up a thousand-dollar bill. HE-roes create themselves. Oh, of course they take advantage of circumstances and profit by events, but they present themselves *to* us. We don't build them to suit our needs. Hell's bells, if we could do that, we would have HE-roes all the time, because it is a damn sight easier for most people to look up than it is to try and look ahead. We want a HE-ro now because the general is here now. If he weren't here, we wouldn't want a HE-ro."

"Judge Pace, will the general always be a HE-ro?" I asked. "I mean, after he gets to be president and everything."

"Probably not. Almost surely not. Pass the hot biscuits, please." I did, and he responded by wiping on great globs of butter and then washing it in the remaining gravy. "You see, the general became a HE-ro in one arena, and is now going to try and switch that over into another. It's very hard to parlay heroism, Donnie-Me-Boy. Hell's bells, it's hard enough to sustain heroism. Ideally, HE-roes should die at their heroic peak. Now that, I think, pretty near all the damn-fool historians agree on—but I still think it's true anyway. Once you hit that heroic peak, it must be all downhill. But great Jesus, boy, that doesn't mean our HE-roes let us down. We understand them. It's only themselves they disappoint."

He shrugged and excused himself, ostensibly to visit the men's room. He returned with a cock-and-bull story about having met a client by chance, and would I mind granting him a half-hour's privacy to handle this nagging transaction? Well, of course I would have anyway, but by chance, Mrs. O'Reilly had suggested that I might spend this time watching a television set in her office. I was also provided with considerable amounts of sherbet ice cream and cookies. Since we did not yet even own a TV set, I hoped the judge's business meeting took all evening; in fact, it lasted a good hour before he returned, redolent with some new men's cologne. The mysterious client never did present himself to me, but Mrs. O'Reilly, a handsome woman of ample proportions with the rosy cheeks of a rag doll, not only came by to wish me well but gave me some licorice to enjoy on the balance of the trip home and some Sally Lund bread (a Southern specialty) for my mother. Even I, in my abject small-town teenage naiveté, knew that there was something here that didn't quite meet the eye, but it was some time, yet, before I perceived everyday truths. The larger ones, about mankind, were much easier to come by.

I HAVE GOTTEN away from where I started here: having coffee with the judge a couple weeks before the Sugar Bowl. When it was apparent that he had concluded his thoughts about the nation's capital, I made my apologies and prepared to leave. He put down his pipe, accompanied me to the door, and picked up his rake there. "Merry Christmas, Donnie-Me-Boy," he said. "Or are you already looking past Christmas to the Sugar Bowl?"

"I guess I am, sir. I didn't know you cared."

"Gavin Grey and his Tarheels are such a ubiquitous concern, no one can escape it," he said. "When in Rome . . . "

"I just hope he plays."

The judge positively beamed at that. "Donnie-Me-Boy, is that what's bothering you? Well, rest your mind. He will play, and he will play well." Here was the subject that a state debated; the judge not only dismissed it with absolute authority, but with the most casual air, as if he were telling me the time of day.

"But how do you know, sir?" (God, but the judge was brilliant at obtaining straight lines.)

"Most of it is simple empirical evidence," he replied, leaning on his rake now, and peering at me over his glasses. "Virtually every time there is a question about a star—an athlete, actor, dancer, what-have-you—appearing at an important performance, the star will make it."

"Is that so?"

"It's certainly my experience. It's also the case that the greater the star, the more likelihood that he will overcome his injury and participate. The historians and journalists call that courage, but hell's bells, courage is too rare a thing to pop up that way most every Sad'dee. These fellows play because they must—and the greater the player, the greater his need to play. I am told that an animal that tastes blood will kill again, and adulation is merely a better taste of blood. Your Grey Ghost will play on New Year's Day."

I smiled wanly, for while I should have been thrilled at this assessment of the situation, this absolute guarantee that Gavin would lead the Tarheels into the Sugar Bowl, I did not like the way the judge characterized Gavin and interpreted his motives. He recognized my expression and laid a hand on my shoulder. "Please, Donnie-Me-Boy, I'm not being unkind to your uncle. Surely, he is an honorable young man. It is not calculation that motivates him. He will never again in all his life have a stage like the Sugar Bowl, and deep inside he knows that and—"

That blasphemy was sufficient to overcome even my timidity. "He's going to be the first draft choice in the pros," I cried out.

"Why, the *News and Observer* says he'll make at least twenty-five thousand dollars."

"Yes, I'm sure, and I'm sure Gavin'll make a fine professional player. But I'm not talking about his pure abilities here, Donnie-Me-Boy. I'm talking about the crest of his wave. And rest assured that Gavin Grey senses that in his bones, better than you or me. You know, there are in nature various of God's creatures who give up their lives to give birth. They know very well what they are doing, but they go right ahead. They proceed. We have something not unlike that here. You cannot donate too much to youth and expect to sustain yourself in long life.

"Rich children are spoiled by wealth. Those that God has blessed with physical talents, like your young uncle, are just as cursed, for what they are given must be too early spent. Look ahead in your life, Donnie-Me-Boy, for whatever you *achieve* as a child is merely something to overcome as an adult."

He stopped abruptly, and I assumed he was through; the judge knew how to conclude. But suddenly, he started up again. "Did I ever tell you about Mrs. Pace?"

"Your . . . wife, sir?"

"Yes. She was the most beautiful creature that God ever put on the face of the earth."

"Yes, sir."

"She was in an automobile accident." He paused and kicked a little at his leaf pile, rather like an animal might pay at the ground. He smiled then. "Isn't that funny? I never thought of that before."

"Sir?"

"*Automobile* accident. That's the only time anymore we ever use the word 'automobile.' We don't say, get in the automobile, or I just bought a new automobile. We say car. We say car everything except when there's an accident. Then we say automobile. We buy cars, we drive them, we worship them. Then we have automobile accidents."

Something triggered in my mind. "It's kinda like the way we talk about the South before the war," I ventured.

"How's that?"

"Well sir, you know, even though we lost the war—"

"The Civil War?"

"The War between the States, yes, sir. Even though we lost it, we talk about it and we're proud of how we fought it, and we talk about 'after the war,' but whenever we talk about 'before the war,' when it was different—"

"When there was slavery."

"Yessir, we always call that 'antebellum.' It was only the last year or two I learned what antebellum was. It's like—"

"Yes, Donnie," said the judge, placing a hand on my shoulder. "It's exactly like automobile accidents. That's a very profound analogy. Very profound." He never made a declaration of it, but he never did call me Donnie-Me-Boy again. He took off his glasses and rubbed his eyes. He was balding, but in an altogether manly way, the pate going back cleanly. There were none of the scraggly hairs, and certainly no odd strands nurtured to great lengths and brushed over, desperate footprints in the snowstorm. No, the judge was going bald, and he was going to make that baldness as proud a part of him as the rest. He wore his baldness just as other men wear turtlenecks or tweed coats.

"So, in any event, Mrs. Pace was in a car accident." He held up his hand like a traffic cop. "No, not that: I wasn't driving. That's not the point of this. She was quite alone, on a slick road at dusk, cutting across on Rout' Forty-two by Buckhorn Cross Roads. Her face was horribly disfigured, and I think it was good that she died, for she could never have handled that. It would have been a lingering death for her, for forty years, for fifty, had she lived with an ugly face." He stopped and looked away, then came back to me: "And I don't know whether I'd've been very good at it either."

"I'm sorry, sir?"

"Well, it's not nearly so significant, but not at all unlike why I left show business." I tensed with excitement, that he would bring this glamorous subject up. Why, till now, till this very moment, he had never even verified the fact.

"Yes, sir?" I said, nearly spitting it out.

"I played the piano and sang," he replied. "Did you know that, Donnie?"

"I've heard tell around, but you never know what to believe."

"Very wise of you."

The judge reached into his pocket, pulled out his pipe again, and took an interminable amount of time tending to it. I panicked; I could not take the chance that he would let the subject fade away. So boldly, I volunteered, "Yessir, I heard you were the only person from Lenoir County ever to win *Ted Mack's Original Amateur Hour.*"

"Yes, that's essentially correct," he said. "Only, a gentleman named Major Bowes was the impresario at that time. I beat a harmonica player who played "Mairzy Doats" and a pair of twins from Wilkes-Barre, Pennsylvania, who tap-danced. I could play a mean piano, Donnie. It just came to me. And I had a sweet voice. I was a tenor—what was called a crooner in those times. I wasn't really an amateur, either. I had sung with bands all over eastern Carolina. Where talent is concerned, there is no such thing as amateur."

"When did you stop?"

"Singing?" I nodded. "Oh, after I went to Hollywood." I blanched. Why, he said that as easily as if he had told me he had been to Raleigh or Rocky Mount.

"Hollywood? Really? The movie capital of the world? That Hollywood?"

"Oh, yes. After I won the *Original Amateur Hour*, I was, as they say, discovered. I went to Hollywood on the Santa Fe, and they changed my hairstyle into more of a pompadour and put me in a movie that was entitled *Singers on Parade*."

"You were in a movie!" If Judge Pace had advised me that he was the Lindbergh baby or Judge Crater, I could not have been more excited. I literally tingled. I had little tingles all over my body. I lost complete control of myself. "A Hollywood movie!"

"One feature-length motion picture and two shorts, entitled *Here Come the Melody-Makers* and *Let's Hear It!*"

"Two shorts, too!" I cried out.

"Yes, I was very well received. I had my hair then, Donnie, and this was not an unagreeable countenance. And, as I said, I had a sweet tenor voice. The studio—"

"You were at a *studio?*"

"Warners."

"Gee, a studio!"

"Yes, they were going to feature me in my next movie, I wasn't just going to sing and play the piano. I was going to be an actor as well. There was even a love scene scheduled for me. I was to kiss the leading lady while in a rowboat on a lagoon. Bing Crosby was doing this kind of thing at about this same time. They called me Frankie Pace, the Carolina Moon Crooner." By now, I could only stare at him, open-mouthed, dumbstruck. Judge Frank R. Pace had lived next to me all my born days, next door, a movie star, one in a million, and I hadn't known it. It was earth-shattering. He messed with his pipe again. "That's when I came back home," he said.

"You left Hollywood?"

"I did. I was making an unheard-of amount of money. Hell's bells, I bought a flashy convertible roadster, all the most fashionable sports clothes, and it's fair to say that I found a great deal of female companionship. Gorgeous women, Donnie. Gorgeous."

"Yessir, in Hollywood."

"Well, yes, I was in Hollywood. But gorgeous women are everywhere. You'll discover that."

"Yessir." The judge was right, too. Wherever I go, the two things people always assure me is that their place has the greatest sports fans and the prettiest women in the world—and they're always right, it seems.

"It's just that more gorgeous women were available to me in Hollywood. My next movie was going to be entitled *Take the Town,* but they couldn't decide on the leading lady, the one I was to smooch with in the rowboat. There was some fuss 'n' feathers about her contract, which I was never privy to, but the upshot of the matter was that production was delayed for a week or so. And perhaps, despite myself, it gave me time to think . . . unawares. And one morning I woke up at about ten o'clock, the sun sneaking through the venetian blinds, and I went to the window and opened them up, and the light just came pouring in on me. It was a secular kind of revelation. It was so bright it was white. Stark white, Donnie. And the green palm trees, my shiny red roadster parked under them. Not a cloud in the sky, either. The sky was Carolina blue that day in Hollywood, California."

"Yessir, the Southern Part of Heaven."

"And I thought to myself, Haven't you had enough of this illusion, Frank Pace? Haven't you been a child here long enough? What more could happen? I could fail as a featured performer and come home, or I could be extremely popular and move on to untold success, with stage, screen, and radio, as our friend Der Bingle had. And between you, me, and the lamppost, I believe that would have happened. I had great confidence in my voice. But either way, it seemed to me, would be equally destructive to my whole life. And so I turned away from the window. . . . " He paused and considered me.

"Yes, sir?"

"To be perfectly candid with you, Donnie, there was another soul there with me in the room. You're old enough to know: a woman. You understand?"

"Oh, yes, sir. You told me about all the gorgeous women."

"Ah yes. So I was standing there, naked as a jaybird, and I turned to her in bed, and I said, 'Denise—' Her name was Denise Del Canto. She was an aspiring starlet at the studio. I said, 'Denise, I'm not going to make *Take the Town*. I'm going back to Carolina.'"

"What did she say, Judge?"

He frowned at that. "I really don't remember, Donnie. I'm not so sure that's the point. I don't remember palavering with Denise Del Canto even under more optimum conversational circumstances. But if you want to know, I believe she said something on the order of, 'What?'"

"Oh."

"I left on Route Sixty-six, headin' back to Carolina later that self-same day.

"Gee, you made Hollywood and you gave it up."

"I've never sung or played the piano since."

"Not ever at all?"

"Not in public. Sometimes for Mrs. Pace when she was alive. Every now and then for Clarissa, on her birthday and what-have-you. Once at her church—hmmm, I guess you could call that quasi-public. And sometimes I do play for myself. Just to see if it's still there."

"Is it, sir?"

"Oh yes. The good Lord gave it to me. It was just a thing he gave me, and so there was no obligation for me to exploit it. It would keep."

"You could have been famous and everything."

The judge just shrugged at that. "Well, that's me," he said. "You needn't worry that my experience must apply to anyone else, namely your fabled uncle. The Grey Ghost can have fine, glorious times ahead of him, and if he possesses the strength and horse sense that you assure me he does, then he'll endure. All he really has to understand, Donnie, is that this glory now will be his burden thereafter."

THE TENSION GREW throughout the state as New Year's Day approached. For Christmas, a great number of Carolina families bought new and larger television sets in order to watch the Sugar Bowl—God willing, The Grey Ghost's collegiate farewell. In Wilson, there was no other topic of conversation, except briefly, when it was announced that the widowed Mrs. S. E. Flowers III, the former Darlene Merrihew, would wed Bolling Kiely, president of Kiely Chevrolet. The nuptials, as weddings were always characterized in the local press, took place on December 28 so that the happy couple could honeymoon in New Orleans and attend the Sugar Bowl.

The judge, of course, was correct about the Sugar Bowl. Gavin played, courageously, it was said, overcoming pain, with great desire. And so forth. He played as if there were no tomorrow. An injured knee? He ran seventy-three yards from scrimmage the second time he handled the ball, and the rout was on for Carolina. It was 27–7 in the middle of the last period when the coach took the first string out. Well, he did not actually have to take them out. It was just that when Carolina regained the ball, the second team ran onto the field.

The fans accepted this, if grudgingly, but the team had to give up the ball. When Carolina got the ball back again the second unit returned, but this time shouts of "Ghost . . . Ghost . . . Ghost" began to fill the stands. Gavin Grey's college career was ending with him on the bench. No doubt rattled by this chant, the Tarheel second string did no better this time and was required to punt again after only three downs. The clock was running out, but then—who says there is no Providence?—with barely two minutes left in the game, the opposition fumbled on their own twenty-six-yard line, and Carolina had the ball back one last time.

Now the coach, a sportsman to the end, sent in his third offensive team. The issue was settled, so he wanted all his boys to be able to tell their grandchildren that they had played in the Sugar Bowl. But the crowd would have none of it. "Ghost . . . Ghost . . . Ghost." The din must have rattled all New Orleans. Even the other team's people wanted to see Gavin back in there. In all the Sugar Bowl, I suspect only Babs was not chanting for him.

At last, with fifty-four seconds remaining, the Tarheel coach signaled the quarterback to call time-out, and then he approached Gavin, where he sat on the bench, hunched humbly beneath a cape. Every schoolchild in the great state of North Carolina knows the dialogue that transpired at that moment. It was in all the papers, verbatim, the next day. "Go in for Wells," the coach said.

"My unit is through for the day," Gavin replied.

"The crowd wants you, Ghost. Just one play," begged the coach.

Indeed, the crowd was on its feet now, verging on the hysterical, merely on the assumption that the coach must be ordering The Grey Ghost back into the game. The poor third-string Carolina quarterback looked over vainly to the bench for guidance. In all the stadium, only the referee failed to stare at Gavin Grey. He checked his watch. "Okay, son," he said. "Time-in."

"Time-out," said the quarterback.

"You just had a time-out," said the referee.

"All right, we want another," said the quarterback.

On the bench, the coach kept pleading with his star. "They want you, Ghost. One play. Go in there and tell Murray to call forty-eight-sweep for you." That was a pitchout to Gavin around right end. The coach had some sense of drama after all. Whatever happened on the play, the action would go to the far sideline. The Grey Ghost would then have to traverse the whole field to get back to the bench. It would make a proper valedictory. "You owe it to these people, Ghost."

Gavin relented some. "I ain't goin' in alone, Coach."

That was all he needed to hear. Lawrence and Finegan flanked Gavin on the bench. The coach tapped the one with his left hand, the other with the right, and said, "Okay, you two boys go in there with your friend." At that, Gavin smiled at them, reached down for his helmet, threw off his blue cape as he arose, and froze there for an instant—the Colossus of Rhodes, the fourth wonder of the world—as he waited for Lawrence and Finegan to join him in posterity.

Many of us, myself included, began to cry, as The Grey Ghost ran onto the field between the two hulks. It was surreal, and gave the sense of slow motion. They took up their places in the huddle, replacing the three third-stringers. Gavin did not speak up. It was Lawrence who addressed the quarterback. "Coach says run forty-eight-sweep for The Ghost."

Suddenly, Gavin's hand darted out and grabbed the quarterback by the wrist. "Unh-uh," he said. "The four-hole." Forty-eight would take him wide around the end. The four-hole was much more up the middle, right between where Lawrence and Finegan lined up.

The quarterback didn't argue. "Forty-four straight," he said. "On two."

"Wait," Gavin said, and he reached across the huddle to the linemen, and—first Finegan, and then Lawrence—he touched them on the chin strap, held his fingers there and looked them directly in the eyes. It was a very dear thing for a man to do, and daring, too, for what people would say. Maybe only The Ghost could have gotten away with it. It was a caress he gave them both; he was telling them that he loved them. And then he took his fingers away from Lawrence's face and nodded to the quarterback. He clapped his hands once and the huddle broke up.

The Tarheels lined up, and there was not a soul there, in the stands or on the field, who did not know that the ball was going to Gavin Grey. It did not matter, either, for, obviously, fate was at work. He took the handoff at the twenty-three-yard line, and dashed through where Lawrence and Finegan had rammed their men aside. The end brushed the linebacker just enough so that Gavin cut by him, pulled away from the one hand he laid on his leg, and then bolted downfield, weaving in and out, running the last few yards to the end zone all by himself.

The tumult was exceeded only by the emotion. Even Babs could not contain herself. She cried in her seat, just as the judge himself cried before his television set. Lawrence and Finegan reached Gavin first. They embraced him, and then they steered him back, through the third string, which jumped up and down and pounded him on the back as he went by. The three emerged into the open for only a moment or two but, long before they reached the sideline, the rest of the Carolina team had flooded onto the field to greet Gavin. He took off his helmet and threw it into the air as a sign of joy, and, simultaneously, he found himself being lifted off his feet. Hardly breaking stride, Lawrence and Finegan hoisted him onto their shoulders. This was the famous picture that was in all the papers the next day and in all the photo annuals the next December.

I look at it now, in my scrapbook of The Grey Ghost. What a glorious photograph it is. The only face is Gavin's. Those of Lawrence and Finegan are lost in shadows beneath their helmets. Gavin's countenance shows such peace amidst all this exultation.

PART TWO

THE MOTHER OF FOUR

8

Nobody except Stuart himself possessed any real confidence that he could go around McClellan and circle the whole Army of the Potomac altogether. But Stuart had surprise as well as twelve hundred sabers at his command. When his troops skirted the little hamlet of Yellow Tavern that first morning, even the Confederate infantry stationed there assumed that the cavalry was heading for softer duty up in the valley, supporting Stonewall Jackson. The ground troops hooted good-naturedly at the glamorous horsemen, and one of Stuart's old friends hollered, "How long you gonna be gone, Beauty?"

Stuart had been gibing back at the infantry cracks, but this time he only turned in the saddle and roared happily. Then, for a reply, he remembered a refrain from an old song, and he sang out in his baritone, "Oh, it may be for years, / And it may be forever." And, enigmatically, he laughed again. Immediately, Joe Sweeney, the old minstrel man, who had worked blackface music shows before the war, strummed the melody on his banjo. The general always had Sweeney ride near his side. The whole troop sang, then, all of them:

"Kathleen Mavourneen, the grey dawn is breaking,
The horn of the hunter is heard on the hill."

It only made the infantry hoot more at the fancy-dan cavalry and their music men, who seemed to be riding off to Ivanhoe more than to battle. Stuart himself was impeccable: the gray coat buttoned to his chin, high boots highly shined, the saber at just the right cant, the black plume perfectly arrayed in his hat. He had taken to signing letters, "J. E. B. Stuart, The Knight of the Golden Spur," and as he had become known as "Jeb" for his initials, now he was called Beauty for reasons just as obvious.

The men about him appeared to take on his qualities, too. It was said by Lee himself (they said) that General J. E. B. Stuart was a legion, for while he did not select the bravest men or the boldest riders, soon enough only that breed rode with him. It was Stuart's own view that armies developed in history to give men something to work at together . . . away from the women. Since soldiers on all sides were in it with common cause, it was just a damn shame they had to kill one another to justify their existence.

Stuart bade Joe Sweeney to drop back in the ranks, strum some for the men to the rear, and to find John Pelham and send him up. Pelham was a new lieutenant, so young he had still been a plebe at West Point when Sumter was fired on only fourteen months before. And he looked younger still: blond, almost pretty, a lapidary face. But the general had taken to him right away, perhaps because he saw so much of himself in the kid; he was a spiritual heir, as important to Stuart the professional warrior as were his own children to the man.

He had taken Pelham with him on a lark two days before. A beautiful lady from the Eastern Shore of Maryland had sent Stuart a huge bay— it must have stood seventeen hands—and he wanted to try it out. He was seeking a chance to examine the mettle of his baby-faced new trooper, too, so he had taken the big bay and the boy lieutenant and ridden out toward the federal lines. At one point, the two Rebels had burst right upon an enemy patrol, but the Yankees had been so surprised that they barely had time to leap for cover, much less to fire upon the intruders. The Yankees finally managed to loose a few token rounds upon Stuart and Pelham, but only after they were well beyond effective range.

The bullets whistled harmlessly overhead, and the general was so amused, that, to Pelham's astonishment, he pulled up his bay, rose up in the saddle, and waved his plumed hat gaily at the poor befuddled Yankees. Then Stuart trotted away at his leisure, laughing and chatting with Pelham. "I should have told you not to worry," he said. "Those fellows get the least bit excited, they fire high. Don't ever let this out, Lieutenant, but all this war is is a race, a race against time. The whole trick is for us to get it done before the Yankees learn to hold steady and lower their sights."

Now, this new June morning, as the troop wound past Yellow Tavern, Pelham reached the top of the file and saluted the general. Stuart returned the gesture. "Lieutenant, do you know what you learned on that little frolic with me the other day?" he asked.

"Well, sir . . ." Pelham began, searching for the right answer.

"You learned that a good man on a good horse can never be caught."

"Yes, sir."

"If you're going to be an officer for Jeb Stuart in the First Virginia, I want you to know one thing."

"Yes, sir?"

"A gallop is an unbecoming gait to a soldier at all times but one: when you're going toward the enemy. The First Virginia can trot away from anything. Steady, without breaking ranks. Remember that, Pelham. We gallop toward the enemy, and we trot away when we've finished our task. Remember that, and you'll make a good horse trooper."

"Yes, sir, I will," Pelham said. "I never thought of it quite like that before, sir."

"No, I don't imagine you've been at it long enough," Stuart said, and he reached over and patted the lieutenant's mount on the withers. "Lis-

ten, John"—and the boy's head shot up, surprised that the general had
addressed him by his Christian name. "Listen, you've got a fine horse.
That's the glory of the cavalry. A man must depend completely upon his
horse and completely upon his fellow troopers, yet with no loss whatso-
ever of his own self. And self is a better thing to cling to than life. Oh,
John, for certain, God never devised a better game for men to play."

—DONALD MCCLURE,
The Life and Death of the Knight of the Golden Spur

I DROVE UP FROM CHARLOTTESVILLE TO WATCH
Gavin's farewell from football early in December of 1964. He
had been in the pros for an even ten seasons, the last seven in Washington, and the Redskins were giving him his "day." In all other
pursuits they honor the departing with dinners and luncheons; in
sports they give you a day. It only takes a few minutes, but they call
it a day. It is a wonderfully selfless and altruistic venture on the part
of the ball club, especially if they can sell more tickets and increase
concession sales. I'd seen a couple other star athletes' days, and
Gavin's was typical of the genre—in sum, I would say, about the
most pagan ritual I have ever witnessed in this nation under God.

And so The Grey Ghost's career concluded. The judge had
been right about it, too. The heroic Gavin Grey of the Sugar Bowl
was never again. Oh, he was a star in the pros. Two of the three
years he played in Canada he was the league's Most Valuable
Player, and before his knee injury in 1960 he made all-pro his first
two seasons with the Redskins—an impossible achievement considering what an awful team it was. He set rushing records that
stand to this day; twice he scored four touchdowns in one game;

he was honored with selection to the Jantzen board, thereby earning a handsome stipend for wearing bathing suits in magazine advertisements; he made even more on the side endorsing a potpourri of products and services in Washington, and he continued, year in and year out, to receive the use of a brand new Chevrolet from Bolling Kiely (so long as he used the use himself), for lending his good name to Tarheel Deal advertising. (Unbeknownst to Mr. Kiely, Gavin also began to obtain the use of Mrs. Kiely on a regular basis, as well.) He was hired by Carolina Life & Casualty, ostensibly to sell policies, in fact to play golf and drink bourbon with jock-sniffing clients and legislators. For many years, too, Gavin and Lawrence had been partners of the Grey Ghost Inn, a steak house near Chapel Hill; Gavin had put up the capital, while Lawrence managed the establishment.

So, by any measure, it had been a successful professional career. But there was a paleness to it compared to what had come before, in Carolina. Yet when Gavin stood at the microphones before his last game, I cried. Oh, perhaps I cried from memory, but somebody had to cry, and Babs, standing next to him, was supposed to smile, which she did as well as ever. Their three children—Thomas Langhorne Grey, age eight; Allison Rodgers Grey, age seven; Russell Finegan Grey, age three—wore shiny new clothes for the occasion and shifted about restlessly as various gridiron pooh-bahs read proclamations and trotted out the likes of TV consoles and power mowers, in appreciation. The fans responded perfunctorily, anxious for the kickoff.

There are three types of ovations at sporting events. The first is the most common, the spontaneous happy roar for when the home team does well. Number two is the best and warmest cheer, and comes only in rare moments, when people are touched. It is not necessarily so long or so loud; indeed, it swells in choppy bursts; hollering is out of place, and the fans pause from their clapping to exchange happy talk with their neighbors: "Isn't that great?" or "Good for him!" Cheerful observations such as that. But no matter who is being honored, nobody responds that way to ceremonies.

No, for them there is the third kind of cheer, one of studied courtesy (or maybe it is simply phony). It is awarded to opponents who get up after an injury, to officials who retrieve errant paper napkins, to servicemen who intone the National Anthem. It is tendered with the same kind of dutiful, affected attention that is awarded when the PA announcer asks for a moment of silence, and I don't think Gavin could tell, but it made me sad that this was the only cheer they could muster for The Grey Ghost at the end.

The last gift for him was from his team. It was a rich set of golf clubs. Henry Brezicki, the defensive captain, and Bobby Sample, the quarterback, made the presentation. Brezicki was what Lawrence or Finegan would have become if they had been good enough. He weighed two hundred and sixty-five pounds and had no neck, and he loved his work, falling upon people and farting in the locker room. Gavin was himself the captain of the offensive unit, so the young Sample had been pressed into service in his stead. He had been the league's first draft choice three years previous (the Redskins invariably finished last, and thus earned the first pick), signed out of Kansas, where he was everybody's All-American. He was as handsome as Gavin, taller and rangier, as quarterbacks tend to be, with a well-promoted Christian faith and a shy, sincere countenance that made people in Washington think of a prairie even if they had never seen one.

Gavin had always liked Bobby Sample and had taken him under his wing from the day he arrived in Washington. It was not only that they were both backs—some guard or tackle simply could not have been Sample's mentor no matter what his age or wisdom—but the two shared the even rarer common experience of being everybody's All-Americans. Babs and Gavin had Sample over for dinner occasionally, but they had to pick their spots, inasmuch as he did not drink and was afraid that he might enjoy himself. He made Babs especially uncomfortable because he was one of these people who always refer to Jesus as if he were a guy from the neighborhood, who even now was down at the Sunoco station or mowing the lawn next door. For her part, Babs played her own private little game with Sample, always dressing as sexily as she could and going right to the brink with daring discourse. The one time the year before when I showed up to make a fourth, Babs, as fetching as I ever saw her in some low-slung hot-pink hostess gown, purposely used the expression "cold as a witch's tit." Gavin, shoveling down the food, took no notice, but poor Sample about choked on his broccoli, and, I swear, could not bring himself to look beneath Babs's forehead the balance of the evening lest his eyes be drawn to her ——. Babs peered mischievously over at me, delighted at how she had discombobulated Sample.

But notwithstanding his innocence, he could pass the ball and lead what there was of a team, and by the time Gavin retired there was no question but that Sample was the dominant figure for the Redskins upon the field and in the locker room. Gavin did not know it, but already Sample had been approached by Jantzen to take The Grey Ghost's place in their bathing-suit ads the next year.

For the official retirement ceremonies, Brezicki, by prearrangement, let Sample make the little presentation speech, and his words resounded about the stadium: "Gavin, now that you'll have more time on your hands on Sunday afternoons, we, of the Redskins family, hope you'll get a lot of use and enjoyment out of these."

And he handed Gavin the golf clubs. Gavin chuckled at this humorous remark, and then thanked everyone who had been responsible for this occasion. He thanked God and his family for their roles in his life, and then he posed for pictures with Babs and the kids, the five of them standing before the golf clubs and the console and all the other bric-à-brac.

I turned to watch Sample and Brezicki run off. After just a couple steps, Brezicki leaned over and patted Sample on the rear. It was a reflex. Here Sample had only given a little speech, said a few words into a microphone, but the other player patted him on the rear, just as if he had scored a touchdown. Athletes are like that. They're like other people who kiss whomever they meet. I don't mean there's anything sexual to it; it's more like a secret handshake. Then Brezicki and Sample came over to the sideline and started hooting and hollering with the rest of the Redskins, banging antlers and carrying on.

I was standing there with Finegan, and with Bolling and Darlene—the Kielys. Gavin had asked me and Finegan to come, and Bolling had extracted invitations for himself and the missus. Finegan called out, "Hey, you got a lot of good shit," when Gavin came off the field. He stopped and looked at us, and nodded, but then he went over to the team. He was smiling, but there were tears in his eyes, as any boy would cry if he knew exactly what day it was that he had to walk away from his childhood.

Babs came over to me and took my hands in hers, and I could see that she was starting to cry too. "Oh, Donnie," she said. "It's over. All the games are over."

"Hey, come on, Babs," I said, and I leaned down and kissed her on the cheek. I had finally gotten old enough and bold enough to do that sort of thing with her by now. And then she took my arm, so I could escort her off the field, and just then the band, attired in Indian war bonnets, struck up "Hail to the Redskins!," which is a bouncy march, as good as any college song, one that calls for vic-tor-ee, and I could feel Babs pick up her step—and the children, too, following after us like baby ducks—and she brightened, as of old, and out of the corner of my eye I could see the kickoff unit run onto the field while Gavin walked up and down the sidelines, patting all the Redskin rears that were left there and calling out cheers to the luckier players on the field.

I WAS, AS you might expect, overcome by nostalgia this day. It was just enough, sitting at a football game again with Babs—and never mind that now there were also three children with us, not to mention Finegan and Bolling and Darlene. Only I had changed. I had grown up, departed Fike High, matriculated and graduated from Carolina, had taken a master's at Vanderbilt, and now I was going for my doctorate in the Civil War and Reconstruction at the University of Virginia. But as sensible and organized as all that sounds, I was also adrift in many ways. My father had died of a heart attack almost five years before, and, after a time, Mom had sold the house in Wilson and gone back to her roots in Charlotte, where she opened a secondhand shop. She would call me on the telephone every week or so around six or six-thirty.

Widows and divorcées are worst around that hour every day. That is when they used to sit down for a drink or dinner with their husband, and when they want so to talk to somebody. My difficult times were vacations—holidays especially—for I had no real place to go back to. There were still many old friends in Wilson, but I couldn't stay with them, and while there was family in Charlotte, the place was foreign—and depressing, from my younger days. As long as I was still attending college at Chapel Hill and Babs and Gavin's kids were still babies, I could go over to their house and attach myself to the family (at least in the off-season, when they were back from Washington), but since I had left Carolina, I had lost that right just to pop in. I really didn't know where to go. I would have been best to leave school and go a-wandering for a while, but you couldn't do that then or they would draft you.

But if I had changed and ostensibly grown up, Babs appeared as she always had, the most beautiful creature on the face of the earth. Oh, the dresses had come up a bit, to near the knee, her hair was somewhat shorter, and possibly she was a half-size larger across the beam. She had learned to drink a little whiskey by now, did not blush before the milder risqué expressions, and might even utter the odd one herself on the order of "cold as a witch's. . . . " After all, if what I had read in all the dependable books was correct, Babs should have been just about at her sexual peak now, which titillated me as I sat with her, even if I did not accept that claim completely at face value, inasmuch as, in my own case, from what I had read in the same books, it seems that I must have been on the far side of my sexual peak before my voice changed.

But never mind: It was just so odd to be back with Babs, watching a football game again, and that it was the last one The Grey Ghost would ever play made me feel very close to her once again, as the pretend lover of hers that I had been in Chapel Hill that fall so long ago. I reached over and took her hand and squeezed it near the end, and she looked me in the eyes, looking back, I think. I don't think athletes and their women ever really look ahead.

GAVIN HAD NOT signed with the Redskins right out of Carolina in '54. They drafted him, the first player in the nation, and then they invited him up to Washington and wined him and dined him and got him a first-class whore for the night when they divined that he was that kind of growing boy. But they never paid him much mind when he made references to playing in Canada. The Redskins thought he was holding out for another $2,000 bonus, which they finally made a great to-do about offering him, and were flabbergasted then when he still kept on talking about going to Canada.

"It's be absolutely un-American for a boy like you to take your God-given abilities to a foreign country," the owner said.

Gavin replied: "Well, I see it like this, Mr. Marshall. It's like an expression we have about women down in Carolina. We say, Turn 'em upside down, they're all about the same."

"We say that about them in Washington, too."

"And every place, I reckon," Gavin said. "Well, sir, my point is, cheering's the same. When you're on the gridiron, it sounds the same whether you're in Carolina or the nation's capital or Canada or where-all. You see now, fans don't understand that, because they always cheer for the same bunch every year. The folks who cheered for me with the Tarheels will cheer for the Tarheels next year when I'm gone. And the same folks who cheered for the Redskins are going to holler for them whether I'm there or not. I may be the HE-ro, Mr. Marshall, I may be the one actually gettin' the cheers, but I'm the one just passin' through. So long as I gotta leave Carolina, it don't make a whole lot of difference where I go to. I might as well get me top dollar."

Gavin told me all about this a couple weeks later when the whole family met in Charlotte when his mother (my grandmother) celebrated her sixtieth birthday. My folks and I drove down from Wilson; Gavin came from Chapel Hill, picking up Babs in Greensboro at the W.C. She was already considered family, more or less.

We all just did make it into Charlotte, too, because it snowed like hell late that Friday night all across the state. It doesn't snow much in Carolina, but when it does, it throws everything into complete chaos. It is a pleasant kind of disaster, though, because it is guaranteed to be short-lived: The sun comes out the next day and melts all the snow, and that's all there is to it. Gavin and I went outside right after we had breakfast Saturday morning, and you could hear—*hear*—the snow melting. It was up to our calves, and we didn't even need to put jackets on.

He told me, without much enthusiasm, how he had negotiated himself a little more bonus money from the Redskins. "So you'll sign now?" I asked.

"I reckon," he said, making me very relieved, because, like every other red-blooded American boy, the thought of The Grey Ghost playing football at a foreign port of call was more than I could bear.

He leaned down and packed a snowball, whipping it across the lawn to a tree trunk, where it splattered dead center and left a bit white patch. I made a snowball myself and chucked it at the tree, just nicking it. "Nice shot," Gavin said, and he picked himself farther along in the snow. "The trouble is, Donnie, what can I do? I don't know nothin' about negotiations and contracts and what-all. And I sure don't know nothin' 'bout this DO-minion of Canada. Where's this Toronto at, anyhow?"

"That's the team wants you?"

"That's what the telegram said. I just know it's someplace up yonder. And everyone I talk to says, You are sure right, Ghost, not to jump into this thing. But while they says that, the last place on the face of the earth they want me to go to is the DO-minion of Canada, because if I go to the nation's capital, they get to see me play on the TV and can even drive up in a few hours' time to watch me play. It's like that Chevvalay man, Donnie. Everybody wants a little somethin' of me. The only one I really trust is my daddy, and what does he know about all this?"

"Judge Pace," I said instinctively.

"What?"

"Judge Frank R. Pace, Jr.," I said.

THE PART ABOUT the judge that Gavin liked best was that he really didn't care much about football. He was so excited, the more I told him about the judge (especially the part about Hollywood, the studio, and Denise Del Canto) that we left with Babs the next morning and drove the whole state to Wilson. We only stopped twice, at two Stuckey's, pre-interstate roadside oases that always advertised "Free Ice Water" down the road in order to lure the unwary traveler in, there to tempt him with more commercial confections.

On the phone, the judge had seemed most receptive to meeting with Gavin, showing concern only with assuring the most decorous dormitory arrangements: Babs would be sequestered in his house, with Clarissa, while he would move next door and bunk with Gavin and me at my parents' house. And when he came out to greet us, he instantly lived up to all my advance billing. First, of course, he attended to the lady: "My gracious, you're even more beautiful than Donnie has described you."

I blushed uncontrollably, but it really mattered none, because Babs paid me no mind whatsoever, taking it for granted, as ever, that it was the natural state for people to be passing on reports of her pulchritude.

And then the judge turned to Gavin: "It's so nice to meet you. I've heard so much about you."

I about to died: *heard so much about you!* It was as if he was meeting a fellow at the Tuesday Rotary luncheon. Even Gavin was impressed. Years later, at a reception in Washington, I was introduced to Jackie Kennedy. I wished so much to have the nerve to say that, but I didn't dare; it passed: "How do you do. . . ."

The judge was just about to usher us inside when Clarissa came tearing out of the kitchen, wiping her hands on her apron. She skidded to a halt before us. "Lord, Cake, you done jes what the judge say. You done brought us The Grey Ghost hisself."

"This is one of your greatest admirers, Gavin," the judge said. "Mrs. Clarissa Ellison."

"Lord 'a' mercy, it *is* my pleasure, Mister Ghost," Clarissa cooed, and she curtsied before him. I think that was the only time I ever saw a grown woman curtsy.

The judge went on, "And this vision is, of course, Miss Rogers, Mr. Grey's intended."

"How are you, Clarissa?" Babs inquired nicely.

"Lawd, Miss Babs, you must be the prettiest white woman I ever did see." That was a new compliment, even for Babs, but she managed to accept it with her usual aplomb. She had very little time, though, for in the next moment Clarissa had turned on the judge: "Judge Pace, I ought to knock you upside the head. You ain't got the manners of a billy goat, keepin' these young folks standin' out here in the draft where they can catch their death o' cold."

The judge was used to such chastisements from Clarissa, and so he merely smiled at her and ushered us into the living room, making sure to shut the door securely in order not to suffer any more of her wrath. "We're going to have Clarissa's famous chops," he said. "Will that be all right with everybody, Donnie?"

"Yes, sir!"

"With sweet potatoes, kale, and biscuits. How's it coming, Clarissa?"

"It's a fixin' to be done presently."

"Well, don't rush it any, because I'm sure our travelers want to get the dust outta their throats. I'd like to spend a little time before dinner myself with Doctor Dant," he said. Babs and Gavin both looked a little puzzled, and so the judge picked up the bottle of J. W. Dant bourbon from the bar and showed them. "What will it be? Bourbon and branch? Or perhaps something milder and less convivial? I have some beer, some sherry."

Babs and Gavin looked at each other and shrugged, with a smile, that they would go with the bourbon. "Highball?" the judge inquired, and they nodded further at that. I don't believe Babs had ever before taken a drink of hard liquor outside her own home.

"Good," said the judge gaily, doling out three tall glasses of J. W. Dant and water. "Beer amongst the boys and sherry amongst the ladies are tolerable, but neither is the right kind of axle grease where either strangers or men and women together are assembled."

He beckoned them to seats, escorting Babs to the wing chair Mrs. Pace used to favor by the fire. The room—the whole house, for goodness sake—was untouched since her death, so far as I could tell; it remained terribly out of fashion, and so terribly feminine for such a masculine male as the judge. The fire was the most manly thing he ever had in the house. His piano was over in the corner, covered by a mélange of family photographs, everything from formal wedding portraits to summer barbecue scenes. It was, at that time, a fair measure of a family's social standing to count how many photographs cluttered a house. Nouveaux riches could be instantly identified on account that objects of art and expensive accessories schematically decorated their houses, leaving no room for intimate photographs of the habitants and their relatives. To this day, the most magnificently appointed houses and condominiums strike me as barren.

Gavin took his seat on the sofa, carrying his drink with him. The judge turned to me. "I haven't forgotten you, Donnie. I think of you pretty near as family. Now, I wouldn't offer you a drink anyway, but just for the record: You don't drink yet, do you?"

"No, sir!"

"Clarissa!" the judge hollered, and she scurried in. "What sort of soda pop do we have for Mister Donnie?"

"Well, what do y'all want, Cake?" she asked me. "We done got Co-Cola, Nehi orange, and Dr Pepper."

"Nehi, please," I said, and she left to fetch it, but I could see Gavin snickering over on the sofa.

"She call you 'Cake'?" he giggled, beside himself. "*Cake.*" I was mortified. I could imagine him calling me Cake for the rest of my life. And everybody else picking up on it, since that was what The Grey Ghost preferred to call me. Nothing could ever make me Donnie again—and I would never ever make "Don." Everybody calling me Cake, wherever I went. "Lieutenant Cake McClure, you take that machine-gun nest." "Do you, Cake, take this woman to . . . ?" "Cake, the president wants you to run for the Senate in North Carolina." CAKE M'LURE DEAD AT 75.

Mercifully, the judge came to my assistance. "Clarissa tenders such appellations to infants, strictly on first impressions," he explained to Gavin. "The Anderson boy down the street is even older than Donnie, a freshman at State, lean as a rail, and Clarissa still calls him Fattnin', from their first meeting, him at six weeks of age. And there's an adorable creature 'cross the way, Doris Weymouth, just now blossoming into a young woman, and Clarissa still addresses her as Puddin'. All things are relative. I'd say Cake is about the best a body could expect from Clarissa."

This seemed to satisfy Gavin, at least until Clarissa returned with the orange drink and said, "Here 'tis, Cake."

"Cake!" I heard Gavin say.

The judge poured me my Nehi into a highball glass. "I'm glad you're not what they call ex-per-I-ment-ing with whiskey, Donnie. It just ain't a fit thing to do at your age. When did you first have a drink, Gavin?"

"Not till I was at Chapel Hill. My daddy would have busted me good if ever I'd drunk in high school."

The judge nodded a benediction at this. "Remember how much damn time you have, Donnie," he said. "No, not Donnie—all of you. You're all so young. Ever'body in this world is forever carryin' on about how time flies. Well, as Clarissa would say, Stuff and nonsense. Right, Donnie?"

"Yessir."

"You'd be surprised at how much time there is. You have no idea. There ain't no need to rush into anything." Slowly, he began to walk away from the mantel, back over to the bar. Gavin and Babs never took their eyes off him until his back was completely toward us. Then Gavin glanced toward me and lighted me up with his smile: He approved! However much I had failed him in introducing Bolling Kiely to his life, now, with the judge, I was redeemed in spades. Judge Pace turned back by the bar. "When I was about your age, Donnie. No, no, a little older. Probably sixteen or so. How old are you now?"

"Fifteen come May."

"Yeah, I was older. I just stayed a little bitty thing. I couldn't grow an inch. My voice stayed just as high as a sparrow's, my face as smooth as a baby's bottom. I couldn't perform well in games, and the young ladies towered over me, whenever in those rare moments they deigned to be seen in my diminutive company. I was what was known then as a pipsqueak."

I tried not to look too attentive; this was hitting too close to home, and I was especially anxious to find out how the story concluded: happily, I prayed. "My daddy . . . yes, even an old coot like me had a daddy once. My daddy came into my room one afternoon when I was especially upset. I believe I might even have been crying. Sniffling, by all odds. And he inquired what was wrong, and I gave him an answer—although probably an obtuse one. But he caught on, 'deed if he didn't already know.

"And he sat down there on the bed with me where I was all sprawled out, and he said, 'Boy, I know it's a reg'lar hurtin' thing now, but you're lucky because you ain't dumb, and you're just goin' to have a little bit longer to look around and study before you get in with the others. I don't mean book study. I mean studyin' folks. And that's gonna be one great advantage to you, because the best way of all to live life is to catch on early and grow up late.'"

The judge spoke those last words with great emphasis—"*catch on early and grow up late*"—but somehow when he did, and without making a point of it, he shifted his eyes from me to Babs and Gavin, and I could detect the edge of sadness; for they, most of anyone, had been denied this luxury of time.

"Well, now," the judge said quickly, taking up another beat. "If I'm not mistaken 'bout how long Clarissa's chops take, I believe we have time to visit the good doctor one more time before dinner." Gavin, catching on fast to the code, nodded enthusiastically and polished off the rest of his drink, then sprang to his feet, delivering his empty glass to the bar. In tacit approval of the plan, Babs took another swallow of her own. The judge took Gavin's glass and poured in more bourbon. "Tell me, son, what're you studyin' at Chapel Hill?"

Gavin just threw back his head and roared, causing the judge to turn around in wonder. "Judge, I 'spect you're the first person in Carolina, on the face of the earth, ever asked me that."

"Then we're gonna get along just fine," said the judge.

IT WAS AMAZING; we ate the whole dinner without the subject of football ever so much as arising. Babs was clearly in love with the judge by the end of the meal, and Gavin was in his thrall. He treated them both so differently from how anyone else did, and while in one way he overshadowed them so with his breadth and intelligence, at the same time he managed to raise them a notch. For the first time, Babs was not a beauty and Gavin not a star—and they loved it. At least for the evening; I doubt if they would have wanted to make a habit of it.

Clarissa brought us coffee, back in the parlor. The judge stoked his pipe then and got down to cases, listening to Gavin about the Redskins and the Canadian business. He paused only to lay another log on the fire. "Now listen to me," he said at last. "I'm going to say some things, and you be sure to keep them in perspective." Babs and Gavin both nodded; he sounded so ominous. "There's an expression I heard long ago—that an athlete dies twice. I thought about it myself when I was in Hollywood, because I thought it might apply to me as well, to an entertainer. I came home because I was scared that I was going to spend a lot of my life dead on my feet. You understand?"

"Yes, sir," Babs and Gavin said in unison. They were listening without hardly breathing.

"You're going to die three times, Gavin Grey. It can't be helped." God, but the judge *could* be ominous when he put his mind to it. Gavin looked as if he had just been handed the death card in a gypsy salon.

"I don't understand," Babs said for him.

"All athletes die when they have to leave the game. That's their first death. But you're going to have an earlier one too, because what you achieved at Carolina cannot be continued or duplicated wherever you play next." Gavin's mouth dropped a little at that; Babs was more plainly hurt. The judge saw. "But I hasten to amend that, to add that it has nothing whatsoever to do with your abilities; it has nothing to do with football." He pointed a finger at Gavin. "Do you know what you've been?" Gavin shook his head, not knowing the answer any more than he did the question. "You've been playing a role. The Grey Ghost is a role."

"Like in a play."

"Absolutely. Gavin Grey was a football player. But The Grey Ghost was a character. And, my God, but you played it well! No man ever played Hamlet better." The judge chuckled. "No, Dwight David Eisenhower didn't play Ike so well, nor did Charles Lindbergh play Lucky Lindy so well as you played The Grey Ghost. Nobody is ever really a HE-ro, Gavin. Someone just plays the part."

"And The Ghost is dead," Gavin said softly, a calm smile crossing his face. There was obviously a certain peace within him that at least one other soul had learned the secret he lived with. Gavin had known. Babs hadn't; she looked very nearly ready to cry, and the judge noticed that and attended to her mourning.

"Don't fret, my dear. He may be better for it. The French have an expression that an actress is more than a woman, but an actor is less than a man. Gavin is freed from acting now, so he can be a man altogether." Then he turned to the object. "And you perceived this, didn't you?"

"I reckon," Gavin replied.

"When Donnie talked to me on the phone, when he told me you had misgivings about the Washington Redskins, I gathered this might be the case. It isn't the money. It isn't that they're a bad ball club. It's that you know you can't keep on playing the role there."

"Yes, sir, that's true."

"I don't know how smart you are, Gavin, but by all odds you're wiser than I imagined." Gavin blushed, and there followed, after a discussion on the properties of brandy and its value as an "aphrodisiac of the mind," a dispensing of the liquor to the three of them. Then the judge sat down on the sofa next to Babs; he stared into the fire for a moment before he continued. "Remember that old lady you met?"

"Mrs. Stringfellow from the Civil War?" Gavin asked.

"Yes. It was really very appropriate identifying you with old Jeb Stuart. A HE-ro not unlike you, upon another stage. Donnie and I have touched on this, haven't we?"

"Yes, sir."

"They call quarterbacks field generals, so it is all the more apt that someone should find some dramatic commonality in you and our greatest cavalry leader. Halfbacks are the cavalry, like great riders upon the beasts up front."

"The offensive line?" I asked, to be sure.

"The fellows who block, those slugs, yes. Stuart was lucky. In the dramatic sense. He was shot and killed just as the wave crested. In the most literal sense of the cliché, he just didn't have the horses anymore. He was physically incapable of any more heroics, at least on the scale we were accustomed to. So his death made the legend all the stronger. You have the same kind of choice, Gavin. If you were never to set foot upon the gridiron again, it would be the best for The Grey Ghost. For remember that each game you play hereafter as Gavin Grey must diminish the legend of The Grey Ghost. You know that?"

"Yes, sir."

"But hell's bells, you'll make a lot of money as a player. You'll raise your family and keep a wife in grander style than you might otherwise manage. You'll still be famous. You'll be in the public eye so long as you play, but you'll be selling out the legend. That's the price."

"I gotta play, judge. I didn't set out to be a legend. I set out to be a football player."

"Of course. Athletes play. They are utterly seduced by their games. I knew you would say that. My point is, though, that if you must sell the legend, then find the highest price for it. If you can get that in Toronto, then go there. The Redskins will give you a lot of who-shot-John about how much more important it is to play in the United States, about how much more exposure you'll get, the television back to Carolina and so forth. But what of that? It'll just tarnish The Grey Ghost all the quicker."

"And they ain't got nobody to block on that team," Gavin said.

"How much more could he get in Canada?" Babs asked, striking to the heart of the matter.

The judge looked into his brandy snifter for just a moment, swirling the drink about. "I've thought about that and played with some figures, and I don't see why we can't get you a twenty-five-thousand-dollar bonus, with a three-year contract of thirty-five-thousand the first year, then forty and forty-five." Babs and Gavin about fell out of their chairs; the Redskins were taking about a twelve-thousand-dollar bonus and a four-year contract topping out at thirty thousand. The judge explained how he had arrived at his figures, how the Toronto team could afford them by selling so many more season tickets on the strength of The Grey Ghost's name, not to mention so many more parking spaces, hot dogs, etc. (He was right, too; Gavin got almost exactly what the judge mentioned to us here.)

"What do I have to give you for handling this, sir?" Gavin asked cautiously.

"Hmmm," Judge Pace replied, drawing on his pipe. "One form of remuneration would be that I'd like you to guarantee me seats on the fifty-yard line whenever it is that I pass through Toronto on the way from Wilson to Rocky Mount. And then, you'd also have to promise me that you'd come over to the piano with me now and accompany me in a few songs." My mouth flew open. The judge called for Clarissa to put the dishes down and come in and help us get the luggage from the car, so we could finish the evening in song.

He began, appropriately, with "Carolina Moon," went from there to "Whispering," "Shenandoah," "Ragmop," the fight song for the Virginia Military Institute, "Baby Face," "The Yellow Rose of Texas," "The Indian Love Call," which Babs sang with him, and "The Church in the Wildwood," where Clarissa made the duet. I added the logs to the fire and sang selected choruses. Gavin kept the doctor on call. And the judge never let up. At one-thirty, he had just moved from "Pennies from Heaven" to "That Old Rugged Cross" when the phone rang, but, unperturbed—who would be calling at this hour of the morning?—he nodded at Clarissa to answer the phone, and kept right on playing. "The Eyes of Texas" was next on his list.

But just then, the door to the kitchen flew open, and Clarissa returned at a gallop, her face beaming. "Judge, Judge, you stop that playing. Miss Dolly has done had her baby!"

He dropped his hands to his lap. "Well, isn't that lovely? Dolly's my niece. This gives me—what is it, Clarissa?"

"It's a beautiful baby daughter."

"This gives me a grandniece, and makes me feel very ancient."

He got up then, and went to talk to his sister, the grandmother, on the phone. I knew Dolly. She lived in Rocky Mount and often came to visit with the judge. She was a few years older than me, and I had certainly noticed her these past few years. Dolly was no match for Babs, to be sure, but she had a fair enough country visage, and a lean, fine body, the sort that men come to admire as they grow older and learn to put large breasts into proper perspective. Unfortunately for Dolly, she had not bided her time until she reached her best advantage, and had let herself go with a dull young local fellow named Stevenson, who worked at a tobacco warehouse. They had had a small September wedding and now a large February child.

The judge returned and hoisted his glass from off the piano. "It's really quite an omen that you're here, Gavin, at the birth of my niece's child." Gavin raised a quizzical eyebrow. "You see, in a sense, she named the little girl after you."

"After me?"

"A girl named Gavin?" I piped up.

"No, not quite. Dolly is, I'm afraid, something of a romantic, which of course largely accounts for this whole business. I never did meet a practical woman in eastern Carolina who had a, uh, 'premature' baby. Only romantics." I steered my eyes away from Babs, for this was as delicate an adult conversation as ever I had experienced in mixed company. "In any event, while she was carrying the child this fall, she read the accounts of you, Gavin, and the old lady who knew General Stuart, and Dolly was so generally imbued with tales of The Grey Ghost, of Carolina, the Confederacy, and the Tarheels, the glory of it all, that she decided to name her child Jeb if it were a boy, and Stuart if it were a girl."

"Stuart Stevenson," I said.

"It has the added advantage of alliteration," the judge said.

"It's a pretty name," Babs said.

"Yes, it is," the judge went on, "and I take it as a most felicitous sign that Gavin was here in the family when she came into this world. Perhaps Stuart Stevenson will capture the spirit of The Grey Ghost instead of that of her physical father. So I'll drink to you both—to Gavin Grey's future and to Stuart Stevenson's." And he raised the doctor high in the air, polished off what was left, and suggested that we call it a night, which we did, upon the recessional he chose, General Stuart's old favorite, "The Girl I Left Behind Me."

9

EXCEPT, PERHAPS, FOR THE THREE YEARS THEY were in Toronto, I always saw Babs and Gavin regularly. I felt close to them, and, especially after my father died and my mother left Wilson, it was somewhat a matter of needing them too, for I was, really, lonely during those years. Perhaps I was lucky. Had I been good with girls I probably would have turned to that completely and ended up with a teenage bride. But I never had any facility with girls; it never dared occur to me that they might actually be as interested in me as I was in them. I always thought of myself as about midway between a sex maniac and an imposition, and so I devoted myself more to my schoolwork. How else would anybody decide to become an historian?

I was the godfather of Tommy, Babs and Gavin's oldest, named for Thomas Langhorne, Gavin's maternal grandfather, and I dutifully remembered all birthdays and Christmases and roughhoused with him and his sister for hours on end whenever I visited. No doubt because I was such a willing playmate for a small child, they invited me to come to the beach with them the summer of 1960. That was right after my father died, too, and I needed someplace to find myself. I had always loved my father, although we had never been especially close in the way of fathers and sons who go rabbit hunting or build cars together. But we had a shared interest in Mother and a mutual respect for one another, and I was shattered by his death—for losing my father and for death itself. I was two weeks short of my twentieth birthday when he fell dead, and I hadn't really ever known anybody else who had died.

"Don't say such things as 'left us' and 'passed away,'" Mother had advised me years before when some doddering distant cousin departed Virginia for heaven. "If you have faith, don't pretty it up, Donnie. We're mortal. We die."

Babs and Gavin had rented a house on the Delaware shore, at a Washington resort named Bethany Beach. The idea was that I could earn my keep and a suntan by baby-sitting and generally helping out, especially from the middle of July on, when Gavin had to go off to the Redskins' training camp in Carlisle, Pennsylvania. The 1950s were over now, an era ended, and it was getting hard already to get reliable colored help to travel.

The first two weeks, when Gavin was with us, I did my best to accompany him in training. We'd run along the beach together, in the soft sand, then sometimes in and out of the surf, working on building up his legs. This would be his sixth year as a pro, his third with the Redskins, and he was all-pro, at the height of his powers. His leaving for training camp was nothing short of cruel, leaving me alone, as it did, with the girl of my dreams. Babs did not help matters, either, by treating me sort of, nearly, almost as family. Nights she would almost always be in her shorty pajamas, and worst of all, when we would come back from the beach, she would take the children into the outdoor shower with her, send them scurrying out, naked and de-sanded, and then ask me to pass her a clean towel, which she would *parade* to her room in. I had erections most of that summer. We called them huskies. I had a permanent Delaware husky.

Alone each evening, when Tommy and Allison were in bed (the last child, the one named for Finegan, came the next year),

Babs and I would sit out in the courtyard together and talk. There was no television, no friends. There was just the two of us, beer and gin. Alternately, I would barbecue or she would cook— steak and crab cakes for the most part—and then we would talk some more. It was the summer John Kennedy was approaching the Democratic nomination, and she listened carefully to my explanation about how the Pope would soon be installed in the Pentagon were Kennedy elected president. We also spoke of Communists, Earl Warren, Sputniks, the fate of Gary Francis Powers, and sit-ins.

I did not know it—I was just being myself—but, apparently, I quite astonished Babs, because on each and every subject, I not only spoke with authority, but I offered different considered opinions from everything else she had ever heard before. For example, I believed that colored people should be allowed to eat at lunch counters, so long as they behaved themselves in an exemplary fashion, and in a week or so I had brought Babs far enough around so that she agreed this was certainly a possibility to consider some years down the road if things were not rushed precipitously.

One night at dinner she suddenly reached out and put her hand on mine, and said: "Oh Donnie, I've loved having you here. I've never talked like this to any man before." Looking back, I suspect this was primarily a discreet circumlocution, meaning every other man eschewed conversation in order to try and put the make on her, but at the time I took it at face value.

"You talk to Gavin, don't you?"

She looked away. "Gavin and I talk about . . . Gavin and me."

"I guess that's what happens when you're married, huh?"

"I guess so," she said, and then she ate another mouthful and thought about it. "No, Donnie, I 'spect that's just me and Gavin.

Because everybody's talked about us. We're used to talkin' 'bout us. You're different. You talk about *things*."

This was an enormous revelation to me, that Babs Grey would rate me over her husband, if even in just the one obscure category: Discussion of Things. But it served to give me the edge on myself that I needed with women, and back in Chapel Hill that fall I actually seduced one from Asheville named Sue Ellen. Oh sure, I don't want to hide my light under a bushel, I had indeed been formally laid before, but always with sad little things like Turtle that somebody threw me in with at a party. Sue Ellen was not a virgin, but she was a very tough nut to crack, a regular conquest, and since I had been certified so outstanding at talking about things by Babs herself, I kept talking about things with Sue Ellen almost to the very moment of consummation. I'm not quite sure whether I dazzled her or distracted her into sin, but it was altogether wonderful, and I always remained grateful to Babs. She had shown me that women would listen to me, as I showed her that a man could be proud to talk to her. I believe we both grew up some on account of each other that summer at the beach.

AFTER GAVIN HAD been away at training camp for a couple of weeks, he called up, in the middle of the day on July 26, a Tuesday. He told me that it was Babs's twenty-seventh birthday, which he had plumb forgotten until a few moments before, when his mind had begun to wander in a passing drill, and he wanted me to take her out to dinner. Of course, he said, he would reimburse me, and for me to spring for champagne, too. So we got a lady at the real-estate office to find us a baby-sitter for the evening, and we dressed up in our best summer finery and made our way up the coast to a restaurant in Rehoboth Beach named the Corner Cupboard. I was

sure that everyone was looking at her, and then at me, trying to figure out what I was doing with her.

I was going on twenty-one, my majority, halfway through college, but I was still skinny and young to look at; my madras jacket
hung over my shoulders like a serape. Across from me, Babs was
dark from a month of sun, and her eyes trapped all the summer
glitter. Her dress was a cream white, cut high across the neck,
sleeveless, with a full skirt, and the stark contrast with her tan and
her black hair made her seem almost naturally a black-and-white
photograph. Certainly, I saw no color in all the world that night, for
there was no color in Babs, only the most magnificent shades.

We stayed late after dinner, finishing the champagne, my en-
thralling her with considered opinions. But suddenly she had
enough of that, of my being the cynosure, and she moved to re-
gain control and return us to her sway. She spoke my name and
looked across the table into my eyes. I stared back, dauntlessly. Like
most men in the path of a beautiful woman, I was self-conscious,
but I was also always confident that if there was one part of me,
one iota, that was passable, it was my eyes. Most people are this
way. In all the surveys, people invariably swear that when they
meet a member of the opposite sex they notice the eyes first. That
is patent nonsense, of course, but it is good general advertising for
the eyes. Just about everybody is convinced they have terrific eyes.

Babs sighed at last, probably bored with my eyes. "Can I ask
you a very personal question?" she asked, in her breathless way.

"Sure," I replied boldly, scared to death at whatever it might be.

"Can . . . can you twist?"

I could not believe my good fortune. Could I twist? Is—as we
were wont to say at that time—is the Pope Catholic? Or: Does a
bear shit in the woods? Could I twist? The wonderful thing about

the twist is that once you learned the trick—which was usually compared to drying your ass with a towel—that was the whole shooting match, like staying up on a bicycle. It was the most magnificent dance ever created for people who could not dance, and I suppose it was so short-lived a craze because the people who could dance, the ones therefore in charge of authorizing and popularizing dances, discovered this and went back to inventing more authentic dances that only they could pull off. What is the point of being a good dancer if everyone can dance?

Never again (or before) had I sought to expose myself upon a dance floor, but now, for this one brief moment in time, yes, you bet I could dance. Bet your ass. I wanted people to ask me if I could dance. Could I twist? Hey, is the Pope Catholic?

"Well," I replied, dropping my eyes, ever so coyly (is this how girls do it?), "a little . . . "

"Oh, please," Babs said, reaching out a hand to me.

"I'm not very—"

"Oh, please. Gavin never wants to dance. And I'll bet you are too good."

"Well, I—"

"Please, Donnie, it's my birthday."

"Well, okay, Babs, for your birthday." So that's how it's done. That's how they do it.

We went to a place down the Ocean Highway known as the Bottle and Cork. It was a hangout, and there was dancing both indoors and out, under the stars. And it was a starlit night, too, with half a moon leering out at us. Babs took me by the arm, pressing upon me, as we entered, and she lent me such maturity, such sophistication, that my false age credentials received only the most cursory attention, and we were waved on to the finest of tables, outside, close upon the starry dance floor. The band was on break, so we ordered drinks: a gin and tonic for the lady and another for me. This was no time for a boy's beer.

When the band returned, the leader solicited dance requests. The house was clearly divided between those who could not dance and called for the twist, and those who could and pleaded for anything else. There being many more people who could not dance, the band broke into a twist, and Babs leapt to her feet.

We danced, Babs and I. We twisted. She did everything just right, as I must have known that she would. Barbara Jane Rogers Grey was not about to venture into the public eye in any haphazard way; God only knows how long she had stood with a towel, gyrating before her bedroom mirror, before she had got it down pat. And we not only twisted. We were watched. I did not delude myself. I knew everyone was staring at Babs. But I also knew that no one could miss me, and I knew I better be good, because everyone would be wondering why I, this ugly, skinny person (albeit one with good eyes) would be the one with the most beautiful creature on the face of the earth. But I *could* dance the twist. I could twist some. And pretty soon I could tell that everyone knew that she went out with me because I was such a terrific dancer. That obviously explained it. I took off my madras jacket, and did many fancy variations on the twist. I twirled it above my head and cried out "The Lariat," and I swung a make-believe bat like a baseball player and hollered "The Slugger," and chopped wood with a make-believe ax and screamed "The Lumberjack." I performed many of these feats of expert twisting, and Babs laughed at my originality and nodded in wonder at my prowess. I was some piece of work. "Boy, can you twist," Babs said.

"You're good, too," I said. God, but I always hated people who said, "You're good, too."

We won the twist contest. The prize was a magnum of very cheap champagne. Now I'll be perfectly honest. There were several male twisters who were every bit as good as I was. One, possibly two, might even have been a smidgen better, although I'm certainly not going to be categorical about that. But it is a fact that there was a constitutional level for excellence in the twist—a point beyond which no one could be better no matter how hard they applied themselves to that goal. There is such a limit for some things: for Big Macs, for example, for TV anchormen, for suntans. Eventually, you must say, Well, that's it; it just can't be any better, and there are many of them just as good and always will be.

But I am not poor-mouthing. I was excellent at the twist, and if Babs was not quite as good as some of the other female twisters, she was nearly so, and she had them beat all hollow in looks, which was obviously how the twist judge was judging women twisters. Life is like that. Babs and I were an unbeatable combination.

"You're good," said the fellow in the boat-neck shirt who was twisting next to me.

"You're good, too," I said.

In fact, Babs and I were popular winners, and when we departed a few minutes later—always leave 'em asking for more—we were applauded as we departed the premises. I was heady and high, and for the first time in my life I clasped Babs's hand naturally as I took her to the car. It only took the edge off my performance slightly that I had left the car keys back in the Bottle and Cork, inasmuch as I had also left my madras jacket and the bottle of champagne back there. But I went back and retrieved them, intact.

I DROVE UNEVENLY the rest of the way home, because I had this distinct impression that Babs was purposely sitting close to me.

Having large amounts of champagne and gin will, obviously, lead your mind into these kinds of hallucinations. But to be perfectly honest, I was relieved, in an odd way, when we got back to the house and I had to leave Babs and take the baby-sitter home.

When I got back to the house, Babs had changed. She had put on a pair of Bermuda shorts and a man's button-down blue shirt. She also had another gin and tonic, and one for me. She said it was her birthday. I drank to that. I hated gin. This was the only night in my life I ever drank gin. It tastes to me how lighter fluid smells.

"I never, in all my born days, thought I'd be as old as twenty-seven," Babs said.

"Well, what didja think would happen?"

"Oh, it's not like I thought I would *die* or anything. But I just still feel so young. I don't feel twenty-seven."

"Twenty-seven's not real old," I protested, but not very convincingly, I'm afraid. Myself, I thought it was ancient.

"You're not just sayin' that, Donnie."

"No, really, I promise. And you sure don't *look* any twenty-seven."

"When I was changing just now," Babs said, very pensively, taking her eyes away from me, "I looked in the mirror, and I thought to myself, Barbara Jane Rogers, take a long look, because this is as good as you'll ever look in all your life. You'll never look this good again . . . tanned and all," she added. She wasn't ready to write herself off completely.

"There's a lot of movie stars who are at least in their thirties," I replied in vague dissent.

"Who?"

"Maureen O'Hara, for one," I said. I have no idea why Miss O'Hara came so suddenly to my mind. I had nothing against the woman.

"And Donna Reed," Babs said, pitching in. "I'll bet she's past thirty."

"Sure, and look at her."

"Elizabeth Taylor is just about my age," Babs said, really getting into the spirit.

"Yeah, and she still looks fantastic."

"Well, those movie stars can use a lot of makeup and camera tricks."

I had had enough. "Look, you look just beautiful, Babs. You really do." She touched her hair and smiled at me.

Then suddenly she jumped up. "I've got it," she cried.

"What?"

"You're not tired, are you, Donnie?"

I was half drunk and could hardly keep my eyes open. "Oh, no."

"Great, we'll go skinny-dipping." I about to died. "Come on, the kids are sound asleep, and nobody'll be down on the beach now." I breathed, I guess; I must have done something. "Haven't you ever been skinny-dipping before?"

"*Sure* . . . but not with a girl. We used to swim nekkid up in summer camp."

"Oh come on, Donnie. I'm not a girl. I'm practically your sister." My heart was pounding. To see Babs in the altogether was as far as I ever let my fantasies go with her (except occasionally in the fantasy where she was widowed when Gavin's plane went down, but I kept that fantasy to a minimum usage inasmuch as it made me feel so guilty), but I cringed at the thought of her seeing me, standing there, looking completely foolish, with my husky. You are not supposed to get huskies skinny-dipping; I knew that. "Come on, sissy."

"Well, what about Gavin?" I finally asked. I had been dwelling so exclusively on my husky that I had not even brought Gavin to mind.

"For gracious sakes, Donnie, we're certainly not goin' to fill him in on our little secret."

"Oh, no," I said, and I smiled shyly and went and changed into a pair of my Bermuda shorts. For a long time I debated putting on my bathing suit under my Bermudas, because I still questioned, deep inside, whether Babs was serious about this. I was deathly afraid that we would get down to the beach and she would have her bathing suit on under her clothes, and I would take my clothes off, and would be standing there with my husky sticking out, and she would say, Donnie McClure, you are disgusting, you didn't really believe I seriously meant we would go skinny-dipping, how could you think a horrible thing like that of me, and I'm going to call Gavin tomorrow and tell him. But, at last, I took Babs at her word. If I was wrong, if she really had been putting me on, I could at least go swimming in my boxer underpants. I could tuck my husky up under the top of the elastic and remain nearly unobtrusive that way.

We skipped along barefoot to the beach. It was about three or four long city blocks from the house. About halfway we had to cross the Ocean Highway, and then there were a couple of rows of beach-front houses leading up to the dunes; over them was Middlesex Beach. The resort is all developed now, full of high-rise condominiums owned by tennis-playing government workers from the Washington suburbs, but then, in 1960, Bethany Beach was still a sleepy little resort, legally dry and possessing only the most necessary commerce. At two o'clock of a midweek morning we did not see a single light on in any cottage as we made our way to the beach.

The half-moon and the stars were brighter still than even they had been when we had danced at the Bottle and Cork, and when we topped the dune and looked down the sloping beach toward the ocean, the moon was casting its glow across the water, unfiltered by any effluvia of modern urban civilization. The three most beautiful sights in the word are the moon shining across a body of water, the moon shining across a slope of land, and the moon shining across the swell of a woman's breast. That is said with the luxury of some hindsight, but even then, even before I had seen the latter, I was moved to a certain amount of poetry.

"Just think, Babs," I said. "The Indians saw it exactly this way when they first saw the ocean." Well, for nitpickers, the Indians wouldn't have seen the lifeguard stand, which was down the beach aways, but it was the only artifact in view. There was nothing else: no lights, no sounds, no people but us. Just me and the most beautiful creature in the world, about to take her clothes all off.

The tide was out and the ocean was calm, with baby waves that only lapped at the shore. I just kept on walking toward the water, pawing at the cool sand. I had no more training, no more instinct for pausing and stripping before a beautiful older woman on a beach than I did for nuclear physics or waltzing. I was a step ahead of Babs when I heard her say, "Here." She threw her towel down, establishing a beachhead. I threw my towel down. "Come on," she said.

I started to unbutton my shirt. I had, at the last minute, selected a shirt with buttons over a pullover for exactly this reason. It bought me time. I unbuttoned. Babs unbuttoned faster than me. There was nothing to it. She just undid all the buttons and took the shirt off. I was looking right at her. And there was nothing else there! In that day and age, women wore bras all the time. It had just never even crossed my mind that a respectable woman wouldn't wear a bra, even if she were going skinny-dipping and thus was momentarily going to take her bra off. I was staring right at Babs's breasts. At her tits. At her nipples.

Quickly, then, I occupied myself and my eyes with taking my shirt off. She did not wait for me to catch up. Immediately, she stepped out of her Bermudas, and there she stood before me, naked as a jaybird, at the end of where the moon shone. The moonlight ended with Babs. I quickly turned my head away.

"It's okay, Donnie, you can look." I looked, sort of. "I want you to look. The human body is a beautiful thing. It isn't dirty to look at the human body," she said, doing her best to sound like the opening chapter in a teenage textbook on introduction to human sexuality. I nodded, tentatively. I didn't want to muddy the waters by saying that it probably is dirty to look at the human body if the looker is full of incredibly dirty thoughts. Babs reached over, then, and touched my cheek, applying just enough pressure to turn my head, my eyes toward her. "Gavin's the only man in the world ever saw me before, Donnie. I just wanted some other man to see me before I got old."

I understood. She had proceeded to get her clothes off with such dispatch because she knew once I disrobed there would be my husky to contend with, to disrupt the simplicity of the looking. "Tell me the truth now, tell me—"

"Yes, ma'am." And she reached out and took my hand softly in hers, and held it there for an instant, contemplating whether or not to place it on her body, on her breasts. My heart raced, but at the last she thought better of it and let my hand fall away from hers. Then she took her hand, that one that had held mine, and touched it to a breast, drew it across lightly, from the bottom up, moving across the nipple, then out and away.

"Tell me true: My bosoms haven't started to sag yet, have they?"

"No, they haven't, Babs. I promise you, they haven't."

"'Deed, I hope not," she sighed, and she merely stood there for a time longer, letting me drink her in. She didn't know what to do with her hands, though. Finally, she took the right one, and made something of a fist of it, and put it in her left palm, laying them both above the left hip. It was so odd. That is the way little Southern girls—maybe all little girls—are taught to hold their hands when they sit, with their legs properly crossed at the ankles and turned to the left. And now, when she was posing in the nude in the moonlight for a man, that is what came back to Babs.

Finally, not sure what I was to do, I nodded a benediction and whispered, "You're absolutely beautiful, Babs . . . still." And she smiled at me in gratitude, happy with that second opinion. Then she only said "Hurry" and ran off into the water, rushing right along where the moonbeam came down.

I took off the rest of my clothes and ran into the water after her. It was especially cold in the dark, and while we frolicked and splashed (from a polite distance), it was only a minute or two more before both of us were ready to get the hell out and get dried off.

I saw the boys first. There were just two of them, fifteen or sixteen years old, I reckoned from the distance. They were standing where we had dropped our things, and in their arms they held everything that Babs and I had brought or worn. "Hey, want your clothes, lady?" one of them called. It was a teasing voice, not a mean one, but somehow this was not comforting, given our station in life at this moment.

"Oh my God, Donnie, what do we do?" Babs said.

"You stay here in the water," stoutly replied I, noble defender of modesty.

"But I'm cold. I'm *freezing* in here."

"Then stay a little behind me," I ordered. Probably that was exactly the wrong strategy to take. Maybe if I had hung back and sent Babs ahead, sort of a visual human sacrifice, the kids would have been gratified enough with a good look at Babs in the buff to drop all our stuff and take off. But here I came first, as menacing as it was possible for me to seem—dripping wet, tensing visibly from equal parts cold and fear, to all appearances a man in a fury, shielding my lady love, prepared to do battle for her. The kids sized me up, waited just long enough to catch sight of Babs in all her moonbeamed glory, and then, the instant I stepped out of the surf, they turned tail and ran like hell, fading into the dark even before they cleared the dune. They were sure-handed little devils, too, and didn't drop a thing. In another minute we heard a car rev up and peel out, and they were gone, leaving us without a stitch.

"What a revolting development this is," Babs said. That is what Chester A. Riley of *The Life of Riley* radio and television show used to say to his wife Peg or his pal Gillis just before the commercial midway through the show, when Riley found himself caught in some such pickle as we were.

"Yes," I replied, being somewhat short of bons mots at the moment, striving to keep on looking into Babs's face. It also crossed my mind at this time that by far the most logical, the most sensible, the most *healthy* tactic that we could employ under the circumstances would be to embrace: body heat, etc. I also decided that, logic notwithstanding, this probably would not serve to improve the situation, all things considered: huskies, etc. And so, casually as I could, I began to shuck the water from my skin, while outlining the complete set of options of how, it seemed to me, we could best escape this dilemma. We could, I proposed, either immediately strike out for home together, or, I would venture forth on my own, foraging, living off the land, as it were, returning with her car and raiment forthwith. It seemed to me that that was how a gentleman or a knight errant or Jeb Stuart would deal with this predicament.

Unfortunately, Babs responded by looking at me like I was a crazy man. "What in the world am I goin' to do here, Donnie?" she whined, underscoring the remark with a burst of shivers. She had goose bumps all over, the best-looking ones being on her breasts, as you might expect.

"Let's go."

We scampered up the beach, came over the dune, and peered toward civilization. Every single house was pitch dark, not a light on, but, on the other hand, I was sure that we could be spotted a mile away. The problem was our rear ends, which glowed shiny white from the moon. The way I worked it out, to avoid the least embarrassment for her if we encountered someone, I would go first, making a dash from a parked car to a garbage can or whatever, and then I would signal her and she would follow me. It was a little bit like a couple of guys going up a mountain.

Soon, we were both laughing. She thought I was very funny "flapping all around," as she called it, and by the time we had reached the highway, my only interest in Babs's body was tactical, that her bottom and her boobs shone so white. And I told her so. "You look like one of those orangutans where all you can see is the hiney," is how I characterized her appearance. It was getting to be something of an adventure, and now that we were away from the ocean breezes, dried off in the air, it was nearly funny.

Only one major obstacle loomed: fording the Ocean Highway. We studied this hurdle from where we lay in wait, ducked down behind a car that was parked at the house on the side street that ran from the beach to the highway. The open expanse we had to cross consisted of two lanes going north, a median strip of grass, and two corresponding lanes going south, all that bracketed by wide shoulders of dirt and with more grassy flat space on either side, where extra traffic lanes might be constructed in the future. It was truly wide, open—perhaps fifty yards from where we crouched to some scrub bushes on the other side that we had to make for. "We better try this dash together," I said.

"Aye, aye, Sergeant."

The trouble was that every minute or so a car would come in one direction or the other—spaced maddeningly just close enough apart so that we never could have made it to the safety of the bush without being spotted. Like a lot of good-looking women, running fast was not Babs's long suit. And so we stayed, waiting for that moment when at last no car could be seen in either direction. It was another three or four minutes before, at last, the coast was clear. The last car went out of sight around the bend to the north, and no other car was visible on the horizon. "Take off," I cried, and we began to sprint, obliquing, like good troops, to reach the bushes.

"Come on, Babs, we're almost there," I said, drawing a couple of steps ahead of her as we reached the median.

That was when I heard her call out and turned back to see: She had stepped on a little pebble. Running full bore, Babs had trod down on it hard, and it had dug into her heel. She cried, "Oh, Donnie," and started jumping around on one foot, moaning, bare-assed naked in the middle of Ocean Highway.

I turned back to help her. It was at that precise moment, out of the corner of my eye, that I saw the headlights. They were coming down a side road, going toward the highway in the direction of the beach. It could not have been worse had we been cursed: a convertible full of boy teenagers full of beer. The car slowed up before a stop sign two blocks away from us. Perhaps, I prayed, they are planning to turn in the opposite direction up the highway, and thus they will not look this way and will then head off unawares.

But things did not happen as I had prayed.

Can you imagine being a boy of sixteen, beered up, in the company of a bunch of other beered-up sixteen-year-old boys precisely because you can't find any girls, and it is past two o'clock in the morning, and all your options have evaporated, and, to your disgust, therefore, there is nothing to do but go home and go to bed, and you glance up by chance and see an absolutely beautiful woman who is absolutely naked and in distress in the middle of a highway? What would you do? I mean, besides ordering the driver to steer the car over to her as quickly as possible. You would yell and scream and whistle, stand up, lean over the side and throw things. Very quickly, it was like a carload of hollering banshees (as my mother used to say) bearing down on us.

So, I took one look and picked Babs up. Just picked her up. It was like those stories you read inside the *National Enquirer* wherein the seventy-three-year-old man who weighs one hundred and twenty-eight pounds has his huge gas-guzzling sedan start to roll over on his grandchild, and so he automatically reaches down and lifts the whole car up by the fender, with superhuman powers he did not know existed, and which he never again could duplicate. This is how I got Babs out of the middle of Ocean Highway. I lifted her up and spirited her off that road as sure as Gavin ever carried a pigskin.

But that still didn't get us to safety, for we had to pass another six or eight houses before we could reach our own. Soon enough, too, the convertible came up the highway and cut down our side street. I was running on the soft grass on the side of the road, so Babs asked me to let her down, saying she could run now, which, in fact, she did pretty well, too. But we had no chance, and soon the car caught up with us. It rode right alongside of us, with the kids all hollering at us, mostly articulating such thoughts as "tits" and "pussy" and "dork" and "dingus," things of that nature, plus references to my general physical stature which I would prefer not to repeat at this point.

This was tolerable, given the range of alternatives, and Babs and I plodded ahead, eyes straight, but then I heard one of the guys—after all, the car was only about five feet to our side—urging the driver to stop so that he could dismount. "Quick," I said to Babs. I grabbed her by the hand, and yanked her due left down the walkway that led to a house.

This slick maneuver caught our pursuers by surprise. The driver obviously was not a quick-thinking leader. On the contrary, he probably had been included on the night's roster only because he was the guy with a convertible. By the time he had polled his riders and brought the car to a halt, Babs and I were already at the house. I steered her around it, going all the way to the back, where there was one little bush growing up against the house. I jumped in behind it, yanking Babs down on top of me.

In another couple seconds, two kids came around the house, searching for where we might have disappeared to. In the back, where we were, there were tall pines to shut out the moon, and it was blacker still down in the little space where Babs and I were crammed. There was almost no way they could locate us as long as we could lie still and quiet.

"They musta got into their house," one of the boys said.

"Which house?"

"How should I know *which* house? All I know is, we better get all our asses outta here quick before they call the cops."

"Yeah, what fuckin' naked people are gonna call the cops?"

That kid was determined. He was snooping all around. By now, he was only a few feet from where Babs and I lay, breathless, in a little ball. And it was only then when I began to contemplate what straits Babs and I were in, exactly. She had ended up absolutely entwined with me, her face pressed way down into my lap, her breasts so soft and yet so tight upon my chest that I could feel the nipples distinct from the rest of them. And, of course, now as it occurred to me exactly how we were arranged, I began to swell into a full husky. It had no place to go but up, and, trapped in these close confines, it ran up against the tip of Babs's nose. She couldn't move or rustle the bush and give us away. "I didn't hear 'em goin' into the house," the one guy said. I could feel Babs wrinking her nose, as you would if a fly alighted there. If I couldn't get my husky to go down, she was sure as hell going to sneeze.

"Jesus, would I like to see that twat one more time," the one kid said, and he came over and pulled a leaf off our bush in disgust. I could hear him breathing and Babs ready to sneeze. I could feel her fighting to hold a sneeze back; after all, I had a very sensitive connection with her. But just then, the kid threw the leaf down, swatted at the bush and said, "Aw, fuck it, Boots, let's go," and they shuffled off to the car.

Immediately, not a second too soon, Babs and I began to unravel. She was very nice, too; she didn't say anything about my condition, although she did lean over and peck me on the lips and say, "My hero," when we heard the convertible peel away. We were standing up by then, safely separated by space. Then we snuck the rest of the way back to the house through the backyards, threw some clothes on, and knocked off the bottle of cheap champagne we had won for the twist contest, drinking it warm, over ice.

10

GAVIN WAS THERE BY MY BED THE NEXT MORNING when I woke up. He was distraught, a mess, and my first thought was that he was going to kill me for going naked with his wife. "Fuck," he bellowed. And, "Fuck, fuck, fuck, fuck." It was barely seven o'clock, and my head was throbbing from the gin and champagne. I had kicked the sheet off, and was lying there naked, the alcoholic poison oozing out of my pores. "Fuck, fuck, Donnie," he said again.

He was drunk, evidently, and obviously unshaven and stinking dirty. It was also easy to tell that what he had done to his face and his eyes came from crying a lot. He was drinking a bottle of Rolling Rock beer, which is popular in the area of Pennsylvania where the Redskins train and unique because it comes in little green bottles. They call them "pony" bottles. Gavin threw back a whole pony bottle just as I lay there, trying to wake up.

"Oh, those sonsofbitches, Donnie! I'll get 'em. I will, I'll kill 'em."

I could only imagine that he was talking about the kids who took our clothes, or the other ones who chased us, but I didn't want to discuss the subject of skinny-dipping with Babs and how innocent it really was until I had to, so I kept quiet. Gavin popped the cap off another pony bottle, and sat down on my bed and started to curse and to cry again.

Babs appeared in the door of my room. She was dressed, and I pulled the sheet over me. She barely acknowledged me. She just came directly over to Gavin and sat down next to him and hugged him around his neck from in back. For his part, he only kept babbling on about the sonsofbitches. Oh, I had seen him drunk before, a little silly; I had never seen him so foolish in front of Babs, but this was something else again—such a display of vulnerability. I couldn't even stand to look at him, and he collapsed completely, sort of into her arms, but sprawling all over the bed.

I looked to Babs for clarification. "Some niggers killed Lawrence," she said softly.

"Oh, no."

"The sonsofbitches, I'll get 'em."

"What happened?"

"Those niggers came into our restaurant late last night when ever'body was gone but Lawrence closin' up, and they killed him for the fuckin' receipts. The fuckin' day's receipts. They cut him up, they threw him through the glass partition, and then they shot him. Oh, fuck, fuck, fuck."

The cops had reached Gavin at the training camp at three in the morning, and he had just taken off and driven from there, going straight through to the ocean in Delaware, drinking pony bottles the whole way. All he had on was a T-shirt, a pair of burgundy Redskins practice shorts, and shower clods.

"Oh God, I'm sorry, Gavin."

"Lawrence, he was one of the best, Donnie. One of the very best. People always tryin' to take a piece outta The Ghost. Not Lawrence. He was the only one, never. Even old Finegan liked to show me off some to his Yankee friends now and again. But never old Lawrence."

"I'm really sorry, Gavin. I always liked Lawrence."

"Will you come with us to the funeral?" he asked me, reaching out his hand.

"'Course I will," I said, taking it.

"Thank you, Donnie. I 'spect you and Lawrence 'bout the best people I ever could talk with. You ever talk to yourself?"

"Sure."

"Well Lawrence—sometimes, it didn't seem to be no difference, me talkin' to myself or to Lawrence." That got a little sad smile out of him. He took his hand away from me, and patted Babs's, which lay softly over his shoulder. "Come on, Babsie, we better get packed and hit the road."

"Oh, Gavin, that's just too far a drive for the children." Slowly, he turned around and stared at her, unbelieving. "There's nothing I can do down there. And Donnie'll keep you company."

Gavin would not take his eyes away from Babs. And yet, for all this directness and intensity, he was very confused. He wanted very much to hit her, and he could not understand how he could think such a thing. For what it did to him, inside, he might just as well have hit her, too, because the thought was as terrible for him as the action would have been for someone else. And so, at last, he began to cry softly again, and then to shake Babs by the shoulders. Or, it was more that he rolled with her: took her by the shoulders and rolled back and forth with her. Then he stopped and gripped her hard. "Don't you tell me you're not goin' to be with me when I put Lawrence in the ground. Don't you say that to me, Babs."

She nodded with her eyes. I wanted to get up and leave them alone, but they were on the sheet, and I couldn't very well walk away stark naked in the middle of all this. Instead, I spoke: "We could go over to Salisbury and get a flight to Washington and connect down to Charlotte. The kids would like that."

"All right, Babs, you do that right away," Gavin said, and he relaxed his grip on her, rose and walked away. He turned back at the door. "I want my wife there when they bury poor Lawrence. I want my children there. You hear?"

"Yes."

"'Cause he loved me more than you do. If you'd been the one died, he'd a-gone to your funeral."

It was a spiteful, puerile thing to say, and he left with the line, going out to the kitchen and taking another beer from the refrigerator. Babs was hurt, but, wisely, she didn't protest, didn't say anything. She only stared after him with the same sort of forgiving expression I was used to seeing her direct at her children when they were being foolish. Women are the ones who keep a little baby talk around to fall back on, but they stop being children much better than men do. Women turn into women much better than men turn into men.

"I'll call the airline and let you get dressed," she said.

Gavin was out in the courtyard with a beer, flopped in a butterfly chair. I took a beer myself. It was the last thing I wanted, a beer before breakfast, but I knew it would serve as a way of binding us. And it worked well enough. Gavin looked over to me, where I sat down on the stones next to him, and he said hello in a friendly way, as if to intimate that we could start all over again. I told him Babs had not meant anything by what she said.

"Yeah, I reckon not," he said. "But she should know I wanted to hit her. I did, Donnie. I wanted to hit her."

"I know you did."

He nodded, apparently not the least bit surprised that I had gathered that. And then we just sat silently a bit in the sun, listening to the children. They were just four and almost three. The baby wasn't born yet; he was conceived a few days later, right after the funeral.

Then, never looking at me, sort of studying his beer bottle for focus, Gavin said, "You know, Donnie, I met Lawrence and Babs both about the same time, about the same week, my freshman year at Chapel Hill." He stared clear into the pony bottle. "That was before I was The Grey Ghost."

"Yeah."

"So I always knew they both really liked me, and not just The Grey Ghost. I wasn't one of those dumb jockstraps who couldn't tell who just liked them for their glory. I wasn't that dumb, Donnie."

"I know."

"But there's somethin' nobody ever paid a mind to. It was 'bout what might happen when I was through bein' The Grey Ghost, when I left Carolina. With old Lawrence, I went right back to bein' Gavin again. It was like there hadn't never been The Grey Ghost. But with Babsie—" He shrugged and took a long pull on the pony bottle.

"Hey, she loves you, Gavin," I said. "I mean, she loves *you*, the person who is Gavin Grey."

"I know that," he said, and a bit testily. "I know that, Donnie. Gavin Grey came first. But she still can't stop thinkin' of me as The Grey Ghost. You see, it's like the judge said: The Grey Ghost had to die. He did. I know it. I can live with it. But I'll tell you somethin': When you live with a woman, and you love her 'bout to death, and ever'time you look at her you know she wishes you're somethin' that's dead and gone, well, now, that does get to you."

"Yeah, I guess so," I ventured.

"Yeah, it does. When I'm out on that football field, no matter how good I'm doin', I'm still just an old football player. I hear all that Ghost-this, Ghost-that shit, and it don't mean no more to me out there than people comin' up to me at the restaurant and makin' a fuss. But, Lord, Donnie, let me just kiss that woman. . . . " He stared at the bottle, grinning. "Why, there isn't a time I make love to her when I don't think I'm The Grey Ghost again. I wake up the next morning, and I don't care if it's ten, ten-thirty, and I'm still The Grey Ghost."

He shook his head, ruefully, I would say, and blew a spit-beer bubble, like a baby. "It wouldn't be so bad, if it was just me. But it puts her back too. Isn't a time she doesn't go back to bein' the Blueberry Queen. Or more than that"—and now he chuckled out loud—"I must be married to 'bout the only woman in all the world who turns back into a virgin ever' time she gets laid."

"That's unusual," I assayed.

"Well now, thank you for talkin' to me, Donnie," Gavin said, and he unwound up from his chair. Babs was walking across the deck then, carrying little Allison, with Tommy tugging along. "Babsie," Gavin hollered to her, "and you listen to this, Donnie. We're gonna have another baby now, and if it's a boy, I'm gonna name it Lawrence. Okay?"

"Yes, Gavin," she said, although I'm sure that, at her age, she didn't want to carry any more babies in her stomach.

AFTER THE FUNERAL in Rutherford County, Gavin flew back to the Redskins' camp, but Babs and the two kids and I drove up to Chapel Hill for a couple of days, just to check on the house and say hello to friends, since we were down there. Also, Gavin had a chore for me: He wanted me to call on Narvel Blue.

Blue had remained his friend, or as much a friend as you could share across racial lines then. Lawrence or Gavin would call him up whenever they needed new kitchen help at the Grey Ghost Inn, and Blue would send over the best black kids who needed work, that sort of thing. Blue himself was doing very well with the Three Corners now, and he had become a regular entrepreneur, going into a variety of local black enterprises.

Sometime before, the first year after Gavin had gone up to Canada to play, he had gotten his team, the Toronto Argonauts, to bring Blue in for a tryout in training camp. The Argos went along strictly to humor Gavin, since he was the big star, but it only took about an hour of light practice for Blue to turn the team on its ear. He hadn't played for several years, but he had gotten himself in the best shape of his life, and he ran over and away from everybody on the field. The Argonauts offered him a contract as soon as practice was over.

Two weeks later the team played its opening exhibition against the Montreal Alouettes. Gavin himself, as befits a star in preseason, was permitted to come along at his leisure, and he made only a token appearance. But Blue played the whole game, and he ran wild. The *Globe and Mail* headlined: PAINTING THE TOWN BLUE. And so forth. Gavin had been the Most Valuable Player in the league the year before, his rookie season, and before the evening was out, the experts were comparing Blue favorably to The Grey Ghost.

The next morning, Blue drove over to where Gavin was staying with Babs and the baby, and thanked him for the opportunity, and then said good-bye because he was going back to Carolina. Gavin couldn't believe it. "It's too much like high school," Blue explained.

The Argonauts offered him great amounts of more money, figuring that must be Blue's ploy, but he wouldn't have any of it. He was back in the States at Niagara Falls and on his way home to Carolina by the afternoon. "Once you been away from it," he said to

Gavin, "it ain't natural to be a player again. Once you been away, I just don't reckon you can acquire the caring back."

So Blue returned to the Three Corners, bought it out, and began to build it up; previously, he had only managed the place. By now, when I called on him after Lawrence's funeral, it was a very respectable establishment. The road was paved, there was a lighted Coca-Cola sign out front, and the building itself had been refurbished inside and coated with some kind of that Perma-Stone type of fancy exterior, the sort of phony brick that recalls a Hollywood castle. Now, too, the place was being expanded, with a "club room" and a "patio."

It was already well past three by the time I arrived, but something of a lunch crowd still remained on hand, and, of course, all these diners, lounging over their desserts and coffee, or still tending what they had in their brown bags, eyed me curiously, if not suspiciously or fearfully, for I was obviously too young to be any sort of policeman or bureaucrat.

A really beautiful young woman came out from behind the counter, where she had been messing with menus, folding napkins, generally taking care of things. Her skin was light, the color of a ginger snap, and she was built lean, stacked up top, but with a trim bottom that could be sexy on its own without having to be all stuffed into something tight. Her hair was not straightened, but neither could you quite say it was an Afro (had I known what an Afro was at the time); it was just sort of correct, like her rear end. "May I help you?" she asked, not only politely, but without any expression of surprise at my color.

"Yes, I'd like to see Mr. Narvel Blue, please."

"I'm Mrs. Blue. Do you have an appointment?"

"Well, no, but—"

"Could I have your name?"

"I don't think my name would mean anything," I said. "But if you would just tell him I'm Gavin Grey's nephew. Tell him The Ghost asked me to come over."

"All right," she said, and while she could have played the role of secretary much longer for all it was worth, she dropped that pretense the instant she heard Gavin's name, and then ushered me through the kitchen, to the room in back, where her husband had his office.

Blue looked up at me from the phone, where he was speaking in a lot of numbers. He had on an Ivy League shirt and a regimental-stripe tie, but in contrast he wore a goatee, which nobody in the Ivy League (or precious few other places) favored at that time. His black eyes stared out balefully at me, but he offered some comfortable hint of recognition, and, indeed, as soon as he hung up the phone, he stood up, stretched out his hand, and said, "The Ghost's boy."

"His nephew. I'm Donnie McClure."

"My, you be grown," he said, sizing me up.

"You've grown up," Mrs. Blue interjected, confusing me at first until I realized she was not offering her own assessment but correcting her husband. He nodded and repeated her words, to all appearances not the least bit upset at her effrontery. Then he bade me take a seat.

It was a proper kind of office, fashioned out of some old stock room, I would imagine, with a nice, rich desk, excessively soft carpeting, and sorrowful paintings on the wall that appeared to have come from some mail-order El Greco school. They were full of anguished black faces, bandanas, and chains, and succeeded at having me avert my eyes from them. Bridget had decorated the office, Bridget being the gorgeous Mrs. Blue, the former Bridget Davidson Hall of Durham. She had only graduated the year previous from Winston-Salem State, a small black college, and Blue had met her when he had gone to help raise bail for some of the students, her friends, who had tried to integrate the lunch counters in Greensboro.

Bridget came from that rare antithetical elite, being black aristocracy in a society where blacks were systematically abused. Her father could not plop down in empty seats on public conveyances or use grubby rest rooms in backwater service stations, but he drove a Cadillac that was occasionally even chauffeured, and he dressed in Brooks Brothers suits that he would obtain every fall when the family journeyed north on its annual visit to New York City. He was a physician, catering to the rest of the black upper crust in Carolina. Bridget, just as any white debutante, had come out at her own great ball, and when she advised Dr. Hall that she wanted to marry Narvel Blue, her father responded, as sure as if he had been a Grand Kleagle, "I'm not having any daughter of mine marry a blue-gum nigger."

Even after Blue had come and properly presented his case, shown Bridget's parents that he was a real charmer and something of a diamond in the rough, Mrs. Hall still remained greatly distressed at the match because Blue was so dark of skin. The wedding finally went ahead after Blue agreed to accept from the Halls, as a wedding present, money to have his teeth fixed and capped.

No whites were invited to the wedding itself, but a handful joined the festivities at the reception, which was covered by *Ebony* magazine. Babs and Gavin were among the whites attending, and, in a burst of spontaneity, with a deep-seated appreciation for good-looking women of all races, creeds, and colors, Gavin pecked Bridget on the cheek in the receiving line. The action brought gasps from the assembled, and, afterward, Dr. Hall discreetly extracted an assurance from *Ebony* that it would not print such an inflammatory photo, lest it endanger Gavin's standing in the state. Certainly, though, The Grey Ghost's appearance did nothing to harm Blue's growing acceptance within the Hall family, and it was not long before Dr. Hall was certifying his new son-in-law's business acumen by encouraging some of his better-heeled black friends to invest in various local enterprises that Blue involved himself with. He prospered, and even Mrs. Hall came to wait anxiously for the grandchild, however dark the hue.

However, Bridget was not yet pregnant at this time, when Gavin sent me to call on her husband. "I'm real sorry 'bout Lawrence," he said. "I was gonna go down for the funeral, but it woulda just created a fuss, a Negro in the church, so I let it pass by."

"I'm sure Gavin would like it if you called him," I suggested.

"I done that straightaway soon's I heard, but he already left camp," he replied, with an edge. He was telling me he wasn't a common body, no matter the color, and I nodded in some embarrassment, hastily inserting that Gavin had urged me to make this visit. "What about?" he asked, and he went across the way, to where there was a matching bar set next to the bookshelves. Bridget and he had Scotches, me a bourbon.

"Well, it's just that Gavin wants to be sure they get the guys that killed Lawrence, and the PO-lice say it was some Negroes."

"Donnie, you be a smart boy. You ought to know by now that down here the PO-lice say everything was done by the Negroes."

"I know."

"Now it sho' 'nuff may be some bad niggers," Blue said. "But I just don't know. But I'll tell you what: I think if it had been some bad-ass colored done it, I woulda heard tell somethin' by now."

"And you ain't?"

"Not so much as a word. Now that's a puzzlement."

"So you don't have any ideas?"

"Not one iota. You talk to that girl friend of Lawrence's?"

"I didn't know he had one."

"Sure, that big old blonde girl. Leastwise, she's presently blonde."

"Don't be catty, Narvel," Bridget said.

"Sweetness, that girl be no more a blonde than me."

"Well, you know," I said. "I ain't playin' no detective. Gavin just wanted you to get the word out that anybody who helps find the killers, he'll remember. A reward."

"You tell him, The Grey Ghost don't need no sweetener—"

"Doesn't need any sweetener," said Bridget.

"The Grey Ghost doesn't need any sweetener for me or any other Negroes around here to help. I'll let him know the minute I hear anything."

"Hey, thanks," I said, and I rose to go.

"Wait a JU-ly minute," Blue said. "Finish your drink. Tell me now, what's Gavin gonna do with his restaurant without Lawrence to run it?"

"I 'spect he'll just get someone else to manage it."

"Yeah, well 'taint easy, runnin' a restaurant. The peoples work for you, white or Negro, gonna rob you. They are. And the onliest way you can make it go is you be on top of it. If Gavin be playin' football off somewheres, and he ain't got a good friend like Lawrence in charge, he be knee deep in you know what."

"He'll be in deep shit," said Bridget.

"Now, if I was The Ghost, I'd sell soon's I can. Will you tell him that for me?"

"Sure I will."

"Now lemme show you somethin'," Blue said, and his wife went over and took out a large rendering of a small drive-in restaurant and laid it on the desk. "Look at this here, Donnie. I'm gettin' out of this place here—"

"The Three Corners?"

"Yessir, soon's I can get me the right buyer. And The Ghost ought to unload his big old inn. There's a thing be comin' out of California—"

"A thing is coming out of—" Bridget began.

"No, darlin'," he said with a grin. "This one *be* comin'. This be a wildfire. It's called franchisin'. You just got little-bitty hamburgers and Cokes and what-not, and it's the same menu all over. Why, you might have ten or fifteen of these places. Everything be laid out in just such a way. You make your hamburgers thisaway, your milkshakes thataway, so much cheese on the cheeseburgers, so many French fries on every plate. Fast and quick."

"And they'd be as many as ten or fifteen of these places?"

"Well now, I don't mean so many as ten right away. In time. Put 'em right off the new highways, the interstates. A man in the business can see it comin'."

"And you want Gavin?"

"I want his investment money if he's smart, but if'n he's smarter, I want his name too. I got me some Negro money, Donnie. Mrs. Blue's father has got a bunch of Negroes with money. But we need white money. We need whites up yonder, in the front, talkin' to the bankers. If we had The Grey Ghost."

"There's a lot of folks tried to use his name."

"I know that," Blue said.

"Lawrence is 'bout the only one he ever trusted."

"But not to speak bad of the dead," Blue said, "Lawrence wasn't smart. That restaurant was like ever' other one an athlete ever put his name on. This franchisin' be different. It be the future."

"Well, it ain't all that new," I said. "I mean, I been to drive-ins for years."

"No, no," Blue broke in. "That's the old drive-ins, where you order from your cars. You need too much real estate to park the cars all around. You need too much help deliverin' the orders to the cars. What we want is little places where you jam-park the car in and come inside yourselves and get your food straightaway and be gone. And we'll put his name on it: 'Ghost's.' We'll have a sign of one of them ghosts done up in sheets, wearin' a helmet and number twenty-five, sprintin' like, whizzin', carryin' a hamburger instead of a pigskin."

"We'll pay him for his name," Bridget said.

"That's right, Donnie. He don't have to put a nickel in it if he don't care to. But we need white money from somewheres."

"Somewhere," said Bridget.

"Well, I'll sure tell him," I said. "I'll tell him, but I don't know much about money."

"If I was a white man and could build me a chain of franchise drive-ins now, I wouldn't have to know nothin' 'bout money for the rest of my natural-born life, 'cause soon enough I'd have so much I'd never have to fret 'bout the cost of nothin'."

I shook my head with great confusion, some wonder, and no vision.

"Let me tell you, Donnie. What was I sayin' awhile back, 'bout maybe a dozen or so Ghost drive-ins?"

"Ten or fifteen."

"Listen, I ain't studyin' 'bout no ten or fifteen. I'm talkin' 'bout hundreds, Donnie."

"Hundreds?"

"All over. All over Carolina, all over the South, all over America, wherever there's roads, which is everywhere. This ain't a Negro thing. This ain't a white thing. This franchisin' thing is gonna go every whichaway. To tell you the truth, I can see one thousand restaurants with that little ghost man in a sheet and number twenty-five on his back. You tell that to Gavin when he gets over Lawrence better."

I looked back at Blue like he was plumb crazy. As I had pointed out somewhat earlier, I was not very good about money.

11

GAVIN AND BABS WERE HAPPY ENOUGH IN Washington. I asked him once what he thought of the place (he often referred to it as "the nation's capital" as if that were the official name: The Nation's Capital, D.C.) and he replied: "The nation's capital is a funny place, Donnie. You can't stand up to have a drink there." And this certainly was true at the time; there was a law which prohibited anyone in any public place from rising with any glass of spirits in his possession. Still, it surprised me somewhat that a reference to that tame municipal statute was the sum and substance of Gavin's feelings for the town he lived in half of each year and every year. Washington was, I suppose, no more than just a place to hang his hat—fine and dandy so long as there was a team there to play football on.

For her part, Babs was not so easily contented, not by nature, and not especially in this case, for whereas Gavin could still find his place upon the field—GREY STARS AS 'SKINS LOSE AGAIN seemed to be a stock headline in the Washington press—it was not the same sort of shared venture it had been in college. In the pros, there is no place for the wives, no recognition for them. They are only considered collectively, as "the wives," and seated at games in a bunch: *the wives*. If you will note, on television, when a baseball player (or basketball player, boxer, whatever; this also applies to politicians and quiz-show contestants) is singled out for some special attention, the cameras switch to a close-up of his wife, cheering and nibbling her fingernails. In football, the wives are never isolated on. Instead, the cameras light on buxom cheerleaders or anonymous pretty spectators: pussy. When it comes to women, baseball is wives, and football is pussy.

But, of course, there were the children to take care of, and so long as they were babies underfoot, requiring attention, Babs was kept busy and diverted. What the hell: Whatever business Gavin had been in, at this stage of their lives Babs would have been caring for the kids.

So maybe it was good that Babs was pregnant again, the third time, that fall of 1960. Perhaps she wouldn't admit to that, but I think it was so. The last day we were at the beach, I came back from chasing the kids out of the water, and she shook her head and said, "I wish I loved children more."

"You love your children, Babs."

She didn't know for sure if she was pregnant again, but she suspected it, and, anyway, it would happen soon enough because Gavin was determined to have what she called "Lawrence's baby." "Oh, I know that, Donnie. Everybody but monster women love their children. But some women love children. And I'm not that kind of a lady."

"Does it matter?"

"Yes. The wives on the team who do best are the ones who get lost in their children." She played with the sand with her toes. She had on a one-piece flower-print bathing suit. "The wives on the team—we're better at being mothers than wives."

"Yeah," I said, laughing at it. "After all, you're all married to little boys."

"Yes, but it's a fallacy to think we could be their mothers. Now if I were married to you—" (I blushed uncontrollably, and so she amended that to "someone like you, you know, not an athlete.") "I 'spect, yes, I could mother you some. I think I'd like to. Now, Donnie, don't you blush. Some lucky girl is goin' to be perfectly delighted to mother you to death."

"Hey, come on. I don't want anybody to mother me."

"Hush, don't be tacky. I mean, she'll be delighted to sleep with you, *too.*"

"Babs!"

"Oh, don't be so prissy, Donnie McClure."

"Well, never mind me. Why can't you mother Gavin?"

She glanced away, down toward the edge of the water where the kids were trying to dig up sand crabs. It was Tuesday, the day after Labor Day, a perfectly glorious, magnificent sunny day, but there was hardly a soul on the beach. All the regular nuclear families had gone back to work and to school the day before. Nuclear families peak publicly on Labor Day. "Because, silly," she said after a time, "like you said, players are all little boys, and the ones that marry little boys are, naturally, little girls. Who else do you think is goin' to marry little boys? Little girls, that's who. And the little boys keep on playin' their games, and they give us babies so we little girls can keep on playin' with dolls."

Then she sprang up, dusting the sand off her bottom, and took me by a hand and helped hoist me up. "Come on, last swim of the summer," Babs said, and we ran into the water hand in hand and splashed about gaily. The best metaphor in the world—it stands for life, I think; or happiness, or death; for something, anyway—is that the ocean water is always the best at the end of the summer when everybody is leaving the beach. I called to Babs: "Isn't it funny? The ocean water is always the best at the end of the summer when everybody is leaving the beach."

That night, our last alone, we ate more crab cakes and drank entirely too much, and for an instant, a frightened one for me, I though Babs, in her cups, was going to suggest that we go skinny-dipping again. But she knew by now that she couldn't do that to me. Instead, she only reached up and pecked me on the cheek, whispering, "Thank you, Donnie, for the summer," and had I been possessed of more confidence or imagination it might have occurred to me at the time that her eyes were misty. But she turned right away then and went to her room, and it was years later before I realized I had seen Babs's tears that night.

AFTER I DROVE Babs and the kids up to their house in the Washington suburbs, I went back to Chapel Hill, started my junior year, met Sue Ellen, and soon enough began to drive her wild with my body, an accomplishment I have already mentioned, being so proud of that memory that I could not hold the information back for its proper chronological niche. Although Sue Ellen was my first genuine lover (a.) in a bed, not upon a car seat, and (b.) return engagements, I remember very little about her. I remember more about the first girl I ever really kissed, and I didn't even like her. Perhaps with Sue Ellen the problem was that I was always conjuring up Babs in her place.

I do distinctly recall Sue Ellen's pubic hair. In the midst of an emotional, shifting experience, that was a simple, circumscribed item I could focus on; also, and no doubt more to the point, it was the first distaff pubic hair that I had ever had more than a nodding acquaintance with. Ever after, whoever else's pubic hair I encountered, I never failed to instantly judge it by the standard of dear old Sue Ellen's. Finer? Crinklier? Covering more or less real estate? Sue Ellen became my Greenwich Mean time of pubic hair.

Now none of this may sound as portentous as, say, the temperature of ocean water, but it will help emphasize how unbearably disappointed I was when Judge Pace called me up on a Monday in October and invited me to drive up to Washington with him that weekend to visit Babs and Gavin and watch Gavin play. Making love to Sue Ellen and pretending it was Babs was greatly preferred to being with Babs and thinking about making love to Sue Ellen. So I apologized to the judge, mentioning Sue Ellen (if not exactly what we were up to), mentioning the Tarheels' own big game that weekend against Clemson, mentioning that the Hot Nuts were booked into my fraternity. I even mentioned that I had to study. But the judge would have none of it, and, moreover, he got Babs to call up immediately afterward to tell me how much she and Gavin were looking forward to my staying with them.

The judge himself had made reservations downtown at the Shoreham Hotel, because he was traveling with a full family now. The winter before, he had married Jennifer, the librarian, and right after the wedding they had adopted Stuart Stevenson, the judge's little grandniece, who had been born that night when Babs and Gavin first met Judge Pace.

Stuart was going on six now, a beautiful little girl in long pigtails. She was also remarkably precocious, without being a smart-ass miniature adult. I think this came from her upbringing. Stuart's mother had long since divorced, but, as scatterbrained as she could be, she always carried on easily with her little daughter, treating Stuart more as a companion than as a baby. There wasn't anybody much else for her to talk to except for the men passing through her life. So Stuart was really quite advanced for her age. It is also true that some of the brightest adults have dull little children for the same reason in the reverse: They never deign to talk to their kids.

Since the judge never treated anyone as if they were less than sixty-five and a Ph.D., Stuart fit in marvelously with Jennifer and him, which was fine, because Stuart's mother went to California with a girl friend and was never heard from again. In the car, riding up to Washington that Friday afternoon, Stuart solicited my views on the Nixon-Kennedy campaign, offering her own assessment. She also discussed the progress of two stocks the judge had purchased for her on the New York exchange, and she told me, step by step, portion by portion, about her favorite recipes. Furthermore, once she blew her nose on her frilly sleeve.

I waited out in the car while they checked into the Shoreham, but soon enough it was only the judge who reappeared. "The ladies will not be joining us at the Greys this evening, Donnie," he said. "Mrs. Pace is going to get a taxicab and take Stuart down to see the White House and the memorials all lit up at night." I had assumed that we would all be having dinner with Babs and Gavin, and I said so, but the judge informed me that, no, it had been planned this way. "There are some business matters we must talk about," he said.

"Well, maybe if it's business, I ought to stay with Mrs. Pace and Stuart," I suggested.

"Oh no, Babs and I want you with us. And when Gavin heard that I was coming up, he specifically requested that I bring you along. You know how highly he thinks of you, don't you, Donnie?"

"Well, he's my uncle, you know, but we've become kind of friends, too."

"Yes, I know, but it's more than that," the judge said, taking the left onto Connecticut Avenue. I regretted that we had gotten into this conversation in the car. Judge Pace was all right when he was driving on the open road, locked in at his six miles over the speed limit, but traffic and stoplights knocked him out of his rhythm. In the earlier days of stick shift, he would get to chattering and never emerge from out of second gear, and now, without that to contend with, he had taken just to drifting along, with a tendency of stopping at all lights, whether green, red, amber, or blinking, and then just sort of holding there, oblivious. The new Mrs. Pace referred to it as his "idling," and it was in just this way that we idled up Connecticut Avenue toward the Maryland line.

"Well, you know," I said, "you might say Gavin's like an older brother to me."

"No, not so," replied the judge, waiting patiently at a green light. "It's more the other way round, age notwithstanding."

"You mean, I'm his older brother?"

"After a fashion," the judge said, starting off again, as car horns prodded him to action. "So much of Gavin's life—and Babs's too—is frozen back there six or seven years ago in Chapel Hill when he was everybody's All-American. And people they knew are also frozen into that time. But you were a mere boy then and a young man now, and even they can't avoid taking cognizance of that transformation."

"Yes, sir."

"We all, deep inside, want to be Peter Pan, but hell's bells, then if we became Peter Pan, we would be envious of someone like you, someone shucking off pale childhood, growing up to manhood, bright, bold, strong—"

"Strong? *Me*? Come on, Judge."

Even he, at his most hyperbolic, relented some then—although stopping the car, for emphasis, a good twenty feet behind the one in front that was waiting for a red light. "Well, *filled out*. 'Deed, but you have filled out nicely, Donnie. True, you haven't got your uncle's Adonis-like body, but you do have some meat on you now."

"I think the light's changed, Judge."

"All right. Now you keep abreast of these directions. Once we reach Chevy Chase Circle, we have to be on the lookout for that left."

"Yes, sir."

"The point is, notwithstanding the exact state of your physique, but in a very odd way, you supply Babs and Gavin with a little, uh, direction. You're really the only one in the family who offers a certain perspective of time. If they can see you growing up, developing, surviving, then maybe they can manage too."

"Yes, sir. The light's changed."

"Oh, yes. Have you spotted that left yet?"

"No, sir. Not yet. I'm watching."

"Good. You see, most of us marry for the moment, for the present, and Lord knows that's dangerous enough. But in a very real way, Babs and Gavin married for the past, for autumn Saturdays gone. And that's an awful lot to overcome. I'm sure that Gavin sees some future in you, and I 'spect Babs fantasizes 'bout you in the same way."

Now that was going too far. "Fantasizes! Hey, Judge, nobody fantasizes about people like me," I cried out, as we sped by our intersection, unseeing. "If Babs is going to fantasize, she's going to fantasize about Tony Curtis and Troy Donahue, those guys."

"No, you don't understand fantasies, Donnie. Or perhaps, like us all, you don't understand women. We men are the only ones that fantasize for real. Damn women—they fantasize in fantasy. And that's not fair. Why do you think these little girls go out and scream bloody murder in the presence of these whey-faced rock and rollers, these Elvis characters? Because they can't possibly have them. And Babs is still very much the girl. No wonder she feels so comfortable with you."

"Yeah, well, I think we missed the turn."

"Just as good," he said, and he pulled the car over to the side of the road and parked it, formally. Then he turned to look me square in the face. "I must tell you this, Donnie. It's going to be a very tough evening tonight. You drink yet?"

"Well, some. Beer mostly."

"Well, fortify yourself this evening, and then fortify me, Donnie. We're all goin' to need you tonight." Then the judge turned the car around, and we drove directly to the house from there, without incident, and without talking anymore except about the upcoming election and other such minutiae.

THE JUDGE PRESIDED after dinner in the living room. Gavin fixed him a bourbon, and took a beer for himself and sat down, content, over in the corner chair. He loved just to listen to the judge talk. "Are the children asleep?" the judge asked, and Babs said they were, even including little Lawrence, and she patted her stomach for effect.

The judge cleared his throat at that, and Gavin kicked off his loafers. I never saw him look stronger. To be sure, he no longer had that visible tingle of stardust surrounding him, as he had at Carolina, but he was more mature now, age twenty-seven, his hair ran a bit longer, and his face had, in a way, caught up with his body, which had always been ahead of the rest of him. He looked better as a mortal.

He had never played better, either. The season before, he had been acknowledged as by far the best running back in the league, and even with the Redskins' woeful blocking, now he was setting new records. The team had been carried along in his wake, too, and thanks to luck and an easy early schedule, Washington had actually won its first three games. The whole gridiron fandom of the nation's capital was agog, and Sunday's game against the Chicago Cardinals was sold out. Not only that, but the Cardinals were a sorry outfit, and the Redskins had been established as solid favorites to go 4–0. For a team that seldom even managed four wins in a whole season, that was cause enough for great joy and excitement in the nation's capital. Gavin himself had not lost his head to this euphoria, and, in fact, during dinner, he had carefully catalogued the team's many shortcomings, but it was also a fact that he was running with the tide, just aching to play. You could tell it in the way he moved across the room, in how he ate and laughed, even in how he sat still, a spring of kinetic energy.

The judge took a long pull on his bourbon, almost gulping it, it seemed, which was quite unlike him. "I've got some bad news for you, Gavin," he said. Lord, that disappointed me: I always thought the judge could do better than that.

"Yeah, what's up?" Gavin replied, in a jaunty tone that indicated that this information could not possibly relate to him, but rather to some unfortunate mutual acquaintance.

"I mean, it's about you," the judge said, and he took another swallow. Now Gavin sat up, but still more curious, it seemed to me, than affected. "I didn't want to come, Gavin. I didn't want to be the bearer of these ill tidings, but it's no longer possible to conceal this from you."

Gavin shot a look to his wife. "Do you know about this, Babsie?"

She shook her head. "I informed Babs there had been some business . . . reverses," the judge explained. "I never told her how bad it is."

"Well, what is it, Judge?" He was genuinely perplexed.

"It's the restaurant, Gavin. It's gone. The money's all gone." Gavin shook his head, absolutely dumbfounded. "Lawrence was never very good with the books, you know, and I'm afraid it wasn't clear how bad the situation was till only a couple of weeks ago."

"But we were doing fine," Babs said. "We were even going to start making some money this year."

"Get me a beer, Donnie," Gavin said. The judge held up his glass, too, and Babs nodded to me. I fixed them all drinks, and one to fortify me, as well. The judge was on his feet by now.

"Let me tell you how bad it is, flat out," he said. "There is nothing in the bank. Nothing at all."

"There has to be," Gavin cried out. "There's more than sixty thousand dollars in the accounts. There has to be. I have to sign for anything that comes out of the special savings."

The judge dropped his head. "There's nothing in the bank, Gavin. And worse, it turns out that the Grey Ghost Inn owes some bills going back four months."

"Why didn't I ever hear about this?"

"Well, everybody was dealing with Lawrence, of course, and then when he was killed, that Mr. Anderson took his place, and when he began to understand the depth of the situation he came to me last month."

"Ohh no," Gavin said, but I could barely make him out.

"Gavin, I've studied the figures. I don't think they'll be any more surprises. Day to day, the restaurant is not faring badly. We should be able to get a buyer at a fair price, especially if you'll agree to maintain some sort of visible affiliation with the place. With what's left over after we square everything with the bank, I estimate maybe another twenty or twenty-five thousand."

"You mean I'll owe *another* twenty or twenty-five thousand after I lose the place?"

"That's the best I can figure."

Babs began to cry softly. "I've only got another five thousand in our account," Gavin said. "I'll have to sell the house too?"

Babs sobbed harder now, and so I went over and gave her my handkerchief and stood next to her. She looked up at me and tilted her head, like a little lost puppy dog. The tears were just pouring out of her eyes.

"No, you won't have to give up the house, Gavin," the judge said. "If it's only a matter of twenty thousand or so, we're in a position to negotiate with banks. New mortgages and whatnot. People in the Tarheel State have not forgotten The Grey Ghost."

"I don't want no charity. I'll pay it all off."

"I mean that. You have a certain equity in your career. Your contract is up with the Redskins after this season, and as magnificently as you've been playing, I think we're in a position to demand a large increase in your salary. The new league is being formed, too. You would have some leverage."

"But I won't have nothin' left 'sides the house?"

The judge shook his head. "I don't suppose so."

"I just don't see how it happened," Babs cried.

"Old Lawrence wasn't *that* bad a businessman," Gavin said. "I mean, we had accountants helping him, we had that good lawyer friend of his who set it all up."

For just an instant, the judge let his compassion go, and he turned harsh. "Well, first of all, that lawyer did not set it up very well for you. If he had set it up very well, this couldn't have possibly happened." But then, softer again: "But neither could he conceive what did happen."

I couldn't stand it. I couldn't stay silent. "What did?"

The judge turned away from Gavin now, away from us all. Babs had stopped her crying. Gavin drank from his beer can and then used it to wipe across his forehead. The judge turned back. "The PO-lice have a pretty good idea who killed Lawrence," he said.

"They do?" Gavin said, and he sat up in his chair again and even smiled. "If I ever get near those niggers that—"

"It wasn't any nigras."

"How do you know, Judge? Ever'body said it was nigras."

"The PO-lice are pretty sure otherwise now."

"Well, if they're so sure, why don't they go out and arrest them?"

"It isn't that easy. Number one, they don't have any solid evidence, and number two, they don't even know *exactly* who the people are who did it. They just have a very good idea."

"But what's this got to do with the restaurant?" Babs said.

"Whoever killed Lawrence came there after him," the judge replied evenly. "It was not just a bunch of common, ordinary thieves who came to rob the Grey Ghost Inn and ended up killing Lawrence because he was there."

"That's what the PO-lice said," Gavin declared stoutly.

"That's what they *surmised* at first. It was very late at night, the place was closed, nobody expected anyone to be on the premises, so the cops figured that the thieves broke in, started to tackle the safe, and then when Lawrence wakes up—he was apparently sleeping on the couch in the office—and discovers the crime in progress, the thieves panic and shoot the witness. That was the theory."

"Right." Gavin was listening intensely to all this about his friend. It was as if the news about his being wiped out had gone completely out of his mind.

The judge said, "Isn't it strange that the robbers left better than one hundred dollars just sitting in the cash register?"

"Well, like you said, they were after the safe."

"Yes, but human nature being what it is, especially with thieves, it is highly unlikely that they would have passed within a few feet of that cash register without at least taking the trouble to go over there and ring it open and pick out whatever pin money there was."

"They panicked when Lawrence found them."

"Hardly. They took their good old time, Gavin. It wasn't just that they turned around, saw Lawrence, and shot him, which is what you would think thieves would do under the circumstances. They spent a long time beating him up first before they shot him."

"Yeah, he fought like a tiger," Gavin said, missing the point. "Captain Phillips told me the whole place was tore up, chairs knocked this way and that. You know that nice glass partition, Donnie, the one between the lounge room and the Tarheel Room?"

"Sure."

"They threw him clear through that. They lifted poor old Lawrence up and tossed him right through that glass."

"It was a massive fight," the judge said.

"Captain Phillips told me they found four kinds of blood. He blooded four of those bastards. He fought like a tiger, Lawrence did." Gavin turned to the judge. "You know we're namin' the baby after Lawrence, Judge. If it's a boy it'll be Lawrence Grey, and if it's a girl, Lawrence'll be the middle name and we'll call her Laura or Laurel."

The judge dropped his head and let that pass without comment, and instead, purposefully, he took another swallow of his bourbon. "But you see, Gavin, the fight helps prove my point, that they came to get Lawrence. They didn't come to rob the Grey Ghost Inn. They came specifically to get Lawrence."

"Come on, now, ever'body loved that man. Why would anybody want to kill Lawrence?"

"Oh, they *didn't* want to *kill* him, Gavin. If they had wanted to kill him, they could have snuck one man in there and shot Lawrence graveyard dead before he woke up. They came to hurt him, Gavin. They came to teach him a hard lesson."

Babs said, "Why?"

"They didn't want to kill him. They came and they got ahold of him, and they knocked him on the head, and they dragged him out to the main dining room, and the three or four of them somehow lifted his body up—and you know, he must have weighed two-seventy, two-eighty—"

"Maybe even three hundred," said Gavin.

"And they hurled him through that glass partition, and then they came round the other side to beat up on him some more, but he must have come to and somehow he managed to get ahold of one of them, and it was dark, pitch dark, and the others didn't know what to do, and it's probable that Lawrence was killing that other one, choking him to death, and the others tried to save their comrade, loose him from Lawrence, but he was too big, and they were thrashing about, all four or five of them, and as nearly as the PO-lice can tell, he must have thrown one clear up against the far wall, and now it was gettin' noisy, and it was takin' a long time, and—this is all what the PO-lice guess now, Gavin—but it was about this point where one of these *gangsters* realized that the situation was gettin' away from them, and he got clear enough to take a shot at him. There was two bullets that missed, you know. They found them in the wall. The first two shots must have missed. Then they got him. There wasn't three shots they found in him, like it said in the papers. It was thirteen."

"Oh my God, poor Lawrence," Gavin said.

"They emptied their guns into him. He must have nearly killed them all when they were fightin', because they were so scared and mad at him that all they wanted to do was get him. Even after they killed him, they couldn't stop themselves. They just kept firin' away into him."

"God, I never knew."

"Gavin, let me say this about your friend Lawrence: No man ever died a harder, braver death."

Gavin only nodded his head, crying now. He had forgotten all about the restaurant. Babs was the one who plunged ahead, "Judge, why did those men want to get Lawrence?"

The judge was standing behind his chair, hands resting on the top of its back. "About a month ago, there was a typical sort of extradition matter involving some cigarette smuggling, and a PO-lice officer was down in Carolina from New York City, and the cops were talkin' shop, and one of them brought up the Lawrence case. He told the New York man all about it, about the great fight, the murderers tossing Lawrence through the glass. And the New York officer was surprised: Didn't the Carolina PO-lice know what that indicated?"

"You mean it meant somethin'?" Gavin asked. The judge's conversation was taking on a tone he didn't like.

"It seems as if, in New York and some other Yankee places, if somebody owes you money—owes loan sharks money; the underworld—and if they don't pay, the, uh . . . creditors, shall we say, have a special way of dealing with the situation. They throw the welcher through a window. Assault him first, beat up on him, and then, as a fillip, toss him through glass. It's an old custom, and it advises the PO-lice to stay away, that this is a private financial transaction. Obviously, this piece of business grew up when there was a certain honor among the thieves and the constabulary, probably before the I.R.S. had inserted itself as a third force. And I imagine these hoodlums who killed Lawrence were imports who didn't realize that their little calling card wouldn't mean beans in Carolina."

"But why were they after Lawrence?" Gavin asked, leaning forward in his chair, starting to squeeze his beer can.

"All right, Gavin," the judge said. "God forgive me that I must tell you, but Edward C. Lawrence had robbed you blind."

"No," Gavin said softly.

"Yes."

"*No, goddamnit!*" He shouted that.

"Understand, the boy didn't mean to. He didn't set out to," the judge said, coming around the chair, going straight to Gavin. "He started betting a little, and then it—it just plumb got away from him. A snowball. At first Lawrence started dippin' into the register to make up his losses, and then he had to cover that up, and so on and so forth, deeper and deeper. It was this summer he finally started forgin' your signature."

Gavin crushed the beer can with his one hand. "How do you know all this?"

"Well, after the New York PO-lice officer put this bee in their bonnet, the Carolina detectives started checkin'. This was 'bout the same time I started hearin' about debts, about bills that were supposed to have been paid. It all began to fit together."

Gavin stood up and said, "I still think it was some niggers."

"No, Gavin, it wasn't."

He turned back to the judge and snapped, "I don't want to hear another word outta you, Judge."

Judge Pace let it pass in silence. He only looked to Babs, and then, very purposefully, she rose and went to Gavin, and clung to him in support. But she said, "Listen to it all, darlin', and be done."

And after a moment, Gavin put an arm around her and looked back at the judge. "I'm sorry, Judge Pace. You know I ain't mad at you. Don't let me be spiteful and common."

"You can't ever be that, Gavin."

Babs sort of steered Gavin across the room, then, and sat him down on the sofa, where she could be next to him. Then the judge picked up again: "There's really not much more, thank God. There was a woman—"

"A big blonde," I said reflexively.

"You knew, Donnie?" Gavin asked.

"Just that. Blue told me that."

"Yes, from Mee-ami, Florida," the judge went on. "Lawrence'd been buying her things, flying down there, bringing her up. The cops spoke to her, and she verified it all, more or less. He was giving the gamblers information about you, about the Redskins all last season: injuries, morale, whatever inside dope he could supply. That kept him on their good side when he first started going into debt, but then the season ended, and he had no more to give them, and he tried to bail out bettin' baseball and basketball, whatever, but of course all he did was lose more. And finally, they came to teach him a lesson."

"I can't believe it," Gavin said.

"This blonde woman told the PO-lice that Lawrence was just tryin' to hang on for a couple more months, till the football season started, because then he figured he could get you to"—the judge paused—"fix a game," Gavin turned and buried his head in Babs's chest. "The lady said that Lawrence had even already told the gamblers that he had talked to you, and it was all set: The Grey Ghost would fix a game or two to save Lawrence and his restaurant."

Gavin raised his head now. He had composed himself some. In fact, he spoke in a level, faraway tone: "I don't believe Lawrence would say such a thing as that. Do you, Babs?" She shook her head. "How 'bout you, Donnie? Would Lawrence say such a thing?"

"It sure don't sound like him."

"Gavin, I don't support that claim. I'm only telling you what the woman from Mee-ami told the PO-lice. Besides, it's moot now anyway."

"Yeah, I know, a lot of these PO-lice think they're Sergeant Joe Friday, and they get to listenin' to some Yankee cop and some old big blonde, and they take this all in, hook, line, and sinker," Gavin said, somewhat defiantly here at first, then shriller, faster, almost breathlessly as he rolled along. "Myself, I still think it was a bunch of drunk niggers broke into the Grey Ghost Inn, looking to rob it, and Lawrence was there and he caught them and fought them bastards, and they had to kill him, but I will also say this, that if there was any of these underworld criminals involved, what it was, they were tryin' to get Lawrence to talk to me about fixin' games, and of course he wouldn't do it, he told them he was talkin' to me, but of course he never did, you all know that, and when they found out he hadn't talked to me and he wouldn't do such a thing, that's when they came and killed him. Now that's if the underworld was in this, which I don't think it was, just because Lawrence wasn't very good at figures, to say he stole from—" And he stopped sharp there, and then for a few moments he said nothing at all, just stared out ahead, and then all of a sudden Gavin cried out, "Ohhhh," as if he had been shot himself, and he pitched forward down into Babs's lap and cried and cried and cried.

The judge nodded to Babs and beckoned to me, and I followed him to the front door. He told me that he would call tomorrow, and that he must come out again, that it was crucial that they begin immediately to start working things out. "Yes, sir. I'll make sure they're ready for you."

"Good. And you take care of your aunt and uncle. You do the fixin' up round the house and help 'em any way you can, because they need someone, they need family very much right now."

That was odd: "your aunt and uncle." I don't believe there was any other time in my life when I heard Babs and Gavin referred to in that way.

I WOKE UP later that night when I heard a door close and somebody go downstairs. On my watch, it was just before one o'clock, and after a while I got up out of curiosity and pretended to go down the hall and use the bathroom. It was Gavin who was up. He had a light on and he was drinking a glass of milk and talking on the phone—on the phone at one in the morning. And so I listened from the top of the stairs, eavesdropping unabashedly.

It was quickly clear that he was talking to Finegan in New York—and just sort of chatting casually, about the Redskins, about how he was playing, about friends. He was tap-dancing, because then, all of a sudden, from out of the blue, Gavin asked Finegan if he had ever heard this thing about gangsters throwing guys who didn't pay their debts through windows. Finegan, of course, knew everything.

Gavin paused to listen. "Yeah, isn't that interesting. I heard that too," he said, and right after that he concluded the conversation, signing off as if it were the middle of the afternoon. Finegan must have thought he was crazy.

I started to reveal myself then, come down the stairs, but right away, Gavin started rifling through his little address book, and then he began to dial again. He woke up Blue in North Carolina and asked him if there was any more news on whether or not some blacks might have killed Lawrence. And Blue must have said there wasn't, and so Gavin thanked him, said good-night and hung up. Then he took another big gulp of milk.

That was when I came down the stairs. "I just wanted to say how sorry I am," I said.

He cocked his head at me. "Are you really?"

That completely threw me. It wasn't just that he had said it, it was that he was so inept at saying it. Gavin just wasn't schooled in facetiousness. "Of course I am. Why would you say that?"

"Because now I wonder whether anybody ever cared."

"Of course they did."

"Yeah? When you're a big deal, Donnie, when they make you into a HE-ro, the minute you start to go down . . . well, it ain't that they turn on you. It's more just like they're embarrassed. They start thinkin', How did I ever make a HE-ro out of this old pile of shit? Even Lawrence."

"He didn't mean—"

"The judge was wrong what he said way back yonder, Donnie. It wasn't The Grey Ghost died. It was Gavin Grey. Nobody ever saw him again."

"Hey, Lawrence just got—"

"Whatdya think I would have done if he hadn't got killed? If Lawrence had come to me and asked me to fix a game? Come on, you're smart. Whatdya think I would've done?" I was smart enough just to stare back at him, to shrug and not to answer. "Well, I would've fixed the game, that's what I would've done."

"No one could have blamed you."

"Everyone would've," he said, very simply.

ON SUNDAY, AGAINST the Cardinals, Gavin led the Redskins to a 24–10 lead late in the third quarter. He scored that last touchdown on a weaving sixty-yard end sweep. And he had done everything this day: banged straight into the line for short yardage; broke off tackle; he had caught a half dozen passes, leaping to snare them all over the field; he had even *thrown* a thirty-yard completion on a halfback option. It was a tour de force; Gavin showed us at least some of everything he could do on the field. "To think he could squeeze so much out of his mind and focus his whole body," Judge Pace said to me. All of Griffith Stadium would stand and roar every time Gavin so much as touched the pigskin. I'd never seen anything quite like it in the pros: The Grey Ghost rampant once more.

When the Cardinals punted, the Redskins began to drive again. Gavin carried for two first downs—one hundred and thirty-two yards on the day—Hardesty twelve yards on a brilliant second-down fullback draw, and right away on first down, Traynor hit Adezio slanting left, seventeen yards, well into field-goal range. That was the last play of the third quarter; three more points and the Redskins could not possibly lose.

The action moved our way, and on the first play Traynor called the same end run that had brought Gavin a touchdown last time. It worked almost as well once more. He cut sharply up past the line of scrimmage, ducked inside past a tackler, then angled to the right sideline, past the fifteen, inside the ten. But there were two Cardinal defenders waiting for him there and a linebacker sprinting over from the side, so there was no way Gavin could cut back. Even he was stymied. The obvious, wisest thing to do was simply to duck out of bounds. He already had made the first down. Or maybe, if he was especially determined and felt tough, he could lower his head and bull his way into the two men, maybe driving them back another two or three yards.

Instead, with all purpose and without any warning, Gavin tried to leap the men before him. His left foot soared out like a ballet dancer's, and he was flying high. I can visualize him at that moment, a silhouette well up in the air. And then it was as if you had taken a gun and shot a bird. The two men in front just reached up and took hold of him, foot first, and the player from his left caught up and slammed into The Grey Ghost broadside, driving him in another direction. As great as ever he was, as elusive, as nimble, he was nothing but a target this one time. Ligaments, the knee, the ankle, the whole damn leg went. Gavin was out on the ground for ten minutes before the ambulance came, and, of course, he was out for the season. The Redskins kicked a field goal and hung on to win the game 27–24, putting them 4–0 on the season. They finished 5–7, beating Pittsburgh on a fluke in a blizzard.

Babs, of course, went right down to be with Gavin as soon as they took him away. I turned to the judge and shook my head. "Gee," I said, "that's a tough break."

The judge was not fooled. "No, Donnie," he said. "That was Gavin Grey's suicide."

We visited him at the hospital that night, just before he was wheeled in for the operation. There was great pain, but no anguish whatsoever, it seemed, and when little Stuart reached up and handed The Grey Ghost some flowers and lay her head on his breast, it even seemed very much as if Gavin had the privilege of attending his own hero's funeral.

12

I T WAS NOT THE END FOR GAVIN, THOUGH, FOR he still had the games in his system, and he was knitted back to-gether for the next season, the fall of '61. He had to make himself over into a completely different sort of player, though; he had to make substantial adjustments. The great halfback, The Grey Ghost, dashing through the line, cutting this way and that, outrun-ning the secondary, *outdistancing* the secondary, was no more. He had, as he often commented himself, lost a step.

The dazzle was gone, too, and a lot of his old power. In their place, Gavin depended on his hands more. He "developed" them, is what he said on that subject. You lose a step, so you develop your hands. In fact, he had always been a good pass-catcher, but that was only something he did to keep busy between times running with the ball. Now he made receiving his primary function, and it was quite amazing, really, to see how he was able to turn himself into another thing altogether overnight.

Oh, he would still line up in the backfield, and now and again his play number would come up. Once, I remember, he even broke a tackle, stiff-armed another fellow, and rambled for forty-one yards against the Giants. But it was not the same. Gavin was there to catch passes: down and out, safety valve, looping across the mid-dle, slanting to the sidelines. He could catch the ball and drag his feet so that they both touched down in bounds, making it a legal reception, and do it in such a wonderfully adroit way that Bobby Sample declared that he "had eyes in his feet."

Sample made a great difference when he was drafted in '62, because once he got adjusted and took over the team late in his rookie season, he gave the Redskins their first genuine passer since Sammy Baugh, eons ago. This was especially important inasmuch as the 'Skins were invariably behind, with no choice but to gamble and throw. In 1963, Gavin actually led the league in the number of passes caught, and by now, since he played so much with his hands and his head, there is no telling how much longer he might have gone on if his leg had held up at all. But it was forever going out on him, one way or the other, it often hurt a lot, and he grew afraid that he would lose mobility in his everyday life, and so he made up his mind to quit after the '64 season.

The funny thing was, though, that he was pretty happy playing those last few years, after the injury. He could just play the game and let somebody else be the hero. Sometimes, it seemed, Babs was a great deal more resentful of the attention paid Bobby Sample than was Gavin. "He looks so good because you get free and catch everything he throws," she said once to him.

"It's just more media hoverin' 'bout him," Gavin replied.

It did disturb him occasionally when the Redskins would need a few yards and Sample would have to give the ball to the other running back because Gavin wasn't up to the task anymore, and the other running back couldn't get the yardage . . . and Gavin knew that The Ghost could have once upon a time. That would bother him. That would remind him of what he was.

One Sunday, late in '63, Sample chucked him a little swing pass, and Gavin got the one block he needed and broke away. It was a bright blue crispy day, and for an instant you could recall The Grey

Ghost dashing away against Wake or State or somebody the fall of '54. He was TD-bound. And then, out of nowhere, the linebacker from the other side of the field—a linebacker, for goodness sake—cut clear across the field and caught Gavin at the two-yard line, and the Redskins couldn't punch it across from there and had to settle for a field goal, which eventually cost them the game—20–23, I think it was at the end. Gavin was distraught about that. He said dirty words that upset Sample, who was a very religious boy, so much that he didn't want to throw any more passes to Gavin. He also made up his mind to quit right after the season, but Babs talked him out of it because they needed the money. They still had some paying off to do from the Grey Ghost Inn.

That was the sad part. On the field he was fine. He took such a delight in catching the ball. Sample could float it out there like a kite, and Gavin would run it down. Or when Sample threw hard, when he gunned the ball, Gavin would be there, and he would hold on no matter how hard the defenders rocked him and tore at the ball. It always made me think of the word "bisect," from my geometry at Fike High. The Ghost would bisect the path of the ball. "You just got to come and meet it," he said. *Meet it* is, in all the sports world, the most descriptive line there is. Strip everything away, and the ones who are athletes are the ones who meet it. Take me out to a field where kids are playing now. I don't care what it is, football, baseball, basketball, tennis or golf, soccer. Show me the kids, and let me watch them five minutes, and the ones who can meet it will be the players.

But Gavin's joy was only upon the field. To have to play for the money pained him the most of all. To tell you the truth, I believe he would have kept on playing even if there weren't the debts to settle. I believe he would have kept at it just as hard for just as long no matter what the money. People are always disappointed when great players hang on after their finest skills have been eroded by time. They always say: Go out on top. But who goes out on top anywhere? And who in their right mind would go out on top where a game is concerned? Why, if you have any sense at all, you will hang on by your fingernails. The idea is to play. Sure, when Gavin and the others got into the action, they all wanted to win and worked at it. But athletes don't keep on playing in order to win. They keep on playing in order to play.

So the last functional seasons, however pale they must have been next to the lyric ones that had come before, were satisfying just the same. Unfortunately, the rest was not so pleasant. Of all the people in the world, it was Bolling Kiely who bought the Grey Ghost Inn. He had wanted to take Darlene away from Wilson, away from where they were frowned on, and so he had opened a second car dealership, Bolling Kiely's Triangle Chevrolet—the triangle being Durham, Raleigh, and Chapel Hill—and it had prospered so in those boom days that he had ventured into the purchase of the Grey Ghost Inn, too. He liked it that he and Darlene could come there, get the best table, and get fussed over.

Gavin didn't want to make the deal with Kiely, but it was much the best offer. The trouble was, the deal wasn't just for the restaurant. It was a personal note, with Gavin himself. In the off-season, he had to be the host at the inn Saturday nights and twice during the week, and, of course, he was not permitted to lend his name to Narvel Blue's franchise chain lest that conflict with the Grey Ghost Inn. Gavin was obliged to help sell cars, too. Kiely wouldn't buy the restaurant unless that was in the contract.

Most of the nights that Gavin wasn't the host at the Grey Ghost Inn, Babs was required to be there in his stead. It was the first job she'd ever had, at least apart from Junior League work. Kiely made her dress in a colonial outfit, with a big hoop skirt. He thought colonial appurtenances lent the place a lot of style. The menu was in neo-Williamsburg, with a "ye" thrown in here and there, a lot of words ending in a superfluous *e*—"roafte beefe"—and all the *s*'s made to look like *f*'s. ("It musta been hell livin' in them days, Donnie," Gavin said to me once when I was at the inn for dinner, "not being able to tell a suck from a fuck.")

Gavin—or Babs in his stead—would greet diners just inside the entranceway, where Bolling Kiely had assembled an impressive period display: the *Life* magazine cover, the Heisman Trophy, All-American citations, various photographs (many also featuring Bolling Kiely), a genuine number-twenty-five Tarheel jersey, a sliver of a goalpost from the last Duke game, and a recording of the play-by-play of the last touchdown Gavin scored for Carolina, in the Sugar Bowl. The interested listener took earphones off the wall and then pressed a button to hear: "The ten, the five, he's over! The Grey Ghost scores again! The Grey Ghost scores one more for Kowlinah and one more for posterity!"

And then, just past these artifacts, would be Gavin himself, handing out menus on his nights, or Babs, dressed like Betsy Ross, on hers.

After I graduated from Chapel Hill, I was seldom around to go to the inn, but in the summer of '64 I was back for a few days to talk to an old professor of mine about my doctorate program at Virginia. Gavin was already away at Carlisle, Pennsylvania—his last training camp for his last football season—so Babs was the hostess most every night. I called and made a reservation under an assumed name, so that I could surprise her, and I brought along a girl named Leslie. She was nothing special to me, but she was exceptionally pretty, which was important on this occasion; I didn't want

Babs to see me with anything second-rate. Also, it probably didn't hurt my standing with Leslie when Babs screeched and carried on when we came in, hugging and kissing me.

I had purposely made a late reservation, so by the time Leslie and I finished dinner, Babs was pretty much free, and she came over and joined us when we had our coffee. I poured her a bourbon from my brown bag, and she sat back and lit a cigarette. She had started smoking in just the last couple years. Gavin couldn't stand it. Babs had become quite a heavy smoker very quickly, too. She always carried a lighter. Especially in those times before all the cheap throwaway Bics and what-not, you could always identify heavy smokers: They were the ones with lighters.

Babs asked polite questions of Leslie, who had just graduated from East Carolina. "I never graduated," Babs said. "I married Gavin after my junior year."

"You were the Blueberry Queen," I said.

"Yeah, I took a year out for that." She looked away for an instant, thinking about it, about something. "If I hadn't have, I would have graduated with Gavin."

"The wages of beauty," I said.

"I was goin' to finish up at some place like Maryland if he signed with the Redskins—I was—but then he went up to Canada, and it was just a little strange up there. And then, all of a sudden, there were the children."

"How many do you have?" Leslie asked.

"Four," Babs said, turning to me. "Counting Gavin."

"You could finish now," Leslie said. "If you've only got a year, it would—"

"No, it isn't worth it now," Babs said, firing another cigarette with her lighter before I could even reach for a match. The house matches were Tarheel blue, with Gavin's autograph and number twenty-five on one side. The place was absolutely schizophrenic, teetering between the gridiron and the colonial. "But I know what I *can* do now, Donnie."

Leslie snickered. "Babs calls me Donnie," I explained. "I'm mostly Don now," I told Babs.

"Well, I'm sorry, you can't change people's names once you start on them. You'll always be Donnie to me. Ever since I got to be a grown-up, my dear Aunt Juliet says, Babs, stop calling me Aunt Juliet and call me Juliet, but I just cain't. If I live to be a hundred and Aunt Juliet to a hundred and twenty, she'll always be Aunt Juliet to me."

That certainly took care of that subject.

"Babs," I said, "you can call me anything but late for dinner."

"Oh God, Don," Leslie sighed, and she took that opportunity to go to the ladies' room. Babs watched her go and told me how pretty she was, in that academic manner that pretty girls employ for one another—a sort of professional courtesy.

Then she leaned way forward toward me. "Can you keep a secret?"

"Sure."

"Gavin would kill me. I've talked to Bolling Kiely."

"What about?" I poured myself a nightcap, and refilled her glass.

"We've just about paid off the note to him. Oh, Donnie, by the end of the season we'll be out from under for the first time since Lawrence was killed."

"Then what'll Gavin do?"

"That's what I talked to Bolling about." Suddenly, she grabbed at her bodice, as if she were going to rip it right off. "Oh I hate this . . . this getup so. Sometimes I feel like a circus freak. I feel like they put Gavin and me in here like a wax museum."

"I always wondered how you felt."

"Gavin really doesn't mind it . . . once he gets here. He likes the folks comin' in and makin' a fuss about the old days."

"He never did before."

"He didn't have to. Long as he was a star, he'd just as soon talk about the present, thank you."

"Oh."

"But I hate this, Donnie. This—" She fingered her dress again. "And every night I had to come in here, I hated myself, and I hated Gavin, and I hated Bolling Kiely."

"I'm sorry."

"Don't be, Donnie. Cake, I don't hate *this* any more." She swept the room with her arm.

"You don't?"

"No, I found out I'm good at it. I'm very good at it." She stood up and held her glass toward me. "Another ounce." And it's funny: What occurred to me is that she stood up just like a man. Oh, she was no less feminine, but now there was a purpose with the grace, and it was hers. "Oh, if I could just get out of this costume and run this place!"

"A business lady?"

"If I'd ever run this place, we'd never have lost it."

"What'd Bolling say?"

"Oh, he was all for it . . . till I told him we had to have a piece of it. But he should take us, Donnie. He'd profit more in the long run. I could run things, and Gavin could still be out front."

"I think he'd be crazy not to take you up on that."

"Well, maybe he will. But he wants to wait and see how the place goes when we're not here—you know, during the season, when we're back in Washington."

"When are you gonna tell Gavin about all this?"

She sighed and sat back down. "I haven't got the nerve yet. Gavin just hates Bolling so."

"Why?"

"Oh, I s'pose he hates Bolling Kiely because he can't hate Lawrence. He's got to hate someone for what they did to The Grey Ghost."

Leslie came back then, and I was glad, because this was not a very comfortable area for me. The trouble was, Gavin had been screwing Darlene Kiely for some time now, and everyone knew it—well, except, I suppose, Babs and Bolling. It was odd, too, so very much unlike Gavin. Oh, I'm sure he had gotten himself laid now and again, but he never talked about it. Yet he boasted often and graphically of his assignations with Darlene; obviously, the point of screwing her was not in the screwing, but in the cuckolding of her husband.

Gavin and Darlene would meet right at her house when Bolling was at the dealership; occasionally in the motel rooms she paid for; and in the moments of the most anxious ardor, they would hie to the far reaches of the automobile lot and do it there, in various of General Motors' best backseats. It was the commonest thing I ever knew Gavin to do—both the carrying on and the boasting. He did hate Bolling Kiely.

And then, as Leslie sat down, I glanced up, and who should be arriving at this very moment, in person, but Bolling and Darlene. They were expensively dressed, and taste was no object. Darlene was in a silvery sort of gown that slashed down to what is known as "the midsection" in boxing, revealing that her huge tossing breasts had swelled and tanned under the summer sun, like melons left out in the heat. She had a beehive hairdo, too. Bolling had gotten chubbier and had discovered white boots.

They had just come from dinner at the country club, dropping by to "check up on things." Babs introduced us all around, and the Kielys said they remembered me, despite my having shot up so and filled out to boot.

Then Bolling turned to Babs and he said to her, "Sugar, I told you: I don't want employ-EES smokin' on duty."

It was not a nice thing to say, to scold her so in front of friends, and even Darlene (who had been eyeing Babs in a strangely proprietary way) rose to her defense. She said, "Now, honey, Babs was with her—"

"Employ-EES can smoke all they want on their breaks in the washrooms," Bolling declared.

Babs did not blink an eye. She handed me my drink, handed Leslie hers, picked up her own, tucked her cigarettes down her front, and rose. "Would y'all please finish your drinks with me in the ladies' room?" she said, and she turned and marched away.

Though we followed closely upon her, Babs was already in a stall, crying, when Leslie and I got there. In a moment, she came out and traded her empty drink for my full one. But she did not curse, and there was no doubt that she still looked her part.

13

IT WASN'T UNTIL THAT LAST GAME OF GAVIN'S, four months later, that I saw either him or Babs again. And really, before the game, he was so keyed up, he didn't have much to do with me. He told me to be sure and come down to see him in the locker room after the game. I didn't want to, but it was a very special occasion, his last game, so I did.

The trouble with locker rooms is that you always feel so out of place. It's like being in a husband and wife's bedroom, and so long as you are there alone with them, it really doesn't matter whether or not they are making love or watching television; all that counts is that you are a stranger. My wife was reading about the women sportswriters once, about them fighting for their rights to get into locker rooms, and while she sympathized with their cause, she couldn't understand how they could want to be in such a private male preserve, them undressing and generally carrying on like men and boys.

"No," I said, "that's really incidental, the sex. No matter who you are—man or woman—you feel different from the players."

So, when I went down to see Gavin, I made myself as unobtrusive as possible, sitting across the way, rereading the souvenir program, until the last of his press inquisitors had shaken his hand, assured him he had been a credit to the game of football, and departed. He glanced over at me then. His elbows were on his knees, and, still so tired, he greeted me only by holding his palms open to either side of his face, framing it there like a window with the shutters tossed open.

Gavin's chest was bare (with a towel around his neck), but he still had his pants on. I came over and sat down next to him, and patted him on the knee, which was a foolishly avuncular gesture for me, but I've never been up to patting another guy on the rear, so this was the best I could manage in that line. "Good way to go out," I said. The Redskins had whipped the Steelers, and, more, Gavin had scored a spectacular touchdown in the third quarter on a pass from Bobby Sample.

He nodded; for being past The Grey Ghost's peak, it had been a representative game. "It was nice they retired your number," I said.

"Yeah, I gotta give 'em the shirt for like a showcase." He was vague and distant and kept looking around, although I don't know whether he was trying to impress this final scene upon his mind, so that he might keep it there forever, or whether he was using it to help him recall all the other locker rooms. "A bunch of us are goin' out for some beers," he said at last. "You and Finegan come along, you hear?"

"Babs?" I asked.

"No, no. This is just the players. You know: grab-ass. Like they're givin' me a farewell party."

"I'm not a player."

"Hey, that's okay. You know, you're a guy."

"No, it's not okay. I'd rather see you at home tomorrow. Hell, I'm stayin' at your house, and somebody ought to be with Babs."

"These guys—they ain't gonna bite you none, Donnie. They don't care if you're not a player."

"Yeah," I said, "but I do."

He shrugged and painfully forced himself to his feet and started to take off his pants. He said, "I been takin' off football britches for twenty years, and this'll be the last time." He stepped out of the pants at last, and kicked them aside, but, purposely, toward his locker. "I'm gonna take them with me," he told me. "They can have the ole shirt. I'd rather keep me the pants. They wear football *shirts* all over now, girls and ever'thin'. *Pants* . . . " He just nodded his head in approval.

Most of the other players were already dressed by now, and Sample, in a somber suit, came by. "Just throw a robe on and come to chapel that way," he said to Gavin.

Gavin introduced me. "Will you join us at chapel, too?" Sample said right away, instead of hello.

"Well, I didn't know anyth—"

Gavin turned to me. At the time, it happened that he had just taken off his jockstrap. "Bobby here is helpin' me find ways to let Jesus into my life," he said. "Me and Bobby been talkin' a lot. He has a *livin'* Bible, with a modern language we Americans all can understand. I'm tryin' to get to be a whole new person."

"Does that surprise you?" Sample asked me, and I promptly said that it certainly didn't one iota, although of course it surprised me a great deal.

"What do you think about Jesus, Donnie?" Gavin asked me.

"Why don't we talk about it after your shower?" I suggested. To tell you the truth, I don't understand how any sportswriters, male or female, can conduct interviews with athletes in the locker room. You can have some wonderful conversations when both of two parties are clothed and you can have some wonderful ones when both are naked, but, with halfsies, it is invariably difficult to establish any sort of substantive dialogue.

This certainly didn't affect Gavin, though. He had been standing in locker rooms for years, nude, talking to people with their clothes on. "What do you think?" he pressed on, scratching himself.

"About Jesus?"

"Well, yeah, about *me* and Jesus." Sample smiled, beatifically.

"You know, I think it's terrific. I'm really envious of you in a way, because I guess I could never get that close to God myself—and, you know, as religious as Mom is, too."

"Hey, you ought to give it a shot," Gavin said, but now his churchy mien was replaced by some good old-fashioned mischievousness. "Ever since Bobby here he'ped bring me closer to Jesus, I gained a half-step. Ain't that what you said, Bobby?" And he nudged Sample with a friendly elbow.

Sample saw no humor in this whatsoever, however. This was no joking matter, Christ Jesus. It was just good old Gavin kidding with the boys, but Sample perceived blasphemy—and, obviously, I was the agent of the devil, drawing it out of him. So he turned on me.

"You think Christ Jesus was some kinda pussy, huh?" is what he said to me.

"Hey, no, I didn't say that."

"Well, let me tell you for sure: Christ Jesus wasn't no pussy," Sample went on, undeterred by my response. Damn the amateur fanatics, be they laymen of any stripe—clergy, military, long-distance runners, whatever—they're always more overbearing than the professionals. "Listen here, Christ Jesus had hair on His chest and dirt under His fingernails, and if he was alive today, I'm sure he'd be a great athlete."

"Probably a pro-fessional football player," Gavin said, and with such deadpan earnestness that I assumed he must be putting on some.

"A linebacker!" Sample declared, going him one better, and speaking with such finality that I could immediately visualize

Christ up there on the cross, a big number "55" clear across His chest. And at that, for no reason, Sample said, "Praise God." It reminded me of a cat yawning. They do that all of a sudden for no good reason, either. It left me even more uneasy. I know there is nothing wrong with saying "Praise God," and I certainly heard enough of that sort of thing firsthand, growing up in the South, but somehow it always seemed to me to be terribly bad manners, rather like kissing with your mouth open in public.

Then Sample laid a hand on Gavin. "You're goin' to make some kind of Christian," he intoned.

And reflexively I piped up: "But Gavin's already a Christian. He's a Methodist."

Boy, was Sample just waiting for that. "Not a *real* Christian," he advised me, and snidely.

"Oh," I said, cowed, and poor Gavin shook his head at me, too. He was still stark naked, unless you count shower clogs otherwise. It was an interesting attire for a theological discussion.

"I'm joining the AAFC," Gavin told me.

I shrugged, but very apologetically. After thinking Methodists were actually Christians, I surely didn't want to commit another dimwitted faux pas. But I just didn't have the foggiest idea what those initials stood for. Sample, praise God, came to my aid: "AAFC—American Athletes for Christ."

"Oh."

At Sample's urging then, Gavin reached into his locker up by the free bottles of after-shave and hauled out some brochures for me. These pamphlets explained how the pro stars of the AAFC met with impressionable youngsters, instructing them likewise in both how to flare out and how to find inner peace.

"Bobby's the AAFC co-captain for our nation's capital," Gavin told me, and Sample bowed his head, properly humble. "Maybe you can visit with him, so's you can become a Christian too."

Sample raised up on the balls of his feet, ready to pounce on me should I actually lay claim to membership in Christianity. I decided it was better to try and wriggle out gracefully. "But I'm not an athlete," I said. "You know, not a *real* athlete."

Now Sample laid a hand on my shoulder. He began, "Danny—"

"Donnie," said Gavin.

"Donnie," said Sample, clearly annoyed at me for having the wrong name, instead of being peeved at Gavin for interrupting him with this quibbling detail. *"Donnie,* you don't have to be a ballplayer or a home-run hitter or a scratch golfer on the PGA tour in order to find a place on Christ Jesus' team. Because that is the greatest team of them all."

I nodded, and, delighted, Sample left to prepare for the chapel service. But he stopped after a few steps and turned back to us. "Praise God," he said. Then he waited, showing his impatience.

Finally, damnit, I turned to Gavin too. "Praise God," he said, bowing his head. Sample nodded his, pleased, and went away.

For nothing quite else to do, Gavin scratched himself then. Well, when you are being interviewed nude, that is one distinct advantage. It is diversionary, but not seeming so, like the hemming and hawing you must do with your clothes on. Finally, he raised his head, although still clutching his privates. "I am sin-cere," he said.

"Oh, I know. It just doesn't seem like you."

"Well, I'll tell you what, Donnie. You're about the one person— the one person not in football—who knows me. And you know I never took the bullshit in completely. I never went along with all that everybody's All-American crap. Not altogether."

"Yeah, that's true."

"But on the other hand . . . "

"Yeah?"

"Well, some of what Bobby says makes sense. I'll tell you what: I'm not fuckin' around with broads anymore. And I think maybe I'm gonna stay off the fuckin' booze, too."

"Yeah?"

"Well, you know, cut back to beer anyhow."

"That can't hurt."

"I'll tell you somethin', Donnie. I played up here a whole damn decade."

"In the pros?"

"Right, here and Canada, the both. And I seen a lotta guys when they had to give it up, and there wasn't a one who didn't fight to hang on, the one way or the other."

"Don't tell me you're fightin' to stay on. I thought—"

"I'm done," he said, although, of course, the whole point of this was to tell me that he didn't want to be.

"Yeah."

"Yeah, the one way or the other: body or soul, Cake. You either go to the doctors for help. Or to Jesus. It ain't a whole lot of difference."

"So why didn't you go to the doctors?"

"Hey, I just flat out don't like them needles," he said. "Seems to me, I'd try prayer first." And he smiled. But make no mistake: It wasn't Bobby Sample he was laughing at. It was himself. The Grey Ghost never was a complicated man. And a football season is not complicated either—not more so than Bobby Sample's Jesus. The season takes up half the year, and the other half is for preparing for the next season. That is a season, too: the off-season. When you are playing a game, the whole year is a season, and when you're not, the whole year is just a year, like it is for everybody else. This takes some getting used to.

"YOU'VE HONORED ME, Donnie," Babs said, when I got back to the house. "I thought you'd go out with the players."

"No, I just never feel comfortable with the team. You know— any team."

"Finegan went along," she said.

"Yeah, but Finegan played on a team with Gavin once. Besides, he's just not the sort to get uncomfortable under any circumstances."

"Well, you've given me a wonderful surprise, and I'm going to show you how an old lady can dress up for a young beau." She went upstairs and put on a sexy hostess gown, patterned in deep maroons, a color nobody should ever wear unless everything is as correct as it is with Babs. The children were down to bed by now, Tommy sleeping in with his sister, since I had his room, so I mixed the drinks and promised to go out for Chinese food so she wouldn't have to fix any dinner. Then, I don't know why, but I raised my drink in a toast.

"You," I said.

"Well, thank you. Damnit, it's my retirement too. Football was just as much to me, you know."

"Yeah, I know."

"Worse in a way," Babs went on, "because I couldn't play the damn games. People always asked me if Gavin brought the games home. Of course not. He could play the games. I was the one who brought the games home."

She laughed and reached for a cigarette, and I found myself staring at her. Simply staring. It was not the sort of thing we call undressing with the eyes, which I can speak of with authority, because God knows I had done that to her enough in the past. This was more just in the line of admiration, mixed with some wonder. Babs was so very beautiful, still so young, hardly past thirty, every part of her looks as glorious, surely, as ever they had been. And yet, there seemed to me more now, a confluence with all of her. She felt me looking at her, and when she looked up, she blew smoke my way, curled and provocative, like in the old movies. And then she said, "Thank you."

"For what?"

"For what? For looking at me like that."

"Oh. Well, I was just thinking how you've grown so."

"Oh my God, Donnie. Please don't tell me I have more character in my face." I shrugged apologetically. "But I'll accept it from you, *Cake*." I grimaced. "Oh come on: Girls adore men like you. That little Leslie I saw you with last time in Carolina. She was absolutely precious."

"Well, she did approve of my mind," I said.

"She liked a lot more than your mind, honey. A woman can tell." She reached over and tugged at my pants leg. "Did you sleep with her?" she asked mischievously.

"Now, what kind of a question is that?"

"Well, did you?"

"None of your beeswax," I replied wryly, with a suave and Continental grin.

She had me pegged to rights. "Oh, so you want it both ways? You don't want to be accused of tellin' tales out of school, but you want me to think that you must've. Shameful." She sighed for effect. "Oh well, I just asked because I understand everybody sleeps with everybody nowadays."

"No, we haven't quite reached that happy millennium."

"I was born a few years too early. But you know: I had to stay a virgin. I had to wait. I did, too, you know."

"Know? Are you kidding, Babs? I think it was in the *World Almanac*. It was all Gavin ever talked about."

"Well, he was proud of me, whatever he said. He was." She lit another cigarette. "That sounds so foolish to say now. But it's true. The only trouble is, when someone is proud of you for something you *don't* do . . ." and she threw up her hands in some exasperation. "You never escape that. You know, he won't listen to me, Donnie."

"I'm sorry. What?"

"Gavin won't even talk to Bolling Kiely. He won't even consider it." She shook her head in disgust, and in the kind of frustration children exhibit when teachers lay down arbitrary strictures and say, "Just because . . ." Gavin had told her, Babs said, that he would never be a partner of Kiely's, but she knew that, truly, he would not have *her* be a partner. "He doesn't want me to work, and even though he doesn't know what he's gonna do."

"I guess he thinks the kids need you at home."

"The kids need somebody to make money," she snapped. "He keeps talkin' about *in*-surance. He's worked all these summers for Carolina Life & Casualty—but what? Vice-president in charge of golf. He can't sell *in*-surance worth a damn, because he'll only try and sell to friends, to people he knows will buy."

"He sold me five thousand dollars' worth."

"Yeah, so how long will they keep him when he's through playing?"

I shook my head, and backed away a bit, standing up, going to the bar. Goodness gracious, there was an edge to Babs, but what was frightening, perhaps, was that it was not unbecoming. "Aren't they talkin' 'bout havin' Gavin do color on the Tarheel football network?"

"That's not a living, Donnie McClure. That's ten Saturdays in the fall."

"Well," I ventured, "he can keep on sellin' cars for Kiely."

"Gavin can't sell cars any more than he can sell *in*-surance."

"Did he ever do anything with Narvel Blue's offer?"

"No, we had to step out of that because we had to take the deal Kiely offered—which is too bad." Blue had been unable to attract any white backers, so he could not open up his own chain, so he and his father-in-law's syndicate took their poke and bought into a franchise deal named McDonald's when it came into the state. They were in on the ground floor, and made a fortune, so then they sold out and started their own chain. It was named Dreamer's, and it was just now starting to spread beyond its Carolina success and across the country.

"So what will Gavin do?" I asked.

"I really don't know," Babs said, handing her glass over to me. "It isn't so much what he is. First, Gavin's got to understand what he's *not* anymore. He's not a player anymore."

"Yeah, but look at it this way," I said. "The good news is, you're not a player's wife anymore, either."

"I only wish Gavin would understand that, Donnie. Now it's the worst of all. He's not a player anymore, but he's still trying to keep me a player's wife."

BOBBY SAMPLE WAS just leaving, hurriedly, when I came back from the Chinese place over on Wisconsin Avenue. We all three were very sorry for the encounter, as brief as it was, Sample accomplishing his departure without so much as a "Praise God." He was gone even before I could lay the egg rolls down.

Babs went to the bar and poured herself another drink. She was in mild disarray, from kissing him, I imagine. Or from not kissing him. Either way, it was that he had been there. "He came by to say good-bye to Gavin," she said.

I moved up alongside her at the little bar and took some ice, never looking at her next to me. "No, Babsie, he didn't come to see Gavin."

"How do you know?"

"I know, because after chapel today—which he presided over, by the way—Gavin pleaded with him to come out with him after the game, but Sample said no thank you, that that sort of fellowship—that was the word he used: fellowship—was not his, uh, cup of tea. I didn't know that this sort of fellowship"—I gestured, directly and derisively toward Babs, sweeping my hand just before her breasts, indicating that I meant her and sex alike—"was the alternative he preferred."

"All right," she said, and she turned full away from me.

"Is this adultery or is this merely a case of coveting thy neighbor's—"

"All right, stop it, Donnie!"

"The sanctimonious bastard!"

Babs turned back to me, and very directly she said: "Look, Donnie, it wasn't his fault. I *picked* him."

"You did?"

"He's very cute and completely vulnerable. You see, I needed someone every bit as guilty as me."

"Oh my God, Babs."

"I'm sorry, God forgive me, but I hated Gavin so much. I just kept thinking: He can't do this to me." She was pacing now. "Well, they went off for a road game right after we had the big fight, right after he told me, *no,* he would not even talk to Bolling. And the kid, whatshisface, you know—"

"Sample?"

"Yes. He had a slight injury that week, so they left him back, and he and I were there at the airport, saying good-bye to the team. I could see him looking at me. And all of a sudden, I had this horrible feeling that, okay, if all Gavin would let me be would be a pretty girl, then I would be a damned good pretty girl."

I turned from her and headed for the steps straightaway. She called after me, "Donnie." I turned back. "Please don't tell Gavin. If I really wanted to hurt him, I'd tell him. Please."

"I won't. Why would you think that?"

"Well, I don't know. You seemed so upset."

"Yeah, well. . . . " Well, I was upset. Babs was right. Only now, standing there, looking down on her from the second step, I realized that I wasn't upset for Gavin. I wasn't sorry for him. I was sorry for me. I wasn't mad at Babs for what she had done with Bobby Sample; I was only mad that she hadn't done it with me.

"Look, nothing happened," she went on, stepping toward me.

"Whatdya mean?"

"I mean, I put my clothes back on and left his apartment."

"I know how much you love Gavin," I said, although I was not at all very certain any longer on this subject.

"That had nothing to do with it. I went there because I was furious at Gavin and I wanted to hurt him, but then I got there and I realized that I'd never tell Gavin anyway, so what was the point? I didn't want to sleep with that awful Christer from the Midwest." She waved in the direction Sample had gone, even managing to smile. "The poor kid. Donnie, if I went to bed with him, I was just gonna fuck everybody up."

Funny—she said that so naturally, even though I had never heard her say anything like that before, and never did again. "So I put on my clothes and left, and he still thinks it's something he did."

I was very relieved to know that Bobby Sample had not violated the most beautiful creature on the face of the earth.

"The trouble is," Babs went on, "is that I was taught you should only do it for love, and now here I am, a grown woman, trying to cheat on her husband, and I can only cheat for love." I nodded weakly and turned to go. "And I don't think that's really cheating . . . is it . . . Donnie?" I did not understand that she was talking to me.

When I looked back at her, Babs took her drink and put it down very deliberately, smiling by now, not seductively, but as a seducer. Still, I could not believe. When she was near enough to touch me, she reached out and took my hand off the banister, and kissed it. Then, intently, looking me dead in the eyes all along, she took my hand and laid it inside her maroon gown, upon her bra. "Go on, Donnie," she said. I reached inside the bra and cupped my hand about her breast.

Babs nodded, and when I did not move anymore, she started up the steps toward me. There, she wrapped an arm about me and kissed me so passionately that I gasped for breath and nearly fell from the step. I had to take my hand from off her breast to find my balance, and then to kiss her, as I wanted to, holding her tightly to me.

"Oh Donnie, my Donnie," Babs said. "You take me." And then I kissed her in a kind of violent manner that tore at me in two ways, that I was doing this at all, with Babs, and that I was actually capable of kissing anyone so.

BABS CAME TO me minutes later in Tommy's room, where I was staying. The room was leering with posters of cowboys and space pilots and all manner of toys and plastic innocence. She had only taken her bra off from under her gown—nothing more. "No," she said then, shaking her head softly. "You must undress me."

I said, "Sure." She was standing before where I sat on the edge of the bed in front of a large yellow rocket ship that I, as Tommy's godfather, had given him for Christmas the year before. I stood up. I wanted to look her in the face. It was in the shadows, the only illumination from the hall light behind her. I like to tell myself that if she had dared drop her eyes from mine, I would have stopped. But I doubt that. Anyway, she didn't. She didn't take her eyes from mine, and there was no stopping us.

I took my hands and reached up to her gown and pulled it down over her shoulders, down over her breasts, down over her hips. It fell the rest of the way, but she didn't move; she didn't step out of it. She just waited for me to pull her panties down, too. As I did that, I sat back down, looking up at her from the edge of the bed.

I pulled her to me, my head upon her stomach. Then I tilted my head back and kissed her softly upon each nipple, then down and touched my lips upon her crotch. Merely kissed it then. I wanted so much to be gentle, to show her that I was not always the creature that had crushed her so downstairs. Besides, I was scared. If she had been with many men before, I would be another. But there had only been Gavin, so I must be different.

I believe she sighed. So then I drew her to me, down into Tommy's bed, and we kissed some more, touched each other, and, soon, began to make love in a sweet, natural way. We fit together much too easily for what emotions should have grated on us.

And it was nice, for sure, nice in the sense that she certainly seemed to like it and told me she did; and I certainly liked it. But it was odd, too, for I felt so little of Babs. All these years I had dreamed of just such a moment, about touching every wondrous part of her, of kissing her, having her kiss me, of at last actually taking her for myself. My God: me inside of Babs Rogers. The Blueberry Queen.

But in those moments, what I thought of was Gavin. What a misplaced victory. It was of conquering The Grey Ghost that I thought—and of conquering all the goddamn All-Americans, all the heroes, the rock 'n' roll stars, the cover boys, the matinee idols, all the famous bastards I had to pay to see and admire and envy. Never mind that Gavin didn't know. I knew; and that was quite enough.

The judge was absolutely right: Those heroes are too close to us these days for them to survive our own sorry vanities. At last, and once, one time only in my life, I had the chance to make love to Babs, to the girl of my dreams, and I had blown the opportunity, making love to myself as well. Of course, at least in this respect, I came the closest to being like Babs and Gavin, to sharing their love their way.

PART THREE

THE NATIONAL SPOKESMAN

14

Stuart was forewarned about Marshall. It was barely weeks past Gettysburg, and the Southern cause was not yet conclusively ended, but it was certainly apparent that Marshall was more concerned about Lee's posterity than he was about Stuart's—or the whole Confederate army's—immediate status. Marshall had been savage in his criticism of General Longstreet's role on the second day of Gettysburg, and now, just as clearly, he was a one-man grand jury indicting Stuart as well.

Lee himself was not involved in the inquiry, and was certainly seeking neither to shift the blame nor to single out scapegoats. He had, after all, officially tendered his resignation to President Davis, and while the president had promptly rejected it out of hand, the move indicated that Lee understood he deserved to be assessed criticism for the failure in Pennsylvania as much as any man. Colonel Marshall, though, would not accept that possibility; he was a defender of the faith, pledged to make General Lee an avatar.

He accepted Stuart's written report of the campaign, but, without graciousness, chastised him for his tardiness. "I apologize, Colonel," Stuart said, "but I've had other matters to attend to."

"Personal?" Marshall asked, and nearly rudely, considering his lesser rank.

"Not at all," Stuart replied stoutly, retaining his composure. "A great amount of material and horses were lost in Pennsylvania."

"I am all too aware," Marshall said, *and then he pulled out a file, extracting a letter from it.* "President Davis forwarded me this," *he said.* "Could you respond to it?"

"I would respectfully submit, Colonel Marshall, that first you read my report. I'm positive that it will answer any questions about the northern campaign."

"No," Marshall replied, *rising with that, by now quite brandishing the letter.* "This correspondence relates to the events in Brandy Station immediately before you left for Pennsylvania."

"What events, Colonel?"

"The sad events of June eighth." And then he read the letter:

"Sir: If General Stuart is allowed to remain our commanding general of cavalry we are lost people. I have been eyewitness to the maneuvering of General Stuart since he has been in Culpepper County, at Brandy Station. Gen. S. loves the admiration of his class of lady friends too much. He held a review yesterday for the benefit and pleasure of his lady friends, and not for the interest of the Confederacy."

Then Marshall passed the letter on to Stuart, saying, *"It is signed, as you see, 'Southern Lady.'"*

"That is an anonymity," Stuart said sharply, *handing the letter right back without looking at it further.*

"'Southern Lady,' it says," Marshall snapped. *"Would you suggest that such a person would dissemble?"*

"I would suggest only that the person does not live who can say that I ever did anything improper of that description."

"It is a fact, is it not, General Stuart, that the Yankees surprised you and your troops that night, after the full review and after an evening's dance?"

"The cavalry was not surprised at Brandy Station, Colonel Marshall."

"Oh, you expected the engagement?"

"No, I did not. Neither was the possibility unforeseen. I might remind you, Colonel, that the Yankees paid with far greater numbers than we."

"Loss cannot always be measured in terms of even our most sacred Southern blood," Marshall said, and he strode back over to his desk, and snapped up a piece of newsprint lying there. "An editorial of June fourteenth from the Richmond Examiner," *he announced, and he held it up, tightly as a decree, to read from it.*

Stuart reached out, though, just bending the upper corner back.

"If you please, Colonel, the press prints to be read."

"As you like," Marshall said, handing the paper to him.

Stuart read without expression:

"The more the circumstances of the late, sad affair at Brandy Station are considered, the less pleasant do they appear. Our puffed up cavalry of the Army of Northern Virginia seems more intent upon showing its shine upon the parade ground, in the image of its frolicsome dandified commander, than in prosecuting—"

Stuart read no further, and handed the paper back. "Colonel Marshall," he said, "I am here to answer to you, a soldier doing your task. I accept that, however harshly. But I feel no obligation whatsoever to respond to journalists, whose purpose, it seems to me, is to steal onto the battlefield after the fight and shoot the wounded."

"The way our commanders are perceived by the citizenry is not an inconsequential issue," Marshall replied, directly, and then he turned and went around to his desk chair. Stuart took that as a signal that the interview was concluded, and he prepared to salute a departure.

"If there is no more," he said.

"There is one thing," Marshall said. "In your report"—and now he patted it, as one would a pet—"do you deal directly with the widespread inculpation that you disobeyed General Lee's orders in your circuitous, distant march in the days just before Gettysburg?"

Stuart stared fiercely at Marshall this time, and if never before in this meeting had he pulled rank in how he spoke and what he did, now he took it full, merely in how he looked. Marshall sat down at his desk. Stuart said, "I am not familiar with that canard, but were it on the lips of every other soldier in the Army of Northern Virginia, I would not respond to it until the one man so charged me directly."

"Of course, General," Marshall said softly.

"In my cavalry, I have never ridden with those who would mount hindsight," he said.

"Yessir," Marshall answered, and he saluted crisply.

"Until then, Colonel," Stuart said, saluting in return, snapping his boots, and tucking his plumed hat only tighter beneath the crook of his arm, as he whirled about toward the door. He was there, reaching for the handle before he heard an altogether softer voice from Marshall, calling after him.

"Jeb," it called. And then even more intimately: "Beauty." Stuart turned back. "I'm sorry for all of this," Marshall said.

"Oh, I understand, Wade. If you plant swords and roses alike and they bloom in victory, then in defeat—"

"Defeat, Jeb?" Marshall said that almost plaintively. "We weren't defeated at Gettysburg."

"No, and I was not surprised at Brandy Station. So you grant me anticipation there, and I'll grant us victory in Pennsylvania, and we'll all go straightaway home to our farms and our wives."

Marshall smiled ruefully, as he was supposed to. "I wish, Jeb. I've never liked this business of war. I can stand bullets and shells and all that *without flinching, as any man must, but the rest. . . . " He trailed off and fingered his dress jacket. "Gold lace on my coat has always made me feel as if I were a child tricked out for a party in red and yellow calico."*

"Ah, but you see, Wade, that's it," Stuart said. "Wear the gold lace, and put the feathers in your hat, and it makes all of it seem more like child's play. That's the only way I could ever tolerate it."

Marshall nodded. "I'll remember that, Jeb," he said, and he stood up again and thrust out his hand. "And I forgot to congratulate you and Mrs. Stuart."

"The Lord giveth and the Lord taketh away. This one was conceived hardly before we lost the other last winter."

"What are you naming her?"

"Virginia—"

"Of course."

"Virginia Pelham Stuart."

"Ah," said Marshall, and he cast his eyes up in some kind of benediction. "Our brave Pelham. Gallant Pelham."

"Dead at Brandy Station where they would have me derelict and uncaring."

Marshall lowered his eyes. "They say he died a hero's death," he sighed at last.

Stuart replied: "No, Wade, no one dies a hero's death. You may live a hero, and if you die while people still see you dressed in that hero's calico, then you've died a hero. Pelham only died a hero because that's all the time the Almighty gave him time to be. He said to me, 'General, I am dead now.'

"I said, 'Major, the Yankees raised their sights for you.' Time, I'm afraid, will do that to us all in our calico."

Colonel Marshall recalled that remark all too well the next spring when Stuart fell mortally on the Sunday afternoon at Yellow Tavern.

"Once a man becomes a hero, he can never raise his sights any higher," Marshall said. *"But all around him others can, and, ultimately, that is what must bring him down."*

—DONALD MCCLURE,

The Life and Death of the Knight of the Golden Spur

T HE FIRST THING YOU MUST UNDERSTAND ABOUT Babs is that no matter how independent she became, she had nothing to do with the era around her. She did what she had to do, and she would have done that in 1865 as surely as in 1965. She only really wanted to be what she had been scheduled to be, which was the most beautiful creature on the face of the earth. In fact, if she had indeed truly been a "modern" woman, Babs would have left Gavin altogether, but, to the end, she permitted a large part of herself to reside with him in the past, even as she had to manage more on her own. Always, it seemed, Babs felt certain that their dreams could be restored, and that once again Gavin would be everybody's All-American and she would be his girl, with a corsage.

Oh, I said *dreams.* Of course, what those two had once weren't dreams. Those things happened to Gavin and Babs. That is the difference between them and you and me and the rest of us weaned on mother's milk. We dream of the best things for us, they remembered. Dreams we can suffer; memories, I suppose, we can't.

Almost to the end of his playing career, I thought Gavin would adjust better than Babs to the muffled memories. Somehow, I thought, he would stay in football, and his life would be quaint and smooth. But, it turned out, that is impossible if you have been as good a player as he was. It is only the fellows who were mediocre, or worse, who survive as the coaches. If you are a natural athlete, you have been obliged to learn little or nothing, and can impart even less to those who need coaching. The one season Gavin did the technical sidekick stuff on the Tarheel radio network, he couldn't even pull that off. He would say things like, "I don't know why Williams didn't cut left then," or "McNally didn't meet the ball"—not commentary, not critique, but more personal disappointment, almost a pique. Gavin simply could not understand why players didn't perform as he so easily could have. The network let him go after that one season, and, as best I can remember, that was Gavin's last official association with the gridiron. Thereafter, he was just a former player.

If you want to be neat, I think you can say that Babs could not have survived as she did without Gavin failing so. Had he succeeded, had he gone down the path laid out by so many of his contemporaries from college, Babs would have surely ended up like so many of hers, a dull and insipid woman, full of cottage-cheese lunches and that social gauntness, legs skinny and tanned to a glaze like doughnuts. But she retained a nice roundness and a glow to her. Gavin was no more overweight, but he was different; he took on a fleshy aspect, the sort that makes us think first of pastels and salad bars.

But death: Why the one had to die, I've never understood. Probably they should have parted that very first fall he was out of football, when he discovered so quickly that he simply couldn't tolerate life without. And Babs was too intertwined with the game; they were a package in his mind, and, possibly, in hers as well. "Everything changed the minute I left football," he told me.

"Whatdya mean?"

"I mean everybody is different toward me," Gavin said.

"In what way?"

"They don't think I'm as good."

"At what?"

"They just don't think I'm as good. You know, a person."

"Everyone thinks this?"

"Sure seems that way to me."

"Look, maybe because you're not playing, *you* feel different, so it's just *you* think people feel different toward *you*. I mean, Babs doesn't feel any different toward you."

This was not, it developed, the best example I could have chosen to illustrate my thesis. "Bullshit, Donnie," he said. "It's altogether different with Babs."

"Whatdya mean?"

"Bed, for Chrissake."

"Oh," I muttered. I had not meant to stumble into this area.

"She's not interested." I didn't say anything. "When we start and all, I can tell she's not interested. She goes along, but she don't care anymore that it's me. I can tell." He shook his head. "It's getting so, it's tough for me to get a hard-on."

"You can't get it up?" I blurted out. My tongue was loosed by a great deal of beer.

"I get it up," Gavin shot back. "I always get it up. It's just that I've started *wondering* whether I'll get it up. But I always do get it up." He gestured across the room. "You see that over there? I fucked her eyes out the other night."

The lady in question was a waitress. We were in a joint named Sweeney's, down near Memorial Stadium, in Baltimore. The simple reason why we were there was because a week before, September 16, the Colts had called Gavin up at home and asked him if he wanted to join the team. The Colts had reached him in Carolina at eleven-thirty. He and Babs and the three children lived in a new development of "modified ranches" over toward Durham. The development was known as Sherwood Forest Estates, and all the streets owed something to Robin Hood. The Greys were in a house on Maid Marian Lane, just off Nottingham Drive, the main drag.

Gavin was alone when the call came. Babs was out with the baby, Russ, and the older two kids were at school. Gavin packed. When Babs arrived back around noon, he told her he was un-retiring, made love to her, and then he threw his gear in the car and drove straight through to Baltimore. He did not even wait around a couple more hours to say good-bye to the oldest children, who would have been home from school around two. It was at this point that Babs should have left him, and if she had I believe they would both still be alive today.

Gavin went back into football because he missed it terribly. He needed it. He had stayed in good shape, hoping for a call. He made no real effort to look for a serious job outside of football, because if he took such a job, it would make it that much more difficult to accept if a call did come. He never told anyone this—he never actually told himself—but it was so. He would work his nights for Bolling Kiely at the Grey Ghost Inn, and, in fact, as soon as the football season started officially, he would sometimes even go over there extra nights on a pretense, accept a beer or two just to be polite, and talk football, especially if the football talk could be about him.

The reason that Baltimore had telephoned Gavin was also very simple. Unlike the Redskins, the Colts were a superb team, the defending conference champions, and they could find good use for a wise old player. In fact, in the first three games he played with the Colts, Gavin scored two touchdowns and had another called back because of an illegal procedure penalty that did not involve him. The Colts would specifically put Gavin in the lineup in scoring situations, and Unitas would look for him because he knew The Ghost could still catch the ball, even if he couldn't run far with it any longer. In the end zone, all Gavin had to do was catch.

That night I was with him in Sweeney's, he was really feeling wonderful. He had scored a touchdown on Sunday, his first game, the Colts had won, and he felt part of the team already. He could accept his reduced role because he was contributing to a winning effort, so promptly at eleven we left Sweeney's and went directly back to his little furnished apartment out in the suburbs, in Towson. "I gotta get my rest," he explained. Only mothers and athletes ever talk about "rest" any more.

That Sunday, against the Giants, Gavin scored another touchdown, this one on a magnificent diving catch into the corner of the end zone. That made is 21–17 for the Colts, and they went on to win 35–17, so Gavin kept talking about his own TD as "the go-ahead touchdown." I drove him back to his apartment afterward and picked up my stuff for the trip back to Charlottesville. Gavin called Babs and told her that he had scored another touchdown. But, obviously, she started telling him about the kids and what-not. So Gavin told her more about the touchdown. He told her, for example, about the go-ahead aspect. But no matter how much he embellished the play, I could tell that it still didn't make any dent in Babs. I never knew whether she was still mad at him for going back or was merely resigned, but, whatever, she refused to encourage him. Probably it doesn't matter. And maybe Babs knew more about football than she let on.

The next Sunday, against the Rams in Los Angeles, Gavin hurt his leg again. He made the catch, but he hurt his leg, and the doctor said it would be several weeks before he could be quote useful un-quote again. So on that Tuesday the Colts picked up another old receiver from the Pittsburgh Steelers, giving up a twelfth-round draft choice, and then they released Gavin outright. It is always re-ferred to as "released outright."

Immediately, Gavin started making telephone calls to other teams in the National Football League. He worked geographically, and, by the afternoon, he was out to the Rams and Forty-Niners on the West Coast. No team wanted him; not even a nibble. The ros-ters were set, and Gavin was old and easily injured now. So then he started calling up the teams in the American Football League. But nobody was interested over there, either. Halfway through the AFL, Gavin called up Babs and told her what he was up to. "Please, darling, don't do this to The Grey Ghost. Come home and give it up. It's over."

"Listen," he said. "I can still play ball. I only played three games with the Colts, but I scored two touchdowns and really three, only this nigger went into motion, and—"

"Precious, please. The game is over."

Gavin hung up on her, and, immediately, resumed calling what was left of the American Football League. He was down to two teams when he got somebody with the Denver Broncos to agree to say they would take a look at him working out if he would come up to New York, where the Broncos were playing Sunday. The Broncos were the worst team in creation; they were so bad, the stripes on their socks went in the wrong direction—vertical rather than horizontal.

But Gavin was thrilled; when he called me up he made it sound as if the Denver Broncos were the Monsters of the Midway incar-nate. And they hadn't even agreed to sign him; it was just what they call a look-see. "Are they going to sign you for sure?" I asked.

"Just wait'll they see me run some patterns, Donnie. How can they pass up The Grey Ghost?"

At first that saddened me; then it frightened me. Maybe they would sign him just as a sideshow. Come see The Grey Ghost! I could see him outside a stadium, catching footballs on his finger-tips, while amused passersby flipped dimes and quarters into his old hat. "Aw, why don't you pass it up and go back to the family?" I said, trying to be casual.

"Come on, Donnie. I showed the Colts I can still play. I scored two touchdowns, and would've had a third, but—"

"But you retired, Gavin."

"Yeah, but this is an opportunity. The Broncos are building!"

He stayed with Finegan in New York, waiting for the tryout. It killed Finegan. Gavin had too much to drink. He had started falling into that, now that Bobby Sample and his abstinent Jesus were not there to monitor his behavior any longer. And something else, something altogether new: When Gavin drank now he would talk about himself; or, in any event, he would talk about The Grey Ghost. This particular night he was boasting about how he was going to get a tryout with the Broncos, but, unfortunately, many of the barflies did not know who the Broncos were, and Gavin got es-pecially irritated at one point when somebody asked him if they were in the Roller Derby.

Finegan, behind the bar, grew progressively saddened, watch-ing Gavin there, ordering too many, slurring his words, telling everybody that he was The Grey Ghost of lore, and soon he would be starring for the vaunted Denver Broncos. So finally Finegan tele-phoned me.

He had to call someone, under these dispiriting circumstances, and Lawrence was dead and gone, and Babs was out of the question.

So he called me. "I never thought I'd see it, kid," he said. "It's the sorriest thing I ever saw." He wanted me to come up to New York and take Gavin back south with me. "He's always listened to you, kid," Finegan said.

But, as I told him, there was no way that Gavin would listen to me or anybody else now—not so long as he still believed he had a chance to stay in football. I tried to explain this to Finegan. If Gavin left the game, it would be, for him, like leaving his manhood behind, too.

"You mean like losing his balls?" Finegan said, getting it straight.

"Yeah," I said. But that gave me something of an idea. "Hey, Finegan, can you get him a girl?"

"A pro?"

"Yeah."

"Sure. What the—"

"No, no, just listen. Look: He named his baby after you, Finegan. If you never do anything else for Gavin, get the best whore you can and pay her . . . Uh, what time is he trying out for the Broncos tomorrow?"

"Noon."

"Well, you pay her to stay with him in the morning, too. Don't let him make that team. You hear me? It's time Gavin went home and got the rest of his life started."

"Fuckin'-A," said Finegan, and he got the hooker, and paid her extra, and the next morning, when Gavin's alarm went off, she earned her bonus in one way or another. Gavin got to the workout, but just barely on time, and he did not especially impress the Broncos, so they told him, nicely, they were sorry, but they were featuring a "youth movement."

This provided Gavin with a polite excuse to use, but then, as the years went by, the youth-movement alibi faded, to be replaced by an account of his extended adventures with the whore. The reason he didn't make the Denver Broncos, Gavin said, was because he was so damn good in bed that a whore—a whore!—stayed around for something extra. It was symbolic, I suppose: sex for football. And as the years passed, it got so that when Gavin fell into his cups, he would not only tell the tale about the long night with the whore in Queens, but he would relate it in approximately the same tone that he usually employed to describe his best game with the Redskins, when he scored four touchdowns and rushed for two hundred and thirty-two yards. Once an All-American, you must remain an All-American, one way or another.

At the time, though, he was hurt, and he ricocheted his way aimlessly down the eastern seaboard, stopping over to commiserate and carouse in Baltimore and Washington. He called me one midday as he passed through Richmond, and already, it seemed, he must have knocked off a few beers. I imagine, too, he had some more, driving the rest of the way, down to the Chapel Hill area. Certainly, a cold sober man would not, as Gavin did, go directly to Bolling Kiely's house around four o'clock in the afternoon and begin making graphic overtures to the lady of the house. Neither would a sensible woman have let him in the house, but Darlene Kiely did, always being tremendously flattered by his attentions.

Momentarily, they were in her bed.

Nothing that followed was at all pretty. Bolling Kiely arrived home a bit early to discover The Grey Ghost and his wife intertwined, so occupied with one another that they did not even realize that he had entered the room. Enraged at the sight, Bolling reached for the nearest object that he might turn into a weapon, which was a lamp. He ripped it from the socket, and this, at last, alerted the two lovers. But they had time only to try and roll aside, and not quite quickly enough, as the lamp clipped Darlene on the side of her head and caught a glancing blow off Gavin's rear end.

Gavin then rolled clear off the far side of the bed, while Darlene screamed in pain between the two men. Kiely still held the lamp and faced a choice: go after the powerful football player or a cowering and somewhat wounded woman? He chose the latter, and raging now, he swung at her again. Gavin stared, unbelieving. Darlene was able to shift herself back just enough for the lamp to miss her head, but it came slicing down across the top of her body, opening it up like a large tin can, one great long gash over the swell of both her breasts, the blood gushing out from her.

Gavin was horrified, struck dumb. Say this for him, though: Hereafter, he was the gentleman warrior. He lunged at Kiely across the bed, just in time to deflect the next blow. Kiely had aimed the lamp—swinging it by the neck, using the base as a clubhead—squarely at the defenseless Darlene, and surely he would have bludgeoned her to death had not Gavin leapt in. As it was, this last blow fell so hard upon her that it cracked her collarbone clean.

She cried out again, the most piercing shrieks of sheer agony. But in counterpoint, Kiely, shamed, frustrated, now berserk, began to holler louder still, incredible vulgarities and imprecations and the din and the blood was such to make the place over into an abbatoir. The dogs howled. The frightened maid, downstairs, called the police and then fled; two other neighbors phoned the cops as well.

Kiely threw the lamp toward Gavin, and then dove upon his wife, trying to strangle her. The blood from her chest wound flowed more, covering him and the bed, so that the carnage appeared, if possible, even worse than it was. Gavin tossed the lamp aside and came back into the fray, knocking Darlene to the floor, as well as Bolling when he lunged at the man. Then he fell on Bolling, and screaming himself now, he began banging the man's head against the floor. This part was quick; Bolling fell limp, mouth open, and Gavin stopped immediately and stood up and away from him. In fact, he paused for the moment and pulled on his trousers.

Gently then Gavin reached down and picked up Darlene and placed her back on the bed. She was not screaming now, only sobbing, hurt and frightened alike, calling for a doctor. Gavin rushed into the bathroom, wetted a towel, and returned with it to pat at her gash, to try and stem the blood and comfort her. He did not even notice that Kiely had got up when he was in the bathroom, and had left.

"I'm dying, I'm dying," Darlene cried. "Please, call a doctor."

"It's the blood. It's not—"

"Please, please, Gavin."

"Okay," he said, and he went to the phone. It was while he was standing there, dialing, on the far side of the room, that Bolling Kiely came back. This time he was brandishing a pistol, and this time he chose to attack Gavin first.

"I'm gonna shoot you in the balls, you cocksucker," he said, and he fired then straightaway, before Gavin could react.

The bullet creased his outside right thigh, and while it turned out to be an inconsequential flesh wound, the force of the shot, the sound and the shock of it all, was enough to collapse Gavin to the floor. The next shot landed higher, just above where he had fallen.

Kiely either thought he had done in Gavin with these two bullets or had least put him away sufficient for him to ignore him for the moment. Whatever, now he turned the pistol upon his wife, point blank, maybe two feet away. He was completely crazed by now and would have killed her in the next moment, but for the fact that, at that very instant, a policeman arrived at the top of the stairs and cried out, "Stop or I'll shoot!"

Within the hour, Bolling Kiely had accused Gavin Grey of breaking and entering, assault and battery, rape and sodomy, attempted murder, and a variety of other crimes. The good news was that it happened just a bit too late to make the six o'clock news.

15

T HE JUDGE CALLED ME WITH THE NEWS BEFORE he left Wilson. He wanted me to come down and be a comfort for Babs, a buffer, whatever. It was late when I got to their house, but the phone was still ringing—although nobody that you wanted to speak to (the press mostly)—so dealing with the outside world became my job. Darlene was remaining in the hospital overnight, but she would be all right. The police had let both Gavin and Bolling go home until they figured out what to do. Darlene was the only one hurt, and she didn't want to press charges against anybody. Still, Bolling's pride was fractured, and he was determined to bring Gavin down.

The judge was closeted with Gavin in the family room, and Babs was saying good-night to the older children. When I got off the phone from the Chicago *Tribune*, no one else called for a while, so I dialed out myself. I phoned Bobby Sample in Washington. He was very surprised to hear from me, because he had already heard about Gavin's "travails."

I said, "Bobby, it sure would help if you people could get somebody down here."

"Oh, you'd have to call the Redskins' front office about that."

"I don't mean the team, goddamnit. I mean the American Athletes for Christ."

"You mean have a squad member from the AAFC come down there?"

"Exactly. If one of you—an athlete, one of your preachers—could come down here and stand by Gavin now, it would mean a great deal."

There was a pause. "Well, I don't know," Sample said.

"Look, it would help Gavin and it would help with, uh, public opinion. You know, Bobby, he's not guilty of anything *illegal*. It's just very sordid."

"He's guilty of fornication," Sample told me.

I couldn't believe the man would say that. I said, "Let he who has a pile in his own eye not fuss over the speck in his brother's." I knew that wasn't quite right. I knew the word "mote" was in there somewhere, but I couldn't remember whether a mote was a big or a little speck. So I just said it quickly; speed counts for more than accuracy when you are trying to impress somebody with Bible quotations, and that Sample didn't counter indicated that he had been suitably impressed (and/or wasn't sure about the size of a mote either).

"Well, I'll tell you what," he said. "I'm sure gonna be praying for our brother Gavin, and as soon as I get off this phone, I'm gonna call AAFC captains all over America and establish a nation-wide prayer alert."

"Bobby, he doesn't need a prayer alert. He needs good people to stand up for him in public."

There was another pause. "Prayer is powerful," he said at last.

"You won't come to him?"

"Look, you've got to understand. Young athletes the nation over look up to us doing Christ's work in the AAFC. If we identify with Gavin in his travails, it can damage the whole cause. I don't think Gavin wants that. But I'm sure he'd be real pleased to hear about the nationwide prayer alert. Could you tell him about that when you visit with him in fellowship?"

"Well, he's just in the next room, so I can get him on the phone, and then you can visit with him in fellowship yourself."

That did not go over well. "No, I think it's best to keep it just to the family members now," Sample said.

"Yeah," I said, and I could actually hear him sigh over the phone. "And Bobby . . ."

"Yes?"

"Fuck you, Bobby," I said, and I hung up the phone. As nearly as I can remember, that's the only time in my life I really ever said that to anybody.

Babs came into the room at this point. "It's that kind of day," she said. "An awful lot of fucking."

"I'm sorry," I said.

But she waved my sentiments away, flopping down in an easy chair. "He hurts, Donnie. He really hurts. I understand." She lit a cigarette with the table lighter there.

"You can forgive him?"

"I didn't say that. I said I understand him. He was a fool to try and go back to the game, and they rejected him. The Grey Ghost, rejected by football." She shook her head. "You don't have to forgive a man out of his mind. Look, a rational man does not go to his boss's house—to *any* man's house—late in the afternoon and start to screw the man's wife in the man's own bed."

"I guess not."

"Any more than a rational woman takes her husband's nephew to bed in her child's room."

"Babs, for Chrissake!"

She looked across to me in silence for a long time. "It's all part of growing up," she said, facetious with her expression even before she spoke the words. "When you play football or you're a football wife, you're just a little late getting around to things." She blew smoke rings, which is rare for a woman, whatever that means. "I can't be righteous, thank God, so I can look at this head-on. It clears the air, somehow. If we can just get Bolling to drop all these damn charges, then maybe we can go on fresh, *grown-up.*"

"Maybe."

"I think I'll tell him about us."

"About *who*?" I fairly gagged.

"You know, about you and me. That night."

"Jesus, Babs."

"Oh, I don't have to involve you. That's not the point. I won't say who the man was. I just mean me. What *I* did. If Gavin knows that I've been unfaithful too, then he won't have to feel so guilty about all this."

I came over to her. "No, you can't do that," I said, and pleading. "He's distraught because football has turned on him. Now if he learned that you too—"

"Exactly," Babs snapped. "It's time he learned that I'm not a goddamn game either."

"No, no, Babs, it would break his heart. The football is enough."

"The football! What *is* the great football tragedy, anyway? For Chrissake, he always knew he'd have to leave it sometime. He knew at some point he'd have to be too old for it. What's the big deal?"

"Still, whenever—"

"But me, Donnie. He never knew I'd be unfaithful. That didn't *have* to happen. So if I told him that, told him the God's truth, maybe then he'd grow up."

"I wish," I said. "But it would just destroy him. Don't do it, Babs."

She stared at me, but just then the doorbell rang. "Oh, that's probably another casserole," she said. The only people who had called were a couple of neighbors, friends who had brought food by, as if there had been a funeral. "Tell 'em I've gone to bed," she said, and she snuck out of the room. I went to the door. Narvel Blue was standing there.

"Hey, Donnie," he said. "The Ghost here?"

"He's with his lawyer."

"Could I see him for a moment?"

"Of course you can," Babs said, coming back into the room. She proceeded directly to the door, took both Narvel's hands in hers and clasped them, a gesture that, given the time and place, meant a great deal more than it sounds. There was a real affection in how Babs held his black hands and stared into his black face. "Thank you for coming, Narvel," she said.

We took him in to see Gavin. "Blue!" he cried, jumping up.

"Hello, Ghost."

Gavin introduced him to the judge, and they both said they had heard of one another. Babs asked Blue if he wanted a drink, but he declined. He spoke with great self-assurance, all inflection gone from his mouth, as sure as the teeth were now capped and straight, almost too neat. But his manner was not falsely stylized; Bridget had only improved him without having to mess with the foundation. In fact, Blue could shift fluidly back into a black argot when it served the purpose of emphasis, rather like a Continental lover turning to French in moments of artful persuasion or a priest falling back upon Latin to intimidate sinners.

"What's the situation now?" Blue asked.

"Well," said the judge, "Darlene is going to recover, and the police would honestly prefer to dismiss the whole episode as just a family fracas. Unfortunately, Mr. Kiely has been cuckolded, and seeks legal redress for that personal issue."

"I sure didn't rape her," Gavin said. Blue nodded.

"The truth, alas, is not likely to appeal to a jury in an instance where a man had bedded another's spouse between his own sheets. And, at the best, ruffled linen is no better to hang out than dirty."

Blue nodded. "Judge," he said then. "I'm going to ask you to leave the room. We have something to discuss."

"Gavin is my client."

"He *be* my friend."

The judge considered that. "Why do you want me to depart?"

"Don't ask me that, Judge. If I told you, you might as well stay."

"I want nothing illegal transacted here," the judge said.

"No, sir."

"All right, but Babs stays too."

Narvel shook his head. "This isn't illegal, but it isn't pretty, either."

"All right, Donnie stays," the judge said, starting for the door.

"Wait a minute," Babs said. "There have been enough . . . uh, indelicacies that this little woman has been treated to today. I'm not leaving."

"Let 'em both stay," Gavin said. The judge shrugged and went out and visited with the good Doctor Dant.

Blue wasted no time. "There's a young lady in Durham name of Billie Simpson. Colored girl. Her daddy works for Triangle Chevvalay, cleaning cars and what-not. There's been a lot of times when old Bolling Kiely, uh—"—he was deferring to Babs—"uh, takes up with Billie Simpson. Know what-all I mean?"

"Perfectly," Babs said.

"Now, Billie Simpson, she is one good-lookin' woman. Only she ain't no woman. She sure looks like one and she dresses like one and she *charges* like one, but she's still only fifteen years old. And that be against the law."

Gavin broke into a Cheshire-cat grin. "What you aimin' to do, Blue?"

"Well, if you'd have a mind to, I'd like to make a phone call to Mr. Kiely. As a public-spirited citizen, I'd tell him that I might have to inform the PO-lice of this situation. I can't abide no lawbreakers."

Gavin looked over at Babs. She merely nodded. "When?" said Gavin.

"Soon's I leave."

"Thank you," said Babs, and Gavin rose to open the door.

Blue paused, though, and clapped him on the shoulder. "Listen, Ghost," he said. "There's one other thing. You need a job now. You're done with football. Now I got just the right job for you."

"What're you talkin' about, Blue?"

"You know, I'm in this franchisin'. We own these McDonald's restaurants. You know them?"

"Sure I do. So many hamburgers sold."

"Yeah, Well, we're selling out and starting our own chain. Calling it Dreamer's. I'll be honest with you: We need some white folks. You've been in the restaurant business. I need me a regional manager for eastern Carolina. Good money, Ghost, good benefits. It be a good job for you."

Gavin was nearly in shock. "You want me? After today?"

"I need a good man right away," Blue said.

"Oh, that's wonderful, Narvel," Babs said, and she came over to him, and, as she had at the door, she took both his hands in hers.

"God bless you," she said, and Narvel nodded. And suddenly then, she leaned up and kissed him. "We'll never forget this," she said.

"I be glad to he'p an old friend," Blue said, looking past Babs, directly into Gavin's eyes. But then, as another old football player, Blue looked away, because he didn't want Gavin to suffer that a man would see him crying.

BLUE MUST HAVE gotten through to Kiely that night, because the next morning, very first thing, the police notified us that, pending further investigation, all charges were being dropped. Billie Simpson's father was given a demonstrator to drive to and from work at Triangle Chevrolet. The Grey Ghost Inn was renamed the Triangle Tarheel Inn, and all references to Gavin were immediately excised. On the judge's orders, I went over and retrieved the Heisman Trophy and the uniform shirt and the goalpost sliver and all the other All-American memorabilia.

That was about the end of it. Gavin did get a few letters. Carolina Life & Casualty wrote to say there had been a shake-up in his department. "I'm the only one in the department," Gavin said. He was right. The shake-up meant that he would no longer be paid to play golf with clients. Two other Carolina firms that he did commercials for also canceled his contract. He received a letter from the head preacher at AAFC headquarters advising him that, thanks to a caring Bobby Sample, a nationwide prayer alert had been called and everybody connected with the AAFC had, privately, been praying their fool heads off for him. Gavin also got one nice letter, from Stuart Stevenson, the judge's ward. Stuart wrote that she was "mighty glad" that Gavin had not been hurt, and she welcomed him back to the Tarheel State. She also enclosed her official fifth-grade individual portrait. It was not lost on Gavin that "the only two folks down here still care about me are a colored man and a little girl."

About this time he went to see Blue about the job. It was, in fact, the only opportunity he had. Blue outlined the job responsibilities. "That's fine, Blue," Gavin said. "The only thing is, I got a lot of teams in both leagues still interested in me, you know, when my leg heals, and I'll probably have to leave for a few months to play next fall."

Blue only shook his head. "Ghost," he said. "That part's done with."

"I scored two touchdowns when I was with the Colts, and it woulda been three, but there was this colored boy on the flank, and they got him for illegal motion."

"There's no more time for football, my man," Blue said directly.

"But I can still play, Narvel."

"Maybe. But I doubt it. And 'sides, even if you could, you ain't got no right to no longer."

Gavin didn't understand. He could not comprehend what Blue was talking about, and he considered it ridiculous that he would not hire him under these circumstances. It would only be a few months a year he wanted off. He came home and told Babs how utterly perplexed he was that Blue could lack such understanding. "I'd be back in January at the latest," he said.

"You damn fool, Gavin Grey," Babs said. Only that; she didn't bother arguing. He was explaining to her how he was still only two pounds over his playing weight from college when she just up and went to the bedroom.

When she came back downstairs, Gavin was sipping on a beer. Babs had a wool suit on, with a white silk satin blouse and a pocketbook with sharp corners—very businesslike. She said: "I'll be back in an hour. I'm going to see if I can get that job."

Blue was busy when Babs arrived at his office. He was meeting with Bridget, who served as his executive assistant. When Bridget came out, she was astonished to see Babs there. "I'm here to see your husband," Babs said.

"I'm sorry," Bridget said. "Don't bother. There's no way we can hire Mr. Grey if he's going off to play football."

"I know that," Babs said. "Your husband is right, and my husband is a damn fool." And with that, for the only time during this whole affair, she lost control of herself. Suddenly, without any warning, even for herself, Babs began to cry—great wracking sobs that gathered in her chest and made it hard for her to breathe.

Bridget stepped forward and took her in her arms and let Babs cry on her, and Babs started to come around, because she could not help but thinking that when she was a very young girl, she had an old black nanny, and she would go and cry to her when her parents punished her, and here she was, so many years later, crying her eyes out on a black woman's shoulder. She was still sniffling in her arms, though, when Blue came out of his office. "Get Mrs. Grey some coffee," he told his secretary.

Babs stood up and tried to make a smile. "Get Mrs. Grey some whiskey," she said.

Bridget handed her a handkerchief, and Narvel ushered her into his office, and beckoned for her to sit down on the couch. It was good black leather.

"I apologize for breaking up," she said at last.

"You have every reason to. Don't be embarrassed," Blue said.

Babs laughed. "No, I was trying to make a very mature impression." She looked him dead in the eyes. "Narvel, I want that job."

"You serious?"

"Of course I am. It wasn't Gavin ran that restaurant. I did."

"I 'magined that."

"Then let me have the job."

"It's a man's job. It's travel all over eastern Carolina, two, maybe three days a week."

"I can do that. For Chrissake, I can drive a car."

"There's men to meet with every day. White men, Negro men. You know what people gonna say."

Babs threw her head back and laughed sarcastically. "After this week, do you really think there is anything anyone could *say* that would bother me?"

"Bridget, honey, tell her there's better jobs suited for a woman."

"Why do you want this job?" Bridget asked.

"Because it pays good and because I know I can handle it, and because—" Babs stopped and looked back over at Narvel. "Because I know you understand."

"I do? I'm a black man from Rutherford County, and I'm supposed to understand you?"

"I know that's funny," Babs said, "but it's true. You understand Gavin better'n anyone, and then, you understand me."

Blue nodded, not necessarily agreeing, but accepting what she had to say. Then he stood up at his desk, brandishing, as he did, a pile of papers. "You know what these are?" he asked, and Babs shook her head. "These are four damn good résumés. Any one of these four men is highly qualified for this job. And they're all four Negro men, with families. And I'm supposed to hire a white woman?"

"You need white folks. You said that."

"I said that to The Ghost. I owed him a favor. That's paid now."

Babs clenched her fists. "Damnit, Narvel, I can help you. I can do the job. I can."

He tossed the résumés gently to his desk, and looked away from her. When he turned back, softly, he said, "I know."

"You do? Then hire me."

"That's why I don't want to hire you. I'm afraid you will handle the job."

"What does that mean?" Babs asked.

"It means if you succeed at this job, The Ghost'll never really work again."

"That's not true!"

"Yeah, it is. Oh, he'll do this and that, but he'll never work. Not really. He'll never stop living the football."

"Please hire me," Babs said, and this time Blue nodded back, as if to say, *The blood is not on my hands.* Babs started work the Monday following, and was extremely successful from the first. And Gavin never really did work at a job after that, although every year, as the football season approached, he would begin to rush downstairs when the mail came and riffle through it quickly, certain every day that this day someone would invite him back into football. So, much of his life took on the curious shape of an interim.

16

IT IS NOT AN EASY TRIP FROM CHARLOTTESVILLE, Virginia, to Wilson, North Carolina, but I gave myself plenty of time so that I could not possibly be late reaching Judge Pace's house. Sure enough, as I had ventured that I would arrive "around four," he was perched on his front porch, waiting for me, when I rolled in at three forty-five. He was nodding there in the angled afternoon sun of autumn, a copy of Plutarch's *Lives* by his side. But he had not worn out; it was his own decision to put his reading aside for a while and "accumulate his thoughts."

This was now the first week of October 1979, many years had passed, and he was genuinely an old man, but his faculties had not dimmed, and he was still as independent as ever. But he had become old, and the problem with the judge becoming old was that he had always been wise, so he had nothing more to gain by growing old. "The reverence of elders has faded so in this republic," he complained later that night, "but the last straw had been this much-publicized revelation in the popular press that the aged—" He stopped. "Don, if I ever hear you employ the expression senior citizen—"

"Or golden-ager," snapped Mrs. Pace.

"Or oldster," added the judge. "Or say I'm so-and-so many years *young*."

"Old-timer?" I inquired.

He pursed his lips, considering for a moment. "Old-timer I can live with," he declared then. "It imparts a certain grizzled, sage quality I fancy for myself."

"Well, old-timer, what is this alleged revelation about—"

"It is this discovery that we ancients are not above the carnal, even as you and whey-faced adolescents, wrestling with zippers in the backseats of cars."

"Now, Judge, I would think that you would like the younger generations to be impressed that you are still—"

"Don't say 'active sexually.'"

"No, sir," I laughed. "I wouldn't dare say that."

"Hell's bells, it always says in these articles that 'senior citizens remain active sexually.'" He shook his fist in mock disgust. "The last refuge should be dignity. Our Roman Catholic brethren understood that about celibacy. God in His heavens knows you're not any better for being diminished in that way. Probably the worse for the frustration and wondering."

"Curiosity killed the cat," Mrs. Pace added.

"Exactly. But the nuns and priests appear above us erotic animals, and that is to the Church's benefit. And here I always thought I was going to receive as much due when I neared the end of the winding trail, but all these damn articles appear about my crowd remaining active sexually. The leering I must endure now. Why, I merely go to the supermarket, and I can tell everybody there cares not a whit for the wisdom and nobility accumulated by me through the ages. No, I can see. They all are only visualizing me copulating."

"Oh, Frank!" Mrs. Pace cooed, and proudly.

"This whole damn nation," he went on. "We talk about planned obsolescence in our appliances. But it's people who are made to become expendable too early, and if our survival as a race depends upon us all imitating teenagers, then God help us. I always thought one salvation of life was that eventually I could get old and cranky and thumb my nose at the world. Now here I am, safely as old as the hills, and I'm still obliged to take on appearances, even as a sex object. Damn! 'Youth and the dawn of life are vanity!' Ecclesiastes Ten, eleven."

"Never heard that before," I said.

"Revised Standard Edition. Greatly ameliorates the King James in spots, Ecclesiastes being one. Listen, I've never said that antiquity is sacred and can't be improved upon. What I am saying is that youth can't be improved upon, but the vanity of these times is that a lot of older people think they can."

This was late in the evening. Actually, when I had first arrived and spotted the judge dozing, I had delayed coming to his house, seeking a brief personal reverie. I parked the car down the street aways and walked back up it, the path of my childhood. It was exactly a quarter century since that fall of 1954 when Gavin was everybody's All-American. This was no coincidence, either: He and the team were being saluted this weekend in Chapel Hill on the occasion of this "Silver Anniversary," and I was here in Wilson to pick up the judge and escort him down to Chapel Hill. There would be a public fete Saturday at halftime of the Carolina-Virginia game, and the formal Silver Anniversary Dinner that evening at the Carolina Inn.

All this institutionalized nostalgia heightened my sense of the past, but the autumn is always the time for remembering. Christmases make us remember, but they only make us remember past Christmases. But the fall, those first few weeks of school when the smells of summer fade, is when the world begins to resettle and renew itself every year. It is the actual beginning of an annual life that we have nominally assigned to January 1 and which nature gives to the spring.

I have always suspected, too, that us males, for all our alleged toughness, make better children than do women. Girls always play mothers; I leave it for others to tell me whether that is biological or cultural; for here, I am only interested that it is so. A girl's family is the one she rears, not the one she is born into. But boys, yes, will be boys. Girls will not. Girls will be mothers. Boys know that once they are done being boys they will be breadwinners, and what is that to pine for?

So I welcomed the opportunity to retreat to my childhood at the right time of the year and relive what I could of it with the judge, who was a living conduit to the past. I suspected, too, that this might be the last chance, there. Mrs. Pace indulged him to keep the house; she wearied of all the time she had to put into it, because help was hard to find nowadays, with Clarissa long dead.

But as soon as I parked the car and started up the old street, I knew I had come back just for me. I looked at our house. We had been gone from there twenty years, and it had changed hands twice since then, so the present owners probably didn't even know that people named McClure had ever lived there. Standing there, looking past the big maple in front, I wished I had carved initials. But never did; never fooled much with penknives as a child; and never as a grown-up had the slightest interest in obtaining one of those Swiss army pocketknives when everybody was raving about all their many uses. So I just stood there, studying the house—I did not approve of the shade of blue they had chosen for the shutters—and then went along to the judge's.

Mrs. Pace played a supporting role for much of the evening, allowing the two men to have some boy talk. The child they had reared, Stuart Stevenson, was originally supposed to have joined us for the evening, but she had, at the last, been unable to get away from work a whole day. She would meet us in Chapel Hill. Stuart was a grown woman now, approaching her own silver anniversary come February, and she was a feature reporter with an Atlanta television station. At this time, she was working on a continuing series entitled *The Unchanging Changing South,* filming vignettes which illustrated how the South had, in many ways, retained distinctive characteristics—notwithstanding the more celebrated regional homogenization it had supposedly undergone. So Stuart was coming to Chapel Hill to film the silver anniversary salute, and to study Gavin in particular, as a perfect specimen for her series. Besides, although she had not seen him since she was a little girl, Stuart had always felt a certain identification with The Grey Ghost, for she had always heard the tale of how his exploits inspired her very name.

The judge was not especially keen about Stuart's involvement, though. He did not even want to attend the celebration himself, but I convinced him that he simply could not reject Gavin's invitation. Still, he kept complaining. "I'm sorry," he said, later in the evening after Mrs. Pace had excused herself and gone to bed, "but I just instinctively object to these kind of artificial jubilees. What more do you want of me? I endured that cursed Bicentennial, didn't I? And I vowed then that that would be the last hokum revival for me."

"Oh, come on, Judge, don't be a cantankerous senior citizen," I said. "Our lives are jam-packed full of anniversaries of all sorts, and Gavin and the others would feel hurt if some attention wasn't called to their old exploits."

"Normally this is so," he replied. "Unfortunately, in the case of your uncle the whole business has been blown out of proportion.

Sometimes I have felt that Gavin has finally found a certain peace, but this contrived emphasis on the past is unhealthy for him. He drinks enough of memories without having us pour that wine down his throat. Hell's bells, I've got nothing against remembering, but what with all these photographs and television tape, we're making the past too literal. The present has always been oppressive enough."

"Well, after all, it's a happy time Gavin will be recalling."

"That's what scares me. Exalt in the good old days, and despise the present all the more. You know, of course, that nature has a way of saving us from pain. If we suffer too much, we black out. Time fulfills the same sort of role with memories. People say time heals. Hell's bells, time doesn't heal. Not unless you are also prepared to say that pain heals. In either case, beyond a certain point, time or pain blacks you out.

"But we've started to monkey around with nature. Pain tells these athletes, Don't play. So they give 'em drugs to fool the pain, and they end up injuring themselves all the more. Same thing with time. We have all these devices to restore the past in living color, and I fear for people like Gavin—and Babs, too, perhaps—that we are making memories too vivid for them."

We said good-night then, and I told the judge that I wanted to take a little stroll before retiring. In fact, I took a kitchen knife, and with it, I carved my initials on the maple tree in front of my old house. I was motivated by a certain mischievousness—the present residents would go nuts wondering, Where did this DM come from? Who is DM? Why here?—but I also was bemused with the idea of tinkering with time. I should have carved my initials on that tree as a child; I was only correcting an oversight. And it was a valedictory, too; I knew that I could not come this way again. It was somebody else's road now.

NARVEL BLUE HAD been absolutely right about Gavin. He wouldn't work, not really. Yet it was not all for the same reason, for, as Gavin perceived it, The Grey Ghost possessed a certain legendary stature, and thus, almost by reason of birthright, it was proper that he be rewarded with appropriate work—as a color announcer, endorsing products, putting his name on a restaurant. That was correct. That was one thing.

But where the occupational line was blurred, where the particular work was unrelated to his institutional fame, then Gavin felt that The Grey Ghost had no business intruding. He wanted it both ways, really. He was like a blond bombshell who yearned to play Ophelia, but then, given the chance at last, played her topless.

On one occasion a few years ago Gavin was given a substantial opportunity to enter the bowling-alley business; the industry was in the process of refurbishing its image, calling them "lanes," and installing automatic pinsetters in the place of little colored boys. A fellow named Timmy Christian, from Atlanta, who had been the Tarheels' head team manager Gavin's junior year, gave him the chance, making him regional manager for all the lanes in the Carolinas.

Now Timmy Christian adored Gavin; always had. But he made Gavin a square offer: a good salary, straight up; a chance to buy into the parent company after a time; real responsibility and a company car. Babs was so excited, but almost from the first Gavin started to threaten to quit. The problem was that Christian was always introducing him as The Grey Ghost to associates, and this irritated Gavin. "Why can't he just say, This here is Gavin Grey?" he asked.

"Well now, what good would that do?" Babs replied. "Then the person is just gonna say, Are you the real Gavin Grey—somethin' like that. So why not lay it right out there?"

"It's the principle of the thing," Gavin said.

"Oh come on, darling, there's still some people who remind folks that I was the Blueberry Queen when they introduce me."

"Yeah, but nobody makes you think they hired you because you used to be the Blueberry Queen."

"Look, it's a real job," Babs said. "Do it right, and then they will forget you were The Grey Ghost, and you'll just become Mr. Grey, the Carolina manager."

For the moment this mollified Gavin, but a couple of weeks later there was a sales conference at Sea Island, Georgia, and Babs could not get away from her work at Narvel's to join him. And every time Christian would introduce Gavin to someone new, he would introduce him as The Grey Ghost, and Gavin began to simmer and to grouse.

In fact, Christian was often very complimentary, and The Grey Ghost stuff was only in passing. For instance, he would say, "The Grey Ghost here is in charge of our best region." Or: "Say hello to The Grey Ghost. He's as good at bowling lanes as he ever was at carryin' the old pigskin." But Gavin hated the football references.

The final afternoon of the conference, he was on a panel for prospective new investors. Christian introduced him as The Grey Ghost, and added that the example he was setting up in Carolina was a beacon light for them all. Gavin then gave a little speech about bowling lanes and called for questions. The first man to respond said, "I saw you play Tech against Bobby Dodd's boys your sophomore year."

Gavin just gritted his teeth. Another man said, "I saw you on *The Ed Sullivan Show* that time."

A third said, "Why'd you go up yonder to Canada outta Carolina?"

That really upset Gavin. Try as she might, Babs could not talk him out of quitting when he got back home. He told a befuddled Christian to come and pick up the company car. And then, after that, there was nothing special; he was *almost* involved in a variety of enterprises. And, in the meantime, he played golf and hung around the nineteenth hole for much of the rest of the days; in a way, the nineteenth hole was wherever Gavin was.

But the golf turned out to be a blessing in disguise. St. George Randolph, Gavin's old Tarheel teammate, started up a large "mature adult" community on the other side of Durham. Each and every town house overlooked a golf hole. In fact, more than that: Most of them overlooked a water hole, inasmuch as that is the most desirable golfing vista. St. George's course boasted, to be precise, eleven water holes of one sort or another, the water a brilliant artificial azure blue, of the same hue you can make the water in your toilet bowl if you purchase the most popular retail dye. The water hazards were so blue they didn't look like water, but they looked like what water is supposed to look like, and, better, everybody could overlook one. The development was known as Pine Lakes Estates.

St. George invited Gavin to join on as a special vice-president in sales. He would receive a small salary, but there was the promise of runaway commissions. In fact, this was true, too. Several of the professional salesmen made great amounts of money, but Gavin sold no one. Oh, to be sure, some of the fans who remembered The Grey Ghost rampaging over the gridiron and who had already decided that they wanted a town house overlooking a water hole eagerly bought from him. But to those who had to be convinced, Gavin was not convincing.

It wasn't either, that he hadn't done his homework. Instead, what it was that he had was an odd fear of trying too hard, of achieving some success, because he was positive that nothing he ever could do would be so accomplished as doing the football that he had already done. So what if he sold one condominium overlooking a water hole—they would just assume that it was a sale because someone wanted to buy from The Grey Ghost. If he sold a lot of condominiums overlooking water holes, why then he was merely doing a better job of portraying The Grey Ghost.

One time, late at night, Gavin said, "You know, Donnie, sometimes I think I've become Babsie."

"What in the world does that mean?" I asked. It was only the two of us; the wives and children had all gone to bed.

"Well, the way it used to be, Babsie didn't really exist by herself. You know, she didn't have any—what do you call, you know, call what you are?"

"Identity?"

"Yeah, right. She didn't have any herself. She was just The Grey Ghost's girl friend and then The Grey Ghost's wife."

"Okay," I said. "Now what?"

"Well now, you know: She's herself. But I'm not. I'm just the guy who used to be The Grey Ghost."

"Is that what you want, Gavin?"

"Hell no. But that's all people want me to be."

SO, FOR THE "season," which ran from March clear into November, Gavin preferred to play golf. Pine Lakes had hired a "name" pro, old Charlie Eversoll, who had won a number of tournaments years before on the PGA tour, and Gavin enjoyed hanging around with Charlie, betting Nassaus and so forth. Charlie had an assistant, but he quit, and the way it happened then, quite unintentionally, Gavin just sort of turned into the assistant. For something to do, he began to run the golf shop, to assign caddies, and to fill in whenever members were looking for a fourth.

For the first time in many years, certainly for the first time since he left football, Gavin was happy. "Damn," he told Babs one night, "now they've started talkin' about goin' out and hirin' a new assistant for old Charlie."

And so, the next day, after her work, without a word to Gavin, Babs called up and then went over to see St. George Randolph at his office out at Pine Lakes. St. George was a clever fellow, a man born to the salt, but, largely through his playing football with the hoi polloi, he had learned what the middle-class masses wanted. "What I am, Donnie, I'm a pimp for taste," St. George succinctly explained to me once.

He had known Babs for years, of course; for a time he had even had a romance with a classmate of hers at the W.C. and so he had double-dated a lot with Gavin and her. So he was delighted that she had dropped by, and they had a drink and cut up about old times. This was fine with Babs, too, because she was nervous to bring up right away what was on her mind. Under more normal circumstances, though, she was confident and self-possessed now, for she had been an immediate success working for Blue in eastern Carolina—had done so well that, after a year or so, when Bridget Blue got pregnant, Blue had brought Babs into his office to replace his wife as his executive assistant. As Blue's franchise operation expanded, there were times when he was away, going after new business, and Babs became, in effect, the head of a large operation herself.

Finally, another bourbon in her, Babs got up her nerve. "I came here to ask you a favor, Saint," she said.

"Sure."

"Hire Gavin as Charlie Eversoll's assistant."

"Jesus, I can't make The Grey Ghost some kind of goddamn caddy master."

"But that's what he *wants*. Just let him keep the title. Let him stay as vice-president of, uh—"

"Water holes," Randolph laughed.

"That's right," Babs said. "Pay him whatever an assistant pro gets, and introduce him as a vice-president. Nobody gets hurt."

"Well, if that's what The Grey Ghost wants," he said, clucking approval. He got out of his seat now and came closer to her, bending down. "But Babs, I want something from you, too."

St. George Randolph would no more proposition Babs Rogers, The Grey Ghost's girl, than he would try to fly to the moon. But his words were poorly chosen, and Babs took them for that. "Saint, you sonuvabitch, you," she said, and she smacked him flush across the face.

Randolph was completely taken aback, because he did not know what had set Babs off. Instead, he just stood there, buffaloed, his mouth hanging open, staring at her. Babs only stared back, defiantly, and then she rose and turned her back to him. "Go on, you bastard," she said, gesturing to the zipper up the back of her dress, "take it off."

At last, now St. George understood the confusion. "Babsie," he said softly, "for God's sake, I didn't mean that."

She was so worked up she didn't really hear him. "What?" she snapped.

Gently, making sure there could be no mistake, he put one hand on her shoulder, turning her toward him. As soon as she was facing him, he quickly withdrew his hand. "How could you ever think I would say a thing like that?"

"You didn't mean that?"

"God, no, Babs!"

"Ohhh, no," she sighed, and collapsed back into the chair. "I'm sorry, Saint. I—" And she lowered her head into her hand.

But now a larger realization hit Randolph. "But you would have done it . . . to get Gavin that job." Babs raised her head; she said nothing, only looked at him. "Oh my God, I'm sorry for you, Babsie," he said at last. "I didn't know it was that bad."

"He just can't find himself," she said. "It's only . . . uh, a . . . phase."

Randolph nodded, to be polite. Then he went over to his desk and poured another drink for himself. "Okay, the job is his. The title, everything. All right?"

Babs managed a smile. She was crying a little, too. "I better go," she said. He nodded, and she rose. She paused, then, remembering. "What did you want of me, Saint? I mean, really."

"Maybe we ought to forget that for now."

"No, please. This was all my fault."

"Well, I know what kind of job you're doing, Babs. We have a position that's about to open here, and it's yours if you want it." The job was as director of food operations for all of Pine Lakes. There was a restaurant, a club lounge, snack bars, and a great deal of catering. There was also more money in it for Babs, and, as Randolph said, "I think you'll be more congenial here than working for those nigras."

Babs accepted the job, but she did not tell Gavin, or anyone else (except Narvel) for weeks, because she did not want people to think that her arrangement had anything to do with The Grey Ghost becoming the assistant pro.

GAVIN BECAME, OF course, a superb golfer, scratch, and I'm certain that he was accurate in believing that had he played golf as a child he could have made the tour and proved every bit as good on the links as he had been on the gridiron. "And then I'd still be playing," he said, brightening. I let that pass.

The golf was healthy for him. It kept him out-of-doors and relatively trim. When the Tarheels celebrated with their silver anniversary reunion, a great many of them were horribly over-weight. Part of this was a function of what they had been as players—stuffed. Finegan, for example, resembled a beached whale. He had moved to Arizona and opened up gay bars there, and now he dressed in all that shiny, plasticky Sunbelt white, neo-rhinestone, which only accentuated his size. But, then, a great many old athletes seem to let themselves go once they re-tire just because there is no practical reason any longer for stay-ing "in shape." They had grown up impressed with the under-standing that to stay svelte and strong was singularly beneficial for them as a player, and so, ipso facto, once you were no longer a player there was no need to trouble catering to your body, your player's shell.

Gavin was a little pudgy in spots—let's say ruddy—but only from frequenting so many nineteenth holes. He drank too much in the sense he took too many drinks, but he didn't drink too much, to excess. Babs didn't drink nearly as much as Gavin, but she drank too much, sometimes. She would come home—well, after a hard day at the office—take care of the kids, fix dinner, and then kick off her shoes and make herself a drink, waiting for Gavin. But he would still be at the nineteenth hole, so she would have another drink or two.

He would come home happy, not a worry in the world this side of par, and try to take her to bed. And she would not want to go. "I've been sitting here, and I had three drinks just waiting for you."

"Hey, that's not my fault. I have to stay with the members. That's part of my job. I can't just play eighteen and then walk away like I'm gettin' off a bus."

"I'm sorry, Gavin, I haven't even had dinner yet."

And he would stop pawing at her and storm away. "Goddamn women, if they didn't have cunts, we'd have a bounty out on y'all." So Babs would have another drink and go to bed without her dinner.

But, everything is relative. Gavin's real narcotic was nostalgia, and on account of that, everybody around him drank more. Listening to him. He also took to diagramming old plays on tablecloths.

I arrived at Pine Lakes one day direct from Charlottesville, and though I saw Gavin ensconced at a table across the way, I went first to the men's room. Two guys were at the urinals there. "A moment's peace at last," said one.

"Jesus, I feel sort of sorry for the old guy," said the other. "He can't get out of 1954."

I ducked into a stall until they were gone. *Old guy.* This was 1973 and Gavin was barely past his fortieth birthday at that time, and yet there was indeed the sense that he had lived so long ago. To look at him as he talked was disconcerting, for the voice, the memories, seemed to come from somewhere else, disconnected. Occasionally he would outright refer to himself in the third person, as if he really were talking about somebody else, but most times he was more subtle, and he developed this gimmick, whereby he recreated a great deal of verbatim conversation, with these other third parties constantly calling him by his legendary name: The Ghost, The Grey Ghost—he would find ways to say it.

"So Paul turns to me in the huddle, and he says, 'What about it, Ghost?' And the other guys are saying, 'Yeah, give it to The Ghost again,' stuff like that. And he calls the play for me, and we come outta the huddle and Finegan says, 'Go get 'em, Ghost,' and he took the big guy outside and I cut past the cornerback, turned on the gas and went for six. And get this: You can hear the PA. He doesn't say, 'Grey scores.' No, he just says, 'The Grey Ghosstttt!' Like that." Gavin slapped his knee at the fond memory, and the words sounded so good he smiled and said them again, ostensibly quoting the PA: "The Grey Ghosstttt!"

The others nodded, and the best of them forced smiles. Babs was with him this night. Her face was vacant, her mind off somewhere, and she very much resembled a politician's wife, listening to her husband deliver his stock stump speech for the four-hundredth time. So, practically speaking, however large the crowd, Gavin soloed. His reminiscences neither had anything to do with response nor did they possess any natural flow to them. And Gavin never related them to anything else in the universe. None of the people in the stories, the other players, were ever identified as anything but what they were in 1954—players. Gavin never said, "Terry Winstead, the left end—you know Terry's president of Wachovia Trust in Charlotte now." Nothing like that. Terry Winstead was only and forever number eighty-three, frozen.

After this one particular evening at Pine Lakes, listening to Gavin, Karen and I went back to their house and just fell into bed. It had been a long day, and Karen was still dead asleep when I woke up the next morning, so finally I got up myself and went downstairs. Babs was fixing breakfast, alone. "Oh, Cake, I'm sorry about last night," she said, even before "good morning."

"What?"

"Oh, you don't have to be polite on my account. Gavin just about drove you two to bed."

"No, we were just exhausted, from the drive and everything."

She shook her head, woefully. "You know, if he just wouldn't be so repetitious. I know every wife has to put up with every husband being boring about *something*."

"Well, he only does it when he's had a couple drinks."

"Hmmm. That's the benign view, I'm afraid. The booze doesn't change him, it just unleashes him. Given his druthers, I think he'd like to talk about the past all the time."

"Oh, come on, don't be so harsh."

"I know, I know, Donnie. Gavin doesn't own the exclusive rights to tedium. Good God, I've got friends who jog, and who *must* tell you about that, and they're ten times more boring than Gavin. It's just that when he gets going, the past excludes everything else." And softer now, looking away: "It's so ironic, too. People imagine that when you're famous, when it's happening to you, that then you're vain. He wasn't."

"Not at all."

"No. That's the funny thing. He took it all in stride then. He cared so much about other people. Remember?"

I nodded; I sure did remember. "He took a great interest in me then, when I was a kid."

"Yeah, and everybody. And he still loves you, Donnie. He loves you and respects you, and he's so proud of you, what you've be-come. But it's detached. He really doesn't have an interest in you anymore. Not in an involved way."

"Damnit, Babsie, you're being unfair. He always asks about Karen, about the kids, about Mom—"

"His own sister. Big deal." She shrugged, backing off a little. "Well, all right, he's best with family."

"Your kids all love him. They adore their father," I said.

"Yes, he's a good friend to them," Babs said—pointedly, no more—and she turned back to the stove. She knew she didn't have to say any more to me. She ran the house and ran the family, and Gavin never really exerted himself as a father. With Tommy, the oldest, my godson, he was the least close. But that was not all bad, and, even, somewhat calculated. Tommy was born in 1956, when Gavin was at the height of his powers and fame, and as a little boy he was very cognizant that his father was a sports star; and Gavin understood that Tommy understood this, appreciating that the closer he grew to the boy, the harder it would have been for him, the more pressure he would have felt to be like the father.

Tommy was not badly coordinated, either. For all I know he might have become a fairly good athlete, but Gavin—and Babs too, in her way—never encouraged him at sports, and it passed him by. There were even times when Gavin would say, "Tommy, be like your Cousin Donnie." And once, after I came in from chucking a baseball around with the kid, Gavin told me: "Hey, I hope you're not doin' that for my benefit. I'd rather you read him something."

"He's not a bad player."

"Listen, Donnie, Tommy's never gonna be as good as me, and if he's just a little good and likes sports, it'll kill him."

"Are you sure?"

"Yeah," he said. This was his last season with the Redskins. "Because I'm just a little good now, and it kills me to be compared to me." And he winked.

As I said, the best players almost never make the best coaches. But say this: The best players make better sports fathers. It's analogous to stage mothers: It's the ones who never really succeed on the stage who become the stage mothers. And it's the athletes who rode the bench or failed to make the team at all who invariably take an overriding interest in the athletic well-being of their sons and their alma maters. But by the time Russell Finegan, the youngest of the three children, started to grow up, just enough time had passed; Gavin had left the limelight, and he was not afraid to encourage the boy some in sports. But never football. Not that. Shoot baskets, play baseball catch. But not football, not even touch.

Russell became a good soccer player, and was good enough at lacrosse, eventually, to start at midfield for the Washington and Lee varsity. And strictly from playing with his father, Russ developed into an outstanding golfer; he had a helluva good short game. Father and son suckered a lot of people, playing best-ball foursomes, because Gavin was long off the tee, and then Russ would get it on in two, and they could both putt well.

Gavin loved that more than anything, playing golf with his boy, and sometimes, if they won a close match, he would rush over and hug and *kiss* his son. In front of strangers. Russ was sixteen or seventeen at this time, and that would absolutely mortify him. Finally, he told his father that in no uncertain terms: No more kissing at all, and, ideally, if you can possibly manage it, no more hugging either. "For Chrissakes, Russ," Gavin said, "nobody's gonna think you're a faggot just because your old man kisses you."

"Yeah, Dad, but everybody knows you're not a faggot because you were an All-American. They don't know about me." Gavin roared at that and blew him a kiss with a limp wrist.

Allison, the girl in the middle, was the spitting image of Babs, and the two of them were much closer as mother and daughter than Gavin ever was to either of his sons. Nonetheless, it is especially revealing that when Allison got knocked up her senior year in high school, she went to her father. He was at the clubhouse at Pine Lakes when she came in out of the blue and asked to talk to him. Gavin just about guessed what it was going to be about, and so he took her for a walk out on the eighteenth fairway, by the water hazard there. And when Allison told him, he didn't swoon or criticize her or ask her a bunch of stupid questions; he didn't even ask her who, because she was only going out with the one boy. He just hugged her and promised her that he would get it taken care of right away.

Then Gavin called Finegan and got him to arrange for an abortion in New York. Gavin told Babs that he was being honored with a memory-lane award by the New York football writers, and he was going to take his daughter with him instead of his wife, because Allison had never really spent any time in New York. Babs thought that was sweet of him and never even imagined a thing. Gavin and Allison had an especially good time, too, because, as it turned out, she wasn't pregnant after all; she had merely overreacted. She was hardly back to the hotel from going to the doctor in Queens that Finegan had set up, when her period started. Gavin had to run down and buy some Tampax.

Finally, chagrined, Allison came out of the bathroom. "Well, anyway," she said, "now you know about me and Blake, Daddy."

Gavin was lying on the bed, reading the sports page. "Yeah, you sure let the cat out of the bag."

"Daddy. . . . " Allison said.

"Yeah, sweetheart?"

"Mom never did it when she was my age, did she?"

"No, not till she married me."

"I guess she's better than me, huh?"

"Naw, honey, I reckon it's just that Blake's better'n me." And he got up, laughing, and hugged Allison.

When they got back to North Carolina, though, Gavin told Allison he wanted to see the boy, and when Blake came to the house, he was, naturally, scared to death. "You tell your daddy about this?" Gavin asked.

"No, sir."

"Your momma?"

"Oh, no, sir."

"Well then, I ain't gonna tell 'em either."

"You aren't?" the boy cried. He could hardly believe it.

"Unless maybe you told somebody else," Gavin said.

"No, no, sir. I didn't," Blake said, lowering his eyes.

"Because if you told another soul, I'm gonna go to your father, and I'm gonna tell him, and you know what I'm gonna tell him?" Silence. "Do you know?"

"No, sir."

"I'm gonna say, 'Mr. Porter, you are common as cat shit.'" The boy gasped. "What do you think about that?" The boy shrugged, hopelessly. "Yeah, that's what I'm gonna tell him, because it means he didn't teach you any manners. Hey, we all got peckers, son, and sometimes they get hard, and a hard-on ain't got no conscience, and I ain't sayin' maybe Allison got carried away too, so that's one thing, but if you go around runnin' off at the mouth about it, then you can't use your hot pecker as an excuse. Then you're just common and your daddy's common for not teachin' you any better manners."

The boy was turning white. Gavin went on: "But since you didn't tell a livin' soul, then we got nothin' to worry about. Right?"

"That's right," Blake said, but barely.

Gavin stood up then—made a big show of it, as a matter of fact—and came over to where the boy sat. "You're lyin' through your teeth, son."

Blake swallowed and tried, with only some success, to shake his head.

"Yeah, you are. I'll tell you why. Because you're a good-lookin' boy, and you're popular, and you're a hot-shot athlete, and you got a lot of friends, and even with all that, it took you some kind of long time to get my daughter's cherry, and there wasn't no way, once you did, you weren't goin' to tell *some*body. Now isn't that right?"

Blake thought the former All-American was going to do him in. He cowered. "Yes, sir," he breathed.

"And then when you thought you knocked her up, you were scared out of your mind, and you had to tell someone that, too, didn't you?"

"Yes, sir."

"Was it the same guy? One good friend?"

"Yes, sir."

"What's his name?"

"Eddie."

"Eddie who?"

"Eddie Steele."

"Does Eddie go runnin' off at the mouth?"

"No, sir."

"Are you positive?"

"Pretty."

"Well, let me ask you this, Is Eddie getting any pussy himself?"

Blake looked up, mouth opened. This was a line of interroga-tion he had not anticipated.

"Well, is he?" Gavin asked.

"I think so," the boy said.

"Think so, my ass," Gavin replied. "If he knows you're getting it, you goddamn well know whether he's getting it. Right?"

"Yes, sir."

"Well, is he?"

"Yes, sir."

"Is it one girl, or is this Eddie a read stud?" Blake didn't say any-thing. "Come on, is it one girl or is Eddie fuckin' everything that moves?"

"It's one girl."

"Yeah, what's her name?"

Blake looked up, but he only set his chin. "Do I *have* to tell you?"

"I asked you her name."

"Please, Mr. Grey," Blake said.

Gavin looked at the boy, but slowly his expression softened, metamorphosing into an avuncular grin. Then he laid a kindly hand on the boy's shoulder. It was the first time he had touched him, and, reflexively, Blake jumped. "It's okay, son," Gavin said. Blake stole a look up again. "I don't want to know her name." And he patted him again. "You're a good man." The boy bowed his head. "It's okay now. If you wouldn't tell on your buddy, then I think you're tellin' me the truth; I don't think you told anybody else. And if Eddie's gettin' it from the one girl, and you know about that, and you don't wanta tell about him, then I don't think he's gonna talk about you and Allison. Right?"

Blake sighed. "God, you know everything, sir."

"I didn't play football *all* the damn time," Gavin said.

"Yes, sir."

"Now, when you leave here, you make a beeline for Eddie, and you tell him that if he ever opens his mouth—"

"Yes, sir!" Blake cried out, taking that as an invitation to clear out. Gavin stopped him. "You bring Allison in here first."

Blake edged back in the room with her. "Now," Gavin said, "this is our little secret. We ain't tellin' anybody. Not Mrs. Grey, not your parents, not nobody. Now, besides me, Allison, did you tell anybody?"

"Well, you know, Deidre."

"Oh, yeah," Gavin said. "I know Deidre. She goes out with Eddie Steel, doesn't she?"

Allison said, "Yes," but Gavin had already turned to look to Blake. They started giggling. "Daddy! What is it?" she cried, mystified.

"Just between us men," Gavin said, laughing all the more. "But listen"—he turned back to Allison—"you get in touch with Deidre and get to see her doctor."

"What doctor?"

"The woman's doctor, for Chrissake, Allison. To get some pills or somethin'!"

Allison looked horrified. "Blake!" she screamed. "What did you tell him about Deidre?"

The boy looked, hopelessly, to Gavin, and Gavin looked at Allison. "He didn't tell me anything. Nothing. This is a good man, sweetheart. And lemme tell you both somethin': No man—*no* man—is a gentleman below the belt. You understand that?" They both nodded. "You see, I sympathize with you two," Gavin went on. "Back when I was a kid—and your momma, sweetheart, and your momma and daddy, son—it was much easier. There was only two kinds of girls. There was nice girls and there was punchboards. And you never said a bad word about a nice girl. You know why?"

They both shook their heads.

"Because you couldn't. If you screwed a nice girl—pardon my French, darling—but if you did, then that made her a punchboard. So you couldn't say anything bad about a nice girl, because if there was anything bad to say about her, then she wasn't a nice girl. She was a punchboard."

"You mean, I'm a punchboard?" Allison gasped, nearly coming to tears.

Gavin put his arm about her. "No, no. That's what I'm sayin'. You would have been a punchboard if you lived in the olden days. But not now. That's my point. It's changed. The nice girls screw now, too. Just like the nice boys. It's just that you guys—you gentlemen—have got to keep on treatin' 'em like nice girls—like ladies—even after the screwin'. You understand, son?"

"Yes, sir."

"Okay," Gavin said, and with that, Blake started to head out again. "Where ya goin'?"

"I'm goin' to talk to Eddie . . . sir."

Gavin laughed. Then he turned to his daughter. "Don't you ever do anything like this to me again."

"Do . . . what, Daddy?"

"Do somethin' so I can't tell your mother somethin'. Okay?"

"Okay." And Allison fell into his arms and told him he was the best daddy in all the world.

I DIDN'T KNOW that story at the time I was talking to Babs in her kitchen that morning. I didn't hear it until about five or six years later, when Allison was out of college, a grown young lady. That was the first time Babs heard of it, too. Allison told it to both of us at the same time.

But in the kitchen, I only said to Babs, "Well, so long as his family loves a man, it can't be much worth worrying about him."

"Yeah, I know, Donnie, but I still wish he took more interest in people."

"What people?"

"People people. People in 1976. He doesn't care about our next-door neighbor, but he can tell you the name of the third-string fullback for Maryland in 1953."

"Oh, come on," I said, and since we were standing there together, next to the stove, I kind of threw my arm around her, and she nestled for a moment on my shoulder, being careful not to hit me with the spatula.

Gavin said, "It's kinda early to y'all to be talkin' about a body behind his back, ain't it?" I don't know how long he'd been standing there at the door, unshaven, in his pajama bottoms.

I flushed and smiled foolishly, withdrawing my arm from about Babs, but she replied directly to him, and without any embarrassment, "I've told you before, Precious, you get a few drinks in you, and you start to talk too much about yourself, the past."

He stepped into the kitchen. "The trouble with you, Babsie, is that you just don't understand. Folks enjoy hearin' about The Grey Ghost." she didn't respond, so he stepped closer. "Yeah, the trouble is, Babsie, you're just plain jealous."

"Oh, get lost, Gavin," Babs said pleasantly, "I haven't got time to hear that when I'm trying to make breakfast."

"No, I'm serious. You were the goddamn Blueberry Queen, and you wanted to be Miss North Carolina, and just because you met me and never got to be Miss North Carolina, you're mad because I was everybody's All-American."

"Well, if it means living in the past, then I'm glad I was never Miss North Carolina."

"You're just not a sports fan, Babsie. Sports fans like to, uh, you know—what do they call it? Come on, Donnie, you're the professor. What do they call it?"

"Reminisce?" I ventured.

"Yeah, right." He came over and swiped a piece of bacon and kind of jabbed it at me before he ate it. "Damn you two. Always *talkin'*. In here huggin'. If you weren't my kin, Donnie, I'd have to worry." He laughed heartily. "I gotta shave."

He left. I looked at Babs in horror. "Oh, don't worry. He doesn't have any idea. I promise," she said, and I walked away from her, to the other side of the kitchen, as if it were proper to keep our distance when discussing our night of glorious sin from long ago. Then she turned to face me. "But let me tell you something, Donnie McClure. I should have told him. I should have told him about me that time I wanted to."

"After the thing with the Kielys."

"Right, then, honey chile. I knew I should've, and you talked me out of it."

"If you'd've told him, he'd've left you."

"Maybe, maybe," Babs said. "Maybe that was the price. But it would've been worth it, because he never would've taken anything for granted again, and he would've grown up."

"I guess I was wrong then."

"You were. Oh, it would've broken Gavin's heart, but hell, he would've gotten over that. And it would've buried The Grey Ghost for good. Amen."

So probably Babs was right. All that seemed to concern Gavin anymore was his place in history, especially as defined by modern measures. What he longed for most of all was to be featured in a commercial, coast-to-coast. His cap was really set for Miller Lite Beer. That was his goal.

It is against ethics-and-standards practices for athletes to endorse beer, but since beer drinkers are so attuned to sports, ad agencies do the next best thing and search out former athletes for these sudsy testimonials. It would destroy Gavin when he would turn on the television and see some old colleague pitching for beer—or cereal or tires, antifreeze, whatever. "Why would they use Nick?" he would moan. "That sonuvabitch wasn't half the player The Grey Ghost was." Sometimes, then, Gavin would go on to cite statistics and specific play-by-play highlights to buttress this judgment.

"Well, you know, it's not just how good a player he was," I would say, trying to explain, gingerly. "It has a lot to do with his image, where he played, crap like that."

"The Tarheels were national champions! And I was the MVP in the pros. One of the best. With a cellar team."

"Well, you know, Gavin, a lot of it has to do with who you know. They probably picked Nick just because he drinks with the right guy at the ad agency."

"Shit, that's just not fair," Gavin said. "I deserve it." The great American dream, once removed to the late twentieth century: the little boy who dreams about growing up to be president so then he can write his White House autobiography and make millions. Or the athlete who thrills a nation with his exploits so that he might qualify to make a commercial in his middle age.

After I explained to Gavin about how personal contacts were crucial to getting on commercials, he would ask just about everybody he met, especially those from New York—and never mind if they happened to be dentists or airplane pilots on early retirement—if they knew the people responsible for casting celebrity commercials, especially the Lite Beer commercials. "I could do the Tastes Better part or I could do the Less Filling part," Gavin said. "I could do either."

Even better, he allowed, he would like to be the national spokesman, alone, for some coast-to-coast product. A lot of old athletes were coming up with this kind of plum. Gavin would turn on the TV to watch the football or the golf, and not only would he go berserk with envy watching the Lite Beer commercials, but some other commercial would come on, with another, less prominent former athlete front and center, touting it.

"Goddamn, look at that," he cried. "Why would they pick his ass, Donnie? Him? You'd think someone who saw me when I was playing would pick me as a national spokesman. Or a national spokesperson. Either one. Wouldn't you think?"

17

THE REASON WHY KAREN AND I WERE VISITING the Greys this particular time was because Gavin was being taken into another hall of fame. There are a wealth of sports halls of fame in America—and a number of walls of fame, as well—and, at a certain point, once a decent interval had passed from his active playing days, Gavin would be, as he always referred to it, "inducted into the shrine."

You would have thought that this would have soothed his ego, and, temporarily at least, it would. Better, of course, to be acknowledged seriously, to be asked to hustle after-shave on national television; better still to be a national spokesman, or national spokesperson; but, lacking that, halls of fame had to do.

My role with The Grey Ghost had been formally certified. While it is true enough that Gavin's interest in me may have dimmed, one aspect of my professional life had come to enthrall him. He had always thought of me as a member of the intelligentsia—a student, and then a professor—and if he took any note of my early published historical treatises, he never mentioned it. They were merely printed extensions of the classroom. But a book I wrote about Jefferson Davis and Abraham Lincoln had a certain widespread appeal, at least in the South, and it appeared in a smattering of commercial bookstores. Like a country-and-western crooner who made it with a song on the pop charts, I had "passed over." One day, when Gavin entered his neighborhood bookstore to pick up a Hallmark birthday card for one of his children, he was amazed to see my book there alongside bona fide titles with half-dressed women on the dust covers. The very next time he encountered me, he suggested we write a book together.

"Oh what?" I said, puzzled altogether.

"On me," he responded. "You know, on The Grey Ghost. On my life and times."

"Oh, yeah."

"It's easy," he explained. "I'll talk into the tape recorder, and then you write it down."

Luckily I had just agreed to do the work on Jeb Stuart, which had always been in my mind, and not only because of the similarities that the judge had distinguished for me between battlefield and gridiron cavaliers. "I couldn't do it till I'm finished the Stuart book, Gavin."

"Sure, how long'll that be?"

"About three years, I guess."

"Three fucking years? To write a book? What the fuck you gonna do, carve it in stone?"

"Well, I still have some research to do, and I can't work on it full-time. I have to teach, too."

Gavin shook his head. "Well, I'll tell you what, Donnie. We can start to work on it now. You know, whenever we see one another, we can do some of the recording. I can start to relive the memories on tape."

I shrugged. Since this is what Gavin already did much of his time, on an amateur basis, he might as well turn pro at it and play for pay. Besides, for my part, the exercise would hardly be unpleasant; after two more years of General Stuart and the Army of

Northern Virginia, I would welcome a respite from the War between the States. I'd worry about a publisher then. Gavin, though,
jumped right in. He began referring to me, rather grandiosely, as
"my autobiographer."

Gavin had already been accepted in the Professional Football
Hall of Fame, which is located in Canton, in northern Ohio. This
took place shortly after he had induced me to become his autobiographer, but I was unable to attend the ceremonies. But the very
next year, 1976, he was chosen to enter a college football hall of
fame, which proudly belongs to southern Ohio, and Gavin was so
insistent on me attending that it was impossible for me to avoid.
Besides, as it occurred to me, I wanted my children to see something of The Grey Ghost's glory, even if it was only him being
handed a scroll, and so we all drove down from Charlottesville to
Chapel Hill and flew out to Cincinnati from there. It was Babs
and Gavin, Karen and me, our two kids, and young Russell, who
was fifteen then and would serve as something of a baby-sitter
for our pair.

This particular hall of fame was located as a classy adjunct to an
amusement park, just off the interstate somewhere between
Cincinnati and Columbus. The hall was down the road from a
campgrounds and the sprawling motel where we stayed. For some
reason, the motel was done in a German motif, but the hall of
fame was in the red-brick colonial style, calling up more dignified
and very collegiate images.

It was the middle of the summer, broiling hot when we arrived,
and Gavin and I went out by the pool with our tape recorder. We
took a quick dip, then found a place in the shade and Gavin started
telling me about the Maryland game his senior year. We were up to
that by now.

This particular contest was, you may recall, one of his most pedestrian adventures. "You know," I said, "the Maryland game came right after you hurt yourself racing Narvel Blue. Let's talk about that some."

Gavin was flabbergasted at this bizarre suggestion. "Why?"

"Well, you know, that was interesting, beating Blue out there at the Three Corners."

"Ain't nobody know who Narvel Blue is."

"No, a lot of people who saw him say—"

"He only played at that little nigra high school."

"Yeah, but he's gone and become real successful. There's even talk Blue's gonna run for Congress."

"Hey, I like that old boy," Gavin said, "but none of that got anything to do with my life and times on the gridiron." He was truly mystified at my introducing this totally extraneous matter.

"Well, you know, I just thought—"

"Shoot, Donnie, we don't beat the Terrapins, who's to say we make the Sugar Bowl? We gotta talk about that game."

"Well, okay," I said, and I flipped the tape recorder back on.

"We won the toss and elected to receive," Gavin began, predictably. The trouble was, in his official memoir voice he was even more inclined to speak as if he were announcing, or reading an old newspaper account. "The kicker approached the ball with his educated toe and sent it end over end deep into Tarheel territory. Big Eye-talian, named Battaglia, number eighty-seven for the Terrapins. You can look up his first name. Good kicker. Naturally, he kicked away from me. Emerson took the ball on the five and started upfield. He got to the twenty-two when he was upended, and we—"

Abruptly, Gavin halted his recitation. It was curious. I stopped listening at the very same moment that he stopped talking. All around the pool, there was a rustle, and then a hush. Gavin and I looked up, and we saw that Babs was coming from across the way in a white bathing suit with red trim. This was 1976; I remember that distinctly, because Gavin kept referring to himself as a "Bicentennial selection" of this particular hall of fame, and at that time the prevailing fashion called almost exclusively for two-piece suits.

Babs's was one-piece, almost demure if considered rationally, but, in fact, she appeared far sexier, more ravishing than all the other women about, strings and flesh. She walked on the balls of her feet, as if she were in high heels, coming down a runway, and all that she moved was her head, almost imperceptibly, just enough to avert the eyes of everyone looking at her. She was as gloriously tanned as ever, as much as she had been that summer in Delaware sixteen years ago, and although she was past forty now, there were no flaws I could discern. I looked carefully at her legs, the thighs. They always say about athletes: The legs go first. That is one more thing athletes and pretty girls share. Babs still had her legs.

"Look at her," Gavin said, and in an outrageously lascivious tone, as if she were some stranger he was ogling.

"She's beautiful," I said, but sotto voce, doing my best not to sound lustful—merely objective—myself.

"I tell you what, Donnie, she's as good-looking now as she was when I first seen her at the W.C." I did not dispute this. Even the women were staring at her now, with envy, and in an odd way it seemed as if they were covering themselves up more, as if they were embarrassed to be displaying themselves so prominently in comparison.

Babs broke out in a big smile as she neared us. "Hi, Precious," she said, and I was quick to respond, hoping, as always before, that those about who did not remember The Grey Ghost might think she was addressing me with that endearing name. "What y'all doin'?"

"We're up to the Maryland game, my senior year," Gavin said.

"Truthfully, I don't remember that one," Babs said.

"Oh, it was pretty important," I hastened to say. "The Tarheels don't win that one, maybe they don't go to the Sugar Bowl."

"Well, I don't want to bother y'all," she said. "I'm just going to lay over yonder with Karen and get some sun." My wife was sitting on a lounge across the pool, watching our kids. Babs turned away to go over there.

Then Gavin called to her softly, "Babs." She turned back, and with that, he beckoned to her with one hand. She came over close to him and stared at him for the moment, and then when he reached up and took her by the back of the neck, she bowed down and kissed him hard upon the lips. It was such an odd thing to do, to kiss your wife in earnest, mouth open, in the sun, before a poolside crowd staring at you.

"I love you, Babsie," he said softly. "Always did."

"I always loved you, Precious," she said, and then she turned back and walked away, gliding without a break in her motion.

"Can't believe how good-looking that woman still is," Gavin said. "Goddamnit, someone as pretty as that shouldn't be working."

"She likes to work. She's done well."

"She shouldn't work. I've never gotten over that."

"You could have taken that job she did, with Narvel."

He stared at me, incredulous. "I couldn't go all over eastern Carolina, on the road, lookin' up folks. When you're an everybody's All-American, Donnie, there's only so much you can do."

"I guess that's true," I said.

"Sure. That's why I want to get me one of those commercials. Then you get money all the time. What do you call those things?" I shook my head. "Come on, you're the professor."

"What things?"

"You know, when they show it over and over."

"Residuals."

"Yeah, those. Or even better, if I get to be a national spokesman or a national spokesperson, Babsie wouldn't never have to work again." He shaded his eyes with a hand on his forehead, and looked at her across the way, as she settled down on a chaise. "Good Lord in heaven, she is somethin' for a body to behold. You know what I noticed the other day?"

"No, what?" I asked, really curious now. He spoke so genuinely now after the flat, artificially cadenced account of his old games.

"Her nipples," he declared flat out. I didn't say anything. "Hey, I don't wanna be common, Donnie. But I just hadn't put my mind to those nipples in a long time. Everything else's go good, the nipples just got lost in the shuffle. You know how it is."

"Yeah."

"Now, you see these little old girls walkin' around without any bras, showin' their nipples through their shirts, and I feel like goin' up and sayin': 'Hey, girl, don't show me your nipples. I've *seen* nipples. I've *lived* with nipples.' And, oh, nipples. I'll tell you somethin' about nipples now, Donnie. Not Babs's nipples. *Nipples,* you know?"

"Yeah?"

"I'll bet you never even told Karen how much you admire her nipples."

"Well, I—"

"I mean, I don't know. . . . "

"About Karen's?"

"Right," he said. "But you very rarely see a bad nipple."

"Very rarely," I agreed. And then we sat there, contemplating; penny for your thoughts. I hardly heard Gavin when he finally said: "Turn it back on."

"What?"

"The tape recorder."

"What about it?"

"Turn it back on."

"Oh, yeah." I punched the button, and he took right up where he had let off. "So's after Emerson was upended, we went into the huddle, and Paul says, 'Okay, Ghost, we'll—'" and Gavin was off and running, and he went on for a few more plays until the Tarheels were obliged to punt after a holding penalty, but it was clear that he didn't have his heart in it. And after North Carolina got the ball back and decided to try a flat pass, Gavin gave up the effort altogether. He sat up straight and said, "Ah, fuck the Terrapin game, Donnie."

"What?" I wasn't listening all that closely.

"I'm just tired of all this stuff and nonsense," he said, and he got up from his chair and purposefully, without a word, headed for Babs. The pool was in between. He dove into the shallow end, flat out, his body barely breaking the surface, and he came up stroking—clean, long strokes that carried him to the other side in a flash, and in such a perfect manner that his lead arm ended up on the side of the pool and he was able to pull himself out all in one motion. The sun glistened off his dripping back, and by now, everyone was looking at The Grey Ghost in much the same way as they had stared at Babs. In fact, some of the older people were saying: "That's The Grey Ghost. He's going into the Hall of Fame tomorrow," and things such as that.

Babs was oblivious, eyes closed against the sun, but when he touched her on her shoulder with his wet hand, she did not start. She knew it was Gavin, and she only opened her eyes and smiled. Perhaps he whispered something to her, too, although I could not tell from across the way. Whatever, she quickly got up, and they walked off in a hurry, together. Yet they did not touch: not so much as a hand. There was no need to, for they possessed such a neon sexuality in how they moved, in how they looked, that there could not have been an adult at poolside who did not know that these two people were going off to make love right away. Some of the mothers began to splash about and push at the rubber rafts in order to create a distraction so that the children would be diverted from such a blatantly erotic scene.

A COUPLE HOURS later, Babs and Gavin showed up on time for the cocktail party that preceded the dinner honoring the inductees. They were both dressed to the nines, the cynosure of every eye, Babs exuding the kind of radiance that seemed to shine brighter and reflect on him each time he so much as looked over at her. When the festivities were over, they did not linger so that Gavin might tell more tales to the worshipful cronies, but instead, repaired immediately to their room.

We were next door, our two kids and Russell in another room down the hall. The walls were not thick, and even as Karen and I began to undress, we could hear the sounds of Gavin and Babs. The bed began to creak with their efforts at love. At first, I tried to ignore it. Karen was brushing her teeth, and perhaps quiet would be restored by the time she turned off the water.

She came out of the bathroom during a lull, and I smiled at her. "What are you staring at?" she said.

"I'm not staring," I protested.

"Yes, you are, you're staring at my boobs."

"No, I'm not."

"Don't make me self-conscious. I know they're not much."

I held up my hands in frustration. "No, I've told you, darling. That's not true. I've always liked your boobs."

"You don't have to go on like this just for my benefit," she said.

"I wasn't," I cried. "I wasn't looking at your boobs."

"You were too," she said, and to outflank me, she crossed her arms across her chest.

"No, I wasn't looking at your boobs, because I was looking at your nipples."

That confused her, and she sort of peeked down beneath her arms to check herself out. "Why?"

"I don't know. They're just very beautiful. That's all."

Karen dropped her arms to her side and smiled broadly at me. "You never said that before."

"Well, that's my fault. I guess we all take too many things for granted. My health, your nipples, et cetera."

She stood up straight, thrusting her nipples out, although I'm not sure she was conscious that she was doing that. "Oh, Don, darling, that's very sweet," and she stepped toward me, and reached out to take my hand. But, just at that moment, all hell broke loose again next door. The bed started bouncing this way and that, and there was a great deal of guttural noises and screeches.

Karen withdrew her hand. "My God, what's that?"

"That's just Babs and Gavin."

Babs screamed with pure ecstasy. Karen tilted her head, listening closely. "Jesus," she said, "you never screw me like that."

She was smiling broadly as she said that, but still, you never like to hear that sort of thing, especially when you are standing there naked before the women you are, presumably, about to make love to. "Well, you know," I said, "you're just not a screamer."

She reached out for me again. "Oh, for God's sake, darling, don't be sensitive. But didn't you tell me they did this all afternoon, too?"

"Well, I wasn't there, but I certainly think they did."

"My God," Karen said, shaking her head again. "How long have they been married?"

"Uh. Twenty-one years June."

"Are they like this all the time?"

"No. You know that."

"Well?"

"Oh, it's very simple, darling. Right now, in that room, it's twenty-one years ago again."

"Again?"

"And again."

18

A FTER ALL THOSE YEARS OF WISHING AND WAITING, it was on Friday, the very day before the official silver anniversary celebration, when Gavin was at last invited to be a corporate advertising spokesman. They had just phoned him from New York with the proposal, and then Gavin immediately called Judge Pace with the news. The judge and I were literally walking out the front door to begin our trip to Chapel Hill when the telephone rang. Gavin was beside himself with delight; he wanted Judge Pace, retired or not, to handle the "law papers."

The judge at first demurred to the request, promising to get Gavin the best active attorney in the state, but finally, so effusive was Gavin that he agreed to do the work for him. "All right, son," he said, and he promised to talk about the matter that evening, when we were planning to come over to their house for dinner.

In the car, after I had negotiated the side streets of Wilson, and locked us into the interstate highway, I reminded the judge of what he had called Gavin. "What's that?" he asked me.

"Son. You called him son. I've never heard you call anyone son, and he's forty-seven years old."

"Oh, just because you have a Ph.D., don't be a pedant, *Cake*. I also call sagging old waitresses 'honey' when the spirit moves me," he laughed, and he began to fiddle with his pipe. But, in truth, his response was somewhat oblique. "Gavin's really looked forward to this weekend, hasn't he?"

"Absolutely. He sort of has it in his mind that the silver anniversary is somehow going to reconstitute The Grey Ghost—just add water and mix—like the Bicentennial or the centennial of the Civil War."

The judge nodded soberly. "What *does* Gavin do with himself now, day by day?" he asked.

"Oh, he's not unhappy out there at Pine Lakes," I said, putting the best face on it. "He tends to the golf shop, tests new equipment, shoots eighteen or thirty-six holes every day. He's listed as a vice-president and occasionally he'll go to a dinner for the company, something like that."

"That doesn't sound like a very gratifying existence for a man at his estate in life."

"It is a bit harder this year," I explained. "The silver anniversary came along at a good time. Young Russell went off to Washington and Lee as a freshman three weeks ago, so Gavin and Babs are alone now."

"The start of a new chapter."

"Yes, and Gavin was closer to Russ than the two older kids. He was much the best athlete."

"The boy didn't play football though, did he?"

"Oh, no. He's coordinated, but not quick enough to be a back. The backs are all blacks now. And he didn't have the arm to be a quarterback or the size to be a lineman. He shoots a good game of golf, though. He and Gavin played together a lot. And he took up soccer."

The judge nodded his head, filing this away for the moment. There was something more pressing on his mind: "Hell's bells, Don, what's our rush? Let's stop and have a drink?" Instinctively, I looked at my watch; it wasn't yet noon. "Oh, stop being an old woman," he hollered at me. "We're goin' on a good old-fashioned football weekend, and the rules of proper civilized social intercourse don't apply on football weekends. Whatever else changes, that still obtains, doesn't it?"

"Yes, sir."

"Then, if we want to stop and water the horses, there isn't a wife or a conscience to tell us otherwise."

"Yes, sir!" I cried, and I pulled off at the next rest stop. It may have reached 1979 all over North Carolina, but only down in Mecklenburg County, where Charlotte is the sinful seat, can a man purchase a drink of whiskey in the Tarheel State. No loss this time: We brushed the first leaves of autumn off a picnic table and took our booze bucolicly. The judge poured Bloody Marys from a Thermos. "This was good of Mrs. Pace to fix up."

"Mrs. Pace my eye. Mrs. Pace my foot."

"Well then, I thank you for your foresight."

"As they say . . . and all too often: just looking out for number one," and he laughed, took a swallow, and smacked his lips. "As they also say, That's the bottom line." He put the cup down, so that he could monkey with his pipe. "Hmmm. So neither of The Grey Ghost's boys played football?"

"No, sir. And it's probably just as good, having to carry the name and everything."

"Oh, no doubts about that. But there is also a certain irony, and a rueful significance to what you alluded to about blacks dominating football."

"Well, we do still have our white quarterbacks."

"A quota system in reverse," the judge said. "Who ever thought that we would have to establish a safe station for our own kind in the hope that we might then create a few artificial heroes?"

"Well, if not in football, then we'll just have to get our heroes out of the white sports—tennis, golf, games like that."

"Very unlikely. Those kind of sports can certainly produce stars, and even—that dreadful term—superstars. But the purest sports heroes in America must, I think, be confined to the gridiron, where we have the panoply and sex that remind us of battlefields."

"Yessir. You may be right. But the fact is, white kids shy away from football now. When I was growing up, I finally just *had* to stop playing football. You remember me then: I was skinny as a matchstick, and used to crack like one out there in scrimmage."

"Oh, yes, Don, you were a pathetic figure of a boy."

"Damn, Judge! You never said that at the time."

"Withholding the hard truth is the kindest flattery, especially where appearance and somebody else's grandchildren are concerned."

"Yes," I laughed. "Well, anyway, when I was about thirteen, I finally just quit football, and I'll tell you honestly that I feared that would render me a hopeless, spineless sissy for the rest of my life. I thought that no matter how long I lived, I could never obtain the qualities of courage and guts and manliness except on a football field. Baseball was only a game, a pastime, and so was basketball, or lacrosse, or anything else. But football was a rite."

"Of manhood in America?"

"Yessir."

"And now?"

"It's changed one hundred and eighty degrees. Football is a painful exercise to be avoided. It's soccer in the suburbs now. Football can only hurt you. Unless possibly you weigh three hundred pounds."

"Ah, so it's become a gladiator game."

"Absolutely."

"Hmmm, it sounds mightily like our so-called volunteer army, where voluntary is a slick euphemism for mercenary."

"Yes, sir. Football now is primarily some kind of vehicle for the underprivileged."

The judge puffed on his pipe. "So we have a certain sort of unique identity crisis, don't we?" he mused. "That is, if our sports mean anything at all to us, and I believe they do."

"You've always said to me that sports mean even more these days."

"Oh, yes. But now you suggest that we have a situation where our great glamour game, our make-believe war, is only being played by our poor underclasses. But the rest of us, us white, well-fed middle classes, sit above the fray and watch the wretched devils bash their heads in."

"Like a freak show," I suggested.

"More like a public hanging," replied the judge. "Certainly, it is some form of cultural alienation."

"That we can't succeed at our own game?"

"Exactly. It goes deepest with football, too, because football, you know, for all its violence—it was always the sport of the elite. Baseball and basketball were the town games, workingman's games. The workingman didn't cotton to football largely because life itself was brutal enough without imitating it in a game. But for the well-off, football was some sort of substitute. You could prove your toughness on the playing field. You sensed that very thing back when you were a boy and abandoned the game."

I nodded. The judge grabbed for the Thermos and poured us both one more Bloody Mary. "Can't fly on one wing, Cake," he said.

I stirred with my finger. "You know, Judge, we always used to wonder how difficult it would be for Gavin to survive as a living former *hero*. Better to be someone like Jeb Stuart, dead in his prime."

"Speaking figuratively now."

"Of course. But I suppose it's even harder for him since there are so few traditional heroes left, even of the sporting stripe."

"Yes, very thoughtful, Don. Who would have thought that The Grey Ghost would not only become a vestige, but an anachronism as well?"

BUT, IF NOTHING else, yesterday's heroes can make today's commercials. Gavin had been called that morning and asked to become the bona fide national spokesman for Gray-Away, a new hair dye for middle-aged men. It was, of course, a natural, even accounting for the *e* in Gavin's Grey, and the *a* in the other. But here he was, The Grey Ghost, graying but handsome, and just the right age to address his contemporaries in passage, which the product was designed for. And they wanted him to film it right away.

Ecstatic, after Gavin called Judge Pace, he tried to reach Babs, but she was out on business and would not be back until after lunch. So Gavin got into his car and rushed to Pine Lakes and told the good news to everybody there. "Ain't this some kind of silver anniversary?" he said. "We've got the team salute tomorrow, I'll be a national spokesman, and after that, my autobiography." He went on from there, speculating that these developments could only lead further on, to a color announcer's job for the National Football League games. Charlie Eversoll, the head pro, had long since retired to Florida by now, and Earl Carson, Jr., the 1956 Insurance City Open Champion, had replaced him at the helm. Earl said,

"Ghost, maybe they'll even take you on alongside Howard Cosell on the *Monday Night Football.*"

"Wouldn't that be some shit?" Gavin said. "Dandy Don can't stay there forever." He picked up the telephone. "Hello, Pine Lakes Pro Shop, Gavin Grey."

It was the Pine Lakes office, and they wondered if Gavin could drop over. Of course, he could. "You know," he said to Earl Carson, Jr., "I'll bet those advertising folks up in New York already called down here about my being the national spokesman."

St. George Randolph no longer owned Pine Lake Estates. Sometime ago, he had merged the property into a larger corporation of his, and, earlier this year, the whole company had been bought up by Telemar Industries of Houston, an electronics company that was diversifying into soft drinks, commuter airlines, and leisure time. This was a felicitous arrangement for all involved, and one of the stipulations of the sale was that all Randolph Corporation properties would be allowed to remain "independent, management-wise." Scotty Parker still ran Pine Lakes, and, for that matter, Babs still ran all the food and drink services. She had been called in for a brief, perfunctory meeting a few days before with Sean Prochino, the Telemar leisure-time division head. He was now personally assessing the Pine Lakes operation, talking with a number of the "key personnel."

When Gavin arrived at Scotty Parker's office, Prochino was also there. In fact, he was the one in charge. Scotty sat behind his desk, but Prochino was the one who welcomed Gavin and asked him to take a seat across from him on the sofa. He said he always preferred to be on a first-name basis, and Gavin agreed that that was fine with him. Prochino was an acknowledged rising star in the leisure business; he wore three-piece suits with open-necked shirts and blew his hair into that heart-shaped style, natural, so perfectly coiffured, that it belied all naturalness and suggested that it must be a wig. He began:

"Gavin, I've been here at Pine Lakes a few days analyzing our newest Telemar acquisition, and—"

"Yeah, my wife says you talked with her the other day."

"I certainly did visit with her. She's doing some kind of fine job, isn't she, Scotty?" Scotty mumbled something, and Prochino went to some papers he held on his lap. "You know, Gavin, it certainly is unusual for an assistant golf pro to be a vice-president."

Gavin laughed. "It sure is, ain't it?"

"Yes, and it's hard to continue that arrangement, because Pine Lake Estates really doesn't exist as an entity anymore. It's just part of our new leisure-time division at Telemar."

Quickly, Gavin caught the drift, and he cocked his head a little, wary, right away. Prochino said, "You can't be vice-president of something that hasn't got a president or any other corporate office." And he forced a laugh at this humorous pass that things had come to.

"There's Scotty here," Gavin pointed out.

"No, Scotty's not an officer. He's the general manager of Pine Lakes, but he's not an officer. Right?" Scotty nodded his head, if without much enthusiasm. Scotty's a good fellow, a couple years behind me at Chapel Hill, and he didn't like this a bit.

"Well, look," Gavin said, "the reason I'm a vice-president is not just because I'm an assistant pro. It's because of my name. My name *value*."

"Yes," said Prochino, "I understand you used to have quite a reputation in North Carolina."

Gavin froze and stared dead at Prochino. Scotty tried to help. He said, "You know, Sean, Gavin is The Grey Ghost."

But Prochino only shrugged, either not caring or not knowing, and certainly not wanting to pursue any of this extraneous stuff. Gavin tried to be helpful. "Now I'm gonna be a national spokesman, too," he said.

That interested Prochino. "A what?"

"What's that, Gavin?" Scotty asked.

"You know, a national spokesman. A national spokes*person*. Like Ed McMahon or Dandy Don for Lipton Tea."

"This is something about tea?" Prochino asked.

"No, that's Dandy Don, tea. I'm going to be a national spokesman for Gray-Away."

"What the fuck's that?"

"You know, it's like a new competition for Grecian Formula, for Alberto-Culver Formula. One of those big companies, Colgate or Procter and Gamble, one of them is putting it out. It takes the gray out of your hair." Gavin put his hand through his hair.

"Well, that's terrific, Gavin," Prochino said. "Isn't it funny how life works out with the fuckin' twists and turns and all? Because Scotty and I were just sittin' here sayin' how it would be best for you to get into somethin' else."

It took a moment for that to register. Gavin looked to Scotty. "What?" Scotty only shrugged. Gavin turned back to Prochino. "Wait a minute. I didn't say I wanted to leave Pine Lakes. I don't have to leave here just because I'm a national spokesman."

"Well, Gavin—"

"No," Gavin cried, and he jumped to his feet and approached Prochino. "In fact, it'll be even better for Pine Lakes if I'm a national spokesman. It'll give this place a lotta exposure, coast-to-coast."

Prochino leaned back, folding his arms across his chest. "But I'm not selling hair spray, Mr. Grey. I'm selling condominiums. I'm selling leisure."

"I'm a good assistant pro," Gavin added, softer. He hadn't meant to scare Prochono. The man unfolded his arms, brave again.

"Mr. Grey, we have to look at the bottom line of the big picture. You've been an assistant pro for fifteen years. The way we operate at Telemar is, move up or move out."

"But I like what I'm doing here. And I do a good job, don't I, Scotty?" The manager only bowed his head.

"That isn't pertinent," Prochino said. "We've got a young man as our backup assistant at our development in Paradise Valley, Arizona. Now we can't keep him much longer in that position. We've got to vertical him, and this is the logical slot."

"A lot of people know me here."

"Fifteen fuckin' years, I'm sure they do. But the times, they are a-changin'. It's like, I have to level with you, Grey. I didn't know who the fuck you were. Your name didn't impact on me. Scotty had to explain to me that you used to be a star."

Gavin's shoulders slumped, perceptibly. He could not accept that without some certification, and he looked toward Scotty. The manager nodded; sadly, but he did nod. When Scotty told me all about this episode much later, it took him two stiff drinks before he really got into it.

"How long has it been since you played down here?" Prochino asked, attacking snidely now.

"This is our silver anniversary celebration this weekend."

"See, that's a long time, especially in a youth-oriented culture."

"But in Carolina, these people still want to see me. I was The Grey Ghost."

"I'm sure you were. But I'm not selling memories. I'm selling condos. I'm selling leisure."

"But I thought they promised, when Telemar came in, there wouldn't be any changes."

"We said *right away* no changes. You can't stand still in this economy. Now that we've assessed—"

"People aren't going to like it if you fire me. It'll hurt this place."

That was the wrong thing to say. That straightened Prochino up. "Listen, don't tell me how to run my division," he snapped.

Gavin didn't quit. "You fire me, the folks are goin' to say, hey, stay the fuck away from Pine Lakes because they fired The Grey Ghost."

Now Prochino threw the papers he held down on the table, and pointed a finger at Gavin. "All right, I don't want to hear any more. I think you hit the line too many times, your fucking head first." He rose, and waved with disgust. "You get this straightened out, Scotty."

Scotty leaned forward on his desk, trying to force his presence between the two men. "Gavin, we'll keep you on the payroll through December, all the way through the calendar year," he said, but if Gavin heard, he made no response. He just kept after Prochino:

"I'm just telling you, you little sonuvabitch, this is gonna hurt you. They're a lot of 'Heels out there. A lot of football fans. There are. They'll sell their condominiums. They will."

"Are you threatening me?" Prochino screamed. "Are you threatening Telemar? Well, I wouldn't do that, Mister Jockstrap. You threaten me, I'll get the cops in here, and I don't care if you're the fourth member of the blessed Trinity!"

"You and your cunt haircut! Pussy! Pussy!"

Scotty had to come around between them now, but Prochino was growing bolder. He could see that it wasn't going to be sticks-and-stones, and names could only hurt one of them. He paused at the door.

"So, who is The Grey Ghost anyway? You're yesterday's newspaper, you—"

"You Yankee fairy!" Gavin cried. He spit it out. He was trying his best to think of the worst possible thing he could call this man, and that phrase must have made a deep and lasting impression on him one day when he was going on twelve.

Prochino struck back, all the more confident. "You really think one person is gonna give up their condo just because you scored some fucking touchdown back when Christ was a corporal?"

"You peckerhead!" Gavin cried. "You, you . . . peterbreath!"

"Do you really fucking think anybody's even gonna give up a game of golf on their day off just because you helped beat East Cupcake U. a hundred years ago?" Gavin could only stare back now, in shock. "You really think anybody gives a rat's ass about old Mister Jockstrap?"

Then Prochino just stood there and stared, balefully, at Gavin. Scotty came to him. Gavin fumbled to say something. Finally, he called out, "Up yours!" but it was pale and thin when he finally was able to say it, and besides, by then, Prochino was gone, closing the door on him.

GAVIN HEADED FOR the club bar and started charging doubles. He had four. For the first three, he didn't say a word. Then he told Nick, the bartender, about how he was going to be a national spokesman. He also outlined for him a summary of the next day's silver anniversary ceremonies. He did not choose to mention about how he had just that minute been fired.

When Gavin left the bar, he started back to the pro shop, to clean out his stuff. He was outside, cutting through a little grove of trees by the side of the clubhouse, when a Lincoln Continental drove up to the door. Gavin looked back, idly, out of sight himself, and watched as an older man got out, went around, and opened the door for Babs. The man and Babs smiled nicely at one another, exchanged thank-yous for a lovely lunch, and then, as well, a decorous little peck of a kiss.

Gavin turned away then, and, instead of going to the pro shop, he went directly to his car and drove home, where he napped away most of the rest of the afternoon. When Babs came home from work he didn't tell her about seeing her, or even about losing his job, and that evening Gavin remained morose and bitter. But then, it was not a very enjoyable dinner for many reasons. The judge was tired after the trip in from Wilson, Babs unsettled by the impossibly disparate aggregate she was obliged to preside over: The other guests were Finegan and his "bride." This second wife was a much younger woman, and her interests seemed to embrace little outside of their own little corner of the Sunbelt; she had no interest in silver anniversaries in faraway places . . . and it showed. Finegan, of course, had never been any prize, conversationally, and early on, the judge (at his most diplomatic) absolved the two of them of any responsibility for fellowship by suggesting, "Y'all must have jet lag."

They agreed they did, and this gave them immunity from displaying any visible consciousness. But soon, if not soon enough, dinner was over, and the judge began signaling to me, waggling his eyebrows. He feigned exhaustion and we departed, our leaving unmourned, neither by us nor by those who stayed behind. "Hope you get over that nasty jet lag," the judge said to Mrs. Finegan as we departed.

"What?" she said, unprepared. Her name was Chrys, or "Chrys with a *y*" as she styled it, coming from that growing distaff sub-nation of Americans that shares an almost unnatural relationship with our twenty-fifth letter. But Chrys and Finegan were, of course, staying in the guest bedroom, so rather than crowd the house with visitors, staying in the children's rooms, the judge and I opted for residence at the Ramada, nearby.

Unfortunately, I had hardly reached my room at the motel, after helping the judge to his, next door, when my phone rang. It was Finegan. Almost as soon as we had left the house, all hell had broken loose. Could I drive over right away, and pick Chrys and him up and bring them over to the Ramada too? Chrys would prefer to sleep there than under the Greys' roof.

This is because, shortly after the judge and I drove off, Gavin had fixed himself another tall drink, sat back in his big chair and become despicable. In a loud voice, he informed the Finegans that Babs had enjoyed a lunchtime assignation, although, of course, he expressed this much more graphically.

Chrys, flabbergasted at the language, grew wide-eyed at this revelation. Babs, unbelieving, across the room, could just manage to say, "Gavin?"

Only Finegan displayed some presence of mind. Sharply, he said, "You watch that toilet mouth, Gavin."

But he did not stop. "Yeah, I seen her, Finegan. I saw you, Babsie, with the guy in the Lincoln Continental. You think I was fuckin' born yesterday?"

Babs was still so discombobulated. "No, no, Precious, I—"

"I knew you were puttin' out for somebody's ass."

"No, no. Lunch. We just had lunch at—"

"Yeah, sure. You gonna take on Finegan now?" Chrys gasped, confused and embarrassed, and Gavin made it all the worse by taking his forefinger and, drunkenly, tracing a line in the air, toward Chrys and back to himself, as if to say, *Then us, too.*

"Gavin, please, please, no," Babs cried now, starting to sob some, and with it, helping to provoke Chrys to tears, too. Gavin only spread a silly, satyric grin across his face, and wiggled his eyebrows at Chrys. That, at last, was enough for Finegan; he had restrained himself well. But now, he slammed his beer can down and came directly across the room to Gavin.

Gavin was leaning forward in his chair now, grinning at Chrys, and Finegan took one of his great, meaty hands, placed it upon Gavin's one shoulder, and shoved him back. It required no great effort, and Gavin only crumpled there, still.

Babs closed her eyes over her tears. Worse than anything he had said, she did not want to see this. There was no dignity left at all to him this moment; and worse, none was due him.

"Common," Finegan said, shaking his head angrily. "Can't believe it: The Ghost . . . common as cat shit."

Gavin looked up at his old, old friend, and slowly, the grin dissolved into anguish, and then again into tears, and at that, he reached out and grabbed for Finegan and held him somewhere about the knees, tightly, sobbing more. Then he tried to say something, but he could barely get the words through the tears. Finally: "Job . . . job . . . I lost my job today."

Helplessly, Finegan looked to Babs. She stood up. Poor Finegan: He did the best he could. He patted Gavin on his back, but, of course, he was not good at this sort of thing. Then Babs came and took Finegan's place, and she bent down before Gavin and put her arms about him. "Darling, I'm sorry. No one knew. I'm sorry."

"Silver anniversary. Fire The Grey Ghost on the silver anniversary."

Babs took his head and held it to her breast, and Gavin cried all the more. Finegan watched, aghast, and Chrys stood and began to back away. She had to move off, physically. This was when Babs told them they better call me.

"I knew you didn't sleep with that guy," Gavin said, sucking in gobs of air now, trying to get himself back.

"No, Precious, he's just a friend."

"I knew you could never cheat on The Ghost."

"No," she said.

Gavin pulled his head up. "You could never do that, could you?"

"No."

Then he sat up altogether. "I know that," he said, with absolute conviction.

"Yes, Precious."

And suddenly he grew calm, and almost smugly, with just as much conviction, but in utter contradiction, he said: "You're lying. I know."

"What?" Babs said, reflexively, so surprised.

"I know you cheated on me once. I *know* that. I know who it was."

He was so positive, but by now Babs had caught herself up, sufficient not to respond at all.

"Yeah, I know," Gavin babbled on. "I know who it was." Still, Babs remained silent, and by saying nothing, she led him on. "It was that sonuvabitch St. George Randolph," Gavin declared. She still didn't respond, and her face remained as fixed as she could hold it. "You think I'm dumb, don't you? But, hey, I knew. I've *always* known."

"How did you know?"

"I know."

"But how did you know?"

"Easy. How else did you get that job at Pine Lakes? Let Saint in your drawers, you get the job."

Babs stared at him for a while—the oily smugness of his face—and then, as she told me, without even knowing what she was doing, she hauled off and hit him flush with her open hand. Gavin's head whipped over to the side. Babs had never done such a thing in her life before, and it was Gavin's surprise as much as the force of Bab's slap that whipped his head so sharply.

Nothing he could have said could have hurt her more, and whatever sympathy she had held for him moments before vanished altogether. "You bastard," she whispered. It was hurt for hurt now. "You sonuvabitch, Gavin Grey." She rose to her feet and looked down on him in the chair. "Don't you ever call me a whore. You, of all people. What did you *ever* get that didn't have something to do with scoring touchdowns? Huh? *Huh*? Who's the whore?"

But you can call a man a whore. It didn't seem to faze Gavin. His one hand went up and touched his cheek, cherry red, where she had slapped him. But even if that bothered him, he did not show it. Only one thing mattered. He said, "So you never have—"

"I never said that," Babs snapped back.

"But you said—"

"I just said not St. George."

"But you cheated on me?"

"Yes, I should have told you before. It might have—"

"How many times?"

"Just once. One man, one night, long ago when you hurt me."

This seemed to please Gavin, the number. It was not the principle of the thing. "One question," he said.

"Yes?" Naturally, she assumed it would be: Who?

Instead, it was: "Was it after The Ghost finished playin'?"

"What earthly difference does that make, Gavin?"

"Well, was it?"

"You had retired," she replied, answering literally.

My car lights were just visible now, pulling into the driveway. Gavin nodded. Babs left him to say good-night to the Finegans. She never did figure out for sure why Gavin cared so about time, about *when* she cuckolded him. Was it important to him that The Grey Ghost was not violated while he was still playing? Was that it? Or was it more the other way around, that here it was, proof one more time, that one more person—and his wife, no less—had acted differently toward Gavin Grey after his time in football was over?

She never knew. And I don't know either. Outside, by the car, I told Babs I would stay the night, and I just gave the car to the Finegans and told them to take my room at the Ramada. When I came in the house, Gavin was still there, awake in the chair, staring out vacantly, thinking about things I wouldn't even begin to understand for yet a few more days.

19

I WAS THE ONLY ONE OF US UP THE NEXT MORNING when Stuart Stevenson arrived on the dawn flight from Atlanta. A local free-lance TV crew would join her at the house. "Hi, Don," she said at the door, "it's been a long time." And she reached right up and kissed me, not so much as a gesture of affection, or even of greeting, but, I sensed, to *put me at ease.*

Young women do a lot of this now. Stuart is certainly of this type, what you might call the New Breed, if it were permissible to call females a New Breed. I don't believe it is, or, anyway, has been till now. Stuart understood that a great many men might be put off by her attitudes and her goals, but, unlike her immediate predecessors—the Gloria Steinems and Jane Fondas, that early crowd—she possessed no cutting edge. On the contrary: More can be accomplished if you try to blur and conquer. We're all in this together, humankind.

I remember the first time this was brought home to me most clearly was when a young graduate student, female, of the New Breed, accompanied me (and some others) to a history convention. We were not friends; I don't even recall that any personal exchange occurred, but the two of us found ourselves together at the conclusion of the evening's formal activities, and, as a matter of course, I invited her to join me for a nightcap in the bar. We found a table and sat down, and, even before the waitress sought us out, the student leaned over to me and said, "I'm sorry, Professor, but I just can't go to bed with you tonight."

I said I understood completely.

Now, you see, we were at ease and could carry on in an estate of genderlessness (and, presumably, we would have managed just as evenly had she started off by declaring that intercourse would be included on our agenda). From a woman's point of view, I can see how it would appear to restrict them to the defensive if they can only respond, answer yes or no, to the man's initiative. Unfortunately, I'm not altogether sure that power comes with controlling the questions, but I am certain that romance comes with anticipating questions . . . or answers. Let's face it: Tension is the second-best thing the sexes enjoy. What I really can't abide are those soupy people, male or female, who go around saying how their spouse is "my best friend." What dreary households those must be. Feminists are fine, convinced that men and women should be equal, but the New Breed, like Stuart, is dedicated to the proposition that men and women should be friends. And that is just going to louse everything up.

"How are you guys?" Stuart asked brightly.

This meant either Karen, the kids, and me, or it meant Babs and Gavin and me; either way, I hated it. "You guys, my ass." I wanted to say. "Fine," I did say.

"You don't have to get me anything," Stuart said. "They gave us some breakfast on the plane."

"Damnit, I'd like to get you something. It'll be a while, anyway. Gavin's hung over."

So we went into the kitchen. I looked her over while she reached for some cups. She has a nice rounded body, terrific high bottom, although it would upset her to know that I could not tell you the color of her eyes even if you put a gun to my head. She was overdressed a little, achieved through conscious underdressing, and while she was only going on twenty-five, she looked a bit older. She acted her age, late twentieth century. "How did you get into TV?" I asked.

"Oh, it's a perfect thing for a reasonably good-looking woman with a nice extroverted personality and no distinct talent," she said. "Those sort of men tend to end up as salesmen of some sort, PR guys. But we're better suited for this, women. We're not as threatening to you guys when we're on camera. And, you know, most of the people making the news are men, and men talk better to women. We're sort of electronic geishas. Starting with Barbara Walters."

"That's very astute," I said, finishing with the coffee, starting to peel some bacon strips out of the package.

"You know," Stuart went on, "it's charming having a pretty young thing like me sitting there, chatting you up with the news. It's really very Oriental. Geishas only talk, you know. They don't fuck you."

"Yes, I do know that," I said, laughing at her. The last remark had been totally gratuitous, of course. But Stuart had wanted to say a shocking word to put me at ease. Men tend to get more foul-mouthed as they go along; it is a natural function of familiarity. But nowadays, women usually say something vulgar first, early on in a conversation.

So I said, "Cunt"—although not very loudly.

"What did you say, Don?" Stuart said. She was sure as all hell I'd said "cunt."

"Oh, nothing," I said, delighted that one of us was not at ease. Confused, she popped herself up on the counter and sat there. "Why are you doing this?" I asked her. "Why interview Gavin?"

"Because I heard so much about him growing up: The Grey Ghost. In a way he came to represent Wilson and North Carolina, the South, all of it." She spoke now with relish, with genuine enthusiasm. "He's so representative of something that existed here once."

"Doesn't it still?"

"Maybe. But he's the prototype. And you can't show the past unless you use something sharp and well defined. Gavin's not blurred, is he?"

"No, The Ghost is not blurred."

"Daddy always told me that he was an original."

"Perhaps," I said, "the last of the originals."

"I like that. Can I use that on the air?"

"Credit me."

She laughed and cocked her head some. "He's a little sad now, though, isn't he?"

I turned away from the bacon sharply. "Please. Don't tell me you came up here to show up an old ballplayer."

"No, I didn't. I promise."

"Because if you hurt him, I swear I'll come down to Atlanta and I'll wring your pretty neck."

"No, don't worry, Don. I just want to celebrate The Grey Ghost."

"Well, good, because you'll like The Grey Ghost. And that's who Gavin likes talking about. Try not to talk about him now. Except this celebration, and one other thing"—and I filled her all in on his becoming a national spokesman for Gray-Away. "Hey, the coffee's ready," I added, and she hopped off the counter and went over to pour a couple cups.

It was while she was standing there that Gavin came into view in the doorway. He was a sight—bedraggled, hair askew, unshaven, eyes made out of spare parts. Also, all that he had on was a faded old wrapper, held haphazardly in place by a loose sash, so that all his parts hung out for the world to see at its leisure. Brightly, Stuart looked him over and chirped, "Holy shit, looked what the cat dragged in."

Gavin did not favor her with a reply. He only stared at her, confused. She was a woman; she was supposed, by all that is holy, to turn away, avert her eyes. Instead, Stuart just went about pouring our coffee, glancing over—and down—at Gavin where he stood, a couple feet away. She was going to put him at ease. For his part, he refused to adjust the wrapper to cover himself up. Damnit, she was supposed to turn away. It developed into a Mexican standoff. Finally, Stuart glanced over one more time, gestured right at him, and said: "It's okay. I've seen lots of peckers before."

"Not mine, you haven't," Gavin replied.

"I was in the Atlanta Hawks locker room once. You know, there really isn't a lot of difference."

"Lady," said Gavin, "there is to me," and he patted his penis, even quite fondly, I would say. Then he reached out, took my coffee cup right out of her hand and retreated back upstairs in order to try and put himself together for the more formal interview.

FROM THAT POINT, things at the Grey house did improve. Finegan and Chrys drove the judge over to see his daughter, and he and Stuart went off alone together, happily carrying on till her film crew arrived and she had to go to work. By then, Gavin was dressed, and Stuart started interviewing him, as we all watched.

Gavin was terrific on camera. He recalled everything perfectly, and he absolutely charmed Stuart. "Gavin Grey, you are just an original," she said into the microphone. "Perhaps the last of the originals."

He ducked his head shyly, like a teenager. It had been some time since last I had seen him do that.

Then they took a break, because Stuart wanted to film another sequence down in the club cellar, where all The Grey Ghost's trophies were, but I had had enough, and so I drifted outside. Babs was there, on the patio, reading a magazine in the sun. It was still warm outside if you stayed out of the shade. "How's it going?" she asked me.

"Stuart's good. You can see the judge all the way through her."

"I'm sure. I guess I'm just put off by this whole, uh, retrospective."

"Well, Gavin sure seems to be enjoying himself."

She put the magazine down and beckoned for me to take a seat next to her. "You want to know the truth, Donnie?" I nodded, even though I really didn't know what particular truth it was that we were getting at. "I don't think that what upset Gavin—the most—was losing the job or that business he dreamed up about me having an affair. What's upset him is having to go through all this silver anniversary stuff, getting that commercial—"

"The national spokesman?"

"Yes. Because there's no way he can live up to it in his own mind. And he knows that. It was easy being The Grey Ghost when he was The Grey Ghost, because to prove himself, all he really had to do was carry the football. Oh, there were speeches to make, interviews, appearances—"

"*Ed Sullivan.*"

"Yeah. But even if he didn't do especially well at that sort of thing, it didn't matter, because he could always come through on Saturdays. But now, he's supposed to be The Grey Ghost, but he isn't, not anymore. And what do you do to prove it?"

"I don't know," I said.

"Neither does he. He's looked forward to this for so long, and now that it's here, he's frightened to death." She lit a cigarette, then pulled her legs up on the chaise, wrapping her arms about her knees. She had on blue jeans, and an old peasant shirt. She smiled at me and read my mind.

"Don't worry. I'll never tell him it was you."

"I'm a big boy. Use your judgment."

"No, don't worry. I only told him about me to make it easier for him."

"Easier?" I cried.

"Yes. If he thinks I've been trash, a scarlet woman . . ." She threw the cigarette away, out onto the lawn, and watched it burn there for a moment before turning to me again. "Donnie, I'm leaving him."

"Oh, no."

"I have to, honey."

"There is another man," I said, reflexively.

"Oh, you bastards are all the same. You can't imagine a woman would just walk away, without another man's bed—or wallet—to climb into."

I twisted my mouth, showing my chagrin. "Fair enough."

"And there have always been men, Donnie. *Available.* Always. Marshall would marry me tomorrow."

"Marshall?"

"The man I had lunch with yesterday. He lives at Pine Lakes, a widower. And if I want to marry him, I will. But I don't know. I'm a very confident woman, Donnie. I only lost my youth. I didn't lose my beauty."

"God, no."

"Of course, it took me a long time to understand. I thought the two had to go together—"

"Like youth and football?"

"Of course. So Gavin must go on chasing his youth. There will always be someone to chase a beautiful woman, and when I want, I can slow down and let them catch me." Again, she lit a cigarette, and she read my mind. "Don't tell me I smoke too much."

"You smoke too much."

"Fuck you, Donnie," Babs said genially, and she took a long drag and tossed the cigarette away, with the other. "There, I'll never smoke again."

"Good for you."

"You see, it'll be better for Gavin without having me around to remind him of the past."

"When will you tell him?"

"Oh, I've thought about that for a long time. First, I wanted to wait till Russ was in college, till all the kids were gone. Then all this silver anniversary crap came up, and it seemed like the fair thing to wait till it was done. After Christmas, I suppose. After I explain it to the kids."

"He doesn't have a job now."

"He'll get something. And I'll support him, Donnie. He can keep the house. As long as I can come over and visit the kids when they come back."

"You really have made up you mind, completely."

"Oh, yes. Long ago, really. I decided for good one night about three or four years ago, and nothing has ever happened since then to make me waver."

"What happened that night?"

"You were there."

"I was?"

"Well, sort of, you and Karen both. We were in Ohio, at that Hall of Fame. I was so proud of him. I *am,* you know. How many women's husbands make any kind of hall of fame?"

"Only the best," I said.

"Yeah. And he looked so handsome, too. I thought: All right, Babsie, he's just a guy now, just a golf pro, an *assistant* golf pro, for Chrissake, but he is special, and he's a good man and a good father, even if he drinks a little and chases a little, I can abide it. For everything he wasn't anymore, I was still very much in love with him, Donnie. Can you believe that?"

"Of course I can."

"And, anyway, it was a lovin' kind of day, steamin' hot."

"I remember."

"The sweat came off of you, the way it does, stickin' to you, especially to all the right—or the wrong—places, to your boobs, to your crotch." She drew both her hands across her chest and quickly touched between her legs. "You feel your breasts. You don't need a man to touch them, but you feel them yourself. All you can think of is your body. You know that kind of day?"

"I didn't know women had those kind of days."

"Are you kidding? It's very lustful in the tropics, isn't it?"

"I guess."

"You just feel your body. And we came back from the dinner, when he'd been honored, and we made love, Donnie. God, what love we made."

"You did that in the afternoon, too," I said.

"Heavens, Donnie McClure, what sort of a pervert are you, keeping score on others?"

"It was a very vivid day for me, too," I said.

"Well, you're right. We did make love in the afternoon, too. And then afterwards, that night. There was a light on from the bathroom, and I could see the trophy they gave him for making the Hall of Fame. Oh, I *was* so proud. I was. And God, I don't think I was ever more a woman. Ever more liked being a woman, anyhow. I just wanted to hold him so. Hold my man. And such love we made. Mmmm, it was just wonderful. And I was lying there then, in his arms, all snuggled up, and I was nearly asleep, and he said, 'Babs?' And I said, 'Yes, Precious?' And he said, 'Wouldn't it be great if I still played football, too?'"

"He said that?"

"Yes. Just as simple as that. Look, I never expected anything poetic, but—"

"And what did you say back?"

"Oh, I just said, 'Yes, Precious.' But then I couldn't help it, I started to cry a little, and he assumed I was crying because he couldn't play anymore. And I just said, 'Yes.' I couldn't tell him what it was, and I just knew then, it wasn't ever going to be possible anymore. I had to leave The Grey Ghost."

"I suppose," I said.

20

STUART AND HER CREW WERE GOING TO CLOSE out their efforts by filming the "commemorative" halftime ceremonies at the game at Kenan Stadium that afternoon, so, while the rest of us went ahead, Gavin stayed back at the house. He volunteered to usher Stuart and the others over to the stadium.

As the crew went about packing up their equipment, Stuart went into the living room with Gavin, and they sat and chatted for a while. He told her some colorful stories about the '54 'Heels. Stuart laughed out loud. "You sure are an original," she said again.

Her tone made Gavin out to be some sort of a specimen, but he certainly didn't take it that way. "I'm going to be a national spokesman, too," he informed her brightly.

"Oh, yes, I heard about that."

"I'll have a lot of travel for them, coast-to-coast."

"Well, if you ever get to Atlanta, gimme a buzz," Stuart said, casually enough.

But Gavin figured he knew a bona fide invitation when he heard one. He stopped bantering and looked directly at her. "You bet I will, sugar," he said, and Stuart smiled back, putting him at ease. Gavin, with a gleam in his eyes now, glanced at his watch. It was just past noon. "Pee-em," he declared.

"What?" Stuart asked.

"Drinky time down South," he announced, and he went over to the bar and got out the bourbon. He held the bottle up for her. "If you're the judge's daughter, you gotta be a good friend of the doctor."

"No, not really," Stuart said. "I'm not much of a drinker. But, I tell you what: I'd love a joint." She fished in her handbag and came up with a little pouch and some cigarette paper, while Gavin watched it all closely, with fascination. She noticed. "You want a joint too?"

"Naw, I never messed with any of that dope," Gavin said, and with a certain condescension, too, that was all the more apparent since he was pouring himself a stiff belt of bourbon at this moment.

"Never?" said Stuart, and now her tone was every bit as snotty, as much as if he had said that he had never used soap. The generation gap was very much in effect here, and Stuart appreciated that and quickly put Gavin at ease. "God," she went on, "I mean, it's worth it just to improve fucking."

"Yeah?" This did bridge the gap considerably. "All right, let me try one of those little devils."

Stuart laughed and rolled him his own. Gavin stared at it, holding it almost gingerly, as if it smelled bad or would momentarily explode, like a bomb in a Road Runner cartoon. "Go on," she said.

"Well now, I'm not all that sure that I need any he'p," he said coyly, setting her up.

"Help at what?"

"At what you said." Gavin couldn't bring himself to say that word to the young lady, even though it was the young lady who had said it to him.

"Oh, fucking," said the young lady.

"Yeah."

"Yeah, well I never met a man—even an everybody's All-American—who couldn't stand some improvement." They were skirting monkey business with every line, and in Gavin's own house. "Go on, go on," Stuart said, beckoning to the joint, and he lit it. That was the only part Gavin got right. When he tried to inhale, he could barely even get the smoke in him, except perhaps for just enough in the wrong places to make him cough. Stuart fibbed some and said he *seemed* to be getting the hang of it, but even Gavin, who had never smoked in his life, knew he wasn't smoking well. He coughed again and hustled over to pick up his drink.

Stuart looked at him with more understanding now. "You're telling the truth, aren't you? You really never did smoke before."

"I wasn't lying none. Why would I lie?"

"I don't know. It just seemed so amazing to me. I never met anybody who hasn't smoked some . . . something."

Gavin put the joint down in an ashtray and gave up that ghost. "Well now, I sure ain't no angel," he said, and he took another big swallow of bourbon. "I have drunk some whiskey in my time. But I just never did mess none with cigarettes, because, I didn't want to stunt my growth none or lose my wind. Then, when the marijuana started comin' out, when folks really started takin' to it, there was a party one night and ever'body was passin' one around, and it got to me"—and here, Stuart told me later, he actually picked the joint up again, and pantomimed this old episode, examining it, as Yorick's skull, before passing it on to the imaginary next person— "and I thought on it, and then I just figured, Aw, piss on it, you got enough vices as it is, Ghost."

Then he put the joint back in the ashtray for real and looked back over toward Stuart. "Lemme tell you: The worse you can do is pick up bad habits after you get grown. Those are the ones you can't handle. It's like my old friend, Lawrence. . . . " His voice trailed off.

"Who?"

"Oh, just an old friend."

But Stuart remembered that all vaguely, from having the name tucked away somewhere. "Oh, yeah, Lawrence," she said.

"Yeah. He come outta Rutherford County where they didn't bet nothin' but beers on arm 'rasslin. He got to goin' and—That's what did Lawrence in. That's what-all, Stuart. It didn't have nothin' to do with me or anything at all."

"No," Stuart said.

Gavin took one more long drink of bourbon, then studied the glass, looking for Lawrence there. "Oh, poor old Lawrence," he said. And then: "Well, let's go. We better get our little red 'asses over to the game. I wouldn't want to be late for my own silver anniversary commemoration."

VIRGINIA WAS THE opponent for the Tarheels on this occasion. This was a wise selection, for the Wahoos, so-called, were perennially a doormat, the perfect opposition for a fete, inasmuch as they were unlikely to provide stiff competition—let alone a defeat—that might mar the spirit of the occasion for the home forces. This was a day when ceremony and happy history should not be obscured by the distractions of a good, close game.

And sure enough, Virginia played its role, falling behind by two touchdowns right off the bat. It was, comfortably, 21–3, shortly before the first half ended, when Gavin and the rest of the 1954 team left their seats and began filing down to the edge of the field. Promptly as the action ended the incumbent Tarheels cleared the gridiron, the PA announcer began, in his most sonorous tones: "Nineteen fifty-four: General Dwight Eisenhower was president of these United States."

"I don't believe they're going to bring the vice-president's name to our attention," the judge said to me. We were sitting in the special silver anniversary section, with Babs, Chrys with a *y*, and other family and guests of the championship team. The Carolina marching band, two hundred strong, "Pride of the Atlantic Coast Conference," played "The Caissons Go Rolling Along," presumably in honor of Ike.

"The *Nautilus*, the world's first nuclear-powered submarine, was launched," intoned the public address, and the band struck up "Anchors Aweigh," as Gavin marched the old team out to midfield, where they all lined up. As the band spelled out more historical happenstance—"a young actress from Philadelphia named Grace Kelly won the Academy Award"—the crowd paid a dutiful amount of restless attention. "The heavyweight champion of the world was Rocky Marciano"—herewith the theme from *Rocky* was briefly assayed, confusing pugilistic fact and fiction—"and another kind of rock drew even more attention, thanks to a man named Bill Haley . . . and his Comets!" Whereupon, a group of students, dressed up in exaggerated fifties period garb, a poor man's *Grease* road show, bopped out onto the field and started dancing to "Rock Around the Clock." This was, clearly, the grand finale.

"I was hoping they'd cite Senator McCarthy's censure, so we could hear 'Oh, Wisconsin!,'" the judge said to me.

But, alas, this musical trip down memory lane had concluded, and the public address declared: "But, ladies and gentlemen, whenever we in Carolina speak of 1954, it can mean only one thing. Will you welcome back now, our 1954 national champion Tarheels!" And the stadium burst into cheering, fondly. It was, however, something of an artificial tone, because any ovation milked from a stadium crowd—no matter how deserving—sounds forced aside the spontaneous kind brought on naturally by the action on the field.

Politicians should never hold a stadium rally, because anyone who has ever attended a football game will recognize, by comparison, how hollow that cheering is. Preachers are the only ones, besides athletes, who should ever work a stadium. The one other thing that sounds just right in a stadium is a moment of silence.

Now, there was a moment of silence for the two '54 team members—Lawrence, of course, being one of them—who had passed on.

Then, in turn, by number, lowest first—"number eleven, quarterback, Paul Sanderson"—each player present was introduced, to take a step forward and wave to the crowd. The cheers were warm enough, rising or falling slightly, depending on the player's prominence. Two were left out of the numerical sequence, the co-captains, Roger Barnett, number fifty-six, linebacker for the defense, and "last, but certainly not least, number twenty-five, captain of the offense, halfback, Gavin Greyyyyyy!"

He stepped forward to wave, and the crowd began to respond with its greatest applause, but just then, down the west end of the stadium, the '79 Tarheel team began to pour out of their locker room. The crowd saw them, and the roar rose, thunderously now, and the band broke into "I'm a Tarheel Born." I had the glasses on Gavin. He held his right hand high in the air, moving back and forth like a semaphore, and his face beamed, a bright crescent, for this remarkable crescendo being accorded him. Then, out of the corner of his eye, he saw the first wave of baby-blue uniforms reach the field itself, he realized who the great cheers were really for, and he dropped his hand, slowly, as if he were drawing a line down the thin air, zippering something shut.

His old teammates there, in line, themselves began to cheer for the team. At the far end, someone called to Paul Sanderson, and he turned and began to lead the team off the field. Gavin still stood a step ahead, and he did not see them leave behind him, nor hear Barnett call to him above the din. When he looked around he was all alone, the others yards away now, weaving off the field like a train pulling out of the station, and as the cheers for the returning Tarheel team began to die out, you could hear some titters across the stadium, laughing at The Grey Ghost, for standing there, out of place, on the midfield stripe.

THE MORE INTIMATE, concentrated part of the reunion took place that evening at the Carolina Inn, a black-tie dinner. The Finegans had kept my room at the Ramada, and so Babs and Gavin and I swung by the motel to pick up the judge.

When he got into the car, he said, casually, "Gavin, that was a very touching ceremony at the stadium this afternoon."

Gavin did not reply at all. He was driving, and he made a big thing out of staring at the road ahead. Babs and I glanced at each other curiously in the backseat. The judge tried again. "Yes, I 'spect all y'all were moved by that sort of acclaim."

Purposely, Gavin kept his eyes ahead, pretending as if driving the car required all the attentions of the captain of a battleship negotiating a minefield. "I didn't think it was all that outstanding," he cracked.

The judge nipped his eyes back to us, trying to get some hint as to what he might have said wrong. But Gavin began to explain for us what was on his mind. "I've heard a lot more cheering in my time," he groused.

I leaned forward on the back of the front seat. "Well, you know how it is, Gavin," I said, and then I went into a boring dissertation about games and politicians and preachers at stadiums. Apparently, this made little headway.

"Goddamnit, Donnie, who's talking about a moment of silence?" We drove on a bit, and then he started in more detail. "I just didn't understand all that shit about 1954. We wasn't salutin' 1954, we was supposed to be salutin' the champion Tarheels. That old Grace Kelly got more attention than the whole lineup. And Bill Haley, shit. Here we ain't had a national champion in Carolina, in the whole damn ACC, since 1954, and y'all would've thought folks would've been more appreciative." He drove on again. "You know what I really missed?"

"What's that, Precious?"

"Ostrich feathers. Wouldn't you think they would've had ostrich feathers? In commemoration?"

"Well, they're pretty hard to get, I guess," I said.

"Goddamnit, Donnie, they've had twenty-five years."

Silence. Nobody knew how to respond. I'd never seen Gavin like this. The judge was right (as ever): The silver anniversary was forcing too much of the past upon him. *He drinks enough of memories without having us pour that wine down his throat.*

And it was the judge who at least figured out how to change the subject. "Well, Gavin, Stuart tells me she sure had a good interview with you," he said.

Gavin perked up with that. "Yeah, you ought to be real proud of her, judge. She knew just what questions to ask me."

The judge was clever enough to go over these questions, verbatim, the rest of the way to the inn.

It was a crowded party, for each of the players had been permitted to invite several guests, and, on top of that, naturally, a great many Carolinians had imposed their presence. Plus layers of officialdom. But it was a happy and homogeneous crowd, and the old teammates laughed and pounded one another on the back and poked themselves in their bulging bellies. Finegan was outstanding as a fashion plate, in a rented powder-blue tuxedo, a huge satin bow tie, and a ruffled shirt. He dominated the loudest group, which was stationed most convenient to the bar. The more cerebral of the players grouped in a far corner and talked about interest rates and John Connally for president.

By now, the squad had been together most of the day, and many had assembled informally the night before, too, so that the players had gone beyond greeting each other in the 1954 pecking order, and were beginning to select each other out on the basis of their current status—people, not just teammates. The wives were also involved in this process; some of them didn't even know who had been the stars and who had been the substitutes twenty-five long autumns ago.

In fact, when we entered the room, a lot of people only sort of waved to Gavin, merely acknowledging another guy on the team, but it was just Narvel and Bridget Blue who made an effort to approach him . . . and they, after all, were his guests. Purposely, a handful of official blacks had been included to provide prima facie evidence of the egalitarian changes that had so dramatically occurred in 1954, but I'm positive that the Blues were the only black people actually invited by a team member.

It had been Gavin's idea. When he brought it up, Babs worried out loud that they might not be comfortable, but Gavin replied that, well, they should have the right to choose that for themselves. He never forgot that Narvel was there to stand up for him when no one else would. "A lotta folks would kiss The Grey Ghost's ass, but they wouldn't give Gavin Grey the time o'day," is the way he phrased it himself.

When the Blues rushed up, there were greetings and introductions all around. "Donnie's my autobiographer," Gavin added on my behalf. Then he asked the Blues, "You see the halftime today?"

"Naw, I'm sorry, I just couldn't get out there," Narvel said.

"Well, lemme tell you, y'all sure didn't miss nothin'. They did this salute to 1954, and hardly bothered 'bout the team atall."

"Oh?" Narvel said.

"You know, there wasn't one ostrich feather in the whole stadium."

Babs could tell that Narvel had long since forgotten about the significance of ostrich feathers vis à vis The Grey Ghost, and it was apparent that Bridget hadn't an inkling. So Babs said, "They used to wave ostrich feathers for Gavin."

"Oh, yeah," said Narvel.

"Wouldn't you think they would've thought of that?" Gavin asked, almost whining now.

"Well," said Narvel.

"This is a very nice function," Bridget said.

"Yeah, let's all get a drink," Babs suggested, and Gavin and I began to work our way to the bar. As we struggled back out through the crowd, he headed over to take Babs her drink, and I split off to give the judge his. St. George Randolph passed Gavin. "Hey, Ghost, howya doin'?" he said. He had been over with the interest-rate bunch. Gavin mumbled something back, and Randolph clapped him on the back. "This is great, isn't it?"

"Great?" Gavin said, and loudly. "That was horseshit out there today. All that crap about Rocky Marciano. We were the ones took the national championship."

Randolph cocked his head at Gavin curiously. At first, in fact, he thought he must be joking, and then when he realized Gavin was serious, he wasn't sure what to say. "Right, Saint? Right?" Gavin asked.

Randolph put a hand on Gavin's shoulder, and talked as sweetly as he could to him, as he might to a disappointed child: "Well,

Ghost, let's look at it this way. We're just a bunch of old farts. It was a long time ago, twenty-five years. I think it's great they remember us at all, huh?" Gavin only shook his head, though, so Randolph quickly turned away, holding up his empty glass as an exit visa. "Gotta get a refill." And he was gone.

Gavin looked about. He was all by himself. Roger Barnett and his wife were drifting by, and he got in their path. "You remember my wife, Dede."

Gavin nodded and said, "What'd you think about that today?"

Barnet said: "Oh, we're all havin' such a good time. We were just over there talking to Bob Morgan, and—"

"Who?"

"You know, Senator Morgan," Dede Barnett said.

"Oh, yeah."

"And that adorable Katie."

"Who?"

"Katie Morgan." Gavin still looked blank. "You know, Mrs. Morgan . . . the senator's wife."

"Oh, yeah."

"Well, you know, Gavin, Senator Bob was saying, no matter what you think about Califano and that tobacco thing—"

Gavin turned directly to Dede, and said, "How many times you heard about that flip before the Wake game?"

Dede looked to her husband for help. He shook his head, utterly baffled. "Now what's that?" Dede said.

Gavin flicked at Barnett with his elbow. "Go on, you tell her." And he laughed at the memory.

"No, you tell her, Gavin."

"Well, okay. You know how it is, co-captains. Just one of you can call the flip before the game, and here we get out there and Roger thinks I'm callin' and I think he's callin', and neither one of us call, so Roger real fast says 'heads,' but now I'm saying 'tails,' and—"

"Oh, yeah," Barnett said, perhaps remembering.

"Who's that, dear?" Dede asked.

"Wait a minute," Gavin said. "Here's the funny part, remember? So then I says 'heads' real fast, but of course, Roger here says 'tails,' and that ole referee, he don't know whether to spit or go blind." Gavin laughed uproariously, but Roger only smiled politely, and Dede didn't even offer that much. Either she didn't get it at all or she simply didn't care. She just kept looking right past Gavin, snapping her fingers and shaking her head toward her husband.

"Which one?" he finally said.

"Over there. The tall one."

Roger turned around, and Gavin had to. "Oh," Roger said, "that's Chippy Hearns."

Dede nodded.

Gavin said: "You probably don't remember him. He wasn't but a backup end that season."

Dede said, "Oh, what does he do, dear?"

"You know. He runs Merrill Lynch in Greensboro."

"Yes, of course," Dede said. "We saw him—"

Gavin interrupted. "He did score the one touchdown in the South Carolina game. Bobby cleared out the linebacker, and—"

Dede looked curiously at Gavin for a moment, shaking her head, and then continued on, "Yes, we met him at that mortgage-banking convention in Wilmington." And mumbling an "excuse me," she brushed by Gavin. Her husband followed, and they went directly over to welcome Chippy Hearns, the former backup end.

And Gavin was alone again. He looked about, at all the people, but nobody approached him. Across the way, I spotted Babs, and our eyes met, and we shook our heads. She was ready to cry. Gavin glanced about self-consciously and drank his drink for something to do. Babs's lips said, "Oh, please, somebody." But no one saw him, or, worse, if they did, no one wanted to see him. Certainly, no one knew what to do with him.

"Look at him, judge," I said. "All by himself. Here it is, the silver anniversary, and it's like The Grey Ghost doesn't belong."

"Or maybe none of us do but him," the judge said.

I froze. I should have gone to Gavin, but I froze. He was starting to sweat now. I could see that. He took out his handkerchief and wiped it across his face and looked about, wondering.

Finally, there was one person who went to him. It was Chrys Finegan. Her husband was backed up against the bar by a bunch of the other players, telling vasectomy jokes, and she had been buffeted this way and that, ignored. I watched as she finally decided to come to Gavin, and they eyed each other warily, like a couple of pimply teenagers at a dance who are grateful for the company but sorry to be lumped together.

"Hi," Chrys said.

"Hi you," Gavin replied.

"I'm sorry about your losing your job."

"Oh, that's okay. I'm gonna be a national spokesman."

They looked about uneasily then, hoping someone else would join them. "This is some kind of a real nice function," Chrys said.

"Whatdya say, y'all want another drink?" Gavin said, and for nothing else to do, he started cutting through the crowd to the bar.

THE DINNER, AS befits football, was roast beef, in ample cuts, with a salad and beans and a big baked potato resting in an aluminum-foil casket. Finegan was mighty pleased with this. "Look at that mother," he exclaimed. "No little pussy potatoes." That was the highlight of the meal for me, as I had never thought of potatoes as having either gender or personal characteristics.

There was an invocation, the minister addressing "the head coach in the sky." The master of ceremonies, a major Carolina television "personality" then assumed command and made a couple of jokes at the expense of Virginia's athletic prowess, and another about Billy Carter. The non-football dignitaries were then introduced, although a number of them were visibly disturbed when the television personality suggested that everybody hold their applause until all had been introduced, and everybody did just that.

"Now comes to that portion of the program we have all been waiting for," the personality said, and the lights dimmed and a special film of the 1954 season began. It was entitled *A Team of Destiny*, and the players hooted and hollered as each of their number would be introduced or would do something spectacular. "Hey, Rudy, who's the guy with the hair?" "And y'all thought Finegan was fat *then!*" That sort of thing. But Gavin did not watch in exactly that spirit. I could hear him across the table, talking, ostensibly to Babs, but really to himself. "Here's the first down. . . . Watch the end. . . . If I just got that block there. . . . I had 'em here. Look! Now! Cut . . . !"

One sensed a greater dislocation with time, too, because the film was in black and white, and so the images that crossed the screen reminded us of movie newsreels, and since there are no more movie newsreels, we were carried farther back into antiquity. "Here comes that big draw play," Gavin said, and I glanced over at Babs and him, and with the light from the projector crossing their faces, flickering, they seemed to be in black and white too.

And then, in another minute or so, we were into the Sugar Bowl, the finale, and soon it read "The End" upon the screen, the words superimposed over the famous view of Gavin being toted off the field by Lawrence and Finegan. Everybody applauded wildly. Gavin said: "Who the hell made that? I don't see how they could've left out that sweep I made against Wake for the second touchdown." Babs patted him on the arm.

The television personality then started calling out the names of the players, in the same numerical order as at the stadium this afternoon. Now, though, he would insert some extra identification, "thumbnail sketches," as he called it, a word or two about what the man had accomplished on the gridiron or what had become of him in life at large. Each player would come up to the stage and receive a commemorative gift, an engraved desk set, that was presented by Pinky Satterwaite, a beloved former assistant coach; the head coach was long dead. The players would then remain on the podium, the team growing there before our eyes, the audience cheering louder and louder as the roll was read. And soon, there were only two more Tarheels left in the audience.

Roger Barnett, the defensive captain, rose across the way. He was a distinguished-looking gentleman, and if he was thin on top, he had stayed trim, proud that he weighed a few pounds less now, age forty-six, than he had as a linebacker. He was the president of the largest department store in Charlotte, and in charge of the United Way for the whole state. He was at ease behind the microphone without showing any real facility for the task of speaking, as he explained how playing on the 1954 Tarheel team was an experience that had enhanced his life in many ways and taught him many things. Also, he thanked the Almighty that he could come back and visit with all his teammates again at this wonderful reunion. Barnett then stepped back to join the rest of the team, the audience responding with a warm, and predictable, measure of applause.

The television personality sighed now. "You know we've only got one Tarheel left," he said, and the room laughed. "I could say so many things about this man, but words would only get in the way of his greatness. How do you introduce a legend in his own time? And so, ladies and gentlemen, let me only say what we Tarheels all said then, in 1954: Ladies and gentlemen, number twenty-five in your program, number one in your hearts, our own Gavin Grey, The . . . Grey . . . Ghostttt!"

The spotlight fell on him, and he smiled and bounced to his feet. This time, too, the audience all rose, as well, and rose as one, applauding in rhythm as the band struck up "Mr. Touchdown, U.S.A." They were still up, clapping, tapping their feet now, too, when Gavin reached the stage and took the commemorative desk set from Pinky Satterwaite. He stood there, waiting for the people to sit back down, cradling the present in his one arm, so that it had to remind us, one and all, of a pigskin. Finally, all the people had returned to their seats, and there was silence, but of that unnatural sort that dangles, ready to break from its thread and crash loudly. Gavin looked about the room, but even with a smile upon his face, it seemed as if his countenance was dimmed, rather than illuminated, by the scene before him, honoring him. His eyes took on a vacant aspect, and across the table from me, Babs swallowed hard, and she began to pinch her own hand with the other. Among other things, she longed for a cigarette.

Finally, after what seemed an eternity, longer even than the many minutes it takes to play the last few seconds of a close football game, Gavin spoke. He looked straight out into nowhere and said, "I thought they should've had some ostrich feathers to wave out there today, didn't y'all?"

Nobody responded in any way. The silence hung before us all again. No one knew what Gavin meant. Finally, someone in the crowd decided that he must be trying to make some sort of a joke, and so they began to force a laugh, politely, and others followed their lead, and the room sort of took with laughter, but in a mannered way, of the kind you hear on laugh tracks over television programs, where nothing has been even remotely funny, and the artificial laughter only calls more attention to that fact.

But if this affected Gavin, he gave no notice. He merely waited for the room to quiet, and then he said, "On behalf of the team, I want to thank you for the film, only I don't see how you can make a highlight film and leave out the sweep I made against Wake from their thirty-seven that broke it open, because that sure was a highlight."

This time, there was no reaction whatsoever, and nothing to salvage the silence, either, for no one could even pretend that he meant to be funny, and laugh. Babs lowered her head into her hands, but only briefly, for then she remembered that people would be watching her, and so she looked back up at her husband and smiled bravely at him.

Gavin did not seem to be bothered. He suddenly appeared to discover the old coach there, sitting next to him. "Hey, how you, Pinky?" he said. Baffled, old Satterwaite sort of nodded back, and Gavin took that as encouragement, and kept on, more or less speaking directly to the one man. "I'm not out at the club no more, Pink," he said. "You won't find me at Pine Lakes." Then he turned back, square, to the audience. "I'm still on the payroll there. I'll be on the payroll till the end of the calendar year. But if y'all come lookin' to play eighteen, y'all won't find me there." A few nodded, but most kept their faces set, grim and confused. "But it's okay," Gavin went on. "It's okay, because I'm a national spokesman now. Coast-to-coast."

And then he fell dumb again, only staring out and away. For an instant, I glanced over at the band, the thought being formed somewhere in my mind that perhaps they might have the presence to strike up "The Star Spangled Banner," as they would to calm a riot. Babs was pinching the top of her left hand so hard that I could see the flesh glow bloodless white.

Gavin's mouth formed. "The ostrich feathers . . . " he began, but he stopped again, in the middle of that thought, dead in the water, and now there was no more from him, and the room grew utterly still, to where we found ourselves, perversely, a benevolent mob, not taking strength from one another, but joined in a bond of pathos, social weightlessness.

From out of this helpless anomie, I finally heard one word from across the room. "Ghost," said a voice in a whisper. A pause, then again "Ghost . . . Ghost," but in that husky tone and cadence that recalled for us all that afternoon against Clemson twenty-five years ago. I looked over. It was the judge; oh, God bless the judge. "Ghost," he whispered out again. "Ghost . . . Ghost." And then, from way in the back of the room, on the other side, a second voice joined in the chorus. It was Narvel. "Ghost . . . Ghost." He understood. And so, I came in myself then, and some others, too, and in a moment more the whole room had picked up the chant, and it filled the place.

Upon the stage, Gavin perked up, and across his face now, a smile broke, broader, and deeper, until his eyes lit up too, and he was beaming. Finegan stepped forward, wrapped one great arm about Gavin's shoulders, and, pressing him hard to him, he lifted him off the ground with his hip. The crowd kept on whispering, "Ghost . . . Ghost . . . Ghost," throwing themselves into the chorus in a way that honored the past and could make them forget what had just happened moments before.

21

T HAT TUESDAY GAVIN FLEW UP TO NEW YORK. A limousine picked him up the next morning at eight sharp and took him over to a studio, on the West Side, where his Gray-Away commercial would be shot.

The man in charge, the agency's creative director, who had thought up the campaign, was named Eddie Leopard, although possibly that was not his real name. "The Grey Ghost!" he hollered when Gavin walked into the studio. "Jesus Christ, The Grey Ghost! I saw you in Carolina! I saw you beat the shit out of the Giants!"

Gavin beamed. "Which time?" he asked.

"Jesus, you know," Leopard said. "The time when you, uh—"

"Scored the three touchdowns."

"Yeah, yeah, that time." Gavin was delighted. Leopard threw his arm about him and took him over to show him the story boards for the commercial.

It would begin with Gavin approaching a mock airline counter, rushing to make a plane. The ticket agent, an attractive women, would say, "Don't I know you?"

And Gavin would reply, "I'm Gavin Grey."

Then the lady would reach out and touch his hair, wrinkle up her nose and say, "Yeah, gray and old."

"She says that?" Gavin asked Eddie Leopard.

"Hey, keep in mind, Gavin, we're appealing to an audience about your age. I didn't hire any young chickie. I got a good older broad for this part. And get the tone. All us grew up reading comic books. I want this like an old-time comic book advertisement. That style. Get it?"

Gavin nodded his head, sort of.

"Remember the old Charles Atlas ad?" Leopard asked. "Remember where the big sonuvabitch kicks sand in the scrawny little cocksucker's face?" Gavin nodded for real this time. "Yeah. Well, that's the tone we want here. After the airline broad says she doesn't like gray hair, it's gonna say, right across the screen: ALONE AT HOME, THAT NIGHT. Got it: ALONE AT HOME, THAT NIGHT. And you're there before your mirror, putting Gray-Away in your head, and you're saying—see here—you're saying, 'Just rub Gray-Away into my scalp and watch unsightly gray hairs disappear, naturally.' Get it?"

This time, Gavin did not nod.

Eddie Leopard went on: "Then, we finish up the commercial with you back at the airlines. It says TWO WEEKS LATER across the screen, and you walk up to the broad, only now your hair is black as the fuckin' ace of spaces. And here"—Leopard pointed to the storyboards again—"she says, 'Don't I know you?' and you say, 'I'm Gavin Gray'—"

"Just like I done before."

"You got it. Only now, she says, 'You're not gray,' and she touches your hair again, and now she says, 'Your hair is young and vigorous.' And you say, 'No, no, I'm Gavin Grey, The Grey Ghost,' but she obviously doesn't know what the fuck you're talking about, and all she can do is keep rubbing your hair."

"She doesn't know me?"

"No. But you should see this broad I got, Ghost. She did all the stuff for Pal Dog Foods, the one with the fucking poodle who sings like Caruso, and she is going to be creaming in her goddamn pants over your new hair, and you're saying, 'No, no, I'm Gavin Grey, The Grey Ghost,' shit like that—"

"She still doesn't know me?"

"No, no, that's the point. And finally she says, 'Oh. The gray goes away with Gray-Away.' Get it? Grey Ghost/gray goes. It'll be fucking dynamite."

Gavin said, "She still doesn't know who I am?"

"No fuckin' idea."

"But if she's about my age, she'd sure know who The Grey Ghost is."

"Well, that's half the joke, Ghost," Leopard explained. "All she can do is talk about hair. I mean who really gives a shit whether hair is gray or not? That's the joke, get it?"

Gavin said he did, and they started shooting after they made him up. The woman in the commercial, whose real name was Elaine, did not have a call till eleven, so first, out of sequence, they would shoot the part of the commercial that Gavin did by himself, rubbing Gray-Away into his head at home. This went fairly smoothly, too. Among other things, because the commercial was intended as a parody of the old wooden comic-book style, since Gavin spoke his lines in a wooden manner, that was approximately what was desired. It only took eleven takes before Leopard had it just right, Gavin looking into a mirror, massaging the cream into his hair and saying, "Just rub Gray-Away into my scalp and watch unsightly gray hairs disappear, naturally."

Then, after a break, he and Elaine started filming the opening part of the commercial. She carried him. Elaine was indeed a real pro, and she was excellent at being completely put off by his hair. "This is terrific," Leopard screamed. "This is fucking fantastic. You're both gonna win a Clio."

Gavin then began to look at the script for the final part of the commercial. He kept shaking his head. He had been uneasy all along about the denouement, and now, regrettably for Eddie Leopard, Gavin began to express his misgivings. "I don't like the way she doesn't know me," he said.

"Whatdya mean, Ghost?" Leopard asked.

"I can't believe a girl my age wouldn't've heard about The Grey Ghost. You gotta remember. I was everybody's All-American. I was on *The Ed Sullivan Show.*"

"Ghost, Ghost, we're havin' fun. A lot of this shit is fun."

"Fun for you," Gavin shot back. "Not fun for me. This shit is making fun *at* me."

"No, no. Hey, for Chrissake, trust me."

But Gavin was not appeased. The more he looked at the script and studied the storyboards, the more he grew wary. "Nobody told me when I became a national spokesman that I was gonna have to get pissed on," he said.

"You're not getting pissed on," Leopard said, soothing him, a hand on Gavin's shoulder. A makeup lady was darkening his hair. "On the contrary, Ghost. Mr. and Mrs. America and all the ships at sea watching this commercial are going to like you even better because they'll see that you're enjoying a little laugh. Hey, *they* know you're The Grey Ghost. They remember. They're gonna think, Who is this dumb asshole behind the airline counter who doesn't even remember The Grey Ghost? They're gonna be on your side all the way. This is going to make you more human."

"I don't know," Gavin said. "I got another idea."

"Look," Leopard said, cutting him off. "You know, they take these polls; they're called recognition factor polls. And five or six percent of the people don't even know who Jimmy Carter is."

"A lot of guys don't like him," Gavin said.

"Hey, I'm not talkin' about likin'. I'm sayin': Five or six percent don't even know who the fuck the president of the United States is. So no one can be surprised if an asshole here or there has let you slip out of her mind. Okay?"

Gavin still wasn't sold. "Why don't we do it this way instead? Why doesn't she recognize me when I come back with the shit on my head, the Gray-Away. Then she says, Oh, now I remember you, you're The Grey Ghost. You know, stuff like that."

Leopard shook his head, "I'm sorry, Ghost. You carry the ball. I'll write the commercials."

And, reluctantly, Gavin took his place and moved toward the airline counter. Elaine said, "Don't I know you?"

Gavin, all smiles, said, "Sure, I'm Gavin Grey."

Elaine ran her hand through his hair. "But you're not gray. Your hair is young and vigorous."

"No, no," Gavin said, losing his smile altogether. "Not my hair. I'm The Grey Ghost."

"Oh, I know: The gray goes."

"The Grey Ghost!"

"The gray goes with Gray-Away," Elaine cried happily, but Leopard was not pleased.

"All right," he said, "that's a good start, but you've got to smile more, Ghost."

"It ain't easy."

Leopard took him aside. "Hey, I know it isn't easy. Just pretend like it's your pubic hair she's running her hand through."

"No, no, that's not it."

"What's not it?"

"It's just not right," Gavin cried out. "I'm a national spokesman, and here she doesn't even know who I am. That's not right." Leopard dropped his shoulders, exasperated. Gavin turned back to Elaine. "You know who I am, don't you? I mean, really. You remember The Grey Ghost?"

"Yeah, I do, personally, but—"

"See?" Gavin said to Leopard.

The producer only moaned. "Yeah, but you gotta do it this way, Ghost. This is a commercial, this isn't real."

"But, goddamnit, I'm real," Gavin cried. "The Grey Ghost is real." And he shook his head vigorously, and when no one knew how to respond to him anymore, he turned around and walked away, out the door of the studio.

"All right, everybody, take a break," Leopard sighed, showing his exasperation. "Lemme go stroke him some." But when he went outside to talk to Gavin, he was gone, nowhere to be seen. In fact, Gavin had gone to a bar, and, after a number of drinks, he had taken a cab to the airport and grabbed the first flight to Atlanta.

22

S TUART CALLED ME THE NEXT MORNING FROM
her office at the Atlanta television station. "Please come down
and get him, Don," she said.

"What the hell are you calling me for?"

"Who am I supposed to call? His wife? 'Hello, Mrs. Grey, your
husband just dropped by to screw me last night, and—'"

"Yeah, okay," I said, if reluctantly.

"My father? 'Hello, Daddy, I have The Grey Ghost in my bed,
and—"

"Okay, okay, Stuart, I get it."

"Thank you."

"No, no, wait a minute, don't hang up. Why do you need anybody? Can't you just tell him to get out?"

"No, I can't," she said, softly.

"You can't? Why not?"

There was a long pause. "I don't want to talk about it," Stuart
said. "Please. Please get him, Don. Please."

"I'll try."

"This isn't for me. I promise you. This would be for him. Please."

So, on the flight down to Atlanta, I concocted a cover story to
throw at Gavin.

"Cake! What in the world are you doing here?" he screamed at
me at the door to her apartment.

And I feigned shock that he was there. "Well, I've been over at Athens, you know, the University of Georgia, doing some, uh, research the last couple days, and, uh, you know, I, uh—" Purposely I fumbled and tried to appear off balance. Gavin took the bait.

"Why, you old sonuvabitch! You've been dipping the wick in her, too!" he cried, slapping me on the rear. At last: We were teammates. I shrugged, modestly. "Ain't she somethin', Donnie? I tell you, she 'bout to wore me out last night."

"Goddamn right!" I hollered, and I rapped him on the bicep playfully with my knuckles. I have never been very accomplished at this sort of barracks bravado (possibly because I never have accomplished all that much), but I laid it on pretty thick here. Finally, spent by reciting this litany of ecstasy, I sighed: "Well, if you got me blocked out here, I better get my ass out to the airport and get home to the old lady."

"Home cookin'," Gavin said, commiserating with me as best he could.

"Yeah," I said. He was not budging. So I turned to leave, but then I pivoted back, as if something was just occurring to me. "Aw, come on up with me," I said.

"With you? Where to?"

"Raleigh-Durham. Back to Carolina. I gotta see Professor Gillespie over at Duke sometime anyway. Might as well do it now. Come on."

He paused. It almost seemed as if he was grateful that I had provided him with an out, but he still had to play the game. "Donnie, I know you'd like company, but I hate to give up this kinda stuff."

"Don't I know how good it is. I can't blame you." I clapped him on the shoulder and started for the door again. I didn't know what else I could do. But then, at last, I heard:

"Aw shoot, Donnie, I'll come with you."

"Hey thanks, Gavin. Maybe you ought to give that poor pussy a little rest."

"Yeah, I don't want to *damage* nothin'," he said, as seriously as he could manage. And thus, for stated humanitarian reasons, did we fly back to Raleigh-Durham together.

It was going on to ten o'clock by the time we got back to his house. The porch light was on, and a couple more inside, too, but, we discovered, these had been left aglow merely to fool the more gullible of burglars; Babs was not home. So Gavin and I had a couple drinks, watched some TV, even lit a fire. It was the middle of October by now, and on some nights there was the touch of a chill. "It's good football weather, is what it is," Gavin said. "The Ghost liked this kinda weather to play in." More and more, he was starting to refer to himself that way, imperially, and no longer did he necessarily require a couple of drinks to get him going about his old self.

We chatted about the game that was to be played the next afternoon at Kenan Stadium; the Tarheels were going against State, and first place in the Atlantic Coast Conference was on the line. But Gavin was obviously distracted, and suddenly, almost in midsentence, as he was discussing Carolina's pass defense, he stopped dead and said, "Well, Donnie, I know Babs Rogers pretty well, and I'll tell you what: She's either been kidnapped by pirates and is being held in a dungeon, or she's in another man's bed right this moment."

"Aw, she's probably with a friend," I said. He looked at me, saying with his expression that he did not appreciate my trying to put him on. "Let's go to sleep," I suggested then, but he stayed behind, staring at the fire.

He woke me up around two-thirty. "I was right," he told me. "Babs ain't home yet." He'd obviously had more to drink, and it was with a little difficulty that he fished around in his pockets. Finally, he pulled something out. "You ever smoke marijuana, Cake?"

"Well, now and then. I'm not exactly a junkie, though."

What he had was a joint that Stuart had given him. He held it up to me. "I tried one last night," he said. "Stuart said it he'ped sex."

"That's what they advertise."

"But damnit, Donnie, I just couldn't get it—the smokin', I mean. I just couldn't do it right."

"Well, you just gotta inhale real deep."

"Here, you show me how."

The last thing I wanted, going on three o'clock in the morning, woken up out of a dead sleep, was to start smoking marijuana, but I managed to raise myself up, and, dutifully, I took a big drag. "You see?"

Gavin marveled at my easy expertise. "Damn. Will you just look at that." But that made him even madder when, then, he tried to smoke, but only succeeded in coughing. "Mother fuck," he shouted then, and, petulantly, he thrust the lit joint back in my hand. "You just en-joy the whole goddamn thing." He sat down on the bed. "You know what, Donnie?"

"What?" I said, when I appreciated than an answer was actually required of me.

"I'm just some kind of old dog can't learn new tricks. I was thinkin' 'bout that downstairs. Just some kind of old dog. The only thing is, I was an old dog when I was twenty-two. I ain't been able to learn any new tricks ever since I became The Ghost."

I nodded. I'd always said Gavin wasn't dumb, just deprived by too damn much success, too soon.

He got up from the bed then and started to leave the room, but he stopped at the door, and I could see him there, only an outline framed by a light down the hall. He shook his head and reached for breath, and the whole time he talked, he never looked toward me. This was hard for him, but it was important to him that someone knew and could understand everything better. "You know, Donnie," he said at last. "I lied to you. I didn't do no fuckin' at all last night. I just plain couldn't get it up. I couldn't get it no bigger than a Ju-ly minute."

I didn't know how to react, and so when I looked down and saw the joint in my hand, I took a drag on it, for something to do.

"Ain't that some shit?" Gavin went on. "The Grey Ghost couldn't get it up."

"Aw, come on, don't overreact. You know what they say: Anxiety is the first time you can't do it twice, and panic is the second time you can't do it once." I forced a laugh. He looked at me dumbly. He didn't understand a word of what I was saying. "Aw, come on, Gavin, they say that happens to everybody at one time or—"

He understood that. "Well, it never once happened to The Ghost before."

"Hey, I know it's gotta hurt, but shit, don't worry, you'll get it back, Ghost."

"I don't know, Donnie. The trouble is, I never did get anything back yet. Ever. That's what happens when you're an everybody's All-American. I was thinkin' 'bout this downstairs. You just start losin' things: your legs, your timin', your speed, your hands. And you never get anything back. You just lose the one thing after another."

And without looking back at me, he turned and left. For a moment, I started to get up and follow him down the stairs, but I sensed enough to let him go. This was wise of me. It was later when Stuart told me about this time the night before, at her place. Gavin had failed with her, and for all she did to comfort him, it was to no avail, and she had fallen asleep beside him.

Gavin and I were having coffee late the next morning when Babs came back. She carried a dress on a hanger, in a cellophane bag, and a small overnight case, and she wore her face with a certain resignation. When she said nothing—especially when she said nothing by way of explanation—Gavin turned away from her.

I stayed out of it, and would have left, but I was across the room, and I hoped that somehow it would just all melt away. It did not. Gavin said, "Hey, did you put out good for the guy?"

Babs looked dead at him, but she did not respond. Instead, she turned to address me. "What in the world are you doin' here, Donnie McClure?"

"We bumped into one another," I said.

She asked where, and I just shrugged, but Gavin burst in and said, "Atlanta."

Now she turned to him. "Oh great, Atlanta. You know, those people in New York were looking all over Robin Hood's barn for you."

He shrugged, beneath caring.

"No, that's not good enough," Babs said sharply. "They weren't done filming when you took off."

"Well, I was done with their little red asses."

"You signed a contract, Gavin."

"I didn't sign a contract so's they could make a fool outta me, coast-to-coast."

"Well, they're filming again on Monday, and you're going back up on the Eastern flight Sunday night. They'll be a limousine to meet you, and that gentleman in charge, Mr. Leopard, suggested you call him at home this weekend if there was anything else you wanted, which is a code, I think, for he will get you a woman if that will keep you happy." She talked without expression. "That's perfectly all right with me, Gavin. You have my permission."

"Hey," I said, "let me outta here."

"No, it doesn't matter, Donnie. There is nothing to discuss." She turned again to face her husband. "I love you, Precious, and I'm going to drive you to the airport tomorrow night, and then I'm going to leave you." Then, businesslike, she picked up her dress and her case and started to head for the door.

"I ain't going up for that commercial," Gavin said. He had understood every word that she had said, but could not accept it.

"Suit yourself," Babs said. She stopped now. "But remember this: I'll help you keep this house for the kids, but you're going to have to do *something* to support yourself."

"You're really going? Come on?"

"Oh, really."

"What, you gonna shack up with that old guy?"

Babs put her stuff back down. Now, she was going to have this out altogether, and there was to her a distance and a calculation I had never seen before. Oh, the former occasionally, and the latter once before, when she took me to bed; but never the two together. Anyway: "What old guy?" she asked, knowing precisely whom he meant.

"You know, that old fart in the Lincoln Continental."

"No, I'm not moving in with him or with anyone else. I've got a little place out there, a kitchenette, and I'm going to stay there, all by myself, loving it, until I figure out what to do."

This answered the question, but not the question Gavin thought he was going to get answered. He tried again. "You were with that old guy last night, weren't you?"

"No," she replied, and just to make it more excruciating for him, she paused a long while before going on. "In fact, you want to know who I was with last night?"

That was enough for me. I started to leave the room. I heard all the rest, but I was gone.

"I was with a young guy last night, Gavin. I got a piece of ass last night. I'm forty-six years old, and I never once had a piece of ass before, and so when I had the opportunity, I took it. I got a piece of ass."

She certainly didn't have to say that again, but there was no stopping her now. And, anyway, she did not know how very much she was hurting him; she could not know that this revelation pained him all the more for what had happened to himself, with Stuart. So she just went on: "Does it really matter, Gavin? Do you care, Precious? Does it matter to you if I just got fucked or whether I went to bed and made love to a man I cared for?"

Still, he didn't reply. I doubt that he understood much, or any, of what she was saying. Probably he was only thinking something of himself. So Babs continued: "Well, I'll tell you. It doesn't matter to you. I know, because years ago, when I first understood that you really were playing around, what did it matter to me? It's all the same, and I just couldn't compete with you. Not then. It was all just touchdowns—women, men, fame, everything. It was all just touchdowns."

Finally, Gavin only said, "Please don't leave me, Babsie."

"Don't come near me."

"I just want to put my arms around you and hug you to death."

"No, when you touch me, you— No, I don't want that now."

"I'll go to New York," Gavin said then, and in a real puppy-dog voice. "I'll do just what they say."

"That's good."

"So you won't leave?"

"Oh, no, no, Precious. And damnit, get away. You're not listening. This is for *you*. I'm leaving for you!"

"Why?" He was obviously and totally perplexed.

"Because I have to."

"Why?"

"I said. I just said: It's because once I couldn't compete with you. I know. And now you can't compete with me."

"No, no, Babs."

"Yeah. I stand for all the things you've lost, and maybe, maybe if you lost me too, it would make it easier. Maybe then you could stop rooting around in the past like some old hog."

"Babs, please."

"I said leave me alone, Precious," and in a moment more, she had swooped up her belongings and walked off from him, and there was nothing left but for him to cry there and to resolve that, whatever was taken from him—even memories—Babs would not get herself away.

23

I TALKED GAVIN INTO GOING TO SEE THE STATE game that afternoon. I told Babs I would do my best to keep him occupied before he went back to New York. The game was a sellout, of course, but he had a lifetime pass, and he found someone to let me in too, and we jammed ourselves into the students' section, down around the twenty-yard line. A few of the kids recognized him, and at first they just said, "There's The Grey Ghost" or "Hey, there's Gavin Grey" (and I also heard one whisper, "Didn't he rape a woman once?"), but, in time, the ones made bolder with whiskey took to calling him The Ghost, and asking him football questions, what he thought of the present Tarheels, questions like that.

It was a cool afternoon, even chilly when the sun would stay for too long behind the puffy clouds, but we dealt with that situation by nipping at some bourbon, just like any regular, crazy half-assed alumni might. When the students around us started to scream, "Rip 'em up, tear 'em up, give 'em hell, 'Heels!" I started to cheer along with them, but Gavin only shook his head at me.

"It's sure silly, ain't it, Cake?"

"What exactly?" I asked.

"All this shit," Gavin explained, sweeping his arm about. "You know, I never could quite understand how you folks could watch it. That never made no good sense to me, *watching* a football game."

"Well, you know, we're not good enough to play. If you can't play, you gotta watch."

"Well, I for one never would have," he said, although this stricture did not prohibit him from inspecting the female support troops down on the field. There were half-a-dozen cheerleaders, eight majorettes, and for the pretty ones who couldn't either twirl or tumble, there were sixteen flag girls, the Marching Carolines. "Whenever folks ask me the difference in football from when I played, I always say, now they got more pussy out there than players," Gavin allowed.

State, the Wolfpack, took the ball, and the cheerleaders called for a sophisticated, modern cheer. "Repel them, repel them, make them relinquish the ball!" the students all around us cheered.

"What is this shit?" Gavin said, and he took another nip, and gave me one.

"You know," I said, "I can't remember the last time I took bourbon straight, outside of a football game." I gasped when the whiskey hit my belly and burned it. "There *is* a lot of pussy down there," I said. I felt good, and better when Carolina recovered a fumble.

Now, the Tarheels began to march in earnest, a black kid named Amos Lawrence doing most of the running. "Hey, Mr. Grey," a student behind us called out. "How good is Amos?"

"He's some kind of good," Gavin said, enthusiastically.

"Is he better'n you were, sir?" another boy asked.

"Truthfully, no," Gavin replied, evenly, without hesitation. "He's good, but I was better." And then, turning to me, "'Member the Clemson game, Cake? My senior year."

"I sure do. I came down from Wilson and sat over yonder with Babs."

As soon as I said that I was sorry, mad at myself for bringing up her name, but it did not seem to trouble him. "I was just now thinking about that game," he said. He looked all about. Everyone in the stands was watching Amos Lawrence and the other Tarheels of '79 marching along toward the Wolfpack end zone, pay dirt, but Gavin was apart, alone, looking all around. Kenan Stadium had been enlarged, a deck added on top, but the old covenant had been honored, and the stadium had not grown up until the trees had. They still towered over the place, so that even with all the scrimmaging and all the spectacle, there was still some sense of resting in God's palm. "You know something, Donnie . . . ?"

"What's that?"

"I never noticed those trees, not when I was playing."

"I guess it's different when you're in the stands."

"What are they, anyhow?" He pointed toward the ones to the west, glimmering red and gold in the afternoon sun.

"Sycamores, I think. But I'm not much on vegetation."

"Pines is about all I know, too." He gestured toward them, at the other end. "But I just never took in the trees when I was playing. Just never saw them."

"No," I said.

"What's that thing where you see something, only you don't? What's that called?"

"You mean a mirage?"

"No, that's out in the desert. You know, Cake. You see it, but it's different. A whatdyacallit?"

"An optical illusion?"

"Yeah, that's it."

"Well, what about it?" I asked.

"A game up here, it's altogether different. Like, do you know the field is slanted?"

"What field?"

"This field. *Any* football field. It peaks down the middle, and then it slopes over to the sidelines. For drainage."

"I never knew that."

"I know."

"How much?" I asked.

"Oh, a few feet, I guess. If you was to go down there and kneel on the sidelines, look across to the State side, and if I was over there, kneeling, I don't believe you could see me."

"Yeah?"

"Yeah," Gavin said, and he took another nip. "A football field ain't flat at all. It's like the world, the earth. It looks flat, but it ain't."

He passed me the bourbon, and I took another swallow. Gavin turned around to the boys who had chatted with him earlier. "Hey' y'all, anybody got any marijuana?" he said.

"You want a joint, Mr. Grey?"

"Sure. We're havin' some kinda time, aren't we? It's a football weekend, ain't it?"

Those boys didn't themselves have any, but they turned around and advertised—"Hey, The Grey Ghost wants a joint"—and pretty soon, one materialized and was passed along to him. "Now don't get caught or you'll get suspended, Mr. Grey," the one boy said.

"Don't worry," Gavin said, grinning. "They look out special for football players." All the kids laughed. And he took a drag, did it perfectly without so much as a rasp.

"Hey, Ghost, you got it!" I called, and he laughed with me. Then I took a drag, and handed it back to him so that he could take one more. Then he passed it back.

"That's good stuff," Gavin said, complimenting his suppliers, and the kids smiled back at him, not quite sure what to make of The Grey Ghost.

He stood up, then, rubbing his hands together, in happy antici-pation (of something), and followed that by turning round and holding up his arms, as if to conduct an orchestra. The students waited, and he opened his mouth, as if to bellow, but what came out was only a stage whisper: "Rip 'em up, tear 'em up, give 'em hell, 'Heels!" But all of it—only a whisper. And the kids laughed then, but not at Gavin, for he had not made a fool of himself at all. They laughed for the fun of it. "Rip 'em up, tear 'em up, give 'em hell, 'Heels!" Gavin whispered one more time.

"Yehhh, Ghost!" the students around us yelled.

Gavin sat down, smiling. "You know what-all that is, Donnie?"

"What?"

"Well, if it's an optical illusion when you don't see right, what is it when you don't hear right?"

"An aural illusion, I guess."

"Well, that's what I just done with that cheer. And that's what it is down yonder all the time," he said, pointing toward the field. "You don't hear the hittin' up here. You people in the stands, you think the field is flat, and it ain't, and you see all the activity down there, but you don't hear it. You don't hear the hittin', and it's make-believe when you don't. You know what it's like down there, really?"

I shook my head.

"Every play, it's a crunchin', a smackin', and just some kinda ommphin'. I don't believe you people, all you *fans* would just sit and watch if you could hear the way it is."

"Why not?"

"Because . . . it's like they used to watch wars before the guns come in and made all that noise, didn't they? It would turn off these people if they could *hear* all the meanness out there." He took one last swallow and dropped the bottle.

"Dead soldier," I said.

"Dead player," he said, chucking foolishly.

Amos Lawrence went wide for eight yards and a hard first down on third and seven, and all around us, everyone rose and cheered. But Gavin kept his seat and I stayed down with him. "The smackin' and crunchin', Cake. It just ain't football 'less you can hear it good. I know what they say about me. I know what they say about The Grey Ghost. They say: He never could make it in the real world. But you see, out there, down yonder, that was the most real I ever did come across. Once you heard all that hittin', the rest of the world is just like all these trees, standing still outside the stadium. You understand?"

"Absolutely," I said.

"Good."

Amos Lawrence took a swing pass and went twenty-two yards for a touchdown. We got up this time, enough to see him snake the last five yards into the end zone. "Yeah, that is some kind of player," Gavin said.

"But not as good as you?" I asked.

"No, sir, not nearly as good as The Grey Ghost. I was one of the best. I truly was, Cake."

All around, the kids were chanting, "I'm a Tarheel born and a Tarheel bred, and when I die I'll be a Tarheel dead, so, rah-rah-Kowlinah, 'linah, rah-rah Kowlinah, 'linah, rah-rah Kowlinah, rah rah, rah!"

Gavin was looking away, off toward the trees, when the extra point went through the uprights. "I'm gonna sneak out for a pee before the ensuing kickoff," he told me. Kickoffs are the one thing in this world that are always ensuing.

The clouds had passed over now, so the sky was, by God's will, all Carolina blue, and in the warmth of the afternoon sun, softened by the bourbon that still burned some inside of me, I leaned back and watched the ensuing kickoff in the kind of detached contentment that comes with watching a jet plane trace high across the heavens. I was no more with the players than I would be with such a jet, or with the trees all around the stadium. I was only part of the crowd, of that; for me, it was only the crowd that was real, and no doubt because Gavin had never been a part of that, it took me some time before I understood that he had gone and would not be back at all, for the rest of the game.

I RAN OUT to where he had parked the car; it was gone, as I knew it must be. Perhaps I should have found a phone and called Babs then to warn her. But why? That is hindsight. Instead, I just started running, searching for a moving car. But everything in the vicinity of the stadium was parked. Of course: Why would anybody ever drive to a stadium during a game? Even the cops go inside between the two traffic jams at the beginning and end of the game.

In fact, there's a vast eeriness to being near a stadium during a game, a social vacuum of some sort, because while everything is so still and empty all around, you regularly hear the deep disembodied voice of the public address announcer, and then, at longer intervals, roars and moans.

But at last, some distance from the stadium I was able to hitchhike a ride in a pickup truck, and he took me down the highway to about three or four miles from Gavin's house, and after I walked awhile from there, I caught some cars stopped at a red light and started offering the drivers five bucks to cart me the rest of the way. Most of the drivers were terrified and rolled up their windows; a teenager took me up on it. I didn't make him take me into Maid Marian, but jumped out there, at the corner of Nottingham, and ran the rest of the way. That, it turned out, was not so wise, because if the boy had driven me straight to the door, I could have gotten him to summon the fire department. The smoke was just starting to come out of the second story when I got there.

I ran into the house and called out. No one answered. But they had to be there; both cars were in the driveway. I dashed about on the first floor: no one. It was still free of smoke, but from the bottom of the stairs I could see that right at the top, from one of the children's bedrooms, smoke was beginning to seep under the door. Gavin must have set the fire in there.

I ran up the stairs, past that door, down the hall to the master bedroom. Babs was there, all right. She was lying still on their bed, a white sheet covering her up to her neck, with her arms folded in front of her, crossed at the wrists. He had laid her out reverentially; all that was missing was an orchid.

I screamed her name and ran to her. She did not stir. I leaned down to her, but there was no sense me feeling for a pulse; I have never been able to find my own, much less come across someone else's in a panic. She was just so still, so beautiful, utterly in repose, except, oddly, for as much attention as Gavin had taken with her, her head was turned some to one side.

Closer then, I saw why. He did not want it visible where he had hit her, a blow to the left temple. He didn't want to mar her looks. So he had turned her head just away, to hide that from his own sight. Babs had a dark bruise there, but the skin had barely been broken, and there were but a few specks of blood that spotted her hair there. "Oh my God, Babsie," I cried.

At least, I was going to get her out of there before the fire burned her up. I pulled down the sheet, so I could pick her up, but she was naked, so, quickly, I yanked the sheet back up, tucked it tightly around her and grabbed her up. She was very difficult to carry, heavier than I expected, dead weight, her head flopping. Now, for the first time, too, I could smell smoke.

I got to the door to the hall, but, like a damn fool, I stopped there when I saw Gavin coming from the other direction. It shocked me so. He was shirtless, and without shoes or socks, either. All he had on was his titian football pants, the ones he had saved from his last game with the Redskins.

He was as surprised to see me as me him. "Cake!" he shouted. "You're supposed to be at the State game."

"You've been calling me Cake all day. Cut it out, willya?" It's funny the things people will say.

"I'm sorry," he said. He was clearly apologetic. I also noticed then that he was holding a pistol.

"Why did you kill her?" I asked.

"Babsie's not dead yet," he said, and matter-of-factly.

"What?"

"I just knocked her out."

"Well then, really, let's all get outta here." Behind me, between Babs and me and the stairs, the smoke was absolutely pouring from under the children's bedroom door.

"No," Gavin said, brandishing the pistol a little. "Babs stays." I looked at him, beseechingly. "That's the damn *point*, Donnie."

"Oh no, I'm taking her. You won't shoot me."

That irritated Gavin, and he took another step toward me. He wasn't but a few feet away. "Of course I won't shoot *you*. This ain't got anything to do with you." But then he leveled the gun to where I held Babs's head against my chest.

"Please come with me, Gavin."

"Donnie, damn it, I did this so there wouldn't be no choice. The way I am about fire—you know—you couldn't get me outta here now even if you blindfolded me like a horse."

"Please."

"You leave Babs with me." He said that forcefully, and he started to move toward me again, but at that moment, there was an awful crack, a blast, and the door behind me blew open with the heat, and the flames spit out into the hall. Gavin, looking past me directly at the explosion, drew back in horror. This was my moment. I just whirled around and, holding Babs close to me, I walked to the stairs without looking back, striding past the edge of the flames.

I carried Babs down the stairs and right out the front door. "Babs! Babsie!" Gavin yelled after us. Outside, I laid her on the ground. It had to be some distance from the house. By now, the top story seemed all afire. Neighbors were rushing over, and I called for them to get a doctor, and ran right back inside.

The smoke was darker now, working down, and the flames were darting farther out the bedroom door, snapping across the hall to the top of the stairs. Yet there was time enough for Gavin to dart through them. But he only just stood stock-still, almost exactly where I had left him, in the hall, backing away from where the fire was worst. I called his name, but he only shook his head. So then I ripped off my jacket. I had on a corduroy jacket. I started up the stairs, holding the jacket high over my head. "I'll blindfold you!" I cried. "I will!"

He shook his head, but I kept coming toward the blaze, holding up the jacket. "Stay there!" I cried.

He only held up his hand, like a traffic cop, as I came nearer to the fire. And he shook his head at me again. "Come on, Cake," he said, sharply, stopping me. And then softer, smiling: "Donnie."

He backed up a step then. "Gavin, please!" I held up the jacket one more time, and pleaded, "Ghost!"

He nodded at that, pleased, I think, that I had called him by that name. For then he turned directly to the door, went into the bedroom, and closed it behind.

To that last moment, I could have saved him. Had he wanted to, I could have led him out. I believe that. And I stared after him for a moment more. But then I coughed from the smoke, and I knew I had to retreat. I wrapped the jacket around my mouth and nose, and hurried down the stairs.

The crackling upstairs grew louder now, the sound of kindling, little explosions. But loud as the blaze had become, and through the smoke that tumbled down on me, the sound of the shot was unmistakable to me. Even with it all, I heard that as clearly as the shot that started the race he ran against Narvel Blue at the Three Corners, when I was growing up so long ago and The Grey Ghost still had all his lives and the rich dreams that he passed off as himself.

Babs had Gavin buried Tuesday, on the hillside of a little cemetery in Chapel Hill, a couple miles from the stadium. There was a family plot in Charlotte, but putting him in the earth there did not seem to make a great deal of sense. We had a very large service at the church, which was well attended and even splashy in some ways, for there was a lot of press there and a number of strangers who came just because of the football connection. The crowd overflowed. Almost all of the silver anniversary Tarheel team were assembled all over again in a special part of the church. It was quite a tribute.

The burial itself, though, was limited to the family and the best of friends.

Babs had come to me and told me that then, as Gavin was put into the ground, she wanted someone to deliver a brief eulogy. I winced when she began to speak to me about that, for I thought she must be preparing to ask me. But that was not her idea. "What do you think about Finegan?" she said.

"Finegan?"

"Well, he played football with Gavin, and I think that's what counted the most," she said. "In the final analysis."

"In the final analysis."

It was, of course, a very appropriate thought of Babs, and if Finegan was surprised when she asked him, he was not cowed by the assignment. He spoke crisply, but with great feeling. He said he was sorry for Babs, sorry for the children, and sorry for himself and for all the people "who had the privilege to know and love Gavin Grey, The Grey Ghost." Finegan paused then; he didn't know what to do with his hands.

But when he went on, Finegan said that "to tell you the truth, I'm not absolutely sure I should be sorry for The Ghost." He explained that he said that because he had not forgotten something from long ago. The last time he ever "was so fortunate" to play with Gavin was when the coach put Lawrence and him back in with The Ghost at the end of the Sugar Bowl, and after Gavin scored the touchdown, Finegan was the first one to him, and Gavin hugged him and said: "Finegan, it can't never get any better than this. Never."

And, of course, Finegan's point was that Gavin was right: It never could and it never did and it never would have. And he knew this. Then Finegan ended up, "But don't be sad because The Ghost was one of the best, and he knew that, too." Again, he didn't know what to do with his hands. "Amen," Finegan said. This concluded the service, Finegan squinting out to the rest of us against the midday sun, which shone in an October sky of Carolina blue. It was some kind of day and, among other things, a good one for a football game.